Slicky Boys

Slicky Boys

Martin Limón

Bantam Books

New York Toronto
London Sydney Auckland

SLICKY BOYS
A Bantam Book / June 1997

BOOK DESIGN BY ELLEN CIPRIANO

For information address: Bantam Books.

Library of Congress Cataloging-in-Publication Data
Limón, Martin, 1948–
Slicky boys / Martin Limón.
p. cm.
ISBN 0-553-10443-8
I. Title.
PS3562.I465S58 1997
813'.54—dc21 96–47108
CIP

Published simultaneously in the United States and Canada

Bantam Books are published by Bantam Books, a division of Bantam Doubleday Dell Publishing Group, Inc. Its trademark, consisting of the words "Bantam Books" and the portrayal of a rooster, is Registered in U.S. Patent and Trademark Office and in other countries. Marca Registrada. Bantam Books, 1540 Broadway, New York, New York 10036.

PRINTED IN THE UNITED STATES OF AMERICA

BVG 10 9 8 7 6 5 4 3 2 1

To my parents,
Peter T. Limón and Marie Werner Limón,
who have always been on my side—
no matter what.

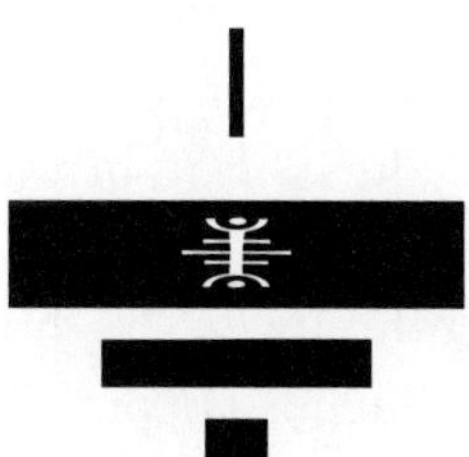

"YOU BUY ME DRINK?"

Eun-hi coiled her body around my arm and leaned over the bar, her shimmering black hair cascading to the dented vinyl counter. I inhaled lilacs.

"*Tone oopso,*" I said. No money. "Payday's not until Friday."

She pouted. Red lips pursed like crushed cushions.

"You number ten GI."

Ernie leaned back on his bar stool. "You got that right, Eun-hi. George is definitely number *ten* Cheap Charley GI." He tilted his head back and swigged from a frosty brown bottle of Oriental Beer.

We were in the U.N. Club, in Itaewon, the greatest GI village in the world. Shattering vibrations careened off the walls, erupting from an out-of-tune rock-and-roll band clanging away in the corner. On the dance floor Korean business girls, clad in just enough clothing to make themselves legal, and American GI's in blue jeans and sports shirts gyrated youthful bodies in mindless abandon.

It felt good to be here. Our natural environment. My belly was full of beer and my petty worries had been flushed away by the gentle hops coursing through my veins. Still, I was surprised Eun-hi had talked to me and I wondered why. Usually she remained aloof from all GI's except those who were willing to spend big bucks, which—on a corporal's pay—didn't include me.

Eun-hi stood up and pushed a small fist against her hip. She was a big girl, full-breasted, tall for a Korean woman. Long leather boots reached almost to her knees and white hot pants bunched into the inviting mystery between her smooth brown thighs. Dark nipples strained to peek out at the world from behind a knotted halter top bundling her feminine goodness. Eun-hi was a business girl. One of the finest in Itaewon. Finer than frog hair, to be exact. A GI's dream, a sailor's fevered vision, a faithful wife's nightmare.

My name is George Sueño. My partner Ernie Bascom and I are agents for the Criminal Investigation Division of the 8th United States Army in Seoul. We work hard—sometimes—but what we're really good at is running the ville. Parading. Crashing through every bar in the red-light district, tracking down excitement and drunkenness and girls. In fact, we're experts at it.

Gradually, over the last few months, more girls like Eun-hi had drifted into the GI villages. More girls who'd grown up in the twenty-some years since the end of the Korean War, when there was food to be had and inoculations from childhood diseases and shelter from the howling winter wind. Eun-hi was healthy. Not deformed by bowlegs or a pocked face or the hacking, coughing lungs of poverty.

She must've felt the heat of my admiration. At least I hoped she did. She took a step forward.

"Geogie," she said. "Somebody want to talk to you."

Ernie shifted in his stool, straightening his back. I stared at her. Waiting.

"A girl," she said.

My eyes widened.

She waved her small, soft palm from side to side.

"Not a business girl. *Suknyo.*" A virtuous woman.

Ernie leaned forward. Interested now.

"Why in the hell would a good girl want to talk to George?"

I elbowed him. He shut up. We both looked at Eun-hi. She shrugged her elegant shoulders.

"I don't know. She say she want to talk to GI named Geogie. In Itaewon everybody know Geogie. So I tell you."

"Where is she?" I asked.

"At the Kayagum Teahouse. She wait for you there."

"Is she a friend of yours?"

"No. I never see before. She come in here this afternoon when all GI's on compound. Ask me to help her find Geogie."

"How'd she know I'd be here?"

Eun-hi laughed. A high, lilting warble, like the song of a dove.

"She know. Everybody know. You always here."

It wasn't true. Not always. Sometimes Ernie and I hit other clubs. But it was true that we were in Itaewon almost every night.

Ernie set his beer down. "What does she want?"

"I don't know. She no say. You want to know, go to Kayagum Teahouse. Find out."

She placed one shiny boot in front of the other and thrust out her hip.

"You no buy Eun-hi drink, then Eun-hi go."

With that, she performed a graceful pirouette, held the pose for a moment, and sashayed her gorgeous posterior across the room toward a group of hell-raising helicopter pilots.

Ernie looked at me, lifting his eyebrows.

"A *suknyo*," he said. "Looking for you?"

"Yeah. What's so surprising about that?"

"Oh, nothing. Except you're a low-rent, depraved GI and no decent Korean woman would get within ten feet of you."

It bothered me. Where did he get the idea that I was depraved? Sure, I preferred girls who were young. Eighteen or nineteen. But I was only a few years older than that myself. What was wrong with that?

"Not so depraved," I said.

Ernie stood up. "Shall we go?"

"Aren't we going to think about this first?"

"What's to think about?" he said. "A virtuous woman wants to talk to you. You think of yourself as a knight in shining armor. Maybe a horny one but still a knight. Besides, I'm curious."

He was right. It was enough to get anybody curious. Itaewon was, by edict of the government, for "tourists" only. Translated—American GI's. And any woman caught in the area of the GI clubs, without a VD card proving that she was a registered prostitute, was subject to arrest. Whoever this *suknyo* was, she had risked losing a hell of a lot of face by coming down here.

"Yeah," I said, standing. "I'm curious, too."

I slugged down the dregs of my beer. We grabbed our jackets off the backs of the bar stools and headed toward the big double doors. Outside, the smoke and noise and smell of booze faded behind us. The young doorman bowed. I figured him to be about thirteen years old, either a distant relative of the owner or some urchin they took in off the streets. He was wrapped in three layers of grease-stained sweaters. A gauze mask protected his mouth and nose from the cold.

I took a deep breath and felt the fresh bite of winter.

Itaewon was layered in crusts of snow. Neon lined the road running up the hill, flashing and sparkling through the latticework designs of frozen white lace. Shivering business girls, half naked, stood in alcoves, arms crossed, peering out over the rims of their dark-lined eyes, searching for the next customer.

A GI winter wonderland.

We twisted up our collars and shoved our hands into our pockets. Ernie blew a great billowing breath through tight lips.

"Cold out," he said. "Colder than a GI's heart."

At the Kayagum Teahouse it was easy enough to spot her. She wore a white cotton blouse buttoned all the way to the neck, and her face was a smooth oval, like an oblong polished pearl. Her mouth was moist and red, and shining eyes gazed steadily at the world in dark seriousness. Her name was Miss Ku.

She handed us a note, intricately wrapped into the shape of a flower, and asked us to deliver it to Cecil Whitcomb, a soldier of the British contingent of the United Nations Honor Guard.

As a civilian, she wasn't allowed on the compound to deliver it herself.

I was hesitant at first but Miss Ku pleaded with her eyes. They'd been lovers. They'd broken up. She wanted to see him one more time.

Each word was pronounced carefully. Precisely. As if the English had been memorized after long hours of study in a library. She told me that she was a graduate of Ewha, the most prestigious women's university in the country.

She apologized for becoming involved with Cecil. It was a mistake. She'd met him at a British-Korean Friendship Day at the British Embassy. He was in civilian clothes and she didn't know he was in the army. She bowed her head.

Soldiers are low on the Confucian hierarchy. Almost as low as prostitutes and actors.

Ernie and I waited. Something was screwy. I didn't know what, but something.

I noticed her hands. Long and slender with short cropped nails and small calloused knots on the fingertips. She slid an envelope across the table. It was stuffed with a short stack of five-thousand-won notes. About a hundred bucks' worth. This changed everything. Greed usually does.

Ernie snatched up the money and shoved it deep into the pocket of his nylon jacket.

I looked around. No Americans in the Kayagum Teahouse. Only young Koreans of college age, boys and girls, hunched over steaming cups of ginseng tea. No one to spy on us. And besides, we weren't taking a bribe. Just working a side job. Nobody could say we were doing anything wrong.

We'd do it. Why not? Easy money.

I picked up the paper flower and slid it into my breast pocket.

When Miss Ku smiled, the radiance of her gemlike face filled the room.

That alone would've been payment enough.

. . .

The next morning we gave the note to Lance Corporal Cecil Whitcomb.

Looking at Whitcomb, I wondered why a woman as gorgeous as Miss Ku would bother with a guy so unimpressive. His body was bony and pale. Dark brown hair fell over eyes that made him seem as if he hadn't quite woken up.

Ernie and I towered over him. Ernie is over six feet tall and I'm almost six foot four, and I was about two shades darker than the nearly translucent Cecil Whitcomb. On duty, CID agents have to wear coats and ties, which is what we had on. Cecil was on a work detail. He wore baggy fatigue pants and a grease-smeared woolen shirt.

He was nervous about two cops cornering him outside the unit arms room, but he unfolded the paper flower and read the message, showing no expression on his long, shadow-eyed face. Somehow he had managed to bedazzle Miss Ku, and now he'd turned his back on her. It didn't make sense. But it wasn't any of our business. Our job was just to give him the note.

I glanced down at the printing. It was in English—in a careful hand—and said something about a meeting downtown and something about "I haven't told anyone yet."

When he finished reading, we waited for him to talk. He didn't. We decided to hell with him and walked away.

Ernie shook his head. "A couple of goofballs."

That summed it up. At least it seemed to at the time.

After work, the sun lowered red and angry beyond the hills overlooking the Yellow Sea. I noticed how cold it was. The temperature must've dropped ten degrees in the last couple of hours. A flake hit my head. White fluff whistled through the air. Snow would complicate things, but it wouldn't stop us from running the ville.

Nothing would.

. . .

A half hour before the midnight curfew, we stood at the central intersection in Itaewon, gazing at the sparkling neon through a steady sprinkle of snowflakes. Kimchi cabs slid on the road and people had to grab handholds to climb up even the most gentle incline.

"Another world of shit," Ernie said.

"Looks like it," I said.

Ernie and I were discussing which bar to hit next, when an ice-laced gust of Manchurian winter roared up the main drag. An Eskimo trudged through the swirling wind. When he came near, I saw that he wasn't an Eskimo at all. Another long nose. And then my eyes focused. It was Riley, the Admin Sergeant from the CID Detachment.

He pulled a thick wool scarf off his neck, scanned the street, and spotted us.

"What does *he* want?" Ernie said.

The first glimmer of worry shot through my brain. "We're on call tonight, aren't we?"

"Sure," Ernie said. "But I left *ajjima*'s phone number." He was talking about the landlady of the Nurse, his steady Korean girlfriend. "She would've come and found us if we had a call."

I wasn't so sure. Not in this blizzard.

Riley stormed up the road, stopped when he reached us, and motioned toward Ernie's right hand. Ernie handed him the liter of *soju*, a fierce Korean rice liquor. Riley rubbed the lip of the bottle with the flat of his palm, tilted his head, and glugged down a healthy shot. His Adam's apple undulated down his skinny neck as the searing liquid fell to his stomach. When he finished, he blew some breath out between his thin lips, thought for a moment, and slugged down another swallow. With red-rimmed eyes, he looked back and forth between us.

"Where have you guys *been*?"

"Right here," I said.

"But you're on call tonight."

"Ernie left *ajjima*'s phone number."

"But she wasn't there when the First Sergeant called and her daughter answered and she can't speak English."

Ernie spoke up. "So the First Sergeant ought to learn Korean."

Riley looked at Ernie as if he just realized that he should be committed to the looney bin.

"You know the First Sergeant hates Koreans."

"That isn't our problem," Ernie said. "We left a good number."

Riley let his head loll on his long neck, as if his skull was suddenly too heavy for his shoulder muscles.

"Okay, okay. So you guys have an excuse. What else is new? But when the First Sergeant can't get through, he calls me in the barracks and orders me out of the rack and sends me down here to find you. At the Nurse's hooch the daughter draws me a map and says *'soju'* and pretends like she's jolting down shots and I wander around the ville until I find you." Riley spread his hands. "So it's over now. So forget it. But we got bigger problems. Problems downtown."

Suddenly I was worried. Not about the First Sergeant or about not being available when we were supposed to be on call—I'd been through that sort of trouble before—but about what had happened downtown.

"What problems?" I asked.

"Dead GI," Riley said.

Ernie and I waited.

"Well, not a GI exactly."

One of the business girls standing in the shadows plucked up her courage and sashayed toward us. Riley saw her coming and waved her off. She pouted, a gentle snort erupted from her nose, then she turned and marched back to her comrades waiting in the darkness.

"They found him downtown, near Namdaemun," Riley said. "Gutted with some sort of big blade. Body in a snowdrift. Blood everywhere."

He was warming to the subject, but I didn't need the details. I'd examine those when I arrived at the site. I interrupted him.

"What do you mean, not a GI exactly?"

"I mean he's not a GI. Not technically."

Ernie leaned forward. "Then what the fuck is he?"

"He's British. Member of the United Nations Honor Guard. A Lance Corporal. Name's Whitcomb."

Mustard gas slammed into my nostrils.

An old man pushed a cart past us loaded with the still-burning cinders of perforated charcoal briquettes. Things that had burned brightly, heating the flues beneath the floors of Korean homes, but that now were dead. And useless.

It took about five seconds for our brains to start working again. We left Riley standing in the snow and stumbled and slid down the hill, running toward the line of kimchi cabs waiting patiently in the somber night.

2

AFTER STOMPING THROUGH THE SNOW TO THE 21 T-CAR MOTOR pool, Ernie flashed his badge and managed to get the keys to the jeep from the half-asleep dispatcher. Twenty-one T-Car is a military acronym that actually means 21st Transportation Company (Car), which maybe makes a little more sense.

Despite the frigid air, the motor started right away. Ernie grinned.

"Amazing what a bottle of Johnnie Walker Black will do for an engine."

The bottle went every month to the head dispatcher who made sure the jeep was properly maintained and always available when Ernie needed it.

We drove through the gate and out into the city.

All vehicles were off the street now because it was past curfew, the midnight-to-four lockup the government slapped on a battered populace over twenty years ago at the end of the Korean War. The theory is that it helps the authorities spot North Korean spies who might be prowling through the cover of night. The truth is that it reminds everybody who's boss. The government and the army. Not necessarily in that order.

We rolled through the shadows.

Seoul was dark and eerily quiet and looked like a town that had been frozen to death.

The jeep had four-wheel drive and snow tires, but still Ernie slid on the packed ice every now and then. He turned out of the skids expertly and I felt perfectly safe with him at the wheel. Safer than I would've felt if I were driving. He's from Detroit. He's used to this kind of thing. But I hadn't learned how to drive until after I joined the army and, in East L.A., where I come from, it doesn't snow very often. Only during Ice Ages.

I thought of the long summer days when I was a kid, running with packs of half-wild Mexican children through alleys littered with gutted mattresses and stray dogs and broken wine bottles. There were no swimming pools in the barrio. We poured buckets of chlorine-laced water over our heads in a futile effort to keep cool. And during the hottest days of the season, when I was fortunate enough to land a job, I breathed in the tang of warm oranges and overripe limes fermenting in a metal pail as I knocked on door after door in Anglo neighborhoods, hustling for a sale.

Every kilometer or so we were stopped by a ROK Army roadblock. The soldiers looked grim and tired. Their breath billowed from fur-lined hoods and they kept their M16 rifles pointed at the sky, which was okay with me. After we showed our identification and the twenty-four-hour emergency dispatch, they waved us through without comment.

Neither Ernie nor I talked. We were both thinking the same thing. We were in deep kimchi, the fiery-hot fermented cabbage and turnips that Koreans love. Kimchi up to our nostrils.

We'd taken money to deliver a note to Cecil Whitcomb, and now he was dead. Military justice doesn't know much about mercy. If anybody found out, we'd be kicked out of the army with a bad discharge or end up doing time in the Federal Penitentiary in Fort Leavenworth, Kansas, or both.

This wasn't going to be a routine case.

I was also beginning to feel a little guilty about maybe getting Whitcomb killed. Maybe a lot guilty. But I decided to put that away for now. I needed to think. And concentrate on the job I had to do when we arrived at the murder site.

Despite all the boozing we'd done in Itaewon, Ernie and I were both sober. But it wasn't from the cold air. It was from the tarantula legs of fear slowly creeping up our spines.

The upturned shingle roof of the Great South Gate was supported by stones weighing more than half a ton each. The gate had been built during the Yi Dynasty about four centuries ago, and was once part of a wall that surrounded the city. Now, in the deepness of the Seoul night, it sat somber and unmoving, as if it were watching us.

We circled the great edifice twice, creating lonely tracks in the snow, until I spotted a glimmer of light in one of the roadways running up a hill.

"Up there," I said. "Vehicle moving."

"Right."

Ernie swerved up the incline and rushed through a narrow road until the walls widened. We turned and almost ran into a gaggle of official-looking vehicles clustered around the mouth of another, even more narrow alley. Ernie found a spot up the road, parked the jeep, and padlocked the steering wheel.

As we walked back toward the lights, a grim-faced soldier stepped out of the night. He leveled an M16 rifle at us, blowing chilled breath through brown lips.

"*Chong ji!*" he said. Halt. "*Nugusho?*" Who is it?

I put my hands up slowly. "We're from Criminal Investigation," I said, "Eighth Army. Here about the body."

When he didn't respond I said the same thing—or almost the same thing—in Korean. The creased brow above the chiseled planes of his face crinkled a little tighter.

Ernie grew impatient. He pulled out his identification and thrust it forward. The soldier flashed a penlight on it, then studied our faces.

He waved his black gloved hand.

"*Chulip kumji yogi ei.*" No admittance here.

Ernie took a step toward the guard, staring at him, talking to me.

"Who does this asshole think he is, telling us we can't go in there? We're on an investigation."

I reached my hand out toward Ernie's elbow. The guard's face hardened.

"Relax, Ernie." I couldn't blame the guard much. We didn't look like investigators right now, dressed in our blue jeans and nylon jackets with dragons embroidered on the back. It was oh-dark-thirty, just a few hours until dawn. We were tired and it occurred to me that we must smell like a rice wine distillery.

"We don't have jurisdiction out here," I told Ernie. "He's just doing his job."

"Fuck his job."

Ernie turned and walked down the alley.

"*Chong ji!*" the guard yelled. When he aimed his rifle at Ernie's back, I stepped in next to him and spoke in soothing Korean.

"We're here for the investigation," I said. "A foreigner has been killed." I raised my open wallet in front of his eyes. "We're from Eighth Army. If you try to stop us, you will have many problems."

The guard looked at me warily. I saw the indecision in his eyes.

"Don't worry," I said. "You won't get in trouble."

I wasn't sure if that was true, but I knew he'd be in a lot more trouble if he shot Ernie—or me.

I backed down the alley, hands raised, identification held over my head. When I was convinced that the guard wasn't going to shoot, I turned and hurried into the darkness.

Korea is a divided country—north and south—and a country under the gun. Over 700,000 armed Communist North Korean soldiers breathe fire across the Demilitarized Zone only thirty miles north of Seoul, the capital of South Korea. It's not surprising that paranoia seeps into everything.

The alley near Namdaemun was like most alleys I've wandered through in Korea. Narrow. High walls of brick or stone or cement on either side. Spikes and shards of broken glass atop the walls to keep out intruders. Flat, uneven stone paving. Water seeping out of open pipes, running freely down the indented center of the walkway, reeking of decay.

Around the bend Ernie waited for me.

"Did you get him straightened out?"

"Yeah, Ernie. Jesus. Why didn't you wait until he checked it out with his Sergeant of the Guard? They would've let us through."

"Fuck that shit. They see a *Miguk* face and they just don't want to let us in."

"They would've had to. Patience pays in Korea."

Ernie snorted.

"You're going to get us shot one of these days," I told him.

He grinned at that. I don't know why the idea seemed appealing to him.

At first glance Ernie appears quite normal. He has short sandy brown hair, combed straight to the side, and a pointed nose and big green eyes that shoot out at people from behind round-lensed glasses. In uniform he looks as if he belongs on a recruiting poster. It's after you get to know him that you realize he's cracked.

A white sign pointed up a flight of stone steps. "Peikchae Yoguan" the sign said. The Peikchae Inn.

Peikchae was the southernmost country on the Korean Peninsula during the Three Kingdoms Period, about 1,300 years ago. Koreans don't forget much.

We walked up the steps. The stone walls followed the stairway and then turned. I felt as if we were in some ancient place. The alley was stuffed with the smell of rusty water and cold stones and frozen hay.

During the Korean War, much of Seoul had been leveled. But many of these old walkways and flights of stairs had survived. Not worth wasting a shell on. New buildings had been constructed on the old foundations. The Peikchae Yoguan was one of those, although the inn was made of cheap wood that was already splintering and starting to rot.

An open spot in the flights of stone stairways spread out enough to make room for a stone bench. Flashlights swirled. Men mumbled. Some squatted and took photographs of footprints or collected minuscule items from the snow with tweezers and dropped them into plastic bags.

The Korean National Police. The all-pervasive law enforcement arm of the government of the Republic of Korea. A federal police force with representatives in every city, town, and village in the country. None of them looked back when we walked up.

The spot was isolated. The high walls around us were the backs of two- and three-story buildings. Tiny windows gazed out on us like half-shut eyes. The entrance to the Peikchae Yoguan was around another flight of crooked stairs with no direct line of sight from the front door. Whoever had chosen this place had chosen it well.

No lighting. At the bottom of a pit of stone and brick in the middle of an indifferent city. The perfect spot for a killing.

We scanned the soot-flaked ice looking for a stiff.

Ernie stepped closer to take a look at a drift of snow up against a short stone wall. He walked back.

"Tried to deep-freeze the son of a bitch."

"What?"

"Yeah. Hid him under the snow."

I sidled my way in closer, watching where I stepped.

In the center of the clustered policemen lay a body, already turning blue. When a beam of light slid over the corpse I saw what resembled the guy we had talked to this morning: Cecil Whitcomb. But it was a lifeless thing. As drained of color as death itself. Eyes wide. Blood spattered like spreading satin on the frozen sheet beneath him.

Whoever killed Cecil had dug out a hole for him in the drift and tried to cover him up. It hadn't worked well because the body made a lump in the smooth blanket of white lace that covered the city. But to the unobservant it would pass unnoticed. And probably all the killer wanted was a few minutes to make his getaway. This frail camouflage had given him that time.

Somebody finally decided to notice us. A tall Korean man. Almost six feet. A long gray overcoat, slicked-back hair, and a hawk nose under almond eyes. I wondered if he didn't have an ancestor who had ridden as one of the Middle Eastern auxiliaries with the hordes of Genghis Khan. He approached slowly. I nodded and we greeted one another. His English was precise. Careful. As were his movements.

"Are you Inspector Bascom?"

Mexican or Anglo, we were all just Americans in the eyes of a Korean policeman. When I was growing up in Southern California that attitude would've come in handy if more people had shared it. Saved me a few lumps.

"No," I said. "I'm George Sueño. This is my partner, Ernie Bascom."

Ernie ignored the tall cop and continued to gaze at the body and chomp on a fresh stick of gum.

"I'm Lieutenant Pak. Namdaemun Police Precinct."

He stuck his hands farther into his pockets and turned his head toward the corpse. "I understand that this person is not an American."

"No. British. Cecil Whitcomb."

"You knew him?"

"I've seen him." Lieutenant Pak waited, as if expecting a fuller explanation. I gave it to him. "He was in the United Nations Honor Guard. Since they're such a small contingent they've turned over police power to us at Eighth Army. They fall under our jurisdiction."

Pak shook his head. "Murders in Seoul fall under my jurisdiction."

He was right. According to the treaty between the U.S. and Korea, any crimes involving United Nations personnel that happen off a military compound can be handled by the Korean National Police if they choose to exercise jurisdiction.

Our role would be as observers, unless Pak asked for our help. I expected he would.

Two men in blue jumpsuits trotted past us, carrying a folded canvas stretcher. They knelt near the body and hoisted it out of its capsule of ice.

Whitcomb's necktie and white collar had been twisted askew. Dressed for an appointment downtown. No American GI would wear a white shirt and tie unless he had to. Who could understand these Brits?

I motioned for the men to wait and knelt near the stretcher. I grabbed one of their flashlights and played it over the body. The sleeves of Whitcomb's jacket had been shredded, as if someone had slashed them repeatedly with a sharp, razorlike blade. His hands and wrists had also been cut, along with portions of his ear and cheek. None of the cuts were deep, except for the big one in the center of his chest.

I pulled open a fold in the white shirt. He wore green woolen underwear. The caked blood made me think of the colors of Christmas. Apparently the knife had entered just below the sternum. One deft gash into the heart.

I lifted his lifeless hand and checked under the fingernails. Nothing. Maybe a lab could find a trace of flesh, but I couldn't see any. I dropped the limp hand and turned back to Lieutenant Pak.

"What have the neighbors said?"

"So far, nothing. My men are out now." He waved at the high canyon walls surrounding us. "Asking questions."

In the flickering beam of the flashlight, I studied the footprints in the crusted snow. "There was a fight. Someone must've heard something."

"Maybe." Pak looked at me steadily. "But sometimes men fight and don't make noise."

He was right about that. Sometimes you're too preoccupied with saving your life. Screaming can wait.

Ernie checked the body as the men with the stretcher lifted it up. He sniffed the air above it, as if examining a side of beef, and chomped more furiously on his wad of gum. He didn't say anything.

I glanced up the stairway leading to the *yoguan*. A light blazed yellow and the front door of the inn was open. At least someone in the neighborhood had taken note of all the commotion. I started up the steps. Ernie followed. So did Lieutenant Pak.

The big wooden double doors of the rickety wooden building were unbarred, and an elderly man and woman peeped out around the entrance. They stood at the end of a long wood-slat hallway that had been varnished and revarnished maybe a million times. The floor squeaked beneath our feet.

The woman wore a long cotton housedress and folded her arms over a thick sweater. A black bandana tied around her forehead hid almost all of her liver spots. The man was thinner, with wispy white hair. He wore the loose pantaloons and shiny silk vest of the ancient Korean patriarchs.

Even though Ernie and I walked in first, they ignored us and bowed to Lieutenant Pak.

"*Oso-oseiyo.*" Come in, please.

Lieutenant Pak nodded back. Before he could speak I shot a question at the couple in Korean.

"*Yogiei junim ieyo?*" Are you the owners here?

Both nodded. Lieutenant Pak leaned back, mildly surprised that I could speak the language. Not many GI's bother to learn.

"Did you see any foreigners tonight?" I asked.

They both shook their heads. The husband smiled, as if he had suddenly encountered a talking horse, but the wife found her voice.

"No. No foreigners."

I twisted my head toward the murder site. "Did you hear anything—shouting, fighting—earlier this evening?"

The woman shook her head again. "Once curfew comes, we lock up and go to bed. We never stay open past curfew."

Not unless they have customers, I thought. The old woman was parroting the lines because of the presence of a Korean National Police officer. Not that Lieutenant Pak would give a damn if the inn stayed open past midnight, but Koreans are a cautious people. Especially when dealing with government officials.

"Did you see a young woman in here tonight? A very attractive young woman. A university student?"

Lieutenant Pak looked at me. Ernie fidgeted. Suddenly, I realized that I'd made a mistake by bringing it up.

"College student?" The old woman shook her head. "No."

"Maybe not a college student, but a young woman. Waiting for someone."

She shook her head again. "There have been no young women here tonight."

Right, I thought. There were probably three or four bar girls upstairs right now. With paying customers.

I asked a couple more questions but the old couple stuck to their story, which boiled down to they hadn't seen anything and they hadn't heard anything. With those big bolted doors it was possible. Maybe.

On our way down the steps, Lieutenant Pak walked next to me. Snow started to fall again, in moist clumps.

"Who is the young woman you asked about?"

I shrugged. "All soldiers—British, American, or Korean—always look for young women."

"Yes. But you . . ." He stopped and searched for the word. "You *expect* something."

"I expect GI's to look for women," I said. "That's all."

The blue-smocked technicians at the crime scene were wrapping up their work. The Korean police—and the U.S. Army overseas—don't rely much on high-tech methods of crime detection. They rely on shoe leather. And on interrogation techniques, the most reliable of which is a fist to the gut.

I turned to Lieutenant Pak and waved my arm toward the jumbled buildings and shacks that ran up the hill away from the murder site.

"Will you let me know if you learn anything from your interviews in the neighborhood?"

"Yes." He handed me his card. One side was printed in English, the other in Korean. It gave his phone number and his address at the Namdaemun Police Station. I didn't have a card, but he knew where he could find me. "Will you be talking to his unit today?"

"First thing," I said.

"And will you tell me what you find out?"

"Yes. I will."

He nodded. Not quite a bow but good enough for cop to cop. I nodded back.

As Ernie and I stepped down the treacherous stairway, Lieutenant Pak stood at the top, hands thrust deeply into his overcoat, watching us.

So far, this case fell fully under Korean jurisdiction. But Lieutenant Pak knew he'd need my help to ferret out information on the military compounds. And I'd need his if the assailant turned out to be a Korean. So far, we were cooperating.

We'd see how long that lasted.

When we got back to the jeep, Ernie unlocked the chain around the steering wheel and started up the engine. "You almost stepped on your dick back there, pal," he said.

"Yeah. You think he was suspicious?"

"Of course he was suspicious. He's a cop, isn't he?"

"But we're the investigators assigned to this case for the U.S. side. He's not going to think we had anything to do with it."

"Not as long as you keep your trap shut."

Ernie backed away from the wall, turned the jeep around, and swooshed through the growing blanket of snow. On the way back to the compound, slush and shattered ice ran after our spinning wheels. Frozen ghosts vanishing in the night.

I thought of Cecil Whitcomb and how pale and shriveled his body looked. Just yesterday I'd talked to him, gazed into his eyes, watched as he dispassionately read a note from a beautiful woman pleading for a rendezvous. And I thought of the two women who'd maneuvered us into this mess.

All the shit started with Eun-hi, the sexiest bar girl in Itaewon. For quite some time I'd wanted to get my hands on her flesh. Before it was for lust. Now I had a different motive.

3

ERNIE AND I WERE BOTH GRATEFUL TO THE ARMY.

It may sound strange when you consider that the last big case I solved got me sent to the DMZ for six months. Standard price for busting a general. But somehow the army always seems to know best. I learned a lot up there, found out what life is like in the hinterlands of Korea, and learned to accept my fate like a combat soldier, facing one day at a time, accepting the few comforts fortune might provide. And it gave me time to cool off.

After I'd done some investigative work for the 2nd Infantry Division Commander, the Department of the Army had questioned what a CID agent was doing in an artillery battery. When nobody could answer, I was transfered back to Seoul. Fortunately, the old 8th Army Commander had rotated back to the States so there was nobody left at the head shed with a hard-on for me. I was assigned back to the CID Detachment and after a couple of days it was as if I'd never left.

The army is always changing, which might have something to do with why it doesn't change at all.

What was I grateful for? For having a real life, for having money coming in—not much, but enough—and for having a job to do. I was an investigator and I wore suits and did important work. A status I never thought I'd reach when I was a kid in East L.A.

My mother died when I was two years old, and my father had taken off for Mexico shortly thereafter. My cousins sometimes told me that he was dead, sometimes that he was alive. After a while I figured that they didn't know whether he was dead or alive and their rumor-mongering was just another form of childish cruelty. A few years later, they stopped mentioning him—and I stopped caring.

I was brought up by the County of Los Angeles—in foster homes. It was a rough existence but I learned a lot about people, how to read them, how to hide when it was time to hide, and how to wait them out. The mothers were all right. It was the fathers you had to watch out for. Especially when they were drunk.

In the summers I was allowed to stay with my Tía Esmeralda, and she and her son, my cousin Flaco, taught me what it is to be Mexican. They taught me what it is to revere a family. What it is to cling to your honor no matter how painful a prospect that might be, even unto death.

What they didn't say to me, what nobody said, was that my father hadn't clung to his. He was a lost man. A man who hadn't honored his family. I learned a GI phrase later that described it perfectly: lower than dog shit.

Ernie was from a whole different world: the suburbs of Detroit. And he was grateful to the army for another reason.

When Ernie had first landed in Southeast Asia he was an eighteen-year-old pup with wide eyes and a sex drive as big as the monsoon sky. He loved it all: the mad convoys of two-ton trucks swerving around children and sharpened spikes on Highway 1, the dugout bunkers wired with rock and roll and shuddering with the pounding of nightly rocket attacks, the taking of women in broad daylight in muddy rice fields, the dirty-faced kids selling moist clumps of hashish through barbed wire fences.

After a year it was over.

When he went back to the States the place seemed bizarre.

Everyone worried about deodorant and cars and mortgage payments. They ignored the fundamental realities of life. Like slaughter. Ernie had to go back to Vietnam. Back to the real world. He did.

But by this time the skinny Vietnamese boys had run out of hashish. All they had for sale were dirty vials of white horse, pure heroin from the Burmese Triangle. The GI's knew it was a weapon, unleashed on them by the North Vietnamese in their desperate attempt to turn the tide of battle. But they took it anyway.

By the end of his hitch in the army, Ernie was strung out.

Back on the streets as a civilian, he was just another junkie and he knew he wouldn't last long. In a fit of sobriety, he popped into the army recruiter's office. Two weeks later he was back in boots. Clean. Quieting the aching need in his gut by filling it with liquor. To the point of madness. A fully acceptable pastime, as far as the army was concerned. They even encouraged drunkenness. They considered it wholesome.

Vietnam was over now but he managed to get an assignment to the nearest country available: Korea.

Right away he loved it: the girls, the bars, the poverty. And as an added bonus there was no heroin. The Korean Government didn't encourage it as the Vietnamese had. To the contrary. Trafficking in heroin in the Republic of Korea was punishable by death.

People argue about the effectiveness of the death penalty but when it's carried out absolutely, it works. I'd never seen any heroin since I'd been in Korea, I'd never even heard about anyone who was using.

Coming from East Los Angeles, that was a new experience.

When Ernie dropped me off at the CID building it was still dark. I used my key to open the Admin Office, turned on the lamp above Riley's typewriter, and sat down to churn out the paperwork the army always requires.

As I pecked out my preliminary report, I thought of what I knew about the British soldiers in the Honor Guard. Their pay wasn't good—probably less than half what an American of comparable rank pulls down—so they often use their ration control plates to buy everything they can out of the American PX and sell it to the Koreans down in the village. Sometimes they barter. Paying their houseboy in the barracks in imported liquor or cigarettes for doing their laundry and shining their shoes. Or buying freeze-dried coffee and hand lotion and tins of preserved meat for the girls in Itaewon who would favor them with those ephemeral charms that a young soldier prizes most.

So maybe this all had to do with some sort of black-marketing scam. Maybe Miss Ku, the gal at the teahouse, wasn't what she appeared to be. Maybe Cecil Whitcomb had gotten involved in a large black market deal and ripped Miss Ku off and she'd hired someone to take her revenge.

Maybe.

I made a note to check Whitcomb's ration control records.

Or maybe they'd been in on something together and pissed somebody off and now Miss Ku was in danger. Or already dead.

I made a note to monitor the KNP reports for the next few days. Tonight, so far, there was nothing on a dead female.

When I finished the report, I pulled it out of the typewriter and checked it for spelling mistakes. I wasn't worried about grammar. Nobody cares about grammar in the army. Only spelling. Spelling is something you can look up. Check out precisely without bending your brain too much. Since I'd been in the army I'd only heard grammar mentioned once. That was in Basic Training when my drill sergeant said, "When I talk, you assholes'd better know what I mean." Somehow we always did.

Whoever read this report would understand its grim message. It was simple enough. A British soldier had been murdered, by person or persons unknown.

What they wouldn't understand—what nobody knew but me—is that I would find the killer.

Ernie and I had been involved. Maybe we'd been double-crossed, used to set up an innocent man. Or maybe Miss Ku had been sincere, maybe she just wanted us to deliver a simple note. If that were true, Ernie and I should've pressed harder, found out why Cecil Whitcomb was so nervous about talking to us. And why he seemed so passive when he read a love note from a beautiful woman.

Either way, nothing would stop me from getting the people who had done this.

Koreans might be inscrutable to most of the world, but they aren't inscrutable to me. I grew up in East L.A. speaking two languages, living in two worlds, the Anglo and the Mexican. More worlds than that, really, if you consider the foster homes: Jewish, Polish, Argentinean. So learning a third language, Korean, hadn't intimidated me. In fact it came fairly easily, especially when the army gave free night courses on the compound and the instructor was young and female and pretty. And living in the Korean world hadn't bothered me either. Their culture was just another puzzle to unravel, like so many that I'd faced when the County of Los Angeles moved me from home to home.

I had time to solve this case. The request for an extension of my tour of duty in-country had been approved for another twelve months. I didn't have to worry about money or food or a place to sleep. The army took care of that. Other than an occasional hassle at work, I had nothing else to do except drink beer and chase women and I could set that aside for a while. I'd catch the son of a bitch who killed Cecil Whitcomb.

And I'd make sure he rotted in prison. Or in hell.

"George! Wake up!"

I raised my head, my hands cold on the sharp edge of the metal typewriter.

"You sleep here all night?"

It was Riley, the Admin Sergeant, the guy who'd first told us about the murder last night. He let go of my shoulder. I shook my head and wiped drool from the corner of my mouth.

"Yeah. I guess I did."

"Better get your ass washed up. The First Sergeant's on the way in and you know he won't tolerate a sloppy troop."

"Yeah. Okay."

I stood up. Riley pulled a disposable razor out of his desk drawer and tossed it to me.

"Here. Use this."

I caught it and grunted. "Thanks."

Down in the latrine I washed up and managed to shave without cutting myself. After I finished, I dried my face with towels of coarse brown pulp. By the time I walked back into the Admin Office, Riley had a pot of coffee brewing. He handed me a cup. I thanked him and sipped on it gratefully.

"Better prepare for heavy swells," he said. "The First Sergeant had one hellacious case of the ass last night."

My head hurt so I said it softly. "Fuck the First Sergeant."

"I wouldn't," Riley said. "Not even with your dick."

The door slammed, heavy footsteps pounded, and a low growl reverberated down the hallway.

"Sueño! You in here?"

I didn't answer. I guess he took that for a yes.

"Get your ass in my office!"

I finished drinking my coffee, set the cup down, and grinned at Riley.

"I hate to see the old boy so worked up before breakfast."

"That son of a bitch doesn't eat breakfast. He gets all his nourishment by chewing ass."

I walked down the hallway, concentrating on keeping my chest thrust out and my shoulders back. I knew I put up a good front. I'd been working on my technique for years. But inside I felt completely alone.

4

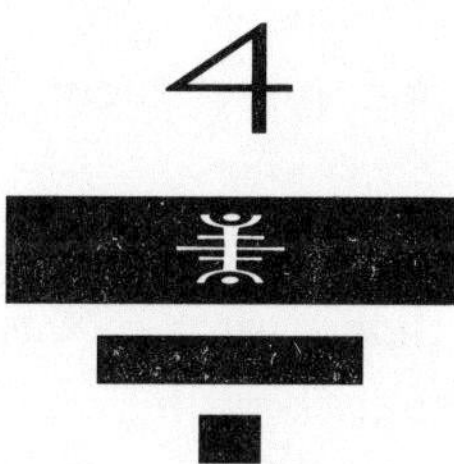

IT WAS A DARK ROOM. WITH SOMBER RED CURLICUES IN THE WALL-paper and a painting of the Virgin of Guadalupe, her halo radiant behind a shawl of purple silk. A tall priest dressed in black gazed down at me, warning me with his eyes to keep quiet. The room smelled of must and baby powder. Old women cried and twisted lace handkerchiefs with crablike fingers.

My mother didn't look like herself. No flushed complexion, no smile ready to break out beneath laughing eyes, no movement in her arms or legs. She lay still on the bed and for a moment I thought she was a stranger, a stranger made of wax.

The priest pointed and nodded his head. I leaned across the damp sheets of the bed and kissed my mother's face. The flesh was cold. I pulled away quickly. Her eyes remained tightly shut but her lips fluttered, like the wings of a dying butterfly.

"*Jorge,*" she said. "*Jorge mío.*"

They took me out of the room.

A few hours later the priest woke me and told me my mother was dead.

I cried for three days.

The First Sergeant and I sat in uncomfortable silence. He puttered with paperwork and occasionally walked up and down the hallway to see if the secretary was in yet. I remained immobile on the hard wooden chair. His little coffee maker gurgled in the corner and I was tempted to walk over and pour myself a cup, but I wasn't about to give him the satisfaction.

We were waiting for Ernie.

The First Sergeant didn't want to waste his breath on just one maggot, he wanted to have us both here for the ass chewing. I knew his game. Keep me here, callousing my butt, so I'd get the message: You can't be trusted to be let out of my sight or you'll wander off and get lost again.

It was a game a lot of sergeants and officers play. Somehow it makes them feel good. Maybe their parents played it on them, I don't know. And feeling good is more important to them than productivity. I was dying to get on with the investigation; time could be everything. The people I needed to talk to could disappear in a few hours like the morning mist. But I wasn't going to beg.

Besides, it wouldn't do any good. He was looking forward to this—in fact he had to wipe his mouth occasionally with the back of his hand because saliva was dripping out—and a First Sergeant with a case of the ass cannot be denied. Not in the army I know.

It was about one minute to eight when Ernie popped through the door.

"About *time* you got here," the First Sergeant said.

Ernie ignored him, walked over to the coffee maker, and poured himself a cup. He hunched over the little counter while he twisted open the sugar jar, scraped some granules off the bottom, and shook a smattering of flakes into his cup. He peered into the jar, trying to loosen the remaining crust.

"Why don't you invest in some more sugar, Top, and a little

cream? You can't keep drinking this stuff straight. Too toxic. Rot your gut."

The First Sergeant stood behind his desk, his fingertips resting lightly on the immaculately white blotter, glaring at Ernie. He wasn't a tall man but he was husky and if it wasn't for a potbelly that was just beginning to grow, he would've appeared muscular. Closely cropped streaks of white hair bookended the sides of his gray crew cut.

Blood rose through his thick neck and settled in slack jowls.

"Bascom," he said, "are you through dicking around with that coffee?"

"Just about."

Ernie clinked his spoon inside the metal cup, slurped on the hot java, and topped it off with just a dash more coffee. Like a potentate about to attend a ceremony, he paraded over to his chair, set his cup down on the cigarette-scarred table, and took his seat.

The First Sergeant leaned over his desk and looked at us both. His voice came out low and menacing.

"Where were you two last night when you were supposed to be on call?"

Ernie sipped on his coffee. I usually let him handle the First Sergeant. He had a knack for it.

"Eating chow," he said.

"At eleven-thirty at night?"

"Sort of a Continental thing with us. We like to eat late."

The First Sergeant looked at me. I didn't move.

"You were out boozing it up," he said, "and running the ville. And when I tried to get in touch with you, you were nowhere to be found."

"We left a number," Ernie said.

The crisp blotter crinkled under the First Sergeant's fingers. "A number where nobody speaks English!"

"Mama-san was out," Ernie said. "Her daughter's a sharp cookie, though."

"But she doesn't speak English!"

Ernie's eyes widened. "Of course not, Top. She's Korean."

"I know that, goddamn it, but when I have to make a call to get ahold of you guys and when I finally get through, I expect to be able to speak something other than that kimchi-eating gibberish."

"When in Rome," Ernie said, "and all that shit."

The First Sergeant took a deep breath. He seemed to be mulling over something, some course of action. He leaned forward.

"All right, you two. From here on out, whenever you're on call I expect you to be in the barracks. Not out in the ville, not in some *soju* house drinking rice wine, but in the barracks. And you'll check in with the Charge of Quarters every hour unless you're actually in your goddamned room asleep. You got that?"

Ernie sipped on his coffee, looked at the First Sergeant, and nodded.

"No sweat, Top."

The First Sergeant looked at me. I nodded.

He'd forget about this latest decree in a month or two and besides, we were only on call every sixth day and we could pay the CQ to call us at the Nurse's hooch if we had to. Not a problem.

"All right," the First Sergeant said. "Now that we have that out of the way. What'd you find out on this Whitcomb case?"

Ernie didn't move, but something in his manner made it obvious that he was through talking. The technical side of things was my responsibility. Ernie was strictly a people person.

"What we found out was in my report," I said.

The First Sergeant stared, waiting. I continued.

"This guy, Lance Corporal Cecil Whitcomb, a member of the British contingent of the United Nations Honor Guard, was stabbed to death in the Namdaemun district of Seoul at some time between ten and eleven o'clock last night."

"How did they fix the time of death?"

"The testimony of local residents. There was quite a bit of traffic prior to ten but nobody saw anything. The body was discovered just after eleven."

"How can a GI be knifed to death in downtown Seoul and nobody see it?"

"It's on the outskirts of downtown, in a residential area, in one of those little catacomblike alleys leading up a hill toward a run-down *yoguan.*"

"A what?"

"An inn. A Korean inn."

It was hard to believe how little Korean the First Sergeant had learned in the almost two years he'd been here. But he was like most GI's. He didn't want to learn.

"Late at night," I said, "a place like that can be pretty isolated. The windows in the buildings around it are mostly boarded up, not used much. Some are warehouses. Others are kept shut during the winter to keep out the cold and to keep out burglars."

The First Sergeant shuffled some papers.

"The Namdaemun Precinct has jurisdiction?"

"Yeah. A Lieutenant Pak will be conducting their side of the investigation. We met him last night."

"What'd he ask you to do?"

"Get information from Whitcomb's unit. Interview his friends. Things like that."

The First Sergeant nodded. "I want those reports sent to him right away. Don't get on your high horse and try to do the translation on your own, Sueño. Have the KNP Liaison Officer take care of it."

"Lieutenant Pak's English is pretty good."

"Good. If we don't have to translate them at all, so much the better. The first thing I want is interviews with everybody in the British Honor Guard. ASAP. Don't concentrate on just his friends. Everybody. I also want interviews with anyone he might've known outside of the British contingent. And I want copies of his personnel records. If they give you a hassle, have them call me. I want this done *now.* Any questions?"

Neither Ernie nor I said anything. It was a lot of work but more importantly it was also stupid. Churning out a ton of paperwork looked good when you sent it up the Chain of Command—they'd be impressed with how much you'd done—but it was more important to get to the heart of the matter. I couldn't be sure yet where the heart of the matter resided but if I had to bet I'd say it resided with Miss Ku. First,

I had to make sure she was still alive. But Ernie and I both knew better than to argue with the First Shirt. That would just set him off. Better to say yes and then do what you want.

The First Sergeant lowered his voice. Confidential now. Buddy to buddy.

"I don't have to tell you this, you guys. You've already guessed that the head shed is about to shit a brick over this. While they're here in the UN Honor Guard, those British soldiers are under our protection. But that's an agreement that can be changed. The British Ambassador has already been on the line to the CG. If we don't catch the killer, and *pronto,* they might pull their troops out of the joint command."

He let that sit for a while, waiting for us to be suitably impressed.

"Politics back home," he said. "One of their own killed over here and they have to rely on us to investigate."

"Tough for the country that gave us Sherlock Holmes," Ernie said.

The First Sergeant studied him, searching for a sign of mockery. He found none. Not in his face, anyway. Mockery was sort of a way of life for Ernie.

"Yeah," the First Sergeant said. "And tough for us too. When the Embassy is interested, you can expect the White House to be interested, and everyone up the Chain of Command is going to be watching us. The Provost Marshal plans to brief the CG on our progress this morning. You two guys are going to be under a lot of pressure, but I'll be here to back you up a hundred and ten percent."

I almost burst out laughing. Ernie's eyes glazed over. The First Sergeant looked at both of us and what he saw gradually made him angry.

"Maybe you don't *want* my cooperation? That's okay too. Either way we'll get the job done. I'll pull you two off the case if I have to."

A snort of air burst through Ernie's nose.

"Not on a case like this, you won't." Ernie put his coffee cup down and leaned forward. "This happened downtown, amongst Koreans, and George is the only CID agent who speaks the language. Besides, we're the best investigators in-country and you know it."

The First Sergeant straightened his back. His hair, which already stood on end, seemed to bristle.

"Don't push me, Bascom. Nobody's indispensable."

Ernie ignored him, leaned back in his chair, and went right on sipping his coffee.

The First Sergeant might want to pull us off this case but I knew he wouldn't. Not now. Not this early. It would look bad to the honchos at the head shed to be shifting personnel for no apparent reason and having to spend the time to get two new investigators up to speed. If the First Sergeant told them the truth, that he had doubts about whether or not he could control us on a sensitive case, it would reflect badly on him. They would wonder about his leadership abilities. The First Sergeant was stuck with us, unless we screwed up. He knew it and we knew it.

"In case you guys have any ideas that you've got me over a barrel," he said, "let's get a few ground rules straight."

A caginess crept into the First Sergeant's eyes. He opened his desk drawer and pulled out a neatly typed sheaf of paperwork. I recognized Riley's handiwork. The First Sergeant placed it in the center of the blotter in front of him.

"Your request for extension, Bascom," he said. "All signed and sealed and ready to go to personnel. Except it won't go anywhere unless this case is handled in the way I say it should be handled."

Ernie's lips tightened. It was a low blow. To overseas GI's like us there was nothing worse than being threatened with going back to the States. Going back to living in the barracks, doing your own laundry, swabbing the latrines, shining your own shoes. Having to put up with all the petty bullshit of the Stateside army that has no mission other than readiness. Which means putting up with any sort of make-believe training a bunch of bored officers manage to come up with.

Off post it was even worse. GI's in the States are considered to be in the same social class as things you scrape off the soles of your shoes. Something to crinkle your nose at. American women looked at us that way too, except for the occasional bar tramp. But here in Korea we were heroes. Feted and looked up to when we went out with the locals. We were, after all, the guys who'd kept the bloodthirsty Communists at bay during the Korean War. And we were still keeping them on their side of the DMZ. Our presence was appreciated. Even treasured. Not so in the States.

"That's all I've got," the First Sergeant said. "Any questions?"

Neither of us said anything.

"Good. After you finish those interviews, report back to me. Then we'll figure out what you're going to do next."

Ernie looked at his coffee, made a sour face, and carried it back to the counter as if it were contaminated. I stood up and followed him out the door.

As we clunked down the hallway, Ernie couldn't help mouthing off.

"If that old tight-ass ever had to run a real investigation he'd probably have his dick tied in knots on the first day."

I grabbed him and shoved him past the Admin Office. Miss Kim, the fine-looking secretary, sat up behind her typewriter. She caught Ernie's eye, and beamed. He winked at her and waved. Riley pointed his forefinger at us and pretended to pull the trigger.

Outside, Ernie started up the jeep and gunned the engine a few times to let it warm up. A smattering of flakes drifted down from gray skies and slowly dissolved on the metal hood.

"Shit!" Ernie said.

He loosened his tie, swallowed, and let his face sag for the first time this morning.

"What is it?" I said. "You've been hard-assed by the First Sergeant before."

He sat back in the seat. "Yeah, but this time he's holding my extension."

The engine churned. The flimsy canvas enclosure was starting to heat up.

"I know how you feel," I told him. "Who wants to go back

to the States? Back there, you're lucky if your monthly paycheck lasts a week. Here we can usually manage to stretch it out to almost four."

"And this time there's something extra."

"What's that?"

"The Nurse. Since we got back together again, she's really trying to make it work."

"What's wrong with that?"

Ernie shrugged. "It cramps my style a bit, but I can live with it. It's just that she's taking it so seriously."

"She wants to get married," I said. "What do you expect?"

"It's not just that. She acts as if this is her last chance. Her last chance to live any sort of decent life."

It probably was, I thought, but I didn't say so. I leaned back. "Yeah, well, they'll put the pressure on you."

"She keeps a razor in her purse."

I looked at him.

"One of those straight razors, the old-fashioned kind that nobody uses anymore, and she says that if I don't get my extension through she'll know it was because I didn't want to stay with her."

He stopped talking. I waited.

"If I don't get the extension through," Ernie said, "she says she'll kill herself."

"Do you believe her?"

"I do. Her family's already disowned her for dropping out of nursing school and taking up with a GI. She'd have nowhere to go."

I wasn't sure if that was true. When the worst happens people always find some path to take. I know. I'd been through it. But I didn't say so to Ernie. He believed the Nurse would commit suicide and that's what was important. And maybe he was right. In Korea, suicide is seen as a romantic act and sometimes a noble one.

Ernie shook his head. "Anyway, we got an asshole to catch. Where to? The Honor Guard barracks?"

"Hell, no."

"I didn't think so."

He slammed the engine in gear and we rolled forward on the slick roadway. At Gate Number 7 the MP whistled us through and we turned left on the Main Supply Route, zigzagging through the traffic toward the greatest nightclub district in Northeast Asia.

Itaewon.

5

THE WINDOWS OF THE KAYAGUM TEAHOUSE WERE DARK AND fogged. Ernie pushed through the big double doors and we were greeted by the sharp tang of ammonia. Standing in the entranceway, it took a while for our eyes to adjust to the darkness after being exposed to the dull glare of the morning snow.

All the chairs were turned upside down atop the tables. A young boy, about thirteen or fourteen, mopped the tiled floor. His mouth fell open and he stopped mopping when we walked in. I went back behind the serving counter with its hot plates and teapots and urns and started rummaging through drawers. Looking for something—maybe a business card or an address ledger—anything that might give us a lead on the woman who had called herself Miss Ku.

I wasn't worried about the rules of evidence. If I found Miss Ku, and turned her over to the Korean National Police, they wouldn't be either.

Ernie waited by the door.

In a frail, frightened voice the boy called into the back room.

"Ajjima! Yangnom wasso."

It wasn't a very nice way to talk. Telling his aunt that a couple of base foreign louts had arrived. But I ignored him and continued to rummage through the drawers.

What I found mainly were knives and spoons and utensils, until finally I spotted a big hardbound ledger. I thumbed through it. It was dogeared and stained with splashes of tea and coffee, and all the entries were dates and amounts of money recorded in won, the Korean currency. I wasn't getting very far.

Someone pushed through a beaded curtain. Apparently this was the boy's aunt. The same woman who had greeted us at the door the night before last when we had met Miss Ku here. But today the woman looked different. She wore no makeup, her hair was tied in a red bandana, and a thick wool dress flowed to the floor. She was dressed for warmth at this time of day, not to impress guests.

Her eyes widened and her full lips formed a circle.

"*Igot muoya?*" What's this?

I opened the last drawer. Spoons, ashtrays, cubes of black market sugar. Everything the well-equipped teahouse would need. I looked at the woman, raised my finger, and walked toward her.

"Two nights ago," I said, "we were here and met a young Korean woman at that table." I pointed to the far wall. "I want you to tell me everything you know about her."

She stared at me, stunned. Maybe by my brazen attitude. Maybe by my rapid-fire Korean. Maybe both. She found her voice.

"I know nothing about her."

"But you do remember her?"

"Yes. I was shocked to see such an attractive young woman talking to GI's."

"She was too high-class for us?"

"Yes."

I didn't take offense. Koreans categorize people by wealth and social position as casually as bird watchers classify red-breasted warblers by genus and species. They don't mean anything by it. Just the facts of life.

"What was her name?" I asked.

"I don't know."

"But she comes in here often?"

"No. I've never seen her before."

"But there's someone else who comes in here often who she knows, who she talked to?"

"No. She came in here alone, said nothing to anyone until she talked to you. After you left, she paid the bill and left without saying anything. Who are you anyway? You're the ones who know her. Not me."

"It doesn't matter who we are," I said. I took a step toward her, pinched my nose with my left hand, then let it go. "You are lying. Tell me how I can find that woman or my friend will get very angry."

Ernie had been watching me closely and spotted the signal. He took three rapid steps across the room, and as he did so the boy shrank back toward one of the booths. The woman swiveled her head. Without hesitating, Ernie leaned over, hoisted the mop bucket, and flung it twirling end over end through the air until it smashed into the stacks of porcelain cups at the end of the counter.

The woman and boy flinched and covered their faces.

"Who was she?" I asked the woman. "Tell me now or there will be more damage."

Ernie grabbed the mop and started smashing the handle into the glass candle-holders on each table.

"Stop!" she screamed. "Tell him to stop."

I grabbed her shoulders. "Who was that woman?"

She was crying now, in fear and anger.

"She came in here before, right?" I said. "She was friends with a woman named Eun-hi who works at the U.N. Club. Isn't that right? Tell me! Who was she?"

"I don't know. I only saw her that one time. She never said anything to me."

The boy scurried away from Ernie, ran toward his aunt, and flung himself into her arms. They hugged, rocking back and forth, tears streaming from their eyes. Crystal and chairs and ashtrays continued to clatter to the floor. I looked at the woman and her nephew, feeling sorry for them. They didn't know anything about Miss Ku and they didn't deserve this type of treatment.

I felt ashamed of myself. I wanted to say I was sorry but fought back the urge. I turned.

"Ernie!"

He smashed one more tray of glasses, lowered the mop handle, and looked up. I stepped toward him and twisted my head toward the door. He held the mop handle out, gazed at it as if disappointed, then tossed it to the floor.

When I hit the door he was right behind me, huffing and puffing, excited by the violence.

"What'd she say? She knows where we can find that broad, right?"

"Wrong." I kept walking. "She doesn't know squat."

Ernie's face soured. He straightened his coat and, like ice quick-freezing on a lake, regained his usual composure.

"Oh, well," he said. "Some of that glassware was due for replacement anyway."

We kept walking. Up the hill. Toward the U.N. Club.

I tried not to think of the tears in the eyes of the woman and the little boy, but instead concentrated on the wounds of Cecil Whitcomb.

The U.N. Club didn't smell nearly as antiseptic as the Kayagum Teahouse. In fact it smelled like a toilet, which is exactly what it was. The aroma of ancient cigarette smoke seemed to seep from the walls even though the cement floors were swabbed with suds. Rotted lemon, stale booze, the reek of the urinals, all of it coalesced to create a blast to the nostrils that I'd never noticed before.

Of course, every other time I'd been in here I'd been drunk. When your belly's full of beer, the place smells like a field of roses.

An emaciated waitress in a blue smock shuffled toward us.

"You too early," she said. "We no open until ten."

"We're not here for a drink," I said. "Where's Eun-hi?"

Ernie sauntered over to the bar. The waitress's tired eyes followed him. She turned back to me.

"Eun-hi?"

"Shit." The tears at the teahouse had made me impatient. I pulled out my identification and shoved it in front of her face. "Where's your VD card?"

All women who work in Itaewon bars are required by the government to have monthly medical checkups for venereal disease.

The girl stepped back and for the first time her face showed a trace of doubt. "Who are you?"

"CID. If you don't show me your VD card, I'll turn you over to the Korean National Police."

"I don't need a VD card," she said. "I'm a waitress."

"Bullshit! Every woman who works here needs a VD card."

A sullen-faced Korean man emerged from the back and stood behind the bar. I recognized him. He was Lee, the guy who poured our double shots of brandy. I walked over to him, hands outstretched.

"She doesn't have a VD card, Lee. Am I going to have to take her in?"

Ernie had plopped atop a bar stool as if he were about to order a wet one.

"No sweat," Lee said. "She newbie. Most tick we get her VD card."

"Better be most rickety tick," I said. "Let me see your VD card register."

Lee smirked, used to GI's trying to throw their weight around, figuring he'd smooth over the whole thing with a free round of drinks.

Ernie lounged against the bar, scanning the room, keeping alert for trouble.

Lee plopped the big leather-bound ledger on the bar. The pages were of thick construction paper. Stapled to each page were black-and-white photographs of the girls who worked here. Next to each picture, handwritten in a neat Korean script, was the name and address, date of birth, home of origin, and Korean National Identity card number. Korea is a highly organized society. Even for bar girls.

Lee stared at me with heavily lidded eyes, trying to pretend that he was extremely bored. "Why you fucking with me, Geogie?"

Ernie shot him a warning look. Lee ignored it. Some of these bar owners in Itaewon were hard-ass little brutes. I'd seen them jump into brawls with GI's twice their size, get knocked down, and bounce back up and slug somebody else. We weren't going to intimidate Lee. He had gone along so far only because he didn't want us to actually sic the Korean National Police on him. That would cost him money.

I thumbed through the ledger but didn't find it right away.

"Where's Eun-hi?" I said.

His face didn't move much but a veneer of knowing condescension passed over it, like a shadow crossing the moon, then disappeared. He thought I was just another horny GI trying to hit on Eun-hi. He wasn't far from wrong so I didn't bother to set him straight.

He riffled through the ledger, found the proper entry, and shoved it toward me.

"Here," he said.

Ernie leaned forward and looked at the photo with me. It wasn't very flattering. Eun-hi's face looked puffed and plain, not at all like the knockout we saw parading around the U.N. Club every night. I breathed deeply, wincing once again at the foul stench of the U.N. Club. If I hadn't noticed that before, maybe I'd never noticed that Eun-hi wasn't all that attractive either. It didn't matter. I was sober now. I'd find out for sure this morning.

"Is this address correct?"

Lee glanced at it. "Yeah. Maybe. Unless she move."

I committed it to memory.

"All right, Lee." I jerked my thumb over my shoulder. "Make sure that girl gets her card right away."

His face didn't move. "You guys want a drink?"

Ernie and I looked at each other. Lee knew we were CID agents and he was a smart businessman. Keeping the police happy was part of his job. At night, with a lot of other GI's watching us, we never accepted gratuities. Ernie didn't wait for me to answer.

"Yeah. Double bourbon. And one for my pal here."

Lee deftly poured the drinks, set them in front of us, and folded up the ledger and put it away. Ernie and I lifted our shot glasses and tossed them back.

On the way out, we saw the skinny waitress sitting in a rickety chair, hugging herself, bare legs crossed, glaring at us.

"Looks like you made another friend," Ernie said.

We pushed through the door and stepped into a slap of cold air.

"Yeah," I said. "So far this morning we're on a roll."

We turned up the hill and trudged past a quiet row of shuttered nightclubs. Behind them lurked a jumbled sea of upturned shingled rooftops. Hundreds of business girls and pimps and hustlers lived back there, in the maze of narrow alleys and shadowed courtyards that is the heart of the bar district known as Itaewon.

Eun-hi was in there somewhere. She knew something. Whatever it was, we'd find out.

6

EUN-HI'S HOOCH WAS IN A NARROW ALLEY IN THE CATACOMBS behind the Itaewon main bar district. We ducked through a doorway cut into a big wooden gate and entered a slender courtyard lined with sliding, paper-covered doors. Upstairs, a balcony with more rooms and hallways wound off out of sight.

Young women squatted on the raised walkway near the kitchen. Steam billowed from the concrete room and the scent of boiling onions filled the air. Pots and pans clanged.

When the girls saw us they let out gasps of surprise and covered their naked faces with splayed fingers.

"*Ajjima!*" one of them said. "*Sonnim wasso!*" Aunt. We have guests.

An elderly woman waddled out of the kitchen, wiping her hands on an apron strapped around her waist. She gawked at us. They weren't used to seeing GI's at this time of morning. Not on a workday.

"*Ajjima*," I said. "I spent the night with Eun-hi but I left something in her room. I came to pick it up."

She squinted. "*You* spent the night with Eun-hi?"

"Part of it."

"What did you leave?"

I did my best to act embarrassed. "Underpants."

The girls laughed.

"Yes, yes. Go ahead." The elderly woman waved her hand toward the stairway behind us. I thanked her and we turned and climbed up the steps.

The splintered wood slat floors creaked beneath our shoes. As we turned the corner we ran into the cement block outer wall on one side and a long line of doorways on the other. We walked forward slowly. Each room was quiet. Not a sound.

"They're all getting their beauty rest," Ernie said.

"But which one belongs to Eun-hi?"

"Take your pick."

Ernie stopped and pounded on a door. When there was no answer he pounded on another. A little farther down the hall a door creaked open.

"*Nugu-seiyo?*" Who is it?

A sleepy-faced girl, wrapped in a flowered robe, gazed with half-closed eyes into the hallway. I walked down to her quickly.

"I'm looking for Eun-hi."

Clutching her robe across her chest, she waved impatiently.

"That door."

Ernie pointed at one. "This one?"

"No. Next one."

Ernie walked over and pounded on the door. No answer. He tried to open it. Nothing. The girl in the doorway waited, the cold air starting to wake her up.

"She's not there," I said to her. "Do you have a key?"

She shook her head. "*Ajjima* have."

Something creaked, squealed wildly, and finally snapped. The girl and I both swiveled our heads. Eun-hi's door was wide open. Ernie grinned at us sheepishly.

"Cheap lumber," he said.

By now a couple more heads had popped out of their rooms. Still no Eun-hi. Ernie and I entered the hooch.

It was a small room. Tiny, to be exact. Just enough space for a Western-style bed and a stereo set and a standing closet jammed with jumbled silk.

The bed was a mess. The embroidered comforter and the stained sheets had been twisted and tossed every which way. Wads of tissue paper sprinkled the room.

"Looks like somebody had a nose-blowing contest," Ernie said.

I turned back to the curious young women peering in the door and held out my hands. "Where's Eun-hi?"

They conferred amongst each other, chattering away in Korean, thinking I wouldn't understand. They mentioned a name: *Suk-ja.* I interrupted them.

"Eun-hi told me that she might be over at Suk-ja's hooch."

They stared at me blankly.

"Can you tell me where she lives?"

They conferred a little more, figuring I must be okay if Eun-hi had told me about Suk-ja. One of them started talking.

Suk-ja was an independent business girl and didn't live here in the house with *ajjima.* Eun-hi often left early in the morning, after whatever GI she had policed up the night before returned to the compound, and visited Suk-ja. The girls were wide awake now and gave me good directions. Suk-ja's hooch was just around the corner. But in these catacombs you could get lost in less than a hundred yards.

I asked them why Eun-hi was visiting Suk-ja so early in the morning. One of the girls shrugged.

"*Jinhan chingu,*" she said. Best friends.

Suk-ja lived on the top floor of a three-story brick walk-up. Ernie whispered to me as we climbed the cement stairway.

"We need to make a quick impression on her," he said.

I thought of the sliced remains of Cecil Whitcomb's body.

"I think you're right."

When we reached the door I prayed the girls had given us the right information. Ernie leaned against the far wall, raised his foot, and leapt forward. The door crashed inward. I rushed past him, into the tiny room, and two startled women sat up in terror.

Eun-hi was naked.

Suk-ja, a tall, extremely thin woman, wore a sheer pink nightgown as if to camouflage her protruding ribs. Large brown nipples stuck out from her flat chest like bullets. Her cheeks were sunken, the planes of her face sharp and angular. She was the first to recover from the shock. Her lips tightened. Her eyes narrowed.

"*Nugu ya?*" she screamed. Who are you?

I ignored her and grabbed Eun-hi by the shoulders and stood her up. She looked up at me, frightened, still struggling to clear her mind.

"Who told you to have us go to the Kayagum Teahouse?" I asked.

Eun-hi shook her head, too terrified to understand. Her English was never good and under these conditions it would be lousy, but I was too angry to speak Korean. Too angry to give her any advantage. I rattled her body and watched her large breasts flop with each jolt.

"Who talked to you about me? Who told you about the Kayagum Teahouse?"

I heard footsteps behind me, then a sharp high cry of pain. I swiveled my head.

Ernie held Suk-ja by the wrist. Her small white knuckles were wrapped around a straight razor. Not an expensive one, just the type with a regular men's shaving blade screwed into a metal holder. She was a strong woman and struggled fiercely but silently. Ernie twisted her arm behind her back until, slowly, she bent forward. Her cordlike body writhed beneath the swishing pink silk. Saliva sputtered over full lips.

"Fuck you, GI!" she said.

Ernie pushed a little harder on her wrist. She grimaced.

"Nice talk," he said.

I turned back to Eun-hi. There wasn't much time. I couldn't wait for her to come out of shock. Someone might call the Korean National Police and they could be here any minute. I slapped her.

Her soft cheeks rippled with the force of my blow. When she recovered she opened her eyes, stared at me, pursed her lips, and spat in my face.

I slapped her again and turned her around and twisted her arm behind her back and lowered her slowly to her knees on the sleeping mat. Once my knee was propped securely on her big round butt, I wiped my face with the back of my hand and pushed a little harder on her wrist.

"I'll break it," I said.

She started to whimper.

Suk-ja growled something to her but I didn't catch it. Ernie twisted her around and slammed her face up against the wall.

I leaned harder on Eun-hi. "Who told you about the Kayagum Teahouse?"

"I told you before," Eun-hi said. "A woman. A Korean woman."

"How did you know her?"

"I didn't know her. She came in the U.N. Club, in the afternoon. Told me to talk to you. She gave me money, so I talked to you."

"How much did she give you?"

"Ten thousand won." She said it without hesitation. Twenty bucks.

"Have you seen her again?"

"No. Never again."

"She told us she was a student at Ewha."

"Humph. No way."

"She's not a student?"

"Only stupid GI think so."

I shoved a little harder on her wrist. "How do you know?"

"The way she talk. Her eyes. She business girl just like me."

I'd totally fallen for the elegant lady routine. But it wasn't the first time I'd been fooled.

"When is she coming back?"

"I don't know. Maybe never."

"Do you know anybody who knows her?"

"No."

I didn't know what other questions to ask. What more could I do?

Doors slammed downstairs. Loud, urgent voices. I looked at Ernie. He nodded. I bent toward Eun-hi.

"If you see her, you'd better tell me. You understand?"

She didn't answer.

We let go of the girls and stepped back. I expected them to embrace, to comfort one another, but instead Suk-ja grabbed her razor and Eun-hi reached behind a small dresser and pulled out a leather strap.

Apparently we weren't the first GI's to give them a hard time. We backed out of the room.

Outside, Ernie and I trotted down the hallway, stepped onto a balcony, and climbed down the rusty fire escape. It squeaked and groaned under our weight but held. The last ten feet we dropped to the cobbled roadway. We rushed through another alley, barely wide enough for our shoulders, emerged between a row of nightclubs, and slid down the ice-covered hill to the Main Supply Route.

Once we arrived back at the jeep, Ernie unchained it and started it up and we both breathed a little easier.

"You think she was telling the truth?"

"I think so. She hit the money she was paid right on the button. Without hesitation."

"Maybe that's how much she charges for a short time."

"Might be. Awfully expensive, though."

Ernie jammed the jeep in gear.

"Worth it," he said. "Especially if you get that skinny-ass Suk-ja thrown in as a bonus."

He swerved into the onrushing traffic, forcing a three-wheeled truck piled high with about half a ton of garlic to slam on its brakes. The driver cursed.

We sped toward the compound and didn't even look back.

7

AFTER STOPPING AT MY ROOM SO I COULD CHANGE INTO MY COAT and tie, we went straight to the Honor Guard barracks. It took about two minutes for someone to call the British Sergeant Major. He stomped down the hallway, fists swinging at his sides, square jaw thrust out.

"Been waiting," he said. "Took your own bloody time."

"Sorry, Sergeant Major," I said. "We had a couple of other people who had to be questioned."

He crossed his arms. Khaki sleeves were rolled up tightly around bulging biceps. Red hairs stuck out beneath his elbows like copper wires.

"Been asking a few questions myself," he said. "Two blokes matching your descriptions were seen near the arms room yesterday, at the same time as Whitcomb. The armorer tells me that you three had a jolly marvelous conversation."

Ernie and I put on our most somber expressions; two guys who had seen it all, so bored with life that we were about to go to sleep. Our professional cop look.

The Sergeant Major seemed vaguely troubled by our reaction but continued to stare at us with eyes as piercing as sniper rounds.

"Sergeant Major," I said, putting as much sloth into my voice as I could, "why don't you let *us* do the investigating?"

Ernie rolled his neck and looked up at the ceiling. I did my best to pin the Sergeant Major with my gaze.

"These are things that don't concern you," I said. "You don't have a need-to-know. I'm afraid we'll have to ask you to keep what you've learned strictly confidential."

He shuffled his brown combat boots, slightly embarrassed now. "Yes. Of course."

I took a deep breath and let it out. As if I were glad to have all the foolishness over with.

Sometimes I thought Ernie and I ought to audition for a play at the music/theater center. We were better actors than any of the clowns who climbed up on stage.

"Can you show us to his quarters?"

He nodded and held out his arm. "This way."

The Honor Guard barracks was one of the old brick buildings built by the Japanese Imperial Army before World War II. Houseboys hustled back and forth carrying piles of laundry and boots shined to a mirrorlike finish. Steam billowed out of the latrine. One Korean man stood in the huge cast-iron sink, pant legs rolled up to his knees, churning his feet as if he were stomping grapes. Another fed laundry and soap into the tub.

Ernie chomped on his gum. Luckily, all the Honor Guard units were out on the parade field, working on their drill and ceremonies. Off duty, they'd been known to get in a lot of fights with the clerks who worked at 8th Army Headquarters. It's natural for infantrymen to think of desk jockeys as not being real soldiers. Ernie'd had a couple of run-ins with them. I hoped it wouldn't flare up here. We didn't need any ill will, and the Sergeant Major already knew too much about our dealings with Whitcomb. I wasn't sure how effective our little act had been. All I could do was pray that the Sergeant Major would keep quiet.

The British section of the building was a long open bay lined with bunks and wall lockers. Equipment of canvas and leather was stored neatly above the lockers or under the bunks. A couple of houseboys worked on boots in the far corner. An old radiator clanged and complained, spewing out sporadic wisps of heat.

The Sergeant Major stopped at one of the bunks. "Here we are."

The bed was neatly made and the equipment display looked exactly like all the others. Still, we went through it carefully. We were looking for anything. Notes, items hidden away, drugs. We found nothing. The last thing left to check was the padlocked double wall locker. I pointed to it.

"Can you open this?"

The Sergeant Major pulled a big ring of keys out of his pocket. The metal doors squeaked open. Unlike the rest of the room, the inside of Whitcomb's locker was splashed with color. The white and red tunics of his dress uniforms. A few civilian shirts and pants. Everything was meticulously neat. We checked it all. The razor blades, the soap, the after-shave. Ernie even sniffed the tooth powder. He was the expert on drugs and if any of it was any good he'd pocket it. He put the tooth powder back.

The big thing that we were all ignoring, saving until last, was the thing that had shocked us initially when we opened the locker. On the bottom, atop some neatly folded winter fatigue blouses, sat a brand-new electric typewriter.

None of us said anything. We knew it couldn't belong to Whitcomb. It was the big heavy-duty type bought by the U.S. Government. Even if Whitcomb wanted a typewriter of his own he would've bought one of the compact, lightweight models out of the PX. This was a monster.

When we'd checked everything else and come up with nothing, I pulled the typewriter out of the locker and looked it over carefully. In indelible ink was a supply number: 49-103. Whatever that meant. I jotted it down in my notebook, along with the serial number.

I stood up and looked at the Sergeant Major.

"Do you have any idea where this came from?"

He seemed genuinely surprised. And upset. "No idea."

He provided a list of Whitcomb's best buddies and promised to send a copy of the personnel records over to Riley at our Admin Office right away.

"What sort of guy was he, Sergeant Major?"

"Quiet fellow. Kept to himself. We never expected anything of this sort. Not at all."

Ernie checked under the bunk, rattled the springs noisily, stood up, and turned to the Sergeant Major.

"How well did you really know Whitcomb?"

The Sergeant Major's face flushed red.

"Not very, I'm afraid."

We thanked him and walked out.

At the Headquarters Supply Room we had to throw our weight around a bit and flash our badges a couple of times, but finally we persuaded an overweight Staff Sergeant to check the records on an electric typewriter with supply number 49-103.

It was tough for him to bend over but he finally found the supply folder in the bottom drawer of a dusty filing cabinet.

"Here it is," he said. "Checked out three months ago to the office of the Special Logistics Coordinator. J-two."

We told him to take good care of the file and left.

The J-2 operation was in a large building right next to 8th Army Headquarters. The "J" stands for joint, since what is commonly referred to as 8th Army is actually a joint staff composed of the United Nations Command, U.S. Forces Korea, and the 8th United States Army itself.

The "2" stands for the same thing it stands for on every army organization chart: Intelligence.

. . .

Captain Burlingame was an air force officer and wore his fatigue blouse loose around his waist. His eyes had bags under them, his skin was soft, and lightly greased black hair hung over his forehead like a batch of spreading hay. He sipped on one of those heavy-duty coffee mugs embossed with a replica of an F-4 Phantom roaring off into the sunset.

"We did have a break-in," he told us. "About a week ago."

"Eight days ago," I said. "To be exact."

Burlingame checked his calendar. "Right."

Ernie and I sat in his office, Ernie fidgeting as usual. Cramped spaces and symbols of authority always made Ernie uncomfortable.

"The MP report said you lost one typewriter and two small jars of freeze-dried coffee."

"That's right. I'd bought them at the PX the day before."

"Who locks up at night?"

"I do. I always do."

The padlock on the office door was pretty flimsy. Not much trouble for someone with the proper tools to pop it open. Other than scratches, the lock hadn't even been damaged, according to the MP report.

"This isn't a secure building, then?"

"Not the whole building. Just the basement."

"What do you keep down there?"

The captain lifted one eyebrow higher than the other and gave me a wry smile. "Do you have a need-to-know?"

"In this case, yes."

"Classified documents. We're an intelligence operation."

"No guards?"

"We have guards at the gates. And guards who make sweeps through the buildings at intervals during the night. That's it."

"Then the downstairs area must be pretty secure."

"It is. Like a vault."

"Besides you, who has a key to the office?"

"Nobody. Except the supply officer."

"Do you ever loan your key to anyone?"

"Why would I do that?"

"Maybe that nice-looking Korean secretary likes to come in late and get some work done."

Burlingame scowled. "What is it you're implying? Miss Ahn is honest. Been with us a long time."

"I'm not implying anything. Just asking questions."

He sipped on his coffee again.

Actually I was trying to rattle his cage, provoke him into saying something unguarded. He'd seemed nervous since we'd walked in. A normal enough reaction to CID agents. But Burlingame was an intelligence officer. An educated man. He should've realized that he had nothing to worry about.

"Before the break-in, or after it, what did you notice that was unusual?"

"Nothing. Everything pretty much routine. Except our typewriter was gone and I had to hustle a replacement. And we had to buy coffee from the snack bar because my ration for the month had been used up."

"Do you always use your entire ration?"

"Hell, no. Are you accusing me of black-marketing?" I didn't answer. His face flushed red. "I don't like your attitude very much."

Ernie rose from his chair. "A man is dead, Captain. Somebody didn't like *his* attitude very much either."

Ernie stepped over to the hot water pot, grabbed the half-empty jar of freeze-dried coffee, and unscrewed the lid. He licked his finger, dipped it in, and tasted the chunky grounds. Moving his mouth, he savored them for a moment.

"He's clean," Ernie said.

Captain Burlingame's jaw fell open. "Now you're accusing me of using illegal drugs?"

Ernie shrugged. "If the shoe fits, wear it."

The captain rose to his feet and pointed his forefinger at Ernie.

"You'll take that back. Right now, Mister. You have no reason to be casting aspersions on a superior officer."

"I'll cast any goddamn thing I want."

The interview was over.

I stood up, grabbed Ernie by the elbow, and yanked him toward the door. He shrugged off my grip and walked out on his own. As we left, Captain Burlingame followed us into the hallway. He stood watching us, hands on his hips.

I pulled Ernie outside into the cold air.

"What the hell's the matter with you?"

"The guy pissed me off. More concerned about whether or not we were accusing him of anything than if we find the guy who sliced up Whitcomb."

We walked rapidly through the redbrick buildings of the 8th Army complex. The snow had let up, for the moment anyway. Naked elms swayed in the breeze like arthritic claws, scratching at the cold sky.

"Give him a break, Ernie," I said. "Most people get nervous when CID agents ask them questions. They start worrying about their own positions. About how they're going to look."

"Yeah? Well, hell with them. I'm tired of that piddly shit."

When Ernie kicked in the door at Suk-ja's hooch I'd figured he was just having fun. Now I realized that this case was already getting to him. He was pissed that our stupidity in delivering a note and not asking enough questions had somehow contributed to the death of Cecil Whitcomb.

So was I.

We had a list of names. Cecil's buddies. I wanted to find out about the real life of Lance Corporal Cecil Whitcomb.

But there was somebody I needed to talk to first. The man who knew more about GI's than they sometimes knew about themselves.

The houseboy.

We slipped in a side door of the Honor Guard barracks and walked down the long hallway. Each room housed eight to fourteen soldiers, broken down by squads. The building was quiet now in the mid-afternoon. Most of the houseboys were finishing up the last of their laundry, and the soldiers were out in the motor pool or on the parade field. Maintenance and training, the story of a dogface's life.

We slipped into Whitcomb's room and waited. A few minutes

later a thin Korean man in baggy fatigue pants and a loose T-shirt shuffled down the hallway, his rubber sandals slapping the cement floor. When he entered the room and saw us, his tired eyes widened slightly. Other than that, his square, craggy face showed no hint of surprise.

"Mr. Yim?"

He nodded. I had gotten the name from the Sergeant Major. I showed him my identification.

"I am Agent Sueño and this is my partner, Agent Bascom. We're here to ask you a few questions about Cecil Whitcomb."

He nodded again, dropped the bundle of underwear he was carrying on one of the neatly made bunks, and sat on a footlocker facing us.

"How long have you worked for him?"

"Since he got here. Three months ago."

His English was well pronounced. Hardly an accent. I knew he'd never gone to high school—probably not even middle school—or he wouldn't be working here. He'd picked it up from the GI's over the years. Intelligence radiated from his calm face. When I first arrived in Korea, I wondered why men such as this would settle for low positions. I learned later that after the Korean War, having work of any kind was a great accomplishment. Even cleaning up after rowdy young foreigners. At that time, the rowdy young foreigners were the only people with money.

"Tell me about Whitcomb," I said.

Mr. Yim raised and lowered his thin shoulders. "He is a GI. Like all the rest."

"But he's British. Not American."

"Same same."

"Does he have a girlfriend?"

"Sometimes he go Itaewon. With friends. Maybe he catch girl. I don't know."

"No VD?"

"No."

So Whitcomb never caught the clap. Otherwise Mr. Yim would've seen evidence of the drip—clotted green pus—in his shorts.

"Did he sleep here every night?"

"Yes. Every night."

His dark brow crinkled.

"What is it?" I asked.

"He sleep here every night but sometime he come late."

"Was he in bed when you arrived to work?"

"Not always."

"What time do you report in?"

"Five o'clock."

The curfew runs from midnight until four A.M., and the MP's routinely open the compound gates for Korean workers at five o'clock in the morning. Houseboys have to report in early so they can shine the boots and shoes of their GI charges before reveille.

"Where did he go late at night? Out to Itaewon?"

"No."

That surprised me.

"How do you know?"

"Because of clothes. When I come in he not in bunk. Bunk no messed up. He down in shower, washey washey. On his bunk is clothes."

"What kind of clothes?"

"Strange clothes."

"Can you show me?"

Mr. Yim got up and walked to Whitcomb's footlocker. He opened it and rummaged through the rolled underwear and socks and towels. He pulled out three items: a pair of dark dungarees, a black pullover turtleneck sweater, and soft-soled, navy blue shoes made of an elastic-type canvas material.

Ernie looked at me. We'd gone through everything while the Sergeant Major was here, but these items of clothing hadn't meant anything to us at the time. Now, when they were displayed together like this, they seemed a little more ominous.

"Maybe he made his own bunk," I said. "And wore these clothes out to Itaewon."

"No." Mr. Yim said it firmly. "He no make own bunk. And he no sleep. He *taaksan* tired."

Very tired.

"How often did this happen?"

"Two, maybe three times each month."

"Near payday?"

He shook his head. "Anytime."

Mr. Yim seemed lucid, calm, smart, sober. An excellent witness, except that I knew from experience that houseboys were so low on the social scale that nobody took their testimony seriously.

But I did. So did Ernie.

"What else can you tell us about Whitcomb?"

"No more. He *potong* GI."

A regular soldier.

"Who killed him?"

Mr. Yim's eyes widened. "Maybe gangster."

"Gangsters?"

He nodded. "In Namdaemun many gangster."

"Do you know any?"

He shook his head vehemently.

We talked for a while longer but Mr. Yim didn't have much more to offer. His life was an endless chain of shining shoes, washing laundry, ironing fatigues, and putting up with GI bullshit. Cecil Whitcomb had been just one more link in those loops of iron that weighed heavily on his soul.

On the way out, Ernie offered him a stick of gum but Mr. Yim refused. Instead, he went back to sorting the folded underwear and placing each item in the proper footlocker.

8

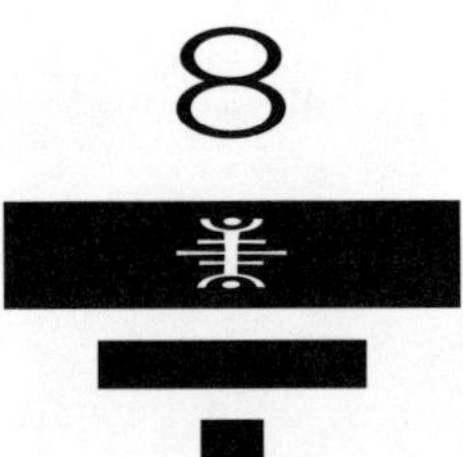

ADMIN SERGEANT RILEY'S THIN LIPS CRAWLED OVER THE EDGE OF the porcelain mug. He glugged down some of the milky coffee, set the mug down, and pulled the pencil out from behind his ear.

"You were right, George. The stats on stolen office equipment have risen sharply over the last three months."

"Up ten percent," I said. "Prior to that, they ran steady for years."

Riley shook his head. "Not the smooth operations we're used to either. Crude. Clumsy. Doors broken. Windows shattered."

"The slicky boys are going downhill," I said.

Riley nodded.

"Slicky boys" was a term that had come into use during the Korean War, more than twenty years before. The entire peninsula, from the Yalu River on the border with China to the tip of the peninsula at the Port of Pusan, had been completely ravaged. Hardly a factory or a business enterprise of any sort still stood. Crops had been allowed to rot in the fields after terror-stricken families fled to evade the destruction by the armies that stormed back and forth across the land. People were desperate. People were starving.

In the midst of this desolation were a few military enclaves, surrounded by barbed wire and sandbags. The only places that had food, that had clothing, that had shelter.

Some of the people would barter with the GI's for the wealth they held. They'd trade anything, even their bodies, for something as insignificant as a bar of soap.

Others took more direct action. These were the slicky boys.

"Slick boys" is what the GI's called them, but the Korean tongue is incapable of ending a syllable in a harsh consonant. They must add a vowel. So "slick" became "slicky." And the GI's picked it up. "Slicky boys" stuck.

And some of them really were boys.

Six, seven, eight years old. They could more easily slip through the barbed wire and hide on the compound for hours and bring out something precious to their waiting families. A handful of dried potatoes, a can of preserved beans.

It didn't take long for their activities to become organized and their thievery to become bolder. The disappearance of supplies and equipment became a serious problem during the war, and the American generals made sure that precious warehouses were heavily guarded. Armed soldiers were given orders to shoot.

As the war dragged on, desperation kept the slicky boys at their work in the military compounds. And there were many compounds to choose from. By 1952, the United Nations had sent soldiers from sixteen different countries to help defend the Republic of Korea from the Communist aggressors.

In one incident, a slicky boy broke into a stronghold of the Turkish Army and was captured. The Turks tried the twelve-year-old on the spot and convicted him of thievery. After being tortured for a few hours, the boy was decapitated. The severed head was set atop a spike at the gate to the compound and allowed to rot until the unit moved back to the front.

Riley rattled the paperwork in his hand.

"This stealing just isn't professional enough to be the work of the slicky boys," he said. "It had to be an amateur."

"Maybe Whitcomb?" I asked.

"Maybe."

We thought about that for a moment. I voiced what we were both thinking.

"Even without Whitcomb butting in, how can thievery statistics stay so constant?"

"That's a hell of a good question."

Riley loved a puzzle. You could almost see him salivating. He picked up the heavy black receiver and started dialing.

I sat back, sipping on my black coffee. Relaxing. Letting him do the work for a while.

After talking to Whitcomb's houseboy, Ernie and I had tracked down one of the guys on the "best buddies" list the Sergeant Major had provided us: Terrance Randall.

The picture Randall gave of Cecil Whitcomb wasn't what we'd expected. Pictures of real people seldom are.

Whitcomb was born into a poor family on the south end of London. His father worked on the docks of the River Thames packing fish and had to make his daily appearance at the market well before dawn. Somewhere along the line, Whitcomb's dad picked up two bad habits. The first was gambling, which didn't do much to help the family finances. The second was rising a little early on a wintry morning to make a stop along the way at a likely-looking household and pick up a trinket or two to help pay for bad habit number one.

Whitcomb's brothers, when they were old enough, picked up where Dad left off and made a full-time business of burglary. As the youngest of the three sons, Whitcomb had been initiated into the family trade but somehow managed to avoid the lengthy police records that his brothers acquired. As such, all the family's hopes were pinned on him. When he was old enough, he enlisted in the Royal Fusiliers.

They all thought of him as the success story of the family and expected him to make a career of the army. Be somebody. Not just another fool in and out of prison.

But Whitcomb couldn't resist the rich pickings on an American compound. There was so much equipment and so much of it just wasn't well guarded. It wasn't fair.

Randall didn't know who Whitcomb sold to, but said he was smarter than most of the other blokes in the unit. Most just black-market with one of the women in the bars. The Korean business girls turn around and sell the PX goods to their mama-sans, and they turn around and sell the stuff to someone else. Everybody makes a profit. Whitcomb decided to go right to the source, keep all the profit for himself.

But he wouldn't tell Randall who that source was. It was Whitcomb's secret and Randall really didn't want to become involved. A few bucks a month for selling booze and cigarettes was enough for him.

For the most part Whitcomb was a regular guy. He hung out with his buddies at the 8th Army Snack Bar on the nights when they sold draft beer, and at the 7 Club in Itaewon while their pay lasted.

Randall claimed Whitcomb bragged about the money he was making. How much he'd sent home and how much he would be able to save, for when he went back to civilian life. But he wasn't planning on retiring from the army for twenty years. A very patient guy. And cautious.

I asked if there was anyone special in Whitcomb's life or if Randall had ever heard of anyone named Miss Ku. The answer in both cases was negative.

He did give me two things I could hold on to. The first was that they never wore civilian clothes on any of their details, and they had never helped set up equipment at the British Embassy. That made a liar of Miss Ku.

Randall also told us that in the shower room he had once noticed welts on the back of Whitcomb's thighs. When he asked about them, Whitcomb snapped at him and told him to mind his own business.

He couldn't think of anyone who would want to kill Cecil Whitcomb. In every murder case I've worked, no one ever can. Somehow, people still end up dead.

Riley spoke in what seemed like code to some guy on the other end of the line: percentages, dates, figures. He jotted everything down as he spoke.

Ernie sat on the edge of the desk of the fine-looking Admin secretary, Miss Kim. They'd had a thing going, unconsummated, for months. In front of them were two cups of coffee and they took turns swirling sugar and cream through the satiny liquid. Ernie watched Miss Kim's slender, red-tipped fingers gracefully rotate. If they were any hotter for one another they would've burst into flames.

"Sure," Riley said. "Thanks, Fred. You got it."

He hung up the phone.

"That was the Eighth Army Budget Office," he said. "The guys who plan for casualty losses and theft losses, things like that. The losses that show up in every annual budget. Casualty's hard to pin down. You never know when there's going to be a fire or a flood on one of the outlying compounds, or when there will be accidents and supplies and equipment will be damaged beyond repair. That fluctuates every year. All these guys can do is plan for an average.

"Theft is a little different, though. For all the years Fred's been here, about four, they've always written in a three-point-five-percent theft loss in the budgets. Why? Because that's what they've been using as far back as he knows about. Almost to the Korean War. What does it actually run? You already know that. Right about four percent."

"Every year?"

"Every goddamn year."

"But that's a lot of compounds. At least fifty, scattered all over Korea. And a lot of equipment and supplies that vary from year to year."

"Can't argue with that," Riley said. "But somehow the theft losses run almost exactly four percent every year."

"Any ideas why?"

Riley sipped on his coffee. "Sure."

"Spell 'em out."

He watched Ernie and Miss Kim for a minute. They'd tossed aside their swizzle sticks and were now dipping their fingers into the coffee. That wasn't so bad. It's when they started to lick one another's fingertips that it became sort of ridiculous.

Riley growled. "You two want to tongue each other to death, fine. But do it on your own time."

Miss Kim turned as red as a silk banner on Chinese New Year's. She reached into her in-basket, grabbed some paperwork, and started fumbling with her typewriter. Ernie sucked off the coffee that remained on his fingertips and stared at her. Smiling. A coyote admiring a chicken.

Riley looked back at me. "Spell 'em out? Okay. Koreans are highly organized. They have been for four thousand years. Nothing they do is freelance. Goes against their nature. Whatever it is, it's got to be done in a group. It might be slaughtering innocent villagers or planting roses for the spring but whatever it is, it's okay as long as it's approved by a group and done by a group."

"So the thievery's organized?"

"Beyond the shadow of a doubt."

"Gangs."

"I wouldn't call them gangs, Sueño. More sophisticated than that."

"But they must get into it every now and then. Like in East L.A. turf battles. The low-riders from one barrio going at it against the low-riders from another barrio."

"No. Never."

"No dead *vatos*? How do they pull that off?"

"Central authority."

"For all of Eighth Army's activities all over the country?"

"Right," he said. "How else do you figure they keep the entire take down to four percent? Everything they steal is pre-approved by a central authority."

I sat quietly, letting that sink in. "Why wouldn't somebody realize this before? And do something about it?"

Riley shrugged. "All of us Americans are here on a one-year

tour. A few more, if we extend. It takes a while to find out about this stuff. The Korean slicky boys don't exactly advertise. And it would take a lot longer than a year to do anything about it. By that time, all you're thinking about is going home. So far, nobody's had the gumption to rock the boat. Not only could it be dangerous to your health but think about it for a minute, we budget for it. The U.S. Government has plenty of money to fight the Communist threat. The American taxpayer is an endless source of wealth. So what's to worry?" He shrugged.

"And that's why the slicky boys keep theft down to just above the budgeted amount?"

"Sure. Nobody notices. The honchos at the head shed don't get upset. Everything's going according to plan."

He picked up his coffee mug and drained the last of the stagnant fluid. When he set it down he looked at me. "You're slow, George. But not hopeless."

Down the hallway, the First Sergeant barked into his phone. Just a matter of time until he started in on us, and I didn't feel like answering any of his questions.

I thanked Riley and gave him a thumbs-up. When I policed up Ernie, I almost had to drag him away from Miss Kim. She pouted and didn't look very happy about him leaving.

To find shelter from the cold we made our way over to the 8th Army Snack Bar. Inside the welcoming warmth of the huge Quonset hut, we filled two heavy-duty cups with steaming black coffee, paid for them, and took a seat at a small table looking out at the passing pedestrians.

I was exhausted. But the memory of Whitcomb's blood-drained body was keeping me going. That, and the fear of what could happen if we didn't come up with a culprit, and come up with one soon.

The coffee went down warm and harsh in my throat. I swallowed and set the mug down.

"Maybe we should interview the rest of those guys in the British Honor Guard like the First Sergeant said."

"Hell with him," Ernie said. "We start doing everything Top tells us to and he'll lose respect for us."

"But the Korean National Police want those reports too. And it takes time to translate them."

"They already have the important ones."

We had given a synopsis of what we had found, which wasn't much, to Riley, who had sent it on to the KNP Liaison Officer.

A couple of Korean women, probably dependent wives, sat at a table near us. Both were attractive. One had long hair and eyes so wide she looked as if she'd paid for an operation to remove the fold of skin above her eyelid. It was supposed to make her look more American. Actually, it just made her look as if she'd taken a terminal hit of methamphetamine.

Ernie stirred his coffee, sipped on it, and gazed at them through the steam. As his glasses fogged up, both women giggled.

I thought of what we had so far. There seemed to be four possibilities.

Ernie listened and occasionally nodded as I ticked them off.

One was that Whitcomb had broken into 8th Army J-2 because he was after classified information. If that was the case, he could've been killed by almost anybody—either an agent from Communist North Korea or a counterintelligence agent from our side, or the Korean CIA, or by a middleman in a dispute over payment.

Spying was a growth industry in Korea.

Since the Korean War ended over twenty years ago, the country had been divided by a brutal gash across the center of the peninsula known as the DMZ—the Demilitarized Zone.

On one side sat the South Koreans, officially known as the Republic of Korea, and on the other sat the Communist North Koreans, officially designated as the People's Republic of Korea. Both republics claimed title to the entire country.

The People's Army of the Communist regime to the north was over 700,000 men strong, backed up with heavy armor and artillery provided by the Chinese and the Soviet Union.

Their largest artillery pieces were emplaced only thirty miles north of Seoul, the capital of South Korea. The North Korean guns were capable of firing shells into the city itself. North Korean aircraft could drop bombs on the downtown business district within two minutes of the first warning of their approach.

Meanwhile, the South Koreans hadn't been sitting on their hands, waiting for the big bad North Koreans to come south and gobble them up. Their army was over 450,000 strong. Every able-bodied man was drafted into service at the age of twenty, and their soldiers were amongst the toughest and best trained in the world.

Between these two snarling dragons sat the 30,000 GI's of the United States 2nd Infantry Division. They were the trip-wire. If the North Koreans ever invaded, their heavily armored legions would slaughter the outgunned and outmanned Americans of the 2nd Division. It was planned that way. Casualties would provide the U.S. President with the ideal pretext to fly in more troops to help defend South Korea from the Communist hordes.

When I'd first arrived in-country, a colonel delivered an orientation speech which summed up the situation we were facing. If war ever broke out again in Korea, he told us, United States soldiers would be involved in the most brutal conflict they've seen since the founding of our nation.

In a tribute to how things change, the poets of ancient China had once referred to Korea as the Land of the Morning Calm.

Did the Communist North Koreans send spies into South Korea? By the truckload. One commando raid had actually reached the grounds of the Presidential Mansion in Seoul.

The spies came in by land, across the DMZ through barbed wire and mine fields; by sea, along the rocky coastline of the Korean peninsula; or by air, with phony passports via Japan.

Still, Cecil Whitcomb being a spy for the Communist North Koreans didn't seem likely. If he was really playing with fire and going after classified documents, why would he have stolen a typewriter and stashed it in his locker? Petty thievery wouldn't pay much and would only bring unwanted heat. Meanwhile, the North Koreans would be paying him big bucks.

It didn't make sense.

There had to be something else happening here.

The second possibility was that Miss Ku was exactly what she seemed to be. A woman in love who'd been wronged and decided to hire somebody to exact her revenge.

That made some sense when you considered the murder site. Whoever had taken out Whitcomb was a pro. The meeting spot was right in the heart of Seoul, a seemingly safe place for a rendezvous, and yet, because of the layout of the buildings, it was actually quite isolated from prying eyes. Someone had carefully selected it.

Also, Whitcomb had not been very effective in fighting back. He had been stabbed cleanly under the sternum and into the heart. A swift, deft move delivered by an expert.

And he had received many light cuts on the arm. Whoever had assaulted him had been so sure of their abilities that they'd toyed with him before killing him. That didn't seem very professional, but I suppose some professionals enjoy their work.

Afterward, the money in his wallet had been removed, but that could've been done just to make it appear that the murder was a common robbery.

Option number two didn't appeal to me much. Miss Ku had seemed like a determined young woman. If she wanted to take revenge on Whitcomb she would've done it herself. Korean women are bold. When they feel they've been wronged, they will attack a man in public, challenge him toe to toe, dare him to hit them, and physically fight if it comes to that. Of course, it's a great loss of face for the man. And if he beats the hell out of her, he loses even more face. That's how Miss Ku would've gone after Whitcomb.

Maybe.

The third possibility was that it was a random killing perpetrated by a thief who spotted a foreigner in downtown Seoul, attacked him, and stole his money.

Two things argued against that.

First, why would anybody have gone to the trouble of sending Miss Ku to hire us to entice Whitcomb to go to the Namdaemun area? Street thieves prowl likely areas looking for random victims. They don't make elaborate plans to entice their victims to certain spots.

Second, if it were a common thief, the Korean National Police probably would've cracked the case already. And so far they had no more than we did. In a high profile case like this you can bet they've already rounded up the known muggers and questioned them thoroughly. The KNP interrogation methods are extremely effective. They don't have to worry about civil liberties. As long as the guy lives through the interview, the KNP's are safe from criticism.

It was the last possibility that seemed most likely to me.

When Whitcomb became a freelance thief on Yongsan Compound he'd elbowed into someone else's territory. He didn't know it, but it was a territory that had been extremely well-organized for decades.

Ernie nodded as I spoke.

"The slicky boys," he said.

"Exactly." I leaned forward. "Think about the bruises that Terrance Randall told us Whitcomb had on his legs."

"They tried to discipline him?"

"Right. And when he kept it up, the slicky boys hired Miss Ku, used her to dupe you and me into giving Whitcomb that note, then killed him when he showed up in Namdaemun."

Ernie sipped on his coffee, set it down. He shook his head. "I don't like it."

"Why?"

"Koreans wouldn't rock the boat like that. They knew Whitcomb would only be here a few more months. They'd try to discipline him but if it didn't work, they wouldn't kill him. Bring too much heat."

"Maybe his sloppy thievery would've brought even more heat. Ruined a sweet deal."

Ernie thought about that. "Maybe."

"And maybe they knew that by compromising us, by getting us to take money from Miss Ku, they'd effectively eliminate the Eighth Army CID from the investigation."

"Because we're the only two investigators who even have a prayer of solving a case off-compound?"

"Right."

"And they wouldn't be worried about the Korean police?"

"No."

" 'Cause they got them in the bag?"

"Right again."

Ernie thought about it. His brow crinkled.

"But that would mean that they would've had to know that the case would be assigned to us. That we were on call the night they killed Whitcomb."

I stared at him.

"Jesus," he said. "That means they must know damn near everything about us."

I nodded. We both let it sink in. Finally, I spoke.

"And they expect us to roll over on this. To protect our own butts."

"Shit."

Ernie glanced at the two women at the next table. They'd been waiting for him to look over. When he did, they smiled and slowly sucked on ketchup-covered french fries. Ernie stared but he wasn't seeing them.

"I'm not worried about protecting my own ass," he said. "It's hung out there often enough before."

"Then we have to go through with it, Ernie," I said. "We have to go after the slicky boys."

"Nobody's ever done it before."

"We'll be the first."

A tremor went through Ernie's body. His lips tightened. I knew he had made a decision. And once Ernie makes a decision he usually doesn't back away from it, even when he gets hit over the head with a two-by-four.

"You're damn right we'll be the first," he said.

We finished our coffee, stood up, and strode toward the door. The girls had finished their french fries and I almost wanted to go back and talk to them, but we didn't have time.

We stepped out into the frigid winter air. I took a deep breath, trying to clear my mind of all the jumbled nonsense that had been tumbling through it before. For the first time since we started on this case I felt as if I knew what I was doing.

Whether or not what we were doing was a smart move was another matter entirely.

We'd be going after the slicky boys, the most highly organized criminal organization in the country, to prove that they murdered a British soldier.

Not exactly a routine case.

9

THE KILLER CREPT FROM SHADOW TO SHADOW AS SILENTLY AS THE night itself. Charcoal smeared his face, and his black clothing made him almost invisible.

It was warm in the midnight alleys. Summertime. Crickets chirped from a row of quivering elms across a broad expanse of road; the raw dampness of the River Han filled his nostrils.

At the back wall of the *yoguan,* the killer grabbed a drainage pipe and probed with his foot until he found a toehold in the brick. In the moonlight he hoisted himself up, inching skyward like a huge, lethal spider.

He passed two windows, making no sound. When he reached the third floor, he paused. Listening.

Heavy breathing. Moans.

"Yobo. Dasi hanbon." Lover. Once again.

Repeated over and over by a woman's voice. A voice the killer knew only too well.

Straining with the massive muscles of his neck and arms, the killer pulled himself higher and peered through the open window, past a curtain of fluttering silk.

The light of the moon shone into the room, bathing the two bronzed bodies in a golden, almost holy glow. He saw her face beneath the man's shoulder, her eyes pinched closed, her mouth cooing soothing words as she ran the long fingers of her soft hands over his back.

Hands that had once touched me, the killer thought.

How many months had she lied to him? Too many. Probably from the very beginning.

The rage bubbled up from his gut like lava exploding from a volcano. Still, his years of training kept his movements deft and silent.

He crawled into the room.

For a time the lovers didn't notice him. They were still too far away, still enfolded in their cocoon of ecstasy. The killer placed himself at the foot of the bed, feet spread shoulder-width apart, watching.

The woman noticed him first. Her eyes popped open. She pushed up on her lover's shoulders, unable to say anything—unable to scream. The lover twisted his head, grunting, and then his eyes widened in shock, finally spotting the dark monster looming over them in the shadows.

Before they could move, the killer's fist shot out like a bolt of black-gloved lightning. The lover's head snapped back. He rolled off the woman, a lewd slushing "pop" ringing through the room as he slid out of her body.

The woman screamed. The killer backhanded her with his iron-like knuckles.

The lover was on all fours now, shaking his head, moaning, but when he started to rise to his feet, the killer shot forward, jabbing his fingers brutally into the man's neck. Slicing deeper, gripping flesh, he jerked backward with all his strength. The lover's throat flopped out onto his naked chest.

Blood splattered everywhere. Against the wall, onto the sheets, along the outstretched arms of the screaming woman.

Choked by her own terror, still, the woman's body moved. Clutching at a blanket. Kicking back toward the open window.

As her spine slid over the wooden sill, the killer grabbed her feet and shoved. The woman fell backward, thudding against brick outcroppings on the side of the building and finally smashing, headfirst, into the street below.

Bone cracked.

She lay silent in the alley. A naked doll, twisted and broken.

The killer shuddered, his body aflame, his manhood engorged and stiff.

People were awake all through the building now. Many of them screamed, and screamed again. Louder and louder. The killer stood by the window, gazing down on the snapped body beneath him in the street. Blood dripping from his hands. Confused.

Why didn't they stop screaming?

The killer jerked bolt upright on his sleeping mat, kicking back the sweaty comforter.

"*Yoboseiyo. Shikkuro. Choyong-hei chom!*" Hello. It's too noisy. Quiet down!

He hopped to his feet, instinctively crouching in a fighting stance. His eyes scanned the darkness. Walls, a sleeping mat, a small cabinet, cold air seeping in through a crack in the window.

Not summer anymore. Winter. Outside the steamed window, snow drifted on a sea of tile roofs. He was in a room he had rented last night. Quickly, he groped in the dark. His clothes were here, his money, the knife. It came back to him now. He was safe. The woman pounding on the door was the owner of this rat-infested hovel.

He cleared his throat and spoke.

"*Arraso.*" I understand.

The owner's footsteps pounded down the hallway. The killer listened at the door for a moment to make sure she was gone.

Bending down, he grabbed the *o-kang*, the porcelain pee pot, held it pressed against his thighs, and took a leak. When he was finished, he replaced the lid and shoved the *o-kang* back into the corner. He squatted back down on the sleeping mat.

The same dream. Over and over. How many times? How long would it haunt him?

He checked the time on the clock radio. Zero five hundred. An hour past curfew.

The killer slipped on his clothes, wiped his face with a damp hand towel, reached under the comforter, and examined the knife. It was long, wickedly curved at the end. The handle wrapped in leather, the steel honed to a razor-sharp edge. Fine workmanship. A Gurkha knife. From Nepal.

Using the hand towel, he carefully wiped off the tiny flecks of blood that still remained. He slipped the knife in his belt behind his back and let his shirt hang loosely over it.

Before leaving, he checked the room to make sure he hadn't forgotten anything. He wouldn't be back.

Outside, bundled up in his down-lined jacket, his feet crunched in the snow on the dark, almost deserted roads. Scattered flurries of flakes powdered the city. Rats scurried off the sidewalk at his approach and disappeared into broad trenchlike gutters covered with perforated cement block.

He should've ditched the knife last night, he thought, but he hadn't been thinking clearly. Too exhausted by the fight.

He shook his head. Not professional. Not professional at all. He'd allowed the fight to go on too long.

He remembered the terror in the Englishman's eyes. He could taste it on his tongue. The delicious terror. The sure knowledge that he was going to die.

The killer fed off of it again, closing his eyes, reliving the final agony of the dying Brit.

He walked for almost a half hour in the darkness until he was two blocks from the site where he'd killed the Englishman. In the distance, blue and red lights flashed. Emergency vehicles.

He found a deserted alley, crouched, and dropped the knife into a rock-lined sewage ditch. The knife fell, cracked a thin layer of ice, and splashed into the filthy water below.

The killer straightened and walked away. They'd find the knife. No matter, he thought. They'd never find him.

An old woman pushing a cart laden with steaming chestnuts

trundled past him. She stared into his eyes and, her face filling with fright, turned away.

The killer smiled to himself.

Terror. Everywhere he went. Terror.

But no time for that now. He had work to do. So much work to do.

His heavy boots plowed through the growing drifts.

10

ERNIE AND I SAT IN THE JEEP, SHIVERING, SIPPING ON HOT COFFEE from a thermos, stomping our feet to keep warm. In the gray distance, the first glimmers of sunlight peeked over white-capped mountains. During the last couple of hours the temperature had plummeted—maybe five or six degrees. Still, an occasional flurry of snow fluttered to the ground.

"Whoever thought of this shit detail?" Ernie asked.

"You did."

"Oh, yeah. That's right. You shouldn't have listened to me."

"You finally said something that makes sense."

We were parked beneath an overhang behind a cement-walled warehouse on a small army supply depot known as Camp Market, situated about fifteen miles east of Seoul. Riley gave us the tip. Electrical equipment had been disappearing from this compound at a steady clip for as far back as anyone could remember.

The pilferage had to be organized and it had to be the slicky boys. We were here to catch them in the act.

Last night, we'd run the ville in Itaewon and called in every favor we'd ever done for anyone, asking about the slicky boys.

The answer was always the same: "*Moolah.*" I don't know.

After applying a little pressure, a few of our Korean contacts opened up with one more thing: Don't mess with the slicky boys, it's not good for your health.

Maybe it was because we'd been drinking *soju*. Maybe it was because we were tired from the long day and pissed off that no one would give us any information and frightened by all the warnings we'd received about the slicky boys. But whatever the reason, last night Ernie and I had come to a conclusion. The only way to contact the slicky boys was to flush them out. Start making arrests, disrupt their operations, force them to talk to us.

Of course, it was risky. How risky I wasn't quite sure.

If nothing else, we'd get their attention.

We didn't know how the electrical equipment here on Camp Market was disappearing, but we did know that there had to be inside contacts involved. The perimeter of the compound was secure: chain-link fence, barbed wire barricade, floodlights, guard shacks every hundred yards.

It looked more like a Nazi concentration camp than a transshipment point for lightbulbs and toilet paper.

The only way to move stolen property off-compound was through the front gate. But in addition to the Korean perimeter guards and the GI warehouse men, there was also a contingent of MP's stationed here. An American MP checked everything that passed out of the gate.

American MP's, like anyone else, can be corrupted. The small village of Pupyong-ni is right outside the gate and it's chock-full of nightclubs and business girls and cheap booze. A little extra money can make life a lot more pleasant for a hardworking MP.

Still, we couldn't be sure exactly how stolen goods were transported off the compound until we witnessed something being moved. That's why we'd been here since before dawn. To catch the slicky boys in the act and stop them.

By the time we had slugged down the last dregs of our coffee, we heard the steady churn of an approaching diesel engine. A truck rolled between us and the next warehouse over, stopping near a cluster of metal drums.

"Trash pickup," Ernie said.

"Let's take a look."

We climbed out of the jeep and slipped through the shadows until we could see the rear of the trash truck.

Four workers, dressed in heavy down coats and pullover caps and gloves, dropped four empty metal drums to the ground, next to the full ones. With deft precision, each of the empty drums was turned upside down. For no apparent reason, two men shuffled off to a nearby coal bin. We followed them. Grabbing broom handles, they poked through a small mountain of coal, raising black dust as they did so.

"This is it," Ernie said.

After rummaging around for less than a minute, both men returned, a coil of copper wire held in each hand.

Copper wire. Not manufactured in Korea. Imported at a big premium. But here it was, on an American army compound. Easy to sell at a good profit margin. Prime pickings for an experienced thief.

My guess was that someone inside the warehouse had slipped the four coils of wire out the back door during working hours yesterday. Not being able to transport the coils off-post through the heavily guarded gate, the crook had stashed his loot beneath the pile of coal.

The trash collectors, armed with this information, had been sent back to collect more than just trash.

Maybe the slicky boys did this every day. Four coils of wire at thirty or forty dollars each—every day—could soon produce a tidy sum.

The two men back at the truck had turned the empty metal drums back to the upright position.

"What the hell are those?" Ernie asked.

On the ground, where the empty drums had been, lay four metal discs.

The four coils of copper wire were dropped, one each, into the four empty metal drums. Then the four metal discs were tossed in after them.

"False bottoms," I said. "The copper's hidden beneath perfectly fitted sheets of metal."

One by one, the workmen dragged the empty drums over next to the full ones. They lifted the full ones and dumped the contents into the drums containing the false bottoms and the copper wire.

"Ingenious," Ernie said.

"Also a hell of a lot of work."

He shrugged. "Hard work, they're used to."

Once the four drums with the copper coils and the false bottoms and the trash were loaded onto the bed of the truck, the workmen climbed back aboard and one of them—the smallest—hoisted himself into the cab, started the engine, and drove off.

Ernie looked at me. "We follow?"

"No. They've got nowhere else to go. We wait for them at the main gate."

"Right."

The trash truck must've had other stops because it took about twenty minutes for it to reach the main gate. The back of the truck was fully loaded now with overflowing drums of garbage. How many of them contained false bottoms and copper wire, I couldn't be sure.

We had parked the jeep in the parking lot of the Battalion Headquarters, engine running, pointed toward the gate.

Ernie said, "Now we see if any of the MP's are in on it with them."

We waited. The trash truck rolled up to the gate and stopped. A bored-looking MP emerged from the guard shack and, carrying a long wooden pole, pulled himself up onto the bed of the truck. The Korean workers shuffled out of his way as he methodically ran the pole down through the trash to the bottom of every drum.

After he'd checked them all, the MP hopped off the truck and waved them forward. A Korean guard started to roll back the big chain-link gate.

"Now!" I told Ernie.

He gunned the engine, shoved it into gear, and we shot forward.

As he did so, I opened the canvas door of the jeep, stood up, held on to the metal roll bar with one hand, clutching my badge aloft with the other, and shouted at the MP at the gate.

"CID! Don't let that truck pass!"

The gate was almost completely open now. Ernie had taken off so fast that the wheels missed their traction on the slick road and the jeep's back end swerved a little. I held on. Ernie regained control in a matter of seconds.

The driver of the truck swiveled around to see what was causing all the commotion.

The MP stepped back from the guard shack, turned, and shouted at the Korean gate guard to close the damn gate.

The truck's diesel engine roared. The big vehicle lurched forward and started to roll through the open gate.

The Korean gate guard stood motionless, not trying to close the gate, pretending he was confused. The tail of the trash truck cleared the gate and sped out onto the main road that runs in front of the compound.

Suddenly, the Korean guard came alive and leaned into it, shoving the gate closed.

Ernie shouted, "Son of a bitch!" and stepped on the gas.

The gate was closing, we were heading straight toward the narrowing gap, and I was standing outside the jeep, the door open, about to have my head smashed against the MP guard shack. I ducked back inside the jeep.

As I did so, Ernie hit the gate, something smashed into our left side, and we bounced against the wall of the MP guard shack but kept moving forward, squeezing through the rolling gate that clanged shut behind us.

"Which way'd they go?" Ernie screamed.

"Right."

He took the corner sliding, forcing oncoming traffic to slam on their brakes. The trash truck was up ahead, only a few yards from us. Ernie shifted and gunned the engine like a maniac, and within a few seconds we were gaining on them.

"Take it easy, Ernie!" I shouted. "They're outside the compound now. No longer in our jurisdiction."

"Fuck our jurisdiction!"

Ernie was just about to swerve to the side of the trash truck and try to force them over, when their red brakelights flashed and they careened left in front of oncoming traffic.

Tires skidded. Horns honked. I screamed.

Ernie didn't slow down. He followed the truck across a short bridge that led into the little village of Pupyong-ni.

The big truck took up the whole road. The traffic here was composed strictly of pedestrians and people on bicycles. They leapt out of the way of the barreling trash truck, screaming and cursing in several languages.

"The son of a bitch is going to wipe out the whole village!" Ernie shouted. But he stayed right on his ass.

Unlit neon and shuttered barrooms flashed past us. Suddenly the road widened. We were heading into rice paddies. But rather than continue toward the open countryside, the driver of the trash truck swerved back toward the cement block walls of a residential district.

Ernie wasn't fooled; he stayed right with him, and now, with the road wider, he made his move, gunning the engine, speeding forward, racing alongside the trash truck.

He started to edge toward the nose of the truck, veering to the right to pull him over, when I saw it.

"Stop!" I shouted.

Ahead was a "honey truck." Workmen stood around it, their faces covered with gauze masks, and a thick rubber hose draped over a brick wall, sucking the filth out of a septic tank.

Ernie slammed on his brakes. The driver of the trash truck wasn't so fast. He sped forward, slammed into the rear end of the honey truck, spun it around, and the rubber hose busted loose. Liquid waste sprayed the air in an exploding brown swirl.

Ernie cut to his right but not fast enough. A stream of shit splattered against our windshield.

"Fuck!"

Ernie switched on the windshield wipers, leaned forward so he could peek through the waste, and kept moving forward.

The stench groped its way into my throat and tried to rip out my stomach.

The trash truck was still floundering in the mud, grinding its way past the smashed rear of the honey truck. When we pulled up alongside, Ernie cut the jeep in front of the truck, bumping it until the trash truck was wedged against a cement-block wall. We shuddered to a halt.

I leapt out of the jeep, holding up my badge.

"Don't move!" I shouted, trying not to gag at the stink. "CID!"

The three workers in the back hopped off the bed of the truck and took off running, splattering shit and mud in their wake.

Ernie ran after them.

People emerged from the gateways lining the street, gaping in awe at the mess, covering their mouths and noses with their hands.

The driver of the honey truck was ranting, shaking his fist at Ernie and the trash truck driver and anyone else who would listen.

Each time I took a breath I felt like throwing up, but I held it.

Instead, I jumped up onto the running board of the trash truck and jerked open the door.

The driver clutched the top of the steering wheel, face buried against two gloved hands.

"CID!" I said. "Climb out of the cab."

When he didn't move I jabbed him in the ribs.

"You're in a world of shit. Don't make it worse."

I grabbed the driver by the shoulder and jerked. With surprising force the body pulled back and the head shot up.

"*Manji-jima sikkya!*" Don't touch me, you bastard!

The face was wrinkled, but the skin appeared soft and there was no stubble of a beard. Climbing out of the cab, a clawlike hand ripped back the wool cap and a flood of gray hair tumbled out.

"Keep hands to yourself, Charley," she said in perfect GI English. "You don't know how treat lady?"

Ernie splashed back through the mud, breathing heavily.

"They got away," he said and glanced at the driver. "Who the hell is this?"

"Nice talk, GI," she said.

Ernie looked at me. "I'll be damned. A broad."

"A *lady*," the driver said. She glanced at the mess. "Smell so bad around here maybe gag maggot."

The snow had stopped. As if it too didn't want to drop into the filth spewed by the honey truck.

I grabbed the lady by the elbow and we sloshed through the sucking muck.

Her name was Nam Byong-suk. We booked her at the Camp Market MP Station, then escorted her to one of the interrogation rooms. Apparently the aroma of the honey truck still lingered in the air around us because the office pukes backed away from us, crinkling their noses, as the three of us paraded down the hallway.

Once we were alone, Ernie offered Nam Byong-suk a stick of gum and I fetched her a cup of coffee. From somewhere within the folds of her filthy jacket she produced a cigarette and I struck a match for her. She took a long drag and blew smoke into the air.

I was right in my evaluation of her. All she really wanted was for us to treat her like a lady. Once we did that, she started to talk.

"I used to be a business girl," she said. "The best-looking girl in Itaewon."

"How'd you get into this line of work?" Ernie asked.

"I can't tell you." She sipped on her coffee.

"This is serious business," I said. "You're about to lose your job."

"No sweat. I get another one."

"It's not so easy to find a job in Korea."

"It is for me."

"Because you work for the slicky boys?"

She glanced at me slyly. "Slicky boys?" She sipped on her coffee.

"That's who you work for, don't you?" Ernie asked.

"Not your business."

"Sure it is," I said. "Between us only. You must cooperate with us. If not, the slicky boys' business here will be shut down. Your boss will lose a lot of money and he'll be very angry."

"We want to talk to your boss," Ernie said.

"Not boss," Nam Byong-suk said. "*King.*"

"King?"

"Yes."

I watched as her puckered lips worked away on the cigarette. The room filled with the reek of cheap tobacco laced with the memory of the honey truck.

I asked, "You mean there's a king of the slicky boys?"

"Of course. How else you think he can control all slicky boys? Without king, without strong man, everybody slicky anything. Pretty soon GI honcho get mad, pretty soon no can slicky anything, pretty soon no more money."

"The King of the Slicky Boys," I said. There was reverence in my voice. She liked that. "Tell us about this king."

"His name is So Boncho-ga."

I nodded. At the time I didn't know what *boncho-ga* meant but I looked it up later: herbalist. She wanted us to call him Herbalist So.

"Where can we find him?" I asked.

"No can find. His place is in . . ." Slicky Girl Nam turned to Ernie, loosely cupping her fist and poking her forefinger into the hole. "What you call this one?"

"Asshole," Ernie said.

"No. Place where *bakchui* live."

Ernie looked at her blankly. I rummaged in my memory for the word and found it. *Bakchui.* Bats.

"A place where bats live," I said. "A cave."

"Yes," she said. "Cave."

"The king lives in a cave?"

Slicky Girl Nam nodded triumphantly. "Yes. A cave. He still does. In Itaewon."

"A cave in Itaewon?" I couldn't believe it. The entire district was packed with hooches and nightclubs and chophouses. And every inch of it had been crawled over by GI's at least a million times. "Where is it?"

She shook her head. "I don't know. Nobody know. It's big secret."

Ernie and I looked at each other and then back at her. She waved her cigarette in the air.

"No bullshit. King live in big cave. Have—what you call?—rats and bats and everything. Beneath Itaewon."

The slicky boys lived underground, she said, like moles. And they came up at night to steal whatever they wanted.

"How can I get in touch with him?"

"I don't know," she said. "Many years I don't see."

"But you work for him."

"Many people work for him. Still we don't see him. Somebody tell us what to do, we do."

Layers of command, insulating the top boss. It made sense. I thought of trying to work my way back, one slicky boy manager at a time. It wouldn't work. They'd never talk to us. Not unless we found leverage to force them to spill their guts, and that would take too much time.

"Who would know how to contact this Mr. So?"

"You no can talk to him."

"Why not?"

"You foreigner, right?"

"Right."

"No foreign bastard ever talk to King of the Slicky Boys."

"Why not?"

"He don't like. If you ever talk to him, if you ever see his face, then you die."

She sliced her forefinger across her throat.

Ernie chomped on his gum furiously. "Knock off the bullshit, Nam. We're CID agents. This Slicky Boy So is nothing but a thief. We'll talk to him whenever the hell we want to talk to him."

"No, you won't. Only one way you talk to king."

"What's that?"

"You keep messing with slicky boys . . ." She waved her hand toward the village, maybe indicating the wrecked trash truck. ". . . then king find you. When king find you, he talk to you, but you no talk to anybody after that."

Ernie leaned forward, nose to nose with the old hag. She didn't back off.

"After I talk to Slicky Boy So," Ernie said, "I'll come back to Camp Market and tell you about it."

"No, you won't. You be beneath Han River. Only talk to fish."

She started to laugh and she kept laughing and she didn't stop until she was hacking away with a smoker's cough. Finally, she spit up phlegm. We had all we were going to get from her.

Maybe she was just looking for attention. Maybe all her years of walking the streets and catching GI's had driven her bonkers. Maybe both.

An hour later we turned her over to the KNP's. Ernie and I handed them our written statements and drove back to Seoul.

"LOOKS LIKE A MARX BROTHERS MOVIE," ERNIE SAID.

"Yeah. Doors slamming, people running in and out. All they need is a bottle of seltzer."

"And a horn."

Ernie and I stood on a hill in Itaewon, hidden behind a dragon-engraved portal varnished in shiny red lacquer.

Six Korean deliverymen pulled wooden crates off the back of a truck, dragged them into a small courtyard, pried them open with a crowbar, and reached in and yanked out the contents.

The customers, a GI and his Korean wife, looked worried. She stood on tiptoes and whispered something in her husband's ear. The GI nodded and stepped toward the Korean man in the blue cap, the head honcho of the delivery team. The GI cleared his throat and spoke.

"*Ajjosi*," he said. Uncle. "Slow down. We need to check each item off the inventory as you open the packages."

The honcho stopped barking orders at the other workmen and looked at the young GI, a sneer quivering on his lip.

"You no trust us?"

The GI lowered his head and stuck his hands deeper into his pockets.

"Sure, I trust you. It's just that with everybody opening crates and grabbing everything, I can't keep track of all the household items."

The elder man waved his hand and turned back to his workers. "After we finish, you checky checky everything. Now we no have time."

The GI glanced around, concerned by the swirling madness of packaging being ripped apart and men running in and out of the front gate with lamps and radios and irons and clothes and nobody seeming to be in charge.

The wife was too good a Confucian to argue with the older deliveryman. She'd already lost enough face just by being married to an American.

Her GI husband seemed on the verge of losing his temper but he swallowed it, figuring, I suppose, that it would just make things worse.

We gazed down on the commotion of the baggage delivery. The snow was holding off but the sky over southern Seoul was gray and brooding.

During the ride back from Camp Market, Ernie and I had decided to hit the slicky boys again on another of their operations. Keep peppering them with jabs. Become a bother. Until they could no longer ignore us.

The GI down below was married so he'd been approved for quarters off-post, and he'd rented this little hooch in Itaewon. The deliverymen were from the 8th Army Transportation Office and it was their job to deliver the GI's hold baggage, personal effects above and beyond what he could carry on the airplane coming over.

The way things should've been done is the deliverymen should hand him the inventory and he'd tick off the items one by one, making sure they're properly accounted for. But by unwrapping everything at once and having some men carry items in and others carry torn packaging back out, and not giving the GI a chance to check all items against the inventory, they were ripping him off.

The CID office had received complaints about this type of thing, but since it didn't happen to officers—the slicky boys were smarter than that—the head shed just figured the young troopers were being hysterical. Or maybe they were trying to pull a fast one. After all, once GI's submitted a claim to the Transportation Office for missing items, they'd be reimbursed, at depreciated value, for everything they lost.

And the expense was budgeted for. Thanks to the largess of the American taxpayer.

"Check it out." Ernie pointed at the flatbed truck in front of the hooch.

At first glance, there didn't seem much place to hide anything. Just two seats in front with only a roll bar on top, no cab, and a flat wood-plank truck bed in back. But as Ernie pointed, one of the workmen lifted the front seat, revealing a space probably designed as a tool storage chest. The worker quickly stashed something inside.

"Toaster," Ernie said.

"They already got the blender and the iron and the coffee maker, right?"

"Check."

"Not a big haul."

Ernie reached in his pocket and pulled out a stick of *ginseng* gum. He didn't offer any to me because he knew I couldn't stand the stuff. Tasted like burnt tree roots. Ernie liked it because it kept his metabolic rate high. Why he needed his metabolic rate any higher than it already was, I couldn't figure.

"Maybe it's not a big haul," Ernie said, "but you pull ten or twelve of these deliveries a day, every day, five days a week. A little here. A little there. Pretty soon you have a fat pile of long green."

"And the GI's don't complain because they get their money back from the government?"

"You got it. And they can buy new stuff in the PX."

"So we're going to put a stop to it?"

Ernie grinned. "Maybe not all of it. But this one."

The head honcho deliveryman supervised the last of the splintered crates and wrapping paper being returned to the truck. Brandishing a clipboard, he handed the GI a pen and pointed to the bottom of the inventory.

"You sign."

"But I don't know if I received everything."

"You think we slicky from you?"

"No. It's just that I don't want to sign until I've checked everything."

The honcho pointed to the truck. "We have six more delivery today. Many more GI wait. We no have time check everything."

The Korean wife stepped forward and grabbed her husband's elbow, the smooth skin of her face starting to crinkle.

The GI still hadn't signed. The honcho pulled out another sheaf of papers and handed them to the wife. He explained in Korean.

"If anything's missing, you fill this out, take to Eighth Army, they will give you all your money back. You cannot lose. Now tell him to hurry because we are busy."

The wife accepted the papers from the honcho, bowing slightly, grasping them with both hands. She turned to her husband.

"You sign. *Bali bali.*" Hurry.

The GI signed.

The honcho grabbed the clipboard, ripped off a copy of the inventory, thrust it at the GI, and hurried out to his truck.

Ernie elbowed me. "As soon as they fire up the engine and roll forward, we take them."

That would be proof of intent to abscond with the pilfered goods.

Ernie trotted down the hill. I stayed on the other side of the narrow road, keeping my eyes open.

As the truck driver started the engine and rolled forward, Ernie hopped up on the running board, holding up his badge.

"CID. You're under arrest. Pull over *now!*"

The slicky boys must all have attended the same training session. They knew that with American rules of evidence, if you escape, and you destroy the tangible proof of your crime, it is much harder to convict you. The driver here made the same move the driver at Camp Market had.

He stepped on the gas.

This time, though, Ernie was already aboard the truck.

I ran after them, shouting. "*Chong ji!*" Halt.

They didn't listen.

The truck careened down the hill. The red brake lights sparkled to life at the bottom of the incline, but only for an instant. The driver jammed the gears and plowed forward, into the heavy afternoon traffic.

Ernie was still holding on. I couldn't be sure but it looked as if he were trying to claw his way over the driver.

When I hit the bottom of the hill, I could still see the truck. The traffic was heavy, as usual on an afternoon in Seoul. Our jeep was parked two blocks away. Too far away to be of any help now. I kept running after the truck, pushing through the crowds.

Ernie punched the blue-capped honcho. The driver was trying to help his boss but couldn't do much because he had to keep his eyes on the swirling flow of traffic. The guys squatting in the back seemed confused at first. Then they started to move forward. One of them clutched a short crowbar.

Shit! Even if they didn't get the best of Ernie, one false move and someone could fall off the truck and be crushed beneath the wheels of the oncoming herd of kimchi cabs.

I wished I had a pistol. Korea is a country with complete gun control. Only the police and the military are allowed to possess weapons. Seldom do we carry arms on a case. Busting a guy for stealing a toaster didn't seem to require heavy armament, but after dealing with these slicky boys for half a day, I was starting to reconsider.

The traffic ahead opened up and the truck zoomed forward. By now, Ernie had rolled the honcho out of the way and had managed to lift up the front seat. The truck was bouncing wildly, and by cursing and threatening and using the vinyl-covered seat as a shield, Ernie somehow kept the irate deliverymen at bay.

He raised a stainless steel toaster aloft in the air. Suddenly, he tossed it forward and the deliverymen flinched. The toaster bounced once on the back of the cab and caromed off into the cars behind. It hit a bumper and bounced back, hit another and started being kicked around like a soccer ball.

Undaunted, the guy with the crowbar moved forward but Ernie flung the blender at him. It hit his shoulder, flew off into the traffic, and the crowbar clattered after it.

After that, Ernie unleashed his entire arsenal: the iron, a radio, a makeup mirror, the coffeepot. All the appliances crashed into the pavement and were smashed to smithereens.

Cab drivers slammed on their brakes, tires squealed, men cursed.

Up ahead the traffic bunched up and the truck slowed.

Ernie leapt off the truck running, stumbled, hit the pavement with his shoulder and rolled, and finally came to a halt.

I plowed through the pedestrian traffic, knocking people over, ignoring their curses. Panting, I finally reached him.

"You crazy son of a bitch!" I shouted.

Ernie ignored me and glanced back at the escaping truck. The driver gunned the engine and pulled quickly away. The men in the back growled and slammed their fists into open palms. Ernie watched them fade into the distance.

"Fuck you too," he said softly.

I knelt down. "Are you out of your gourd? Jumping on a moving truck like that?"

He fingered his head. "No. My gourd's still here."

"And your shoulder?"

He rotated it. "No problem."

"Hey," I said. "No arrest is worth that much risk."

"They didn't get their damn toaster, did they?"

He swiveled toward the road. A half dozen cab drivers had pulled over and were examining the damage to their headlights and grillwork. One of them picked up the dented iron, chattered away to his comrades, and pointed at us.

"Time to fade into the alleys," Ernie said.

"Yes," I said, helping him up. "Let's do that."

12

WE CHECKED THE KNP LIAISON OFFICE ON COMPOUND AND HAD them contact Lieutenant Pak at the Namdaemun Precinct. The homicide investigation downtown had stalled. All leads resulted in nothing so far and they were beginning to discount any thought that the murder of Lance Corporal Cecil Whitcomb might have been a mugging gone wrong.

"They're counting on you," the Liaison Officer told us sourly.

Although it was still midafternoon, we purposely avoided the CID office and slid on back to the barracks. In my room, my soiled blue jeans still lay in a crumpled heap on the floor, and they still reeked of field manure.

I sighed and picked them up and carried them down to the latrine. Using hand soap, I washed them as best I could. After wringing them out, I returned to my room and dried them on the radiator.

. . .

"The guy wants money," Ernie said.

"How much?" I asked.

"Twenty thousand won." About forty dollars. "Just enough to cover his expenses while he sneaks out of town. He's quitting anyway."

"Can we trust him?"

"Shit, I don't know. But it's the best lead we have so far. A contract security guard. Pissed at the slicky boys. It's our shot at catching one of them in the flesh."

We were in my room. Ernie had stopped by and I sat on my bunk in my skivvies. We were both watching my blue jeans dry on the clanging radiator.

Ernie's houseboy had gone on strike against him, too. The word was out, apparently promulgated by the slicky boys. No Korean workers on-compound were to help Ernie or me in any way. A not very subtle message: Leave us alone!

I had never realized how far the influence of the slicky boys reached, but we were starting to find out.

A trickle of smoke slithered its way into my nose.

"Shit! The jeans!"

I turned them over. They were singed by the radiator. Little black lines across the butt.

"Don't sweat it," Ernie said. "Nobody looks at your butt anyway."

"Only your girlfriends."

"Hey!"

"Okay," I said. "Do you think we can write the twenty thousand won off our expense account?"

"Maybe Riley can find a way."

"Yeah. He's a genius at that sort of thing. What time is the meeting set up for?"

"Zero one hundred tonight. We pay the guy the money and he leads us to the slicky boy."

"How does he know the slicky boy is going to strike tonight?"

"It's set up. The medic who provides the medicine works on a rotating shift. He's on duty tonight. He steals the shit out of the one-two-one Evac Hospital, leaves it at a prearranged place, the slicky boy climbs the fence and retrieves it, then climbs back out and turns it over to his fence. Sweet deal."

"And this security guard is supposed to make sure that he's looking the other way?"

"Right. They pay him later. But lately he figures he's been getting stiffed."

"Why?"

"Because the shit they're bringing out is high-grade American primo pharmaceuticals. Products from all the big companies. Antibiotics that they don't even make in Korea because the diseases just recently arrived. Germs carried in on jet planes by tourists with hard-ons and too much money to spend. People need the medicine in the ville. But after customs duties are paid, it's just too expensive. And most of the time it's not even available anyway."

I whistled. "High profit margin."

"You got that right. When a rich guy's caught a case of the creeping crud, he's willing to pay through the nose for the right kind of medicine."

"So what's this guard going to do?"

"He's going back to his farm, he says, down in Cholla Province. He's tired of all this corruption up here in Seoul."

The people of Cholla had always been at odds with the people here in Kyongki Province. For the last few millennia anyway.

"Why doesn't he just do his job," I said, "and quit playing the game with the slicky boys?"

Ernie's eyes widened. "Are you kidding? They'd fire him, if he was lucky. If they thought he was a turncoat, he'd end up in the Han River."

"Next to us."

"Not me," he said. "They're never taking Ernie Bascom down."

I wished I felt as confident as Ernie did. I watched him. I think he was only faking his bravado, but I knew him well enough to realize that he'd never admit it.

"So we have about five hours to wait?"

"Yeah," Ernie said. "Might as well have a brewski."

"Capital idea."

As he rose to walk down the hallway to the vending machine, someone pounded on the door.

"Who is it?" I yelled.

"CQ." The Charge of Quarters. "Someone here to see you."

Ernie and I looked at each other. Without saying anything, he grabbed the entrenching tool stashed with my field gear and padded over to the wall behind the door. When he was in place, he nodded.

I opened the door.

Two MP's, black helmets glistening, filled my doorway, their fat thumbs hooked over webbed pistol belts.

"Sueño?" one of them asked.

"Yeah."

"Your presence is requested over at the Provost Marshal's office."

"I'm off duty."

"I don't think it has anything to do with duty."

"Then what's it about?"

The MP tried to look bored. "Don't know. All we know is that you have to come with us."

Ernie stepped out from behind the door. "What the fuck's going on?"

"Ah, Bascom," the MP said. "How convenient. Your presence is requested also."

"Me?" Without thinking, Ernie raised the entrenching tool. Both MP's stepped back. Their hands reached for the butts of their .45's.

"Drop it, Bascom," one of them said.

Ernie looked puzzled at first but he swiveled his head and looked at the entrenching tool.

"Oh, this. Sorry."

He started to lower it but suddenly reared back and threw it at them with all his might.

"Ernie!" I shouted.

Both MP's dodged and the short shovel slammed against the far wall, gouging a chunk of cement block and kicking up a cloud of dust.

The MP's rushed into the room. They were big and knew what

they were doing, and soon they had wrestled Ernie to the ground and slapped the handcuffs on his wrists. I started tussling with one of them but my heart wasn't in it because I knew it was absolutely the wrong thing to do. Instead I held the MP back a little, yelling at the other one to take it easy on Ernie.

When they had him secured, the MP's stood up and one of them pointed at me.

"Put your clothes on!"

I walked over to the radiator and slipped on the still damp blue jeans. After I had thrown on my jacket and my sneakers, the MP told me to turn around. He snapped the cuffs on my wrists.

They marched us outside to a line of vehicles waiting, red lights swirling.

In the back of the jeep, Ernie leaned over.

"I didn't actually mean to hit them with the entrenching tool," he whispered to me. "I missed on purpose."

"That was considerate of you."

He sat back in his seat.

"I'm a considerate kind of guy."

13

AN MP HELD OPEN THE DOOR AND THE FIRST SERGEANT WALKED into the holding cell. Top's stubbled jowls sagged and he wiped his face with an open palm, as if trying to wake up from a bad dream.

"What's this about you guys resisting arrest?"

"Not so," Ernie said. "They never told us we were under arrest."

"But they did say you had to come with them to the MP Station, didn't they? And that's a direct order, isn't it?"

"Still not arrest," Ernie said.

"Jesus, Bascom, why do you have to make everything so damn difficult?"

"If you wanted to talk to us, Top, why didn't you just swing by yourself instead of sending the MP's?"

"It's not me who wants to talk to you. It's the Provost Marshal."

Somewhere down the hallway someone shouted, "Attention!"

"Carry on."

Boots pounded down the long corridor. The First Sergeant held the door open while Colonel Stoneheart, the Provost Marshal of the 8th United States Army, strode into the cell.

"Good. You're both here," he said.

What the hell did he expect? He'd sent a convoy of armed men after us.

Colonel Stoneheart was a slim man who stayed that way through religious jogging. His hair was short and brown with a slash of gray at the temples. The fatigues he wore were freshly starched. Not a good sign. Apparently, he'd put on his uniform and interrupted his evening at home just to talk to us.

The First Sergeant unfolded a metal chair and the Provost Marshal sat down. We faced him from a hard wooden bench.

"Thank you for coming down," the Provost Marshal said.

I nodded. "Our pleasure."

"I was at the Officer's Club tonight," Stoneheart said, "and this tragic murder of Trooper Whitcomb is quite the topic of discussion."

He looked at us. Neither one of us said anything. Ernie's face was grim. Unreadable. I think we both knew what was coming.

"Well, a British Liaison Officer was there and one thing led to another and . . . Well, anyway, he told me that the Sergeant Major of the British Honor Guard claims that you two talked to Whitcomb, at their arms room, the day before his death." He let that sit for a while, still studying our faces. "Is that true?"

Ernie didn't flex a muscle. He stared at the Provost Marshal, not aggressively but without emotion, as if he were a stone-faced deity from Easter Island. Handling this issue would be my job. We both understood that. It made sense to have one spokesman. If each party involved were mouthing off, almost inevitably you'd trip each other up, even when you were telling the truth. But especially when you're lying.

Maybe Ernie expected me to lie. Maybe I did too. Instead, the truth popped out of my mouth.

"We saw him," I said.

The First Sergeant's face pulled back slightly but he regained his composure quickly enough. The Provost Marshal let out a little sigh.

"Why?" he asked.

"We met a woman in Itaewon. Or I should say she met us. She gave us a note and asked us to deliver it to Cecil Whitcomb."

"What did the note say?"

"Something about a rendezvous."

"Where?"

"In Namdaemun."

The First Sergeant and the Provost Marshal looked at one another with exaggerated surprise. It was clear that they were in the process of washing their hands of us, steering away from any dirt we might be involved in. After this little act, Colonel Stoneheart spoke again.

"Who was this woman?"

"She called herself Miss Ku." I turned my palms face up. "Naturally, since Whitcomb was murdered, we've been searching for her. So far, no luck."

"Why did she give you this note?"

"They were lovers who'd been quarreling. That's what she claimed and, at the time, that's what we believed."

"So you just did her a favor?"

"Right."

"And Whitcomb ends up dead that night, after you delivered the note to him?"

I nodded.

"Why didn't you tell us this before?"

"Well, to be honest, sir, we were afraid you might take us off the case."

"You're damn right I would have." For the first time his voice raised slightly. "To think I had to hear about this through gossip at the O Club."

That was his main worry. That he'd been embarrassed and that it would reflect poorly on his annual efficiency report. Even the slightest bad mark can keep a full colonel from being promoted to general. For him, the stakes were high.

Ernie hadn't moved. I don't think he really gave a shit. Of course, neither did I. Not about the colonel's promotion, anyway.

The Provost Marshal seemed distracted as he spoke. "What about that other issue, First Sergeant. What was it?"

"The SOFA charges, sir."

"Yes." Stoneheart looked at us sadly. "Charges made against you two under the Status of Forces Agreement."

Ernie's back stiffened a little. SOFA charges were bad news. Usually made by a Korean civilian against an American serviceman—for abuse or assault or theft—under the provisions of the SOFA treaty between the United States and the Republic of Korea. Sometimes the GI would end up in a Korean court, but more often everything was settled by an ROK/U.S. mediation board. Either way, the GI usually shelled out a lot of money in compensation to the victim.

"What SOFA charges are those, sir?" I asked politely.

The First Sergeant handed the Provost Marshal some papers and he shuffled through them.

"Apparently you two had a busy day. There was a traffic accident in Pupyong-ni. A female truck driver charges you with reckless driving that resulted in injury to her."

Finally, Ernie spoke. "That was the broad we busted for stealing the copper wire."

"Not proven," the Provost Marshal said.

"The wire was in the back of her truck."

"But you can't link it to her. The other workmen who disappeared, maybe, but not her."

"Sure we can. She helped them load it."

"Maybe. Sloppy work anyway. And another incident here in Itaewon." The Provost Marshal looked up from the paperwork and stared at Ernie. "Some workmen claim you assaulted them after they delivered some household goods."

"Sure, I did. Because they were stealing."

"Stealing what?"

"An iron, a toaster, a blender, shit like that," Ernie said.

"Have these items been checked into the evidence room?"

Ernie lowered his head. "They sort of got misplaced in the heat of the incident."

"Yes. Misplaced. So there's no evidence of any theft. But there is eyewitness testimony of an assault."

"They're all slicky boys," Ernie said. "Their word doesn't mean shit."

"They're what?"

"Slicky boys. The same guys who've been ripping off this compound for years."

A chill crept into the cell. As if the entire force of the Korean winter had busted right through the cement walls. The Provost Marshal lowered his voice. "What do you mean, Agent Bascom?"

Ernie went on to explain about the cartel that began in the Korean War and had been pilfering exactly four percent of U.S. military supplies and equipment ever since. He told the Provost Marshal about their high degree of organization and about how they stuck together whenever somebody went up against them.

After he finished, there was a lengthy silence. Colonel Stoneheart's mouth drew into a thin line. I'd never seen him look so grim. Even the First Sergeant became nervous and coughed and shuffled his feet. Finally, the Provost Marshal spoke.

"Do you have any *proof* of the existence of this cartel?"

Ernie rolled his shoulders. "Proof? Everybody knows about them."

"No," the Provost Marshal said, half rising from his chair. "I'm talking about *proof*. Not some wild-ass speculations. *Proof*, Agent Bascom. That's what you're supposed to provide. You're a professional investigator, not some punk on the block who repeats every ridiculous rumor that comes down the pike."

He stood completely upright and waggled his finger under Ernie's nose.

"Until you get proof, real evidence that will stand up in court, I will not have you spreading wild rumors about some gang of 'slicky boys.' You understand that?"

Ernie was stunned. Finally he realized that Colonel Stoneheart was waiting for an answer. Slowly, he nodded.

The Provost Marshal quivered and his lips almost disappeared altogether. For a minute I thought he was going to punch Ernie. The

First Sergeant's brow crinkled, and he stood and stepped a little closer. Maybe he thought the same thing. Finally, the Provost Marshal swiveled and marched to the door.

"Come with me, First Sergeant."

"Yes, sir."

The First Sergeant shot us a warning look which meant stay right where you are and followed the colonel down the hallway.

"What was that all about?" Ernie asked.

"The slicky boys," I said. "A professional cartel of thieves operating with impunity right under the nose of the Provost Marshal. It's his responsibility to stop them, but he can't even touch them. Therefore, his only recourse is to deny that they exist."

"How can he do that? They're everywhere."

"Nobody realizes that at the Officer's Club. What with servants and drivers and maids, they live a sheltered life. And as long as they're in the dark, the Provost Marshal's reputation stays intact. But if the existence of the slicky boys becomes common knowledge, the first question will be, why didn't he do something about it?"

"And he'll be slapped with a low efficiency rating," Ernie said.

"Now you got it."

"And he won't make general."

"Right."

"And he'll have a case of the big ass."

"Right again," I said.

"At us."

"Correct."

"So I should keep my mouth shut?"

"Correct again."

About two minutes later the First Sergeant came back into the room and sat down across from us.

"Good news and bad news," he said. We waited. "The good news is that you're free to go."

That made sense. There were no criminal charges that could be filed against us. And the Provost Marshal wouldn't try to trump any up. It would make him look as bad as us.

"The bad news," the First Sergeant said, "is that you're off the case. Burrows and Slabem will be taking it over."

"Those two dorks?" Ernie said. "Out in Itaewon, they couldn't find their way to the latrine."

"They're good investigators," the First Sergeant said.

"But the Koreans don't trust them and won't tell them shit."

The First Sergeant raised his voice. "At ease, Bascom! The decision's already been made."

Ernie draped his elbows over his knees and shook his head. The First Sergeant continued.

"Until further notice, you two will be assigned to the black market detail. Unless, of course, Burrows and Slabem dig up something about this meeting you had with Whitcomb. You two want to tell me anything more about it?"

Neither one of us answered. The fact that we'd been paid fifty thousand won to deliver the note would never cross my lips.

"The Provost Marshal expects you to keep your noses out of the Whitcomb investigation," the First Sergeant said. "Bascom, you still have that request for extension pending. Don't forget about it. Not if you want to stay in Korea. And you, Sueño, you can still be sent back to the DMZ. If you have an aching need to walk the line again, staring across the wire at those North Korean Commies, it don't cut no ice with us."

He stared at us long and hard, searching for a wise remark. When he heard none, he clapped his hands. "That's all then. Report to the office at zero eight hundred tomorrow."

Outside, Ernie and I trudged toward South Post, neither one of us speaking.

There was still no snow falling, but the temperature had dropped and the drifts and mangled tufts of ice had frozen into crazy shapes that glistened in the moonlight. Freezing wind bit into my sinuses.

Finally, Ernie said what we were both thinking.

"We're not really going to let Burrows and Slabem handle this thing, are we?"

"Of course not. They're not the ones who convinced Cecil Whitcomb to show up out in Namdaemun that night. We are."

"So it's our responsibility?"

"You definitely got that right."

"So we're going after that slicky boy tonight?"

"Sure," I said. "They're filing SOFA charges against us now. That means that the slicky boys are nervous, on the run."

"We gotta keep 'em that way."

"Absolutely. Keep 'em off balance."

Ernie had left the jeep at 21 T-Car for some fender work, so we had to hoof it. My blue jeans were almost dry. But not dry enough that they didn't start to stiffen in the frigid breeze blowing out of Manchuria. We crunched across a frozen sheet of snow, heading toward the 121 Evacuation Hospital.

14

THE 121 IS A SPRAWLING COMPLEX WITH A LITTLE SNACK STAND out front—closed and shuttered at this hour—a horseshoe-shaped one-story hospital behind that, and a half dozen warehouses scattered about. We waited outside until just before zero one hundred, one in the morning. All the while I wished I had worn about three more layers of sweaters. Once we started moving I was happy about it.

When the army plans for injuries, they think big. The emergency room behind the 121 had not only a helipad but also a huge loading dock and a small fleet of ambulances.

Just let those North Koreans come south. We're ready for them.

We found a dark spot beneath a naked elm tree near one of the warehouses. We didn't have to wait long.

A blue-smocked medic emerged at about ten minutes before one. He was average height and average weight and would've been difficult as hell to identify because he wore a tight-fitting blue medical cap and a gauze mask over his nose and mouth.

"The masked marauder," Ernie whispered. He was enjoying this.

In the medic's hand, nearly hidden behind his body, was a plastic bag stuffed with what appeared to be small boxes and vials.

He slipped out of the floodlight glare behind the emergency room and into the darkness near a line of square metal Conexes. They were padlocked and probably loaded with medical supplies to be airlifted where and when the need arose.

Each Conex was a complete, self-contained unit. Their foundation was two layers of hollow ribbed corrugated metal. The medic knelt in front of one of the Conexes and shoved the plastic sack into an opening in the foundation. From somewhere he grabbed a broom handle and, bending lower, he probed carefully with the stick, shoving the plastic farther beneath the Conex. Soon he had reached in almost all the way to his elbow.

"He's pushing the bag to the other side," Ernie said.

I nodded.

The medic placed the broom handle back where he'd originally stashed it, stood, and brushed the snow off his knees. Looking around, he scurried back up onto the loading dock and into the Emergency Room.

"Neat trick," Ernie said.

"Let's work our way over to the other side of the Conexes and see what happens."

"Let's."

We searched for another concealed spot, this time farther away because we figured the slicky boy would be tougher to fool than the medic. We finally settled on a row of bushes against the cement-block perimeter fence. I squatted down in the snow. Ernie edged in next to me. We had to hold back the sharp branches with our hands.

"Hope this doesn't take long," Ernie said.

My legs had already grown numb when we heard the boots of the perimeter guard crunching toward us. He wore his big gray parka with his hood pulled over his head and an M1 rifle slung over his shoulder. When he walked past, he looked straight ahead, not even glancing in our direction.

About twenty yards away, directly behind the Conex where the medic had stashed the plastic bag, the guard stopped. He slipped off his gloves, reached into his pocket, and pulled out a cigarette. The scratch and hiss of his wooden match was loud in the darkness.

For a moment his bronze face was illuminated in the glow of the flame. I looked at Ernie. He nodded. This was the guard we had paid the twenty thousand won.

The guard took a deep drag, coughed, stomped around a bit, and before he was through with his cigarette tossed it down in the snow behind the Conex.

After he trudged off toward his remaining rounds, the night became quiet again.

Finally, I heard it. Not much more than a scratching. Suddenly there was a thump and Ernie elbowed me. He pointed.

There, along the wall, about ten yards past the Conex, I saw it. A dark spot in the snow. I couldn't believe it. The cement block wall was almost ten feet high and it was topped by metal spikes and coiled barbed wire. Yet somehow, in a matter of seconds, someone had climbed it, making no more sound than a cat crossing a coffee table.

I stared at the blank spot in the snow and started to doubt my judgment. Nothing moved. Was it just my eyes playing tricks on me? Or was there actually a human being lying there?

Suddenly it moved.

Like thought, the shadow drifted across the snow and came to a halt behind the Conex. There was some sound now. Plastic rubbing on metal? An instant later, the shadow was moving back toward the wall.

Ernie elbowed me again. "Let's go."

We were up and moving but my legs were so knotted that I stumbled twice and had to shove myself back up with my arms. Ernie was ahead of me, running at full tilt. Shouting.

"Halt! Halt! Halt or I'll shoot!"

He didn't have a gun, but what the hell. If the ploy worked, good.

Apparently the ploy did.

The shadow had reached the wall and Ernie was coming on fast. As the thief started to climb up, he glanced back and in the moonlight I saw a face. A young Korean man. Calm. Not worried. For a split second he seemed to evaluate Ernie's threat.

The delay wasn't long, but it was enough.

By the time the slicky boy started to pull himself up, Ernie was only a few feet from him. Still, the thief scaled the wall amazingly fast and had a handhold on one of the metal spikes before Ernie grabbed his foot.

Ernie tugged and the slicky boy strained upward. His body stretched taut, and for a moment I thought his leg would snap off until suddenly something popped and Ernie reeled backward, holding an empty boot in his hands.

I hit the wall running and, as the slicky boy rose, I managed to grab hold of his waist, hug, and pull down with all my weight. Ernie was up now and we both had the thief and suddenly the slicky boy's grip gave and we all fell backward onto the hard-packed snow.

The air burst out of me but I rolled and felt myself on top of the slicky boy, and Ernie howled in pain.

"My thumb! My goddamn thumb!"

The slicky boy punched and kicked but I was in too close for his blows to have much effect and my weight was too much for him. As I reached for my handcuffs behind my back, his thumbs gouged my eyes.

I jerked back from the sharp nails and, in less than a second, he was up and heading for the wall again.

I bounded up. I caught him while he was still on the ground and plowed forward, ramming him face-first into the cement block wall.

My shoulder thudded, his head cracked, and we both fell in a heap at the foot of the cement block.

I couldn't move, but he wasn't moving either. Pain shot down my shoulder into my fist. Using my good hand, I grabbed hold of my handcuffs, rolled the slicky boy over, and secured his wrists behind his back.

Ernie cursed softly.

"What is it?" I asked, trying to catch my breath.

"Dislocated my goddamn thumb."

I checked my hand. The fingers were still moving. Just a shoulder bruise. It would heal.

I checked the slicky boy. He was young, probably in his late teens. Thin, almost emaciated, but I knew from our tussle that he was as muscular as hell. A red welt on his forehead had started to puff up like a golf ball. His eyes fluttered and opened. He moaned.

I sighed with relief. He'd be all right.

I crawled over to Ernie. He held out his hand to me. The side of the palm was grossly distorted, bone jutting out beneath the skin at an odd angle.

"Yank on the thumb," Ernie said. "Pop it back in place."

I nodded toward the Emergency Room. "I can take you over there. Get a shot of Novocain first."

"That lightweight shit? It don't work on me. Hurry up. Do it now."

I grabbed the thumb, jerked back on it, and felt it slide, bone on bone, until it crunched into place. Ernie let out a howl, recoiled away from me, and rolled in the snow, cursing.

After a few seconds the swearing subsided and he looked up at me, his eyes watery.

"Thanks, pal," he said. "I needed that."

He held his hand up and wiggled all the fingers including the thumb. "Back in tip-top shape."

I walked to the slicky boy and sat him up. He kicked at me and spat.

"Nice talk," Ernie said, rising to his feet, still wiggling his fingers, pleased, I guess, they were all working. "Why don't we kick his ass here? Nobody's watching."

I'm not sure if the slicky boy understood or not. The stonelike ridges of his face didn't move. I stuck a fist in his face.

"You want that? You want us to hit you?"

When he didn't respond, I said the same thing in Korean. *"Choa hani? Deirigo shippo?"*

I questioned him, but it didn't do any good. He wasn't talking.

We picked up the plastic bag of pharmaceuticals and dragged the slicky boy over to the Emergency Room. I used their phone to call for an MP jeep. While we waited, the medics stood around gawking at us. I tried to figure which one we had seen out on the platform, stashing the drugs, but it was useless. The only ones I could eliminate for sure were the nurses. Ernie was watching them.

When the MP's arrived, we shoved the slicky boy in the back and took him over to the Liaison Office of the Korean National Police.

When he saw the KNP symbol above the door his eyes widened, he tried to swallow, and for a minute I thought he was going to throw up. But he still said nothing.

Ernie and I sat in the waiting room for about forty minutes. During the entire time we heard no screams and no thuds of a body being flung up against the wall. I think the KNP methods were more subtle than that. I would've liked to witness their interrogation techniques—as long as I wasn't the subject of the interrogation.

Lieutenant Roh, the night duty officer, emerged from the back room and sat down next to us. He was a frail man with straight black hair that hung over his eyes, and round-lensed glasses that made him look more like a mathematics professor than a cop. He tapped the tips of his splayed fingers together.

"He's a slicky boy. That's for sure."

"Did he admit to the theft?" Ernie asked.

"No," Lieutenant Roh said. "He will deny. Deny all the way."

"But we've nailed him, right?"

"Yes. Still, he will not talk. Not about the slicky boys."

"Why not? He could get a lighter sentence, couldn't he?"

Lieutenant Roh considered that. "Possibly. But if he mentions anything about his superiors, it would be suicidal."

"They'd kill him?" Ernie asked.

"Of course. And anyway, while he's in prison, they will take care of his family."

I leaned forward. "Listen, Lieutenant Roh. I need to find the slicky boy honcho. To talk to him. I have to ask him some questions."

"Why?"

"It's complicated. Certainly, this young slicky boy can give us some sort of lead."

"No. He will give you nothing."

"Then how can we contact the King of the Slicky Boys?"

Lieutenant Roh studied me for a few seconds. When he spoke, he spoke softly.

"You must not continue in this, Agent Sueño. All Koreans respect Americans. Even the criminals do. We realize how much you've helped our country, and we realize how important it is for you to stay here so we won't be conquered by the North Korean Communists. Still, if you continue to disrupt their operations, the slicky boys will kill you."

I said nothing.

"What I'm most worried about," Lieutenant Roh added, "is that it might already be too late."

He stood up and walked out of the room.

15

MAYBE IT WAS BECAUSE WE DECIDED TO BE GOOD SOLDIERS FOR once. Or maybe it was because Lieutenant Roh's warning the previous night put the fear of God into us. Whatever the reason, we actually spent the entire day working on the black market detail.

We busted three housewives and one buck sergeant. All for buying coffee and cigarettes and liquor and other sundry items and selling them in Itaewon for about twice what they paid for them on post. Resale of duty-free goods is a violation of military regulations. Also of Korean customs law and the Status of Forces Agreement. All four suspects were taken to the MP station and booked. We figured the sum total of the take came to about $346.57.

U.S. goods black-marketed in Korea per year are estimated to run about ten million dollars. From that vast sea of contraband, we'd siphoned off at least a couple of ounces.

The problem was that we weren't any closer to finding Cecil Whitcomb's murderer.

From what Riley told us, Burrows and Slabem had done nothing all day other than review our reports and insist on interrupting Lieutenant Pak down in Namdaemun, demanding a conference so they could be briefed on his lack of progress. Typical bureaucrats. Laying a foundation of paperwork to cover their butts when they failed to solve the case.

I knew it. They knew it. Everybody knew it. But it would also make the CID Detachment look better, because they'd be sweeping a supposedly insoluble case under the rug without raising any more uncomfortable questions about the activities of the slicky boys.

Maybe Burrows and Slabem were right. Despite all our efforts, Ernie and I had been unable to come up with anything. Cecil Whitcomb was dead. Nothing was going to bring him back. The chances of us finding Miss Ku in Seoul, a city of eight million people, were narrow to nothing. And the chances of us finding the leader of the slicky boys, Herbalist So, much less convicting him of a murder, were probably less.

Maybe the best thing was to back off for a while. Let the universe flow on and see what happened.

After all, we'd already tweaked the nose of the King of the Slicky Boys. It was his move.

When the Honor Guard flag detail fired the cannon and lowered the colors at the close of the business day, Ernie and I hustled back to the barracks, changed, and made a beeline for the Class VI Store.

In the old brown-shoe army there were five classifications of supplies: Classes I through V. So when the army set up liquor stores, some joker decided to call them Class VI stores. That's what they had remained ever since.

We bought a case of beer and a bottle of Jim Beam and a case of orange soda and two cans of peanuts and a jar of pickled Polish sausages.

"Supplies for a week," Ernie said.

We flagged down a PX taxi and gave him orders to take us to Itaewon. When we pulled up in front of the Nurse's hooch, she was already there waiting, holding the gate open for us.

A long cotton kimono showed off her curves. The Nurse had broad shoulders for a woman, but a small waist and round breasts. Roundness described her best. Strong but soft and round. Ernie was a lucky man. I doubted that he really understood that, though.

As we entered, the Nurse bowed and grabbed one of the packages out of the crook of my arm. Through powdered snow, she waddled on straw slippers across the small courtyard.

Red tile, upturned at the edges, topped the hooches that were constructed of varnished wooden beams. The smell of charcoal smoke and kimchi, pickled cabbage and turnips festering in earthen pots of brine, filled the cold air.

An old woman carrying a perforated briquette to refuel the underground *ondol* heating system bowed to us as she passed.

"*Ajjima,*" the Nurse said to me. The landlady.

Ernie and I nodded our heads in greeting.

At the front of her hooch, the Nurse stepped out of her slippers and up onto the narrow wooden landing. She slid back the paper-paneled door and motioned with her upturned palm for us to enter.

"*Oso-oseiyo,*" she said. Please come in.

Her unblemished face flashed a full-lipped smile. Long black hair shimmered and swooshed forward as she bowed once again.

Ernie placed his hand on her shoulder and spoke gently. "Do you have any chow?"

"Most tick I get."

"Good. And pop a couple of wet ones while you're at it."

She did as she was told and soon we were sipping on cold beer and sitting on a cushion on a warm vinyl floor. The Nurse brought in a heated hand towel for each of us so we could wipe off our faces and clean the backs of our necks and scrub our hands. I felt cozy. As cozy as I had since the Whitcomb case began.

Ernie sipped on his beer. "A whole day wasted."

"Maybe not completely," I said.

"What do you mean?"

"The word that we want to talk to the King of the Slicky Boys is out. Maybe it will shake something loose."

"Yeah. Maybe." Ernie didn't sound hopeful.

The Nurse brought in a black lacquered tray, inlaid with a white mother-of-pearl crane fluttering its wings. She unfolded the short legs and placed it in front of us. Soon the small table was piled with bowls of hot bean curd soup, a pot of steaming white rice, and plates of diced turnips in hot sauce, spiced bean sprouts, and a roast mackerel staring with blind eyes into eternity.

Ernie rolled up his sleeves and dug in. So did I.

In Korean fashion, we didn't talk while eating. The theory is that it's barbaric to ruin the enjoyment of a good meal by talking about things that might start vile juices rumbling in your stomach.

As we packed away the grub, the Nurse hovered about us, not eating, herself, replenishing the various dishes when needed.

Most of the business girls weren't nearly as traditional as the Nurse. She was doing it to give Ernie good face. And she was doing it to show him that she'd make a good wife. A great wife.

It was hard to believe they were the same couple I'd known a few months ago, when they were on the outs. Then the Nurse had barged into a nightclub in Itaewon sporting a warrior's band around her forehead, brandishing a heavy cudgel, and caught Ernie flirting with another girl. She'd smashed glassware and almost cracked the table in two with the heavy blows from her club. It had taken three strong men to drag her off him.

That wasn't their only altercation, either. Love, between Ernie and the Nurse, was a many splintered thing.

But lately they'd been more sedate. Maybe it was her threat to commit suicide if Ernie left her. Maybe it was that he'd finally come to his senses and was falling in love with a good woman.

After we finished eating, the Nurse cleared the plates and Ernie and I resumed talking about the slicky boys. As she wiped off the last of the sticky grains of rice from the small table, she glanced up and interrupted us.

"You want to talk to slicky boy?"

"Yes," I said.

"I know slicky boy," she said. "He retired now. Old man. Very famous in Itaewon. Everybody say before he number *hana* slicky boy."

Number one. The best. She pointed her thumb to the sky.

"He's retired?" Ernie said.

"Yes. Sometimes can do."

Ernie and I glanced at one another.

I leaned forward. "We want to see him."

"I show you then." The Nurse rose and slipped on a heavy coat and a muffler.

I downed the last of my beer, grabbed my jacket, and stepped out into the cold winter night. Ernie followed, but stopped at the outside *byonso* before we left.

The Nurse led us past the Statue Lounge and Kim's Tailor Shop and down a narrow lane that led into a valley filled with a maze of hovels.

We passed a white sign: OFF LIMITS TO U.S. FORCES PERSONNEL. Being caught in an off-limits area was the least of our worries.

After a few minutes, we arrived at a dilapidated wooden building. The Nurse bounced down a short flight of stone steps, stopped at what must've been the basement level, and pounded on a wooden door the color of soot.

In less than a minute a man opened it.

I guessed his age to be in the late forties or early fifties. The short-cropped hair above his square face was flecked with gray. He was a sturdy man, broad-shouldered but very short.

"*Kuang-sok Apa*," the Nurse said. Father of Kuang-sok. "These men wish to talk to you."

He looked slightly surprised.

"They are good men," the Nurse said. "The tall one speaks Korean. They only want to learn about your illustrious career."

The man bowed slightly, then motioned us inside.

The Nurse smiled and waved at us and trotted off through the snow. Ernie ignored her. I don't know why he didn't treat her better. But it wasn't my business. Not at the time, anyway.

We followed the old man inside. He closed the door.

I wondered why the Nurse had called him "Father of Kuang-sok," and noticed that he walked with a slight limp.

He was dressed in baggy black trousers and a soiled, heavy-knit sweater of gray and bright red. We took a couple of steps down to a cement-floored room illuminated by a naked bulb hanging from a bare rafter. When I exhaled, my breath billowed in the cold air. There was equipment here—wrenches, hammers, nails, old pipes—and I realized that this man must be the custodian for the building.

He slipped off his shoes, stepped up on a narrow varnished wooden platform, and waved for us to follow. Behind the platform, light shone through a paper-paneled latticework door. A shadow stood, rising only halfway up the door. The panel shuddered and slid back.

"*Abboji. Nugu seiyo?*" Father. Who is it?

It was a boy.

Kuang-sok, I thought. The boy had a narrow face, not square and sturdy like his father's, and eyes that were heavily lidded, just slits in a smooth complexion.

"*Sonnim wayo,*" the man said. "We have guests."

The man entered the room and Ernie and I slipped off our shoes and followed.

The room we were in was not much bigger than the toolshed out front, but it was a lot more comfortable. The floor was covered with a soft vinyl padding and I felt warmth beneath my feet. The floor was heated by subterranean ducts flooded with charcoal gas. A six-foot-wide varnished wood armoire covered one of the walls and open cabinets took up most of the rest, stuffed with books and clothes and blankets and a few eating utensils. Cooking was conducted outside, on the cement charcoal pit I had seen on the way in. A tiny TV, imported from Japan, flickered in a corner, beaming out the songs of some Korean variety extravaganza filmed at one of the studios on the side of Namsan Mountain.

The boy had the volume down low. More disciplined than most kids I knew.

The man looked at us with his tired brown eyes and stuck out his hand.

"I am Mr. Ma," he said in English.

We shook. The palms of his hands were as rough as the cement walls of his basement.

Ernie and I sat down cross-legged on the floor. Mr. Ma poured us each a glass of barley tea. The boy sat next to us, his back to the TV, studying us intently. Ernie offered him a stick of gum. The boy glanced at his father, who nodded, and he grabbed the gum with his small fingers.

Mr. Ma waited. I figured it was time to get to the point.

"I'm looking for So Boncho-ga, the King of the Slicky Boys."

I said it in English but there was no comprehension in Mr. Ma's eyes. I repeated it in Korean. He blinked and nodded.

"Why?" was all he said.

"There was a man killed. A soldier from England. I think the slicky boys who work Yongsan Compound will know something about it."

Mr. Ma looked at his son. "Go outside and fetch me a newspaper."

The boy rose to his feet and bowed. "Yes, Father."

After Kuang-sok scurried out of the room, Mr. Ma shook his head and sipped on his tea. He spoke once again in Korean.

"If the slicky boys do know something about this man's death, why should they tell you?"

"Because this murder could cause much trouble on the compound. Much anger amongst the generals who are in charge. Now they sleep. If I give them reason to wake up, they will wake up very angry."

"And the business of the slicky boys will suffer?"

"Exactly."

Mr. Ma nodded. "First, I must tell you that I am not a slicky boy. That was long ago, before God gave me Kuang-sok."

"*God* gave him to you?"

"Yes. I used to be a slicky boy, on your compound, the Eighth American Army. I was a good slicky boy when I was young. The very best."

Mr. Ma gazed past the TV screen, seeing an image much more vivid than the black-and-white electronic flickering.

"It was winter. Cold, much colder than tonight, with a blizzard screaming through the streets of the city. The perfect night for me. The perfect night for any slicky boy. The guards who patrol the compound would be less vigilant on their rounds, more anxious to return to the warmth of their guard shacks. An hour after curfew, I left my hooch."

He waved his hand.

"I had a much bigger room than this one. I was rich in those days. When I reached the remotest part of the wall, I waited in hiding until the sentry had passed and then I made my run on the wall. Before I got there, I noticed something small, something in a box, and it moved. I knelt down and saw that it was bundled up. I brushed away the snow from the box, unwrapped the covers, and when the cold hit the soft flesh, the child began to wail."

Mr. Ma smiled at the fond memory.

"Of course, my night's work was foremost on my mind. In the howling wind the guard would not have heard the child's cry. I could be over the fence in a few moments, steal what I needed, and be gone. But when I was halfway up the fence, the child began to wail again. It was a forlorn wail. The wail of the lost. The cry of those who will never be found.

"It was up there, while the jagged wire dug into my fingers, that I suddenly knew what I had to do. It didn't take long to think about it. It flooded my mind like a ray of light. I knew I had to stop being a slicky boy and start taking care of the child lying below me.

"A shot rang out. One of the guards had been more diligent than I thought. I dropped to the ground, breaking my ankle, and just barely managed to pick up the box and shuffle across the street into the alleys before the guard reached the fence and fired again."

Mr. Ma looked down at his foot. "And now I have two souvenirs of that night. This bad leg, and the strength of my soul: my son, Kuang-sok."

"You never went back to the compound after that?" I asked.

"No. It's been ten years and I never have."

It was an interesting enough story, I had to admit that, but he'd been out of touch too long. The Nurse had thought she was doing us a great favor by bringing us here. But this guy was just a lonely old man who wanted an audience to listen to him rave about past glories. Still, it was a touching little family, and so poor. I knew how that was.

Ernie swirled the brown barley tea in his glass. It was just a matter of time until he grew antsy and did something stupid.

Mr. Ma didn't notice our discomfort. After cleansing his throat with more of the barley tea, he continued his dissertation.

"Slicky boys have been taking money from you Americans for many years."

He smiled at the thought.

"Of course you have plenty. More than you need, and during the war we were starving. Sometimes I think you Americans knew that. That's why your security was never as good as it could have been. Or as good as it had been on the army compounds when the Japanese were here. The Japanese ruled with an iron hand. In those days, to be a slicky boy you had to be very brave because if you were caught you would be either shot on the spot or executed a few days later.

"Now we go to prison. Not such a terrible fate if you're starving to death anyway."

We had to get out of here. Otherwise, this guy was going to chew our ears off all night. But before I could make a move, he was talking again.

"When the war ended there were independent slicky boys outside all the hundreds of U.S. compounds around our country. Many of these compounds you closed up, turned over to the Korean Army, and gradually you consolidated into the fifty or sixty big bases you have now. The slicky boys started squabbling over territory. Many men were killed. This disarray lasted for some months until we had an iron hand again."

I looked at him and waited.

"So Boncho-ga," he said.

I spoke in English. "Herbalist So."

"What's that?"

I switched back to Korean. "I've heard of him," I said.

His eyes widened. "Then you are also a very diligent guard. Not many foreigners have."

"Is he still alive?"

"Oh, yes. Very much alive. Some say he might live forever." Mr. Ma picked up his tea and his eyes smiled over the rim of the cup. "All those herbs, you know."

"The herbs keep him alive?"

"Yes."

I didn't know about that but I did know that the Koreans spend fortunes on *hanyak*—Chinese medicine—and the exotic herbs and potions that go with it.

"How can I meet this Herbalist So?"

Mr. Ma shook his head. "You can't."

"Why not?"

"You are a foreigner."

"Why should that make a difference?"

"It makes all the difference. No foreigner has ever set eyes on So Boncho-ga. No foreigner ever will. That is how he survived so long." Mr. Ma raised his forefinger. "Caution."

"I can appreciate caution," I said. "Maybe there is someone who can tell him of my concerns."

"None that I know of."

"Maybe you."

Mr. Ma laughed. "I am long retired," he said. "And nothing more than a poor custodian and a collector of bottles and cans. Such an important man as Herbalist So would never listen to the likes of me."

"Then where can I find someone who he will listen to?"

"That I cannot answer."

The paper-paneled door slid back. Kuang-sok stepped into the room and sat down next to his father. He hadn't brought the newspaper, I noticed, but that wasn't my problem. Disciplining children was beyond the purview of the Criminal Investigation Division.

I downed the last of my barley tea. Ernie did the same. A waste of time, I thought. Another waste.

I thanked Mr. Ma and stood up. He rose and slipped on his shoes and followed Ernie and me to the door.

When I looked back, the last thing I saw was Kuang-sok peering at us with great relief, his arms clutched tightly around his father's waist.

Outside, stars glimmered. The moon was rising slowly above peaked tile roofs.

We turned down an alley. In it, two men stood with their backs to us. As we approached, they swiveled. In the growing moonlight, I could see they were young, hair long, disheveled. Both wore brightly colored workout outfits. The emblem of a martial arts training *dojang* was emblazoned on the chest.

They stared at us.

Had I been alone, I would've ignored their hard looks. Routine survival procedure in East L.A. But I was with Ernie. I knew he would never ignore them. I was right.

He jerked his thumb in their direction. "What do these dorks want?"

"I don't know, Ernie. Don't pay any attention to them. They'll go away."

Ernie's walk took on more bounce and he thrust out his chest. What a study he would make for some scientist. Dominant male in a pack of baboons.

Something landed heavily behind us. I looked back. More men. Dropping from a tiled roof. Three of them. Four. Five. In front of us, six more figures appeared.

Slicky boys. At long last. Somehow I wasn't filled with joy.

They closed in on us. Clubs appeared from coats.

I stood loose. Trying to make it seem as if I were ready for them.

Ernie backed up against a wall, found a large stone, and knocked it against cement to check its firmness.

"Time for some ass-kicking," he said happily.

"Who's going to be doing the kicking?"

"We are!" He tossed the rock at the first guy coming in and charged. Errol Flynn couldn't have done it better.

No time to think now. I did the same, leaping forward with a solid side-kick, catching a slicky boy in the ribs. Swinging fists crunched skull and jaw.

All in all, I'd say Ernie and I made a pretty good account of ourselves. I remember two, maybe three guys going down. I dodged a couple of bat swings and most of their karate kicks slid off of me like bullets ricocheting off armor. But it didn't last long. The flesh is weak. Especially when you're outnumbered six to one.

Somewhere along the line, I plowed headfirst into the snow. Before I could rise, hands grabbed my arms and punches and kicks rained down on my legs and my spine.

I struggled upward beneath the thudding onslaught, making progress, until something clunked on my head. I felt myself falling. As the world faded into blackness, I wondered what had hit me.

Looking back now, I think it was a brick.

16

ROUGH WOODEN SLATS JOLTED ME SKYWARD. FOR A MOMENT I hung suspended in air until slowly, gravity tightened its grip, jerked me earthward, and slammed me back onto the hard splintered boards.

Churning wheels rolled me forward, gliding over a smooth surface until they hit another eruption of stone or brick. My body was jarred once again.

Musty canvas enveloped my face. I couldn't move. The air was hot and close and laced with dirt and the cadavers of dead fleas.

I started to kick and thrash but when I did the thick shroud around me only tightened its unholy grip. I willed myself to relax. Remain still. Ease my breathing. That helped a little. Not much. I wanted to get that thing off my face.

My palms were numb, pinned beneath my body. Tingling spears of agony shot up my spine.

Someone mumbled above. Men cursed, laughed. Koreans.

We came to a halt for a moment. Whispered conversation. Some sort of go-ahead was given: We rolled forward.

Now the quaking started in earnest.

We were on jagged steps and as we progressed into the bowels of the earth, my spine slapped against the hard wooden boards again and again.

I was in some kind of cart. A wooden cart on wheels. Someone was pushing me, someone else was ahead guiding the cart, and other voices hovered around, fading in and out. Escorts of some kind.

Just another parcel being wheeled through Itaewon. Not anything anyone would notice.

I wasn't sure, but I thought there was another cart behind us. Ernie.

I was wrapped so tightly in canvas I couldn't sit up. If I shouted, I not only wouldn't be heard but I'd waste what precious oxygen was left to me. Already I felt light-headed. I fought back waves of nausea.

What to do now? I tried to remember what I'd learned in training classes out of the CID manual. Mentally, I thumbed through the table of contents. What had the authors advised if you're wrapped in canvas and being transported in a wooden cart through an ancient Oriental city? Nothing came to mind. I must've skipped that chapter.

I decided to improvise. I'd wait, though, until they unwrapped me.

Things got quieter—no more street noises—and a deep chill filled my bones. More whispers.

Suddenly, the cart was in the air. Men had grabbed hold of it all round and were grunting and snorting through their noses. We descended down what must've been a steep flight of stairs. Finally, we reached bottom and with a loud bang, the men dropped the cart.

Now there was more talking. More joviality. I was wheeled along what seemed to be a smooth stone surface. Doors opened and shut. Finally we stopped. The cart behind me rolled up and bumped into mine. Footsteps faded away. All was quiet.

I lay perfectly still.

It was cold, colder than it had been. A vicious thought crept into my mind. Had they deposited me in a tomb?

Maybe they didn't have the courage to kill me, but instead had wrapped me in this canvas and brought me down into some ungodly dark pit and left me here to die. To die of suffocation and starvation and cold.

I rolled slightly in the canvas, feeling with my legs and my arms. No folds. No place to grab onto an edge and pull. I lay still again and listened. No sound.

And then it overcame me, like some drooling monster bounding out of the dark. A horrendous, screaming surge of panic. I rolled and kicked and thrashed against the canvas and then I screamed, hollering out as loud as I could. But the more I struggled the tighter the canvas embraced me. I wiggled and pushed and clawed but nothing seemed to help. Finally, I was exhausted and I could hardly breathe. I lay in the canvas, sweat drenching my body, gasping for air like some enormous landlocked tuna fish.

I closed my eyes. Hoping for oblivion. It didn't come. I realized that somehow, just enough oxygen was seeping into my tight shroud to keep me alive. I wouldn't die and I wouldn't be able to get out. Torture. I could stay here suffering for days.

I would go mad. I was certain that before I died, I would go mad.

My jaw locked open in a silent scream. My body became rigid. I prayed. Not to be saved, but for forgiveness. For all the things I'd done wrong, for all the people I'd hurt.

It was a long list.

It could've been two minutes. It could've been two days. I'm not sure how much time passed. But somewhere deep in the recesses of my mind I heard clicking. Not a metallic click but a softer sound. More like a tap. Shoe leather on stone.

The footsteps stopped. Glass, or maybe porcelain, clinked. The footsteps came closer.

Next to my head, ancient hinges creaked. Something jarred the cart. I felt it, the shift in weight. Someone had dropped the side panel. I felt two tugs on the edge of my canvas. I went with them, rolling now, rolling toward the side of the cart, and then the surface gave way and I was falling.

I twisted and landed on my side and kept rolling, feeling the canvas unraveling and I saw daylight and pushed the last of the covering away and without warning I was blinded by light. Still, I struggled to my feet, wavering like a punch-drunk fighter, shielding my eyes with my hands.

I wasn't angry anymore—at my captors for tying me up so cruelly—but I was tremendously grateful. Grateful to whoever had pulled me out of that living hell. And I was ready to fight. Ready to make sure that nobody put me back inside. I knotted my fists and opened my eyes and scanned for targets.

The light that had seemed blinding before was nothing more than a dim lantern. Guttering. Oil-fed. I seemed to be in some sort of chamber. Rock-hewn. Jagged edges. The space slowly came into focus.

It was nicely appointed, with a comfortable-looking sofa, a pair of lounging chairs, and a coffee table centered on an intricately knit black-and-red carpet. The design of the flooring seemed a jumble at first, but after staring for a while it leapt out at me. Phoenix rising.

Behind, lining the walls, were cabinets. Inlaid mother-of-pearl with intricately wrought metal handles and clasps.

The room didn't make sense. Located in the bowels of the earth. Clean, comfortable, designed for entertaining guests. In it, the dirty old cart and flea-infested canvas seemed bafflingly out of place.

Wood rattled on wood. Something heavy thudded to the floor. A big brown mummy rolled toward me, unraveling, until I saw blue jeans and a pair of sneakers. Ernie!

I helped him to his feet. Blindly, he let loose a couple of roundhouse punches into the air.

"I'll kill the bastards!" he said. "I'll kill 'em."

Gingerly, I patted him on the shoulder. "It's okay, Ernie. It's just me. We're all right now."

He stopped swirling around and grabbed my arm and leaned on me, letting his eyes adjust to the light. Breathing heavily, he took in the room in which we stood.

Standing in the middle of the carpet, her hands clasped demurely in front of her waist, stood a beautiful young woman.

As I gazed at her I realized that she had no plans—nor any

capability—of rolling us back into the canvas. I knew she didn't deserve my gratitude—she had to be a part of the gang who'd dragged us here—but my heart flooded with warm feeling for her. She was, after all, the woman who set us free. Our liberator.

When she realized we could see her, she lowered her large brown eyes and bowed slowly from the waist. Her glossy black hair brushed forward as she did so, covering her soft cheeks and exposing the tender flesh of her neck. She straightened her back and I took a long look at her.

She was not very tall, maybe just slightly above the average height for a Korean woman, but she gave the appearance of being tall. Red silk, intricately embroidered with an entwining gold dragon, wrapped around her slender body. The collar was high, buttoned, in the style of the Manchu Dynasty. A slit at the side of the dress exposed naked thigh.

She smiled at us. Tentatively. Full lips, round nose, big eyes. Cheekbones not sharp but soft and gently contoured. It dawned on me that she wasn't Korean. She was Chinese.

When she opened her mouth to speak, the voice was high and lilting. The words came out in faltering English.

"You must be tired." She gestured towards the teapot and cups on the coffee table. "Please sit. I will pour you some tea."

Ernie's mouth fell open. "What kinda bullshit is *this*!"

He scurried off into the dark crevices of the chamber, checking the two doors, rattling the locks, pacing the length of the craggy stone walls. When he was satisfied that there was no way out, he returned to us, planted his feet in front of the Chinese woman, and held out his hand.

"Gimme the key," he said. She smiled at him. "Gimme the goddamn key to the door!"

"I'm so sorry," she said. "I don't have it."

He bunched his fist and took a step toward her. I rushed forward and grabbed him.

"Hold it, pal. Give her a chance. They wouldn't have left us down here with just her if there was a way out."

Ernie glared at her, murder in his eyes.

In his haste, Ernie had missed a couple of spots.

"Over here," I said.

We trotted to the other end of the chamber and in the shadows found an opening carved out of the rock. Ernie stared down a short stairwell that led into blackness. I turned to the girl.

"Where does this go?"

"Not out. Please, have a seat. You will be taken to my employer."

Ernie peered into the black pit. "It's too damn dark down there."

I looked at the steps. They were carved out of stone.

Who in the hell had built this place?

I didn't have any particular desire to go deeper into the cave. I looked back across the room. There must be a way to pry the doors open. I grabbed Ernie's elbow and whispered.

"She's our best bet to get out of here. Come on back. We'll talk to her."

He nodded and we returned to the center of the chamber.

"Who is your employer?" I asked.

She answered in Korean. "So Boncho-ga." Herbalist So.

The man we wanted to talk to. Might as well have a go at it. We were just as likely to be able to bust out of here later as we were now. Which maybe wasn't very likely at all.

I sat on the edge of the couch, keeping most of my weight on the balls of my feet, my forearms draped over my knees. Ernie joined me, but his head kept swiveling around as if he expected a window to open up in the stone walls any second.

She poured aromatic tea into thick porcelain cups with no handles and offered them to us with both hands. I took my cup from her and as I did I brushed the flesh of her fingers. Amazingly soft. This was a woman who had been bred for graciousness, not work. I looked at her feet. Normal. Soft-soled black canvas shoes with sequins. I'd almost expected her feet to be bound.

I sipped on the tea. The bitter taste of ginseng rolled down my parched throat. Ernie set his on the table in front of us. Didn't touch it.

When I finished, I asked for more. No sense being impolite. She poured with a pleased expression.

Relaxing us like this so soon after our ordeal was obviously her job. And the fact that even I, a half-crazed foreign devil, had responded to her ministrations would give her good face. Demonstrate to her employer the full extent of her skills. Which were extraordinary. Just having her around, with her graceful movements and her beauty and the smooth serenity of her demeanor, had a calming effect.

On me, anyway. Ernie still looked angry enough to frighten Jack the Ripper.

I started to wonder about this Herbalist So. He hires thugs to knock us out and cart us through Itaewon. And then this beautiful woman to bring us back to a semblance of civility. So was used to manipulating people. I'd let him think it was working. For the time being.

After I finished my second cup of tea, the young lady rose and bowed again.

"It is time to see my employer," she said. "Please come with me."

When we didn't move she stared at us, puzzled.

"What's your name?" I asked.

She shook her head and her black hair fluttered like a raven's wing. "Not important."

"You're not Korean," I said. "You're Chinese."

"Many Chinese in Korea. Since the revolution."

"Why do you work for Herbalist So?"

"Who?"

"So Boncho-ga."

"Oh. Because he is a very kind man."

I rubbed the back of my neck.

"Then why did he hit me over the head?"

"He did not hit you over the head. Those boys did." A disapproving expression crossed the soft features of her face. "They are very bad."

"Yes," I agreed. "Very bad."

I pushed myself up. Ernie rose too, still swiveling his head around, looking for a monster to leap out of the dark so he could bust him in the chops.

We followed the beautiful Chinese woman through the carved opening in the stone, into the darkness that led to Herbalist So.

17

WE MADE TWO TURNS, DOUBLING BACK ON OURSELVES THROUGH narrow passageways. It was cold down here and getting colder. I admired the goose-bumped flesh on the arms of the Chinese girl and wondered how she could stand the frigid temperatures.

Our path was lit by small oil lamps flickering out of indentations carved in the granite walls. Whoever set up this operation had little faith in electricity.

Mining must've gone on down here at one time or another. At the opening to an old shaft I spotted rusty rails and what appeared to be a cast-iron mining car. Probably an antique.

A shroud of smoke drifted close to the floor, snaking its way into the dark shaft.

At another carved opening, this one covered only with a beaded curtain, the Chinese girl bowed and motioned for us to enter. I nodded to her and watched as she trotted back into the darkness.

"Nice can," Ernie said.

I grunted. He never lets up.

The beads clattered as we pushed through.

This chamber was even darker than the hallway. Inside, there were no lamps. Instead, the sparse flames of stone stoves sputtered beneath thick earthen pots. The room was filled with the pungent aroma of herbs. Some tangy, some sweet. All types of herbs. Seared, boiled, roasted. I felt as if I had stepped into the den of some long-lost medieval alchemist.

Along the walls were plain wooden cabinets, each lined with hundreds of square panels. A wooden knob poked out of each little panel and every one was marked in black ink with a Chinese character. I couldn't read all of the characters but most of them had the radicals for "wood" or "plant" or "horn." The collection of herbs in the wall of tiny drawers was vast. It must've taken years to accumulate.

Something moved.

At first I thought it was nothing more than a shawl draped over the back of a chair. Then I realized it was a man, hunched over one of the small pots.

"Good evening, Agent Sueño," he said.

His voice resonated with venerable authority. To my amazement he even pronounced my name correctly.

Ernie stepped toward one of the stoves and grabbed a pair of metal tongs.

"Ah," the man said, "and Agent Bascom. So good of you to join us."

Ernie spat on the floor.

I decided to answer in Korean. And not politely.

"*Wei uri chapko deiri wasso?*" Why did you drag us here?

The man known as So Boncho-ga, Herbalist So, stood up. He was tall for a Korean, with a back that was crooked only when he leaned over his pots.

Bulging eyes glistened in the dim light like eggs swimming in water. From a tangled bush of gray hair, a bronze forehead slanted downward, lined with deep wrinkles, making the skull that housed his brain seem as solid and as secure as the steep flight of stone steps which led to his kingdom.

He reached forward with a pair of rusty tongs that were almost as crooked as his fingers and moved a steaming pot from one fire to another. When he looked back at me his full lips moved, enunciating the English as if he had been born a first cousin to the House of Windsor.

"You employ our mother tongue well," Herbalist So said. "Even the indirect insult. Quite admirable."

He puttered amongst his pots for a moment or two, finished some obscure chore, stepped forward, then turned his full attention toward me.

"Are you familiar with Chinese medicine, Agent Sueño?"

I could've tried to hard-ass him. Make him answer my question. But I knew the door behind us was barred and I doubted that there was any other way out of this damp cave. Besides, his boys probably weren't far away. I had to go along with him. For now.

Ernie still stood motionless. I didn't know how long that would last.

"I know that a lot of Koreans believe in Chinese medicine," I replied.

"Oh, yes. They certainly do. And for good reason. There are many secrets locked in these herbs. Secrets that I have spent my life trying to unravel."

"But it's only a hobby for you," I said. "Not your main line of work."

He chuckled at that.

"Yes, you're right. Not my main line of work. It was at one time, though. When I was young. Even our Japanese overlords believed in Chinese medicine. They had no objection to us plying our trade as long as all prescriptions were written in their foul language." He turned, spat on the floor, and stared directly at Ernie.

Ernie tightened his grip on the tongs. Herbalist So looked back at me.

"This chamber." He waved his arm. "It was carved out of natural formations that were discovered when dropping a new well in the area behind Itaewon. The local chief of the partisans decided to use it for his headquarters."

I stared at him, trying to discover the source of the pride that rang in his voice. I said nothing.

"Yes. That's right. The chief of the partisans was my father."

With a damp cheesecloth he wiped residue dripping from an earthen spout.

"We held classes down here. I was one of the students. The Japanese had forbidden us Koreans to speak or read or write our own language. Everything had to be conducted in Japanese. To keep our own culture was risky, but we did it. After four thousand years of Korean history, did they really think their brutal methods could turn us into second-rate Japanese?"

I didn't have an answer for him.

"Of course not," he said. "Have you been to south post on your own compound lately? The old prison there?"

"Yes. I've seen the bullet holes in the wall," I said.

"The Japanese executed many Koreans. Some of them just before you Americans arrived, after their Emperor surrendered. The Imperial Army from your compound made a final raid on Itaewon and the surrounding areas. With the thought that our misery was almost over, my father was careless. They caught him, up above. Two days later they executed him. The following day an American troop ship landed at the port of Inchon."

One of the pots started to bubble. He rushed toward it, lifted it with a thick pad, and with a charred stick rearranged the glowing coals beneath.

I could see more clearly now and I searched the walls. They were mostly carved stone but there were some spots that were darker than others. My bet was that there were back entrances. If these chambers had been used by armed men resisting the Japanese, they would've had more than one means of escape. There had to be ventilation. The smoke from the pots drifted back to the entranceway, toward the old mining shaft we had seen on the way in.

"After the war," Herbalist So said, "we Koreans had nothing. The Japanese, yes, set up some industry. But its purpose was to export raw materials back to their heathen islands. The rest of our economy was utterly devastated. Still, we started to rebuild."

"And then the Communists came south?"

He looked at me sharply, wondering if I was mocking his slow tale. I kept my face unrevealing.

"Yes," he said, nodding. "Armies paraded up and down our peninsula. First the North Koreans, then you Americans, then the Chinese. We were poor before, but after our own civil war we were desperate."

"That's when you started the slicky boy operation."

The pot he had been puttering with must've been done. He poured some of the potion into a thick cup. He leaned forward and inhaled, testing it, pleased. Sloshing it around to rinse the cup, he tossed the rest of it on the ground and poured a new cup to the brim. He held it out to me.

"You have been through a lot tonight, Agent Sueño. For that I apologize. Here, drink this. And sit down. You will find a bench over there."

He motioned into the darkness. I took the cup from him, walked over to the bench, and sat.

Ernie followed, keeping a few feet away from me, heavy tongs still at the ready.

"What is it?" I asked Herbalist So, indicating my cup.

"A concoction of herbs. Designed to restore the harmony of the *yin* and the *yang*."

I held the cup to my nose and breathed deeply. The liquid smelled of ancient things decayed and rotting in the earth.

Herbalist So walked out from behind his pots and sat down on another bench opposite me, ignoring Ernie. Ernie didn't mind. He kept his eyes moving, studying the darkness, expecting more slicky boys to spring out at us at any moment.

At first, Herbalist So kept his back ramrod straight. Then he leaned forward.

"Balance is the key to everything we do. To our health and to our 'slicky boy' operation, as you call it."

"What does 'balance' have to do with thievery?"

He sat back up. "You are bold, Agent Sueño. They told me that you were but now I see for myself."

"A man named Cecil Whitcomb," I said, "a soldier in the British Army, was killed in Namdaemun. Slaughtered by a man expert in the use of the knife. Were you, or any of the men who work for you, involved in his murder?"

Herbalist So seemed amused by the question. "And if I said no, would you believe me?"

I shrugged. "I will believe the facts."

"Wisely said."

I looked into his big eyes. Half-moon lids slid lazily over them, as if he were a lizard with a full belly, about to fall asleep. The steam from the cup drifted into my nostrils. I held the cup away.

"Then tell me the facts," I said.

He set his elbows on his knees and clasped his hands.

"After the war everyone was desperate. People, especially children, were starving in the streets. You Americans did some charitable things, I'll grant you that—much more than the Japanese would've done—but still your compounds were loaded with wealth. Food, heating fuel, clothing, medical supplies. All the things we desperately lacked. It was a matter of balance, you see. You had too much and we had too little."

"So you took the partisan organization that your father left you and started raiding the American bases?"

"It wasn't quite that simple. Like everyone else, our little band had been ravaged by the war. But we had some expertise and, above all, daring. We found likely young boys and put them through a conditioning and training program. Fed them well. Outfitted them with the proper clothing and tools, and sent them forth."

"But you also sent them armed with information," I said.

Herbalist So laughed softly. "Quite. Help from the inside is the only way to keep an operation such as ours productive in the long term."

"And you didn't become greedy. You only took as much as you figured the Americans could afford to lose."

"Exactly. Greed, of course, would have destroyed the balance."

"But occasionally someone did get greedy and had to be disciplined."

"It was sometimes necessary. Unfortunate, but necessary."

"Was the murder of Cecil Whitcomb part of your disciplining process?"

Herbalist So stared directly into my eyes. I felt it then. The intelligence, the determination, the power that was in them. And the ruthlessness. I fought back a wave of fear.

"No," he said.

He stood and walked back to his simmering pots. Ernie paced nervously. Herbalist So adjusted some of the earthen jars over the small flames and shoved fuel beneath others. Smoke from the dry twigs watered my eyes.

"You should drink your tea," Herbalist So said. "It restores balance."

"Fuck your tea," Ernie said.

Herbalist So stared at him. "Yes. Quite." He nodded. Keeping his eyes on Ernie, he spoke to me.

"We did know Cecil Whitcomb," he said. "When he started his amateurish campaign, we were informed about it immediately. I hoped, at first, that he'd stop on his own. His methods were crude. They attracted too much attention. When he didn't stop, we had a . . . talk with him."

"You brought him down here?"

"Heavens, no. He did not rate such a thing. We talked to him on the compound. One of your own contract security guards had a little chat with him. No." Mr. So shook his head. "We didn't bring Mr. Whitcomb down here. You are the first foreigners to have such an honor."

And the last, I thought, but I didn't say it. Now that we knew the secret, how could they let us go?

Herbalist So glanced over at me, a wry smile raising the edge of his mouth. I was afraid to ask him what was so funny. I knew it must be my fear.

"We thought reason would work with Mr. Whitcomb. But apparently he had little regard for the warnings of us Koreans. When he continued, we were obliged to use more forceful methods."

He walked back over to the bench, carrying another cup of tea, and sat down opposite me again.

"The British bruise easily," he said.

I didn't answer. He shook his head.

"Still, Mr. Whitcomb persisted. An obstinate little devil. Tough. Almost as poor as us when he was growing up. In a way, I admired him. If he'd been Korean I might have given him some training and turned him loose. But I could not do that. So we were in quite a quandary. What to do?"

He spread his hands.

I wanted to ask where in the hell he learned all this English. He was a scholar, certainly. A man who remembered things. But still, he would've needed to practice. I thought of the Korean magazines I thumbed through occasionally, the ones with businessmen in photos with American and European wheelers and dealers. I tried to imagine Herbalist So in a suit, his hair properly brushed. He'd fit right in. All the years he'd been making money off of the U.S. compounds, he must have accumulated a fortune. He would've had to invest it, take on a second life. Above ground. For years his organization was one of the top producers of income in the country. His money had helped rebuild the devastated Korean economy. Helped the Koreans climb back into international markets. I was tempted to ask about all this but I fought the urge. My survival, I knew, depended on not knowing any more than I had to.

"When we heard about Mr. Whitcomb's death," Herbalist So said, "we were saddened. Yes, it is true. And quite concerned. Our operation has always run on an unwritten contract of mutual trust. The tenets of that contract are simple. We do not take too much and no one gets hurt. Now, someone had been hurt. We knew you Americans would be upset. And rightfully so."

"And so you started your own investigation?"

"Yes. Of course your name was brought up immediately. And that of your partner, Agent Bascom." He shook his head. "Your violent behavior at the Kayagum Teahouse was the real clue. You really frightened the owner. She did remember you mentioning the name of a woman who works at the United Nations Club. That led us to that charming young lady, Eun-hi."

"You talked to Eun-hi?"

"Not me personally. One of my representatives spoke to her."

"What did she tell him?"

"About fingers."

"What?"

"Attractive young ladies notice things about one another. When Eun-hi was approached by this 'Miss Ku,' they chatted for a while and Eun-hi saw that Miss Ku's manicure was in poor repair. The nails too short. Unsightly lumps of hardened skin at the tips of her fingers."

"Calluses."

"Yes. Eun-hi, not being very diplomatic, mentioned it, and Miss Ku explained that she played the *kayagum* professionally."

I thought I heard the sharp twang of the strings of the *kayagum*, an ancient Korean instrument similar to a zither. But other than the sputter of the bubbling pots, the chamber was silent. The sound must've been generated by my overheated imagination. Or by my taut nerves.

"Well, that's all the information one needs really," Herbalist So said. "An attractive young lady, on an unsavory mission, who is also a professional musician. Seoul is a huge city, over eight million souls, but that narrows down the search considerably. Investigators as talented as you and Agent Bascom here should have had no trouble finding her." Herbalist So shook his head again. "Too bad you decided instead to waste your time disrupting our operation."

"It got your attention, didn't it?" Ernie said.

Herbalist So nodded, surprised that Ernie had said something to him without using a cuss word. "It most certainly did." He pointed to the cup in my hand. "You must drink, Agent Sueño. It will help."

"Help what?" I asked.

"You will go to sleep. Everything will be quite painless."

Ernie inched closer to Herbalist So. The shadows behind the flickering pots shifted.

"We drink that shit you brewed," Ernie said, "it knocks us out, and we never wake up. Is that the idea?"

"Not exactly. You will wake up. Wake up somewhere other than here."

Ernie stepped back. "You ain't putting me back in that canvas."

Herbalist So shrugged. "You brought it upon yourselves."

I felt the same way Ernie did. There was no way I was going to drink this foul potion and there was no way they were going to put me back in the canvas. Besides, how could we be sure that Herbalist So was telling the truth? How could we be sure that we'd wake up at all?

While I was working this out, Ernie surprised me. He let out a slow puff of air. "Okay," he said. "Where's my cup?"

Using a polite Korean gesture, Herbalist So held the tea out to him with both hands. Ernie reached for the hot potion but instead of grabbing it, his fingers flicked forward.

He slapped the burning liquid into the face of the King of the Slicky Boys.

18

HERBALIST SO SPUTTERED AND BELLOWED IN RAGE, WIPING THE steaming broth from his eyes.

"*Sikkya!*" Born of a beast!

Shadows emerged from the far wall. Bodyguards. I expected that. Herbalist So wouldn't be here with us alone, although he wanted to give that appearance.

Ernie kicked over a few of the bubbling vats, grabbed an earthen jar, and flung it at the approaching slicky boys. They jumped back from the boiling spray.

"Come on, you bastards!" Ernie yelled. "I'm ready for you."

I grabbed him by the arm and pulled. He jerked away.

"Why not fight 'em here? There's no escape from this place."

"There might be," I said. "Come on."

We burst through the beaded curtain and, instead of heading back to the chamber where we had encountered the Chinese woman, followed the drifting smoke toward the tunnel with the rusty railroad tracks.

Behind us there was much commotion and cursing. Apparently the bodyguards were helping Herbalist So to his feet, figuring they had plenty of time to deal with us.

Herbalist So, still enraged, hollered orders. All of which amounted to the Korean version of "After them!"

I slowed and grabbed one of the oil lamps. I motioned for Ernie to do the same.

I had a hunch about this particular tunnel. Smoke drifted into it and the smoke had to go somewhere. Apparently the tunnel hadn't been used for a while; that might be a good sign. The slicky boys wouldn't think about it as a possible escape route.

There had to be some way out of this dungeon. Whether we could find it before the slicky boys caught us, that was another question.

The old mining cart was enormous, made of cast iron. I would've liked to have examined it, see if it was smelted here in Korea or in Japan, but there wasn't time.

The tunnel itself was pitch black and just big enough to accommodate the cart. Holding the lamp in front of me, I stepped up on the old tracks and started forward.

Ernie didn't. "I'm not going in there," he said.

I turned. "We have no choice. You pissed them off now." I motioned at the smoke wafting past us. "If there's a way out of this joint, this is it."

Footsteps clattered in the outer passageway. The slicky boys had already discovered that we hadn't returned to the Chinese woman's sitting room, but had foolishly delved deeper into the catacombs. Their voices grew louder.

Ernie asked, "Are there any rats in there?"

"No way," I said.

He swallowed, then followed me into the darkness.

The lamps helped at first. The ceiling was so low that we had to bend at the waist to avoid clunking our heads into low-hanging clumps of granite. A trickle of water seeped from the rock walls. Darting through the air toward us, a bat veered off at the last second. Ernie covered his face with his forearm but kept moving forward.

Was I frightened? You're damn right I was. But now that Ernie had insulted Herbalist So, and they had us down here in this dungeon, and nobody else in the world knew we were here, and we'd already proven that we were going to be the worst thorn in their side they'd ever experienced, their decision about what to do with Ernie and me would be easy. Do away with the troublemakers.

And if nobody ever found our bodies, what would the honchos at 8th Army think? That we'd deserted? That we'd finally given vent to our real desires and become part of the underground scene in Itaewon?

Probably. They'd believe whatever was convenient. Anything would be better than dealing with the embarrassing proposition that we might have been murdered by the slicky boys, whose existence they didn't even acknowledge. And we were officially off the Whitcomb case. That would be the water they'd use to wash their hands of us.

The voices at the mouth of the tunnel grew nearer. They'd realized where we were. Probably from the flickering light of our oil lamps. A Korean word was bandied about. *Hyuu-juh.* Fuse.

The tunnel was dropping slightly downhill. This surprised me. I had expected it to rise, to reach the surface. How else had a draft been created that drew the smoke?

No sense worrying about it now. We kept moving.

Sweat dripped from my face. Although it was cold as hell in the tunnel, the exertion and the tension were causing me to overheat. Ernie was in good shape, I knew, but behind me he too breathed heavily.

Something rumbled. The cavern trembled.

At first I thought it was an earthquake. Metal creaked. The rumbling returned, steady now, like low rolling thunder. Then I realized what it was.

The mining cart.

Ernie stumbled and cursed. "Jesus H. Christ! They're rolling the fucking cart down here."

I searched the shadowy walls. No openings. There hadn't been any since we entered this tunnel. The cart took up every inch of space. There'd be no way to avoid it when it reached us, which it would do in seconds. We'd be run over. Crushed.

"Keep moving forward," I told Ernie. "It's our only chance."

And although I was bending at the knees, hobbling like Quasimodo tending his bells, I started to run. I felt Ernie's hot breath on my neck.

My right foot slammed into something. Pain shot up my leg. I stumbled forward, arms out, dropping the lamp, and splashed face-first into slime. My lamp sizzled, then sputtered out.

Ernie tripped over my feet and crashed down on top of me. Wriggling free of him, I raised my head out of the scum-filled water, gasping for breath. At first I thought my eyes were covered with mud, but when I reached up and rubbed them I found that my face was clear. Now that both lamps had been snuffed out, we were in almost total darkness.

I stared back down toward the mouth of the tunnel. Nothing. Only the huge silhouette of the ancient mining cart, rumbling relentlessly toward us.

Flesh thudded into flesh. I reached for Ernie, felt his hands flailing wildly. He was slapping himself.

"Rats!" he yelled. "Fucking *rats*!"

"They won't hurt you." I stood and pulled him forward. "Come on. We have to move! The cart."

He came to his senses and followed me forward.

The tunnel was rising now. The pool of scum had been its low point, moisture and filth accumulated from decades of stagnation.

The darkness was maddening. Since I couldn't see the overhanging rocks, I leaned forward as I ran, grasping the track rails with my slimy hands, pulling myself ever onward.

But no matter how fast we moved the rumbling of the mining cart kept growing nearer. And faster.

A blade slashed into my eyes. I dropped to the ground and rolled, covering my face with my arms, trying to escape the pain.

Within seconds I was moving forward again. So was Ernie. And when I uncovered my eyes I realized what had happened.

Somebody'd found the fuse box they were talking about and a long string of lightbulbs, stretching in front of and behind us, had been switched on.

Ahead about twenty yards, loomed a wall of stone. Dead end.

I willed my eyes to focus, searching for a means of escape. Two-by-fours were bolted up against the end of the tunnel. Bumpers.

I figured it out. The mining cart had been designed to be rolled down the tunnel and carried by its own momentum up the incline, where it slammed into the splintered lumber.

Not good.

The mining cart was moving so fast now that even the rising tracks wouldn't slow it down. There were no hollowed spaces in the wall, no escape hatches.

Ernie and I were about to be crushed by two tons of rolling metal.

When we were about ten yards from the end of the tunnel, the cart splashed into the pond of scum behind us. By now, my eyes had adjusted to the harsh light and I was able to make out the outlines of a ladder against the far wall. Maybe there was some hope after all.

Reaching for the ladder, I scrambled up and saw the square outlines of a trapdoor in the roof. I shoved upward. The door groaned but wouldn't budge.

Ernie was right below me, glancing back at the rapidly approaching cart. "Push it open!"

"Too heavy!" I yelled.

"Here," he said. "Brace your feet on that rock."

I did as I was told, lifting myself off the ladder. Bolted into the stone wall, it was old and rusted. Using his legs for leverage, Ernie gripped the ladder and pulled. The ancient bolts groaned but didn't budge.

The cart was only yards away now. It was all over.

Then, without warning, the bolts gave and the metal ladder popped free. Ernie shoved it up to me and stabbed his finger at an outcropping of granite.

"Use that as a lever."

I did. With one end of the ladder braced against the trapdoor, the stone as a fulcrum, and Ernie pulling down on the other end of the ladder with all his weight, the trapdoor started to creak open.

Ernie hung from the far end of the ladder like a monkey after coconuts.

"Push, goddamn it!" he yelled. "Push!"

I shoved up on the trapdoor with all my strength. Lumber scraped on lumber, filth fell into my eyes and mouth, and suddenly the trapdoor popped free.

The cart was a moving shadow now, only yards away from us.

I scrambled up, reached back in, grabbed Ernie's outstretched hands, and tugged.

The rumbling was like the approach of death itself. I jerked backward with all my strength, and Ernie's head popped through the opening. His butt and his feet cleared the ground seconds before we were both knocked back by a tremendous crash.

We lay on a dirty wood floor, dazed and winded, peering down into the darkness and the billowing dust. Beneath us, as if its lethal mission had been accomplished, the big cart started to roll back the way it came.

Apparently, someone had been inside it, because four dark figures hopped out onto the tracks.

They were quick and we were exhausted and not thinking fast enough. By the time I pulled myself together they were climbing up the wall.

I shoved the trapdoor. It clapped shut, but that wouldn't be enough to keep them away. Frantically, I searched the space we were in.

Dust, crates, grimy windows. We were inside a warehouse.

Against one wall sat an enormous crate. I forced myself to my feet and stumbled toward it. Stenciling. In English. Pittsburgh, PA. Some sort of machinery. A lathe, I think.

"Ernie! Help me with this."

Together we tried to shove the crate atop the trapdoor. It wouldn't budge. I wedged myself between the crate and the wall, set my sneakers against a wooden beam, my back against the box, and pushed. Ernie and I strained with all our might. The crate started to slide.

I heard the trapdoor creak open.

Ernie told me later that fingers crept over the edges of the opening like tarantulas crawling out of a hole.

The crate scraped forward, slid over the top of the trapdoor, and slammed it shut.

When we staggered back to the Nurse's hooch, she slid back the paper-paneled door, opened her mouth when she saw us, and screamed.

We both crashed face-first onto the warm vinyl floor. Ernie waved his paw, like a canine begging for mercy.

"We're okay," he said. "We're okay."

Ajjima from next door rushed over, and soon she and the Nurse had us out of our filthy clothes. They washed our faces with hand towels and poured barley tea down our throats.

Gradually, the warmth and the hot water and the soap brought us back to our senses.

"What happened?" the Nurse asked.

"The slicky boys," I said. "They kidnapped us."

The Nurse's face shifted from worry to panic.

"They were going to ask for a ransom," Ernie said, "but it finally dawned on them that nobody was going to pay."

For some reason we both found that uproariously funny and we howled with laughter.

Our hysteria seemed to make *ajjima* nervous. She loaded up a metal pan with the towels and the barley tea she had brought over. The Nurse escorted her out and bowed politely, thanking her for her help. *Ajjima* returned to her hooch on the other side of the courtyard.

The Nurse rummaged through her cabinet, pulled out a crystalline bottle of *soju,* and poured us each a shot in small cups. We tossed them down.

After we had calmed down a little, I started to explain.

I told the Nurse about the twelve guys who had jumped us and being wrapped in canvas and the beautiful Chinese woman and Herbalist So and the escape through the tunnel and the trapdoor in the warehouse on the 8th Army compound.

She was astonished. "On the compound?"

"Yes. An old warehouse. GI's never go in there. Koreans do all the manual labor on the compound. Besides, it's very well hidden. Nobody ever would've found it unless they were looking for it. And the slicky boys haven't used it for years. Probably figured it was too risky."

The warehouse was on Yongsan's south post, in an old storage area of brick buildings built by the Japanese Imperial Army. When we left it and walked up behind one of the security guards, we damn near gave him a heart attack. Once he regained control of himself, however, he knew better than to ask questions.

The Nurse was curious about Herbalist So. She'd heard rumors about him, but no one in Itaewon was sure if he really existed. I told her what I had observed and then told her about the calluses he had mentioned on Miss Ku's hands.

The Nurse rubbed the tips of her fingers. "The *kayagum*," she said, nodding. "Very bad for woman's hands."

"We have to talk to Miss Ku," I said. "She could be the key to this entire investigation. And at least now we know how to find her."

"How?"

"There must be places where women study the *kayagum*, where they play it for fun, or to make money entertaining."

The Nurse nodded gravely. "Yes. Many places."

I raised my palms in the air, resting my case. "Then all we've got to do is hit a few spots in Seoul, places where *kayagum* players hang out, and we'll find Miss Ku."

"You must be out of your gourd," Ernie said. "There's probably a jillion joints like that."

"We can do it."

The Nurse nodded agreement. "I can help."

"See?" I told Ernie. "We even have our own native guide."

Ernie groaned and poured himself another shot of *soju*.

The Nurse squeezed my hand and smiled. I knew why. She was thanking me for including her in our investigation. She'd be happy to spend more time with Ernie, no matter what the reason.

Still, I was worried about including her. The slicky boys had a serious grudge against us. We had not only disrupted their operations, but we now knew the general whereabouts of their king and their headquarters. Maybe I should've kept her out of it.

She smiled again and her face took on a deep, satisfied glow.

I sighed. Too late now.

19

THE NEXT MORNING WE MADE AN APPEARANCE AT THE CID office, but slipped away as soon as we could. For two bottles of Johnnie Walker Black, Ernie's jeep had been repaired and looked as good as it did before we crashed into the trash truck. It purred through the evergreen trees of Yongsan Compound's south post toward the redbrick warehouse area.

One of the Korean supply honchos escorted us into the building. He may not have known all the particulars, but he knew this had something to do with the slicky boy operations. His hands shook as he twisted the key on the padlock.

Ernie elbowed me and nodded toward one of the windows. It was the one we had broken last night when we escaped from the warehouse. New glass. Already.

But that was nothing compared to what we found at the spot where the trapdoor had been. The heavy crate had been pushed out of the way and new flooring laid down. The trapdoor no longer existed.

The Korean manager ran his finger beneath his collar, sweating.

Ernie hollered for a crowbar and one of the warehousemen came running. It took us about twenty minutes to rip up the new wooden planks. Ernie climbed down into the crawl space and knelt. He came back up with a claylike substance smudged on his finger.

"Mortar," he said. "The tunnel's closed. Bricked up."

We could've had the new brick broken in, but something told me that all we'd find would be caved-in rock.

I turned to the Korean manager. His entire body quivered.

"When will you talk to Herbalist So?"

He looked at me, stupefied, his throat so dry he croaked.

"Never mind," I said. "When you see him, tell him that his secret is safe with us."

I didn't know if it would do any good but it was worth a try. Let the slicky boys know that our objective was to catch the killer of Cecil Whitcomb, not to expose their operation.

Of course, if Herbalist So had been lying to us and he actually was the one who'd ordered Whitcomb murdered, they wouldn't stop trying for us until they succeeded.

The manager didn't nod. He just gaped at me, beads of perspiration clinging to his forehead.

Ernie tossed the crowbar back to the workman. We climbed into the jeep and roared off.

Ernie pounded on the steering wheel. "Can you believe those guys? They somehow managed to move supplies and a work crew in here in the middle of the night and close up that damn tunnel."

"I can believe it."

"Jesus H. Christ. Is there anything the slicky boys *can't* do on this compound?"

"A few things," I said.

"Like what?"

"Like gain access to classified information."

"Classified information?" Ernie looked at me. A two-and-a-half-ton truck barreled toward us. We slid past it by inches. "What's classified information got to do with the price of kimchi in Itaewon?"

"I'm not sure, but it's something maybe we should check out. Just in case Herbalist So really wasn't involved in Cecil Whitcomb's murder."

"I thought we decided that Whitcomb couldn't be a spy?"

"We did. But maybe we cut off that avenue of investigation too early. We ought to check it out."

"Okay," Ernie said. "We check it out. What with the slicky boys after our butts and the First Sergeant thinking we might've had something to do with the murder and us no longer assigned to the case, no problem!"

I ignored his bellyaching. "Let's go see Strange."

"That pervert? He turns my stomach."

"You always tell him dirty stories."

"The only language he understands."

"No matter how objectionable his personal habits might be," I said, "every classified document at Eighth Army Headquarters passes through his hands."

"Jesus H. Christ," Ernie said. "That figures."

The flagpole loomed above us, fluttering listlessly. Moist snowflakes plopped into the mud.

When we checked at the classified documents center, the civilian clerk told us that Strange was attending monthly training with all the other NCO's assigned to 8th Imperial Army. We found out where the training was being conducted and walked past the parade field and trudged up the hill through some supply huts to the leveled-off training area.

A twenty-man tent had been set up amongst the trees. When someone ducked out through a canvas flap, a smudge of tear gas wafted through the pine-scented grove.

"They're nothing but a bunch of clerks and jerks," Ernie said. "What do they need CBR training for?"

CBR: Chemical, Biological, and Radiological. Three of the army's favorite subjects.

"In case they have to use tear gas to put down a riot or something."

"Strange? Put down a riot? I'd like to see that."

We found him off by himself, under the tree line, smoking a *tambei*. He wore fatigues that were too tight around the butt and too baggy at the shoulders. It wasn't so much the cut of the uniform but the cut of his body. His jump boots were as unscratched as if they'd come out of the shoe box that morning. The highly spit-shined tips pointed to either side at a wide angle. He looked like a web-footed paratrooper with a weight problem. When we came close he peered at us through his tinted glasses and grabbed the cigarette holder in his mouth, tapping it with his pinky, dropping ash onto the ground in front of him.

"Hmmm," he said. "Had any *strange* lately?"

I could've told him about Eun-hi and Suk-ja and wrestling with their naked bodies, but I didn't want to get him all worked up.

"No, Harvey," I said. "No strange lately. We're here for some information."

His real name was Harvey and he didn't like to be called by his nickname, which was Strange. Primarily, I supposed, because people who really are strange don't like to be reminded of it.

"Information, eh? That's a valuable commodity."

Ernie stepped forward. "Have you ever met Annie and Miss Inchon?"

His eyes widened behind the dark glasses. "Who?"

"They work in Itaewon. Let me tell you about them."

While Ernie went on with his made-up story, I surveyed the training site. Men were lined up, white scorecards clutched in their hands. As they took their turns going into the tent they handed their card to one of the cadre NCO's. Before stepping inside, they slipped their black protective masks over their heads, blew out and cleared them, and made sure all the seals were tight. Once inside they stayed for only a few seconds. They had to take off their masks and recite their Social Security numbers or the first lines of the Gettysburg Address or something inane like that. Most of them didn't finish even the most simple dissertation before they burst madly out of the tent flap, coughing and hacking.

The idea was to get you used to being uncomfortable. Sometimes I figured that was the sole purpose of the entire U.S. Army training program.

When I turned back, Ernie had finished his lies, and Strange's eyeballs were glazed over.

"Harvey," I said.

He didn't answer. I tapped him on the cheek. The flesh quivered like refrigerated lard.

"Harvey!"

"What?"

"Tell me about Captain Burlingame."

"Hard-ass," he said.

"What else?"

"Sloppy with his classified documents."

"Sloppy?"

"Thinks his people are above making mistakes. Doesn't like it when we come down to inspect his security arrangements. Thinks he's getting back at us by not signing and dating all the log-in sheets."

"How many classified documents do Burlingame's people handle?"

"Loads. Were you in his office?"

"Yes."

"Then you were sitting right on top of the J-two vault. Access downstairs."

Cecil Whitcomb was into stealing things that he could immediately resell on the black market. He was a petty thief, not very skilled. If he'd been an expert we might not've even noticed his little crime wave. So would he have risked going after classified documents? Probably not. He wasn't stupid. Missing typewriters can be ignored. Missing classified documents can't. Besides, where would he find an outlet for military secrets? They're not easy to sell. Even though there are plenty of spies in Korea, contacting them is not easy. They don't advertise in newspapers.

"Has J-two had any problems? Missing documents? Stuff like that?"

"Nah. They've been lucky. But if they keep up with sloppy procedures they'll get burned eventually. Then they better not come crying to me."

So that wasn't it. The fact that classified documents were nearby when Cecil stole a typewriter was just a coincidence. Anyway, where could he steal something in 8th Army Headquarters and not be near classified documents? The whole place was crawling with them.

Strange pulled on his cigarette. I watched his thin lips crinkle around the tobacco-stained holder. It wasn't a pleasant sight.

"Have there been any other security problems lately?" I asked. "Anything unusual?"

"There's always something unusual in security."

"Here on Yongsan Compound?"

"No. Not here. Other places. Only rumors though."

A gruff voice bellowed beside the tent. "Second squad! Fall in."

Strange plucked his cigarette stub out of the holder and dropped it to the mud.

"Gotta go."

"Harvey," I said. "Check with the other security NCO's. Especially here on compound. Find out if they've run into any problems."

I didn't think there had been any, but since Cecil Whitcomb had broken into at least one office that housed classified documents it had to be checked out.

"I will," he said. "But if you get any *strange* . . ."

"Yeah. Don't worry. I'll tell you about it."

We watched him waddle off. When he was out of earshot, I leaned toward Ernie.

"It's good to know," I said, "that he and others like him are maintaining a constant state of readiness."

"Yeah," Ernie said. "But ready for what?"

I didn't know the answer to that one.

We walked down the hill, away from the burning gas that floated in the gray sky.

. . .

Broad steps between whitewashed brick led down to an open iron grating, behind which sat a counter and a giant reading a comic book. Palinki, unit armorer for the CID Detachment. He looked up from the magazine.

"What's up, brotha? Gotta shoot somebody again?"

Ernie offered the big Samoan some gum and he accepted it in his thick fingers without saying a word.

"I need a pistol, Palinki," I said.

"That's my line of work," he said. "Hold on."

He rummaged amongst the rows of oiled metal until he found something, returned to the counter, and plopped it down in front of me. A .45.

"Got anything smaller?"

"Sure." He looked slightly disappointed. "You're not planning on blowing anybody away?"

"Not today. I want something that won't be conspicuous."

"What?"

"Something that I can hide."

"Sure, brotha. Can do."

Palinki was one of the friendliest guys you ever met. When he was sober. But when he was drunk he could turn into the biggest pain in the ass in the universe. Out in Itaewon, Ernie and I had pulled him away from trouble more than once. Lately, he'd been seeing the chaplain and had enrolled in some sort of alcohol-and-drug rehabilitation program. That's why Ernie wasn't talking to him. He was afraid something might rub off.

Palinki prowled around the gleaming rows of black metal, the aroma of light oil wafting out toward us like a lethal pomade.

When he returned he slapped something on the counter. A small revolver, almost hidden in his huge brown fist.

"Snub-nosed thirty-eight," he said. "Just the thing."

I adjusted the strap around my chest, put my jacket back on, and shrugged my shoulders.

"Fits good."

"Palinki's Fine Tailoring. That's us."

I thanked him and we trotted out of the cement cellar back up into the cold wintry wind and the warm jeep. Ernie had left it idling. When we jumped back in, he let out the clutch and jammed it into gear.

"No more riding in wooden carts," Ernie said.

"Right. And no more letting the bad guys wrap us in canvas."

I tapped the .38. It felt snug and secure against my chest.

20

THE NURSE WORE A BRIGHT BLUE COTTON DRESS WITH LONG sleeves and puffed shoulders, and a single strand of imitation pearls around her neck. A stainless steel barrette held back her long black hair, and she clasped Ernie's hand and smiled and bounced as she walked.

If she hadn't been concerned with appearing mature, she would've skipped like a little girl. That's how happy she was.

The snow had stopped and although the sun hadn't quite decided to make an appearance, it was thinking about it.

We left the jeep behind on the compound because parking in downtown Seoul is impossible, and besides, we'd be asking for information and didn't want to intimidate anyone by appearing too official. The city bus was packed. Bodies pressed against me and the entire rocking enclosure reeked of fermented cabbage and garlic. I kept a close check on my wallet and the pistol hanging heavily beneath my armpit.

The Nurse had marked at least a dozen destinations down on a tourist map of Seoul. Our first stop, a training school for Korean traditional music in Ahyon-dong, wasn't very productive. The caretaker was too frightened when she saw Caucasian faces to talk to us. The next place was a music conservatory in the Okchon District. The headmaster consented to grant us a bit of his time.

I explained the situation as best I could, letting the Nurse translate my English into Korean to give her good face. The headmaster nodded respectfully, checking us out all the while, wondering what two GI's and a business girl were doing in this part of Seoul. Finally, he asked me a question.

"Did you see this woman's calluses?"

I nodded.

"Which fingers?"

I pointed to all the fingers on the left hand and the forefinger and the middle finger on the right.

He nodded. Miss Ku was a *kayagum* player, all right.

He held out his hand. "Were the calluses as big as mine?"

I shook my head. Not nearly. Enormous welts rose off of his skin, almost as if he had two fingertips instead of one.

"Then they were smaller?"

"Yes."

"How small?"

Through the Nurse, I tried to describe the size of Miss Ku's calluses but I wasn't communicating very well. In frustration, the headmaster called for one of his students. A girl of about thirteen trotted over and bowed.

"Myong-chun," the headmaster told her, "hold out your hands."

Obediently, she did. The soft skin was distorted by hard lumps at the tips of her fingers.

"Myong-chun is one of our best students," the headmaster said. "She has been studying the *kayagum* for six years. How did this woman's hands compare?"

I studied Myong-chun's calluses carefully, trying to remember every detail of Miss Ku's hands. I had seen them in dim light, in the teahouse in Itaewon. Still, I remembered because the ugliness of the calluses had contrasted sharply with the general softness and beauty of her skin.

"The woman we are looking for," I said, "had calluses on her fingers about twice as big as those of Myong-chun."

The Nurse translated. The headmaster told Myong-chun to return to her studies. The girl bowed and scurried off.

"Then the woman you are looking for," the headmaster told us, "is a serious student of the *kayagum*. Ten years, at least. If she studied that hard, and if she's as beautiful as you say, she shouldn't have difficulty finding employment."

"Where?" I asked.

The headmaster rubbed his chin. "It is difficult to say, but most young women employ the same method to find a job."

"What's that?"

He answered using a Korean term that I was unfamiliar with. The Nurse, also, had trouble translating it. After a little discussion, we figured it out.

Miss Ku, like most young female musicians in Seoul, would've used a talent agency. An agency organized for the purpose of finding jobs for *kisaeng*. *Kisaeng* are the Korean equivalent of Japanese geisha girls, but theirs is an even more ancient art. They play the *kayagum*, sing, dance, and beat drums, and they have been entertaining royalty for uncounted centuries. Now, of course, they're reduced to performing for tourists. And Japanese businessmen here on sex tours.

Without prompting from me, the Nurse asked the headmaster for a list of agencies. He said there were only three major ones. He didn't have their addresses but he gave her the names. The Nurse produced a small notebook from her purse and, her face crinkled in concentration, scribbled down the name of each agency.

We bowed to the headmaster and thanked him.

Ernie complained about being hungry, so we stopped in a noodle shop with a picture of three frolicking eels over the door. I don't like seafood much, especially if it looks like a snake, so I ordered plain rice with bean curd soup. Ernie and the Nurse both asked for noodles with eel flesh. When the steaming bowls were delivered, they dug in with zest.

Halfway through the meal, the Nurse pointed with her chopsticks into Ernie's bowl. "Your fish not done."

"No sweat," he said.

"No. I send back. Make them cook more."

She started to call for the waitress but Ernie stopped her. "It's okay," he said.

A lot of people stared at us, checking out the Nurse carefully. I didn't want to ruin her good mood but I couldn't resist asking, "Aren't you embarrassed to be seen downtown with two foreigners?"

"No," she said. "Not at all."

"But all the women are looking at you," I said.

"They're looking at Ernie, too," she said.

"Yes. They are."

"That's because they're jealous."

Ernie kept eating.

"They're jealous because you have an American boyfriend?"

"Sure. American man good. Have money. Most don't beat up wife." She waved her chopsticks in a circle above her head. "They're all very very jealous."

She smiled and grabbed Ernie's hand. He jerked it away and reached across the table for more soy sauce.

The first talent agency we visited had closed down. The second allowed us to look through their files, but there was no hint of anyone who matched the description of Miss Ku.

We only had one left.

It was already late afternoon by the time we found it, in the Myongdong District of Seoul, not too far from the huge Cosmos Department Store. Finding the address was not easy, even when we knew we had the right block, because all the buildings were high-rise and there were so many shops and neon signs and barkers with megaphones on the streets that it was difficult to locate the little bronze plaques that gave the names and numbers of the various office buildings.

Finally we climbed a narrow stairway into a foyer with an ancient elevator. The Nurse scanned the directory and pointed.

Heing Song Ki Huik.

The Shooting Star Talent Agency, I told Ernie.

"Rising or falling?"

"We'll see."

Upstairs, in the receptionist's office, the Nurse did all the talking, explaining who we were, what we were after.

Ernie strolled around the small room, studying the publicity photographs of beautiful Korean women in the traditional *chima-chogori*, embroidered silk dresses. A row of celadon vases sat on pedestals spaced every few feet.

The receptionist was a good-looking young woman and seemed amazed to see foreigners in her office. Soon, she disappeared into a back office and returned with a middle-aged woman in a neatly tailored business suit. She smiled and shook all our hands.

I explained again what we were after and, once again, the Nurse translated. The woman in the business suit shook her head.

"The personal histories of our clients are confidential."

"We don't want a personal history," I said. "We only want to find out where she's working now."

"What's her name?"

"Miss Ku. But it's probably an alias. If you allow me to look at your booklet of publicity photos, I'm sure I can identify her."

"I'm so sorry. That's for client use only."

The Nurse started to argue with her but the agency owner cut her off.

"You must understand, our ladies are very beautiful, and sometimes people of low education bother them. Old boyfriends. Or Japanese tourists, or—"

Something smashed. Green bits of porcelain exploded into the air. We all swiveled.

It was Ernie. He stood serenely in front of the publicity photos and reached for another frame. With a deft flick of the wrist he hurled it at the next vase in the row.

"*Yoboseiyo!*" the woman screamed. "*Weikurei?*" You! What are you doing?

She rushed toward him. The receptionist stood up, eyes frightened, curled fists in front of her mouth.

As calmly as if he were playing Frisbee in a park, Ernie grabbed another picture frame off the wall and hurled it at the lacquered vases. More pottery smashed to the floor. The agency owner grabbed him by the arm and jerked back.

"*Tangsin weikurei?*" What are you doing?

That was all it took for the Nurse. Someone attacking her Ernie. Her calm face flickered into a mask of rage. She charged forward and belted the elder woman in the ribs. The owner screamed, clutched her side, and stared at the Nurse in amazement. Before she could react, the Nurse belted her once again, this time in the jaw.

The receptionist ran out from behind her desk and grabbed the Nurse by the shoulders, but she was a frail woman. The Nurse swiveled, elbowing her in the gut, and the receptionist went down.

By now the agency owner was back up, claws bared. She charged the Nurse and grabbed a good handful of her hair. They wrestled back and forth, a match for each other, screaming and shouting curses.

Ernie stood back, arms crossed, grinning. His work done. He loved it when people went crazy. Maybe it was his two tours in Vietnam that did it to him. I don't know.

I wanted to help the Nurse, but instead I took advantage of the situation and stepped into the back office. Behind a polished mahogany desk was a tinted plate glass window with a magnificent view of downtown Seoul. I didn't have time to admire it. Instead, I checked through the bookshelves until I found what I was after. Four leather-bound volumes with mug shots of the talented ladies represented by the agency.

I thumbed through the pages quickly, listening to the crashes and shrieks outside. There were men's voices now. Apparently the front door of the office was open and people from down the hallway had come to find out what was going on.

It seemed to take forever. I flipped through the faces until they became a blur and suddenly I stopped and turned back three pages.

There she was. Her hair piled up and longer than it had been when I'd seen her. Wearing a traditional Korean dress embroidered with white cranes. But it was her, all right. Miss Ku. No one could ever mistake that beautiful smile.

I checked her real name: Choi Yong-ran. Miss Ku must be her stage name. And the name she uses when duping unsuspecting CID agents in Itaewon. Many Koreans change names when they change professions. Especially when the profession is somewhat unsavory. Like being a *kisaeng*.

It was easier finding her folder in the steel filing cabinet because everything was in order according to the *hangul* alphabet. Rather than jotting anything down, I just stuck the folder under my coat next to the little snub-nosed .38.

By now, pandemonium reigned in the front room. Some of the Korean men were arguing with one another, and the Nurse and the agency owner were still locked in a hair-pulling embrace. Ernie stood back out of the way. I nodded to him.

Stepping forward, I whipped out my CID badge. I held it high in the air.

"Nobody move!" I said. "You're all under arrest!" I pointed at one of the men who seemed to be in the thick of things.

"What's your name?" I demanded.

He seemed intimidated by the show of authority and pointed with his forefinger to his nose.

"Yes, you," I said, still using English, figuring it would keep them off-balance. "What's your name?"

"Hong," he said.

"Good." I stepped forward and patted him on the shoulder.

By now Ernie had somehow extricated the Nurse from the agency owner's grasp. She charged again but Ernie straight-armed her and held her back.

"Mr. Hong, I'm putting you in charge."

Ernie knew what to do. He thrust the writhing and screaming agency owner into Mr. Hong's arms.

"Hold her, now," I said.

He nodded. The enraged woman almost wriggled out of his grasp but another man stepped forward to assist.

Ernie dragged the screaming Nurse out the doorway and down the hallway. Following them, I stopped and turned to the stunned crowd.

"The police will be here any minute. No one move."

Ernie didn't bother with the elevator but found the doorway to the stairs and pushed through it. I was right behind him. The Nurse started to calm down, realizing now that disappearing was the wisest course of action. She moved quickly down the cement steps.

"Good thinking, pal," Ernie said.

"Koreans respect authority," I answered. "Someone taking charge. And when you spout it out in English, they're confused. Backs them off for a minute."

Boots pounded on cement. Coming up toward us. Running.

"The police," Ernie said.

The Nurse clung to him. The KNP's would arrest her without questions if they found out what happened.

I shoved past them. "Let me go first."

When the footsteps were two flights below me, I shouted.

"*Kyongchal!*" Police.

I rushed down the stairs, holding up my badge. Two young troopers in khaki uniforms stopped when they saw me, both panting heavily.

This time I spoke Korean. "*Mipalkun Honbyong,*" I said. Eighth Army Military Police. "There's a crazy woman upstairs on the twelfth floor. Already one person has been attacked. We're escorting the victim to the hospital now."

They nodded.

"Hurry! Up to the twelfth floor. What are you waiting for?"

The policemen shoved past me and Ernie and the Nurse.

We trotted downstairs, out the front door, and after sprinting through a couple of alleys, waved down a taxi.

21

HER SILK SHIRT SWIRLED LIKE WHIRRING JADE. THE BEAUTIFUL young woman banged away at a circle of suspended drums as if she were trying to disturb the slumber of long-dead kings. As the rhythm increased she twirled ever faster. I thought she'd go mad with dizziness.

Ernie snapped his gum beside me.

"Does she take off her clothes?"

The Nurse elbowed him.

"No, Ernie," I said. "This is classical Korean *kisaeng*. The real thing. Ancient arts. These girls are dancers and musicians and poets. Not strippers."

"So what's the difference?"

"Jesus. There's no talking to you."

We stood in a carpeted hallway. Beyond us spread a ballroom dotted with linen-draped cocktail tables. Leather-upholstered booths lined the walls. A small stage shoved into a corner supported the spinning *kisaeng*.

The joint was in the brightly lit downtown district of Mukyo-dong. Outside, a hand-carved sign in elegant Chinese script told it all: The House of the Tiger Lady. A *kisaeng* house. Reserved for the rich.

"This place sucks," Ernie said.

He despises opulence.

"You're just suspicious of any place that doesn't have sawdust on the floors," I said.

No one had noticed us yet. Elegant young women, wearing the traditional Korean *chima-chogori*—long, billowing skirts and short, loose-sleeved tunics—paraded across the room like brightly colored flowers of pink and red and sky blue, bowing and serving the men in the audience. All the customers were Korean businessmen in expensive suits. Not a foreigner in the crowd. Not even a Japanese.

The folder I had pilfered from the Shooting Star Talent Agency confirmed my suspicion that Choi Yong-ran—alias, Miss Ku—wasn't what she'd claimed to be. She had graduated from middle school but after that, instead of her continuing on to high school, her family had enrolled her in a music training conservatory. Forget college. Despite what she'd told us in the teahouse in Itaewon, she was no more a graduate of Ewha University than I was an Ivy Leaguer with a trust fund.

After finishing up at the music conservatory, she landed a few jobs as a *kisaeng* and most recently the gig at the House of the Tiger Lady.

The folder didn't tell me much about her personal life. Just the names of her parents—her father deceased—and the fact that she had been born and raised in Kyong-sang Province, outside the city of Miryang, a predominantly rural area 180 miles southeast of Seoul.

Now she was here, playing the *kayagum* in front of wealthy men. A long way from the rice paddies of home.

A tall woman on the other side of the ballroom caught my eye. A magnificent lavender gown embroidered with white cranes flowed down her body. She stared right at us and barked a couple of orders to two girls who also looked at us but quickly turned away. The woman, smiling and bowing to one of the customers, excused herself and made her way around the back of the crowd, heading toward us.

"We've been spotted," I said.

"Good."

The Nurse clung tighter to Ernie. Despite her protestations about not feeling self-conscious when accompanied by two foreigners, I could tell she felt out of place in Mukyo-dong. This was the most elegant district of Seoul. Here, upscale shops and lavishly dressed women and boutiques sported the latest in Paris fashions. The Nurse's plain dress and straight hairstyle made her stand out, especially in the Tiger Lady's *kisaeng* house.

I turned to Ernie. "Any of these girls look like Miss Ku?"

"Not so far."

The young woman finished her drum solo to thunderous applause. Stage curtains closed. The serving *kisaeng* poured the men more scotch, and while they conversed we backed deeper into the shadows. Ernie gazed down the hallway.

"Plenty of rooms. Convenient."

"Cost you an arm and a leg, though."

"Hey, what's money?"

I knew it. Once he gave the place a chance, he started to like it. Ernie was a sawdust kind of guy but if he ever inherited a million dollars, he'd develop expensive tastes fast enough.

When the woman in lavender appeared at the mouth of the hallway she spread her long red nails and looked as if she longed to scratch our eyes out.

"*Weikurei?*" she demanded. "What you do here?"

A little English. She hasn't always catered to Koreans, I thought.

I pulled out my badge and flashed it in front of her face.

"I'm looking for a young woman," I said. "Police business."

She examined the badge and then me, trying to decide whether to listen or kick our butts out. Ernie crossed his arms, leaned forward, and peeked out at the crowd, letting her know she'd have trouble if she didn't deal.

She looked the Nurse up and down, the beginnings of a sneer visible on her lips. The Nurse stood up straighter and held her head up. Defiant.

"You must be the Tiger Lady," I said.

"What you want?"

"Like I said. A young lady." I strummed on an imaginary flat surface with wriggling fingers. "She plays the *kayagum.*"

Before she could answer, the curtains reopened. Three women, dressed in flowing Korean dresses, sat on an elevated platform with stringed instruments in front of their crossed knees. They bowed their heads. Hair as black as raven feathers was tied back tightly by large jade pins. Behind them wavered a painted scene on a canvas backdrop of gently rolling hills, gurgling springs, and groves of blossoming plum trees. The women raised their heads and in perfect unison began to pluck the taut strings of the three flat wooden *kayagum.* A high-pitched wail rose from their crimson mouths.

"That's her," Ernie said. "The one on the left."

We listened to the music.

"Never hit the top of the charts," Ernie said.

I turned to the Tiger Lady and pointed to the woman on the stage. Miss Ku.

"We want to talk to her," I said.

"She don't do nothing bad. I watch my girls."

"Maybe she didn't do anything bad. We just have a few questions."

"About what?"

"We'll tell her."

She thought about that for a moment.

"If not," I said. "My crazy friend here will walk up on the stage."

She studied Ernie. From deep in his throat, he growled at her.

"You've seen crazy GI's before," I said.

"Yes," she said. "I see before."

She was old enough to remember the days when American GI's were the only men in the country who had any money. She'd risen above those days; she didn't want to go back to them.

A group of Korean businessmen strode into the far end of the ballroom. Serving girls rushed forward, bowing and smiling. One of them turned toward the Tiger Lady and motioned, palm down, for her to come over.

"Okay," the Tiger Lady said finally. "You talk to her." She held up a wickedly pointed finger. "But no trouble."

I raised my open palms.

"No trouble," I said.

She returned to her customers. We followed the hallway and turned down another and then another until we found ourselves in front of a walkway that led to the rear of the stage. Women in huge silk skirts gawked at us.

Ernie smiled and offered them some gum. They all refused. He looked perplexed but just shrugged. Generally, Koreans are friendly and open to Americans. But when your presence can piss off a wealthy clientele and threaten their livelihood, they're a little less open. Besides, they were suspicious. What were two big-noses doing behind their stage?

When the *kayagum* number was finished, we allowed the first two performers to swish past us but Ernie reached out and grabbed Miss Ku and pulled her back into the wings. Her heavily lined eyes widened when she saw us.

The Nurse started to fidget. Not liking it that Ernie had a tight grip on another beautiful woman.

The stereo speakers arrayed around the ballroom launched into a stirring rendition of "*Arirang*," an ancient Korean folk song of separated lovers. Two more *kisaeng*, one dressed like a farm boy, the other like a peasant country girl, rushed onto the stage and began twirling in an elaborate dance.

While Ernie held her, I pointed my finger into Miss Ku's face.

"You lied to us," I said.

Her face crinkled in rage. "I no lie," she said. The teeth behind her rouged lips were white and perfectly shaped.

"The guy who broke your Ping-Pong heart," I said, "Cecil Whitcomb, is dead."

No particular remorse flashed across her face.

She tried to step back but Ernie jerked her forward. She looked up at him, turned, tried to punch him, but he caught her small fist.

The Nurse stepped forward but I grabbed her by the elbow,

frowned, and shook my head. She stopped but her body remained tense.

Ernie and Miss Ku struggled for a minute, silk rustling, perfume billowing through the air. She looked desperate but relaxed when a broad smile spread over his face. They stood completely still, staring into one another's eyes. Fear and lust. Goddamn Ernie's an expert at both of them. His favorite emotions.

Blood started to rush up the Nurse's neck. I put my arm around her shoulders, leaned over, and whispered, "He's only working. Don't be angry."

Slowly, Miss Ku pushed herself away from Ernie, her breathing subsided, and she turned back to me, her face serious.

"I didn't know anyone would kill him."

"Who paid you to bring us the note?"

"A man. I don't know name."

"An American? A Korean? Who?"

"An American."

"A GI?"

"I don't know. His hair was short. He was very strong."

"What color was his hair?"

She turned toward Ernie. "Like his."

"His eyes?"

"Like his."

Great. Light brown hair and blue or green eyes. That narrowed it down a lot.

"How tall was he?"

Miss Ku looked back and forth between us. "A little taller than him. Not as tall as you."

Between six one and six four.

"Why'd you do it?"

"He paid me."

"How much?"

"Not your business."

Ernie grabbed her arm and twisted it behind her back. She squealed. I wasn't sure if it was from pain or delight.

As long as Ernie was hurting Miss Ku, the Nurse seemed to like it. A smug expression spread across her face.

"How much did the American pay you?" I asked Miss Ku again.

She grimaced in pain. "A hundred thousand won."

Almost two hundred bucks, depending on where you exchanged your money.

"How did he know you would do it? Maybe you'd just take the money and not talk to us."

"He was watching."

"At the Kayagum Teahouse?"

"Outside."

"And he paid you then?"

"Half before. Half after."

"What's his name?"

"I don't know."

Ernie pushed on her arm again. This time she took a deep breath, closed her eyes, and bit on her lower lip. Her breathing became fast and rhythmic. She seemed to be savoring the pain.

The Nurse appeared happy, but as it dawned on her that Miss Ku was enjoying this wrestling match, she started to frown again.

A group of *kisaeng* gathered in the hallway nearby, murmuring and staring. Koreans don't like seeing a couple of big Americans pushing around one of their own. I decided to hurry.

"How did you know this American?" I asked Miss Ku.

"He came in here," she said, "with Korean friends."

"Who were they?"

"Businessmen. With money."

"I want their names."

Miss Ku shoved her backside tighter up against Ernie's crotch. He leaned into it.

"Their names," I said.

"I don't know their names. Only one of them. Mr. Chong, I think. He owns a print shop on Chong-no, third section."

"What's the name of the shop?"

"I don't know. Something like modern, up-to-date. Something like that."

"Had you seen the American before?"

"No. That was the first time. And the last time I saw him was when he paid me outside of the Kayagum Teahouse."

"Why did he chose you?"

She lowered her head. "Sometimes I help Mr. Chong."

"With what?"

"His problems."

"What kind of problems?"

"Problems with his wife." She looked up at me, defiance flashing in her eyes. "She doesn't give him enough sex."

"And you do?"

"I have plenty."

The music stopped and a stagehand rushed out to change the set.

The cluster of *kisaeng* was growing larger. Time to finish it. I nodded to Ernie.

When he let her go, Miss Ku leaned back toward him. As he took a step away, she clutched his sleeve.

"Why you go?"

He stared at her without smiling.

She pressed her body up against his. Silk rustled against blue jeans.

"I'll be back," he said.

The Nurse bristled and shoved Ernie. "What you mean, you 'be back'?"

Ernie held up his hands. "Hey. Police business. That's all."

She glowered at him. I knew she was contemplating punching somebody. Either Ernie or Miss Ku. The Nurse's face flushed red in frustration and embarrassment. This was a problem that fists wouldn't solve.

Miss Ku savored the Nurse's discomfort.

Trouble brewing. Big trouble.

Smiling in triumph, Miss Ku released her grip on Ernie's sleeve.

I grabbed the Nurse and grabbed Ernie and yanked them both away from the murmuring gaggle of *kisaeng*.

We hustled down the hallway, exited through a back door, and, once in the cold alley, plowed through frozen snow sprinkled with soot.

Bare-bulbed streetlights shone harshly on the Nurse's face, filling the deep shadows with lines that should never have been there.

Ernie seemed lost in thought.

22

CHONG-NO MEANS "ROAD OF THE BELL." AT THE BASE OF THE road, where it begins near the old Capitol Building, is an ornate temple housing a massive bell made of solid cast bronze. Every morning the bell is rung by Buddhist priests. Its low vibrations spread over the city of Seoul, rattling stacked beer bottles and resonating out in circles that bring the citizenry to life.

The alleys shooting off Chong-no contain shops and small factories where, even at this hour, men worked under the glare of floodlights.

Sparks shot out from grinding wheels. Hammers pounded on plumbing fixtures.

We found the Hyundai Print Shop in the third alley we visited. Three men hunched over rattling presses, oblivious to our presence.

"Doesn't look like the owner of this place could afford to go to the Tiger Lady's," Ernie said.

"Maybe this isn't his only enterprise."

"Maybe not."

Ernie had spent almost a half hour trying to convince the Nurse to go home. She didn't want to leave him—danger or no danger. When I finally told her that it was necessary for her to leave, she resigned herself to her fate and allowed Ernie to put her in a taxi and pay for her fare back to Itaewon.

I watched the red taillights of the cab fade off into the deepening night, feeling sad for some reason. This quest for Miss Ku had been the best day the three of us had ever spent together.

A few of the young workmen across the street from the print shop halted their chores and looked at us. When you wander away from the GI bar districts, get used to being stared at. They don't see many foreigners back in these alleys. We stepped forward into the shop.

The three young men inside were still too preoccupied with their work to look up. We wandered around. Browsing.

Finally, one of them noticed movement and took off his goggles. His mouth fell open.

"*Anyonghaseiyo*," I told him. Hello. "We are looking for the other foreigner who usually comes in here."

"*Mulah-gu?*" What?

"The American. With blond hair. A little taller than him." I jerked my thumb toward Ernie.

"No. We didn't see him in a long time."

I turned, as if I were surveying the ink-stained presses, and mumbled to Ernie. "It's the right place."

I swiveled back to the printer. "Are you the owner?"

"Oh, no. Not me." The young man shot his eyes toward Ernie. "What is he doing there?"

Ernie had wandered back through the equipment to a tiny office area with a desk and a file cabinet.

"He's just curious," I told the young man. "Tell me about this American. Did you meet him?"

The other two printers stopped their work. The one I was talking to barked an order to the youngest. "Go fetch Chong."

The youngest man peeled off his filthy gloves and sped through the door. I pulled out my badge.

"This is police business," I told the two printers. "You must tell me what you know."

While they gawked at the badge, not making any sense of the English lettering, Ernie opened the drawers of the desk and searched them. I shot more questions.

"Is the American a good friend of Mr. Chong's?"

They shook their heads, grimacing.

"What's the matter?"

They looked at each other but didn't answer.

"Did he come in here often?"

"Only twice."

Ernie tried the filing cabinet but it was padlocked with a bar down the center of the drawer handles. Somewhere, he found a short metal pry bar, propped it between the hasp and the edge of the cabinet, and levered it forward with both hands. He tried twice but the drawer didn't budge. Lowering himself and rebracing his feet, he gave it a tremendous pull. The lock popped open and clattered across the cement floor until it clanged against a printing press.

"What's he *doing* there?" the printer hollered.

"Police business. Don't worry about it."

Some of the workers across the way started to come out of their shops. I heard the word "*Miguk*" floating through the air: American.

Ernie riffled through the files quickly, checking behind and under each folder. He had started on the second drawer when a man burst into the shop. Red-faced. Hollering.

"What are you doing here?"

The print shop owner was a squat, sturdy Korean man with a square, leathery face that was burning crimson. The youngest printer stood behind him nervously. It looked as if he'd had to drag the owner out of a *soju* house.

"Get away from my files!"

The red-faced man stormed back toward Ernie. I zigzagged through the presses and placed my body in front of him. When he came to a stop, I showed him my badge.

"We're looking for an American," I said. "You did business with him. You took him to see the Tiger Lady."

"What? I don't know what you're talking about."

"Yes you do, Mr. Chong. You introduced him to a *kisaeng*, Choi Yong-ran. She also calls herself Miss Ku."

Worry crossed his scarlet features. "Who in the shit are you?"

"Eighth Army CID," I said.

He turned his face from me, spittle exploding from his lips as he spoke. "*Sangnom sikki.*" Born of a base lout.

I ignored the insult. "The American, Mr. Chong, what's his name?"

"I don't know his name."

"But he's a GI?"

"He *was* a GI."

"Where can I find him?"

"I don't know." The owner pointed a squat finger, the tip swirled with black, at my nose. "But if you do find him, tell him he owes me money."

"How much?"

"Plenty."

"What'd you sell to him, Chong?"

"Not your business." Sobering slightly, he became aware of Ernie again. "Hey! What are you doing?"

Ernie was on the bottom drawer now. Before I could react, Chong shoved his way past me, took three long steps forward, and grabbed Ernie by the back of his jacket. Without thinking, Ernie turned, swung his fist in an arc, and punched the man on the side of the head.

The printers let out a howl. I ran forward and stood in front of Mr. Chong again, but now he was screeching.

"Get away from my stuff, you long-nosed foreign louts!"

The printers started jostling me. Across the street the crowd of workers swelled. They made rude comments about people of nationalities other than Korean.

I grabbed Ernie's arm and jerked him close.

"We have to un-ass the area," I told him. "Now!"

"I'm right behind you."

I made my way through the machines to the front. Some of the workers walked over to block my way. I swerved away but when one shuffled in front of me, I held him gently and said "*Mianhamnida,*" I'm sorry, as loudly as I could. Ernie slipped by me and we were moving down the alley. The crowd slowly flowed toward us, still undecided as to whether or not to attack. I turned and smiled and said I was sorry and bowed repeatedly, like a big overgrown pigeon. When we reached the end of the alley, we started to run.

We strode through the busy nighttime streets of Seoul, avoiding pedestrians, stepping over soot-speckled piles of slush.

Ernie reached in his pocket and pulled out a small plastic card. It was beige on the bottom with a brown stripe on top and a red-and-white cloverleaf in the upper left. The emblem of the 8th United States Army.

I took it in my fingers and studied it front and back. A perfect facsimile of a U.S. Forces Korea ration control plate. Blank. Suitable for embossing with whatever name and serial number you chose to put on it.

The RCP is used by all GI's in Korea when they purchase anything out of military PX's or commissaries. The idea is to limit what they buy so they won't violate customs law and sell American-made goods in the Korean villages.

I pulled out my own RCP and compared them. The forgery was a fine piece of work. The only difference was that the plastic on the authentic one was a little more pliable. I nestled them both back into the folds of my worn leather wallet.

"Nice work," Ernie said. "Get a phony ID to go with that and you can black-market your ass off and clear a couple of grand a month. Easy."

"So now we know why Mr. Chong can afford to spend time with the expensive ladies at the Tiger Lady's *kisaeng* house. He creates and sells bogus documents. And we know that the guy who talked Miss Ku into doing a number on us the other day is into some serious black-marketing."

"Yeah," Ernie said, "but that still doesn't explain why he offed Cecil Whitcomb."

No. Ernie was right. It sure as shit didn't.

Our most promising lead so far had ended in a dead end.

The guy was an American. He had disappeared. The print shop owner said he didn't know who or where he was and I believed him. A serious black marketeer wasn't exactly likely to leave a forwarding address. Especially when he owed money to the people he'd done business with.

We wound back toward Mukyo-dong. I spotted a taxi stand and started toward it. Curfew was close, less than an hour away. Already the taxi line was long. In a few more minutes it would be hell trying to catch a cab and it was a four-mile walk back to Yongsan Compound.

When I queued up at the end of the line, Ernie grabbed my elbow.

"You go ahead," he said. "I'll stay down here."

I looked at him blankly. "Why?"

"The interrogation of Miss Ku," he said. "Got to finish it."

I remembered her flushed face and her labored breath.

"Yeah," I said. "I guess you do."

He shoved his hands deep in his pockets, turned, and waded into the crowd.

It took me twenty minutes to catch a cab, and when I finally found one it was crowded with other customers heading toward the south of Seoul. The cramped sedan reeked of rice wine, fermented cabbage, and cheap tobacco. The driver refused to take me all the way to 8th Army Compound. There were only a few minutes left until the midnight curfew and he had to take his other customers to their destinations. Instead, he dropped me off in Itaewon.

I could've hoofed it back to the main gate—in fact I started to—but when I walked past the alley that led to the main nightclub district, the sparkling neon and the laughter and the rock and roll were more than I could resist.

I stopped in the 7 Club and ordered a drink. There wasn't much time to get drunk before curfew, but I did the best I could.

It was morning. Charcoal glowed inside a small metal stove. The tattered wallpaper and the cold, vinyl-covered floor told me where I was: the hooch of an Itaewon business girl.

I searched frantically for the .38. It hung in its holster on a nail in the wall. I put on my shirt and strapped the leather around my chest.

Other than the stove, the only piece of furniture in the room was a Western-style bed. When you're in business, no matter how low your capital, you must invest in equipment.

Vaguely, I remembered something about two sisters. The younger sister lay under a thin blanket, curled up next to the stove. The elder had exercised her prerogative and snuggled comfortably in the big luxurious bed.

In Korea, the dictates of Confucius still live: Elders come first.

What had I done?

I couldn't remember so I shook it off. No sense even thinking about it.

As I stepped into my trousers, both girls woke up. After they rubbed their eyes and slipped on their robes, I reached deep into my pocket and checked my money. All there. I gave them some of it. I'm not sure what service they had performed for me the previous night, but they'd let me sleep here. Besides, they were both skinny and looked as if they could use a few bucks.

Outside the hooch, I slipped on my shoes and pushed through the front gate.

It was still dark. The road that led back to the compound was deserted, all the shops still shuttered, and the dirty blacktop had been sheathed overnight by a smooth new layer of snow. Only a few curved tracks marred its beauty.

I spotted the sedan about ten yards down the road. A blue-and-white police car. Engine running. Windows steamed.

As I came closer I read the license plate. Namdaemun District, it said. The back window rolled down.

"Geogie."

It was a strong male voice. A voice that I recognized.

"Get in," he said.

The car door opened. A man wearing a brown trench coat slid over on the back seat to make room for me. Lieutenant Pak. He was up early.

I climbed in and slammed the door shut.

The car was warmer than outside but clogged with the smoke of pungent Korean cigarettes. Suddenly I knew I should've stayed outside and talked through the window. Now I was in KNP territory.

Up front, a uniformed driver and another officer stared straight ahead.

Lieutenant Pak reached deep into his coat pocket, pulled something out, and nudged it into my ribs. I glanced down.

The gleaming blade of a wickedly curved knife.

vay that someone can grab your arm or kick it out of your hand. ab with it to keep them at bay, pulling it back quickly when they forward. But contrary to popular belief, he told me, you wouldn't them with a long lunge, you'd catch them when they came to Once they did, grab them by the collar, jerk them forward, and, a short brutal thrust, ram the knife onto the soft flesh above the or slash it across the unprotected throat.

Flaco talked viciously, but he wasn't really cruel. It was the l that swirled around my cousin that caused him to react with a ing savagery. Later, when he started taking heroin, he always ned it had been forced on him.

I believed him.

The gangs in the barrio wanted converts. If they had to hold you n and shoot you up to convince you of the spiritual benefits of the of the poppy, so be it. And then you were theirs. A junkie. A rce of income for the rest of your life.

Now he was in prison. For burglary. Arts he had learned after I pped seeing much of him. After I dropped out of high school and ed the army.

Now, as I gazed at the long, curved blade in Lieutenant Pak's d, I thought of Flaco. And how, in his own twisted way, my cousin l always looked out for me. I mourned for his wasted life.

"This knife killed Whitcomb," Lieutenant Pak said.

I studied it. "A Gurkha knife," I said.

"Yes."

Gurkhas are the Nepalese auxiliaries to the British Army, diers known for their savagery and skill in combat.

The long metal blade in Pak's hand was sharp and curved up-rd at its fat tip. Perfect for slicing into flesh. And prying upward til it popped into the pulsating balloon of the human heart.

Lieutenant Pak reached in his other pocket, then tossed some-ing to me. It was a thin leather belt with a small buckle in front and sliding pouch attached to the rear.

"This Whitcomb wear," he said.

Twisting the blade downward he slid it deftly into the pouch. erfect fit.

23

Most summers the County of Los Angeles deci be okay for me to stay with my Tía Esmeralda. I think i wasn't attending school and therefore a strict enforcer c wasn't so important in my life.

It was during those summers that I felt most co

My aunt enjoyed my visits, too. She worked in a on Wilshire Boulevard and although her oldest son, F years on me, she put her trust in me to keep an eye o kids while she was at work.

During those long summer afternoons, when supervised by anyone, my cousin Flaco took it upon him me the skills of survival in East L.A.

Flaco was good with a knife. With one backhand send it twanging into the bark of the old avocado tree ou he could swing it loosely in his fingers and slice unripe a crooked branches without nicking a leaf.

He also taught me how to fight with it. Keep it in c

"We found the knife in gutter, maybe one hundred meters from body."

Gutters in Korea were stone-lined trenches with vented covers on top, perfect for hiding just about anything.

"Whitcomb's unit was last assigned to Hong Kong," I said. "He probably bought the Gurkha knife there."

Lieutenant Pak nodded.

"Any blood?" I asked.

"Yes. Already been to laboratory. Same type as Whitcomb."

He pronounced the name *Way-tuh-comb.* Koreans have to break down harsh consonant endings into separate syllables.

I said, "Way-tuh-comb met someone who was very tough."

"Yes," Lieutenant Pak agreed. "Maybe Tae Kwon Do."

The Korean form of karate. A lot of kicks used.

Lance Corporal Cecil Whitcomb, although not a big man, had been a trained soldier. Whoever met him in that dark alley and took his knife away from him must've been a skilled street fighter indeed. I started to form a picture in my mind. A picture that corresponded with the cuts I'd seen on Whitcomb's hands and arms. Whoever had attacked him, once they had his knife, performed a deadly dance with him first. Sliced him lightly on the arms and wrists and hadn't moved in immediately for the fatal blow. Maybe taunting him for fun? Or trying to obtain information from someone who, at the moment, must've been a terrified man.

I knew martial arts experts who claimed they could take a knife away from a grown man. I'd never seen it done, except in movies, which are all bullshit. In training we used wooden knives and the instructor went through the moves of snatching a blade from an armed man step by step. But I never believed it would work. One jab in the calf or the forearm and all the lessons in the world would bleed right out of you.

Whoever had taken this knife from Whitcomb had to be not only highly skilled but also as fast as an enraged cougar. And he had planned it carefully. Isolated spot, an open level area, about the size of a prizefighting ring. The killer had looked forward to this. And enjoyed it.

And when he tired of playing with his living ball of yarn, he had killed Whitcomb as easily as biting into the neck of a helpless kitten.

But why had Whitcomb decided to carry his Gurkha knife that night?

Supposedly, he'd been on his way to see an old girlfriend. Not a meeting that usually requires being armed.

But now I knew that Whitcomb didn't even know Miss Ku. I closed my eyes and tried to picture the note she'd paid us to deliver to Whitcomb. I'd only glanced at it briefly but I remembered a few of the words. One of them was "secrets."

Whitcomb had gone out to Namdaemun, armed, probably for some reason having to do with these "secrets."

So the killer knew that Whitcomb would be on guard.

Without any visible signal from Lieutenant Pak, the driver shifted the car into gear and we rolled forward. We drove down the Main Supply Route, past all the shuttered shops and chop houses and past the Itaewon Police Station. At the main drag of the nightclub district the driver turned right and the engine churned steadily up the hill. All the hot joints sat quiet and dead, shrouded in fresh snow. At the top of the hill, we made a slow U-turn. Tonight these alleys would be staffed by dozens of half-naked business girls.

"You never call me," Lieutenant Pak said.

I didn't answer.

"So we come Itaewon, look for you."

Lieutenant Pak laid the knife down on the seat, pulled out a pack of cigarettes, and offered me one. *Kobuk-son.* Turtle boat brand. I turned it down. Nicotine is one of the few bad habits I never acquired.

He lit the cigarette with a wooden match and snuffed that out with a fierce wave. The harsh aroma invaded my nostrils. I tried not to snort.

"You like tea, I think," Pak said.

I gazed out the window, letting him get to the point in his own good time. Like the killer of Cecil Whitcomb, he was toying with me. I wasn't going to play along.

"You and your partner," he said, "you went to the Kayagum Teahouse. Owner there was very frightened by two big-nose foreigners give her hard time. She say you break all her teacups, frighten her nephew. Keep ask about someone named Miss Ku. Owner went to Itaewon Police Station. Cry very much. They call me."

That was sweet of him. He already had feelers out here in Itaewon in case Ernie or I drew any attention to ourselves.

"The lady, she frightened but she have very strong mind." He pointed to his temple. "She remember another name you mentioned. Eun-hi. In the U.N. Club."

I turned slowly to look at him, trying to keep my face composed. Pak would know about how we roughed up Eun-hi and her girlfriend, Suk-ja.

"Eun-hi is a very big woman," Pak said. "Big *jeejee.*" He cupped his hands in front of his chest. "Big *kundingi.*" He patted his rump. "Like an American woman. I think that's why GI's like her and that's why she work in U.N. Club."

I didn't comment on his social observations. Eun-hi worked in the U.N. Club because of poverty more than anything else, but he already knew that.

"I have long talk with Eun-hi. And her girlfriend called Suk-ja." He shook his head. "Oh, she don't like you very much."

He peered at me curiously. "Geogie, you shouldn't punch woman."

"I didn't punch anybody," I said.

"Okay. Maybe your friend did."

"What'd Eun-hi tell you?" I asked.

"She said that woman paid her to give you message. To meet her at Kayagum Teahouse."

"Happens all the time."

"And this woman must be Miss Ku who you asked Kayagum Teahouse owner about."

"That might be her name. I forget."

"What'd Miss Ku want from you?"

"The usual."

His eyes widened in mock curiosity.

"She wanted us to black-market," I said.

"Yes. Good money. What did you say?"

"We said no. Forget it."

"Then why you go back and bother Eun-hi day after Whitcomb was killed?"

"Look, Lieutenant Pak. Are we supposed to be cooperating on this case, or are you investigating me and Ernie?"

He pulled deeply on his cigarette, held the smoke for a long time, and let it out. Sometimes I swear Korean cops must study old gangster movies as part of their training.

The driver had slowly cruised back down the Main Supply Route. The barbed wire atop the walls of Yongsan Compound loomed ahead.

"One more thing, Geogie."

"What's that?"

"Your interrogation technique, not too good."

"What do you mean?"

"Eun-hi. She told us something that she did not tell you."

"Like what?"

"Like in U.N. Club that night there was a strange man."

I snapped my head and stared into his face. "What strange man?"

"The night she gave you a message. An American was there. Someone Eun-hi never see before."

"What was he doing?"

"Nothing. Just watching. And after you left, he left, too."

Maybe he was the same foreigner who had paid Miss Ku to deliver the message to us. "Has she seen him since then?"

"No. Never."

"What did he look like?"

He shrugged. "Like GI. Big nose."

"Brown hair? White hair? Black hair?"

"Maybe light color. GI haircut. Tall, like you. Strong. Not fat. Blue jeans, shirt, jacket." He shrugged. "Like all GI's."

"Did she talk to him?"

"No. Another girl served him. She don't remember anything either."

"You believe her?"

"Yes. Just another customer. He did nothing unusual."

"Then why did Eun-hi remember him?"

"Because he stared at you. When you left, he leave full beer. Follow."

She'd remember a full beer. Your typical Cheap Charley GI would never walk off and leave a virgin bottle of suds.

The police sedan pulled up to the front of the main gate of Yongsan Compound. I opened the door and started to climb out.

"Remember, Geogie."

I looked back.

"You off case now. But maybe this man, maybe he don't know that."

"Yeah," I said. "Maybe he doesn't."

I grabbed the handle and slammed the door.

The guy in the U.N. Club whom Eun-hi had seen could've been just your regular lookey-loo. Ernie and I attract a lot of attention everywhere we go. Most people don't have their own life; they like to stare at ours. I'm dark, tall, big, Mexican, and used to being stared at. Ernie is always doing something weird. And girls like him. Why, I've never been quite sure. But when women look at him, guys will be jealous and stare.

Leaving the U.N. Club after we did could've been just a coincidence, and not touching a full beer could've meant that the guy either had a sour stomach or suddenly decided to reform.

Maybe.

And maybe he was following us.

I sat at Riley's desk with a big, steaming cup of snack bar coffee, reading the just-flown-in-from-Tokyo edition of the *Pacific Stars & Stripes*. I had stopped at the barracks, showered, shaved, and changed into my coat and tie. I felt a hell of a lot better. Revitalized.

The big double door down the hallway creaked open, then banged shut. Footsteps clattered down the varnished wood slat floor.

When he burst through the door, he looked as pleased with himself as a deacon on his way to church.

"Ernie," I said. "What the hell you doing in so early?"

He marched straight to the unplugged coffee urn and rattled the empty shell.

"Jesus, no java. How do they expect a man to live?"

I realized that although he was clean and dressed neatly, his eyes were rimmed with red and his cheeks seemed to be sagging a bit.

"She kept me up all night," he said.

"Miss Ku?"

"Yeah. Crazy broad. I thought she was going to scratch off my third layer of skin."

I shook my head. This meant more trouble with the Nurse. She'd attacked him with sticks and knives before. All I could do was pray she didn't get her hands on a bazooka.

In the distance, doors slammed open. Upstairs, shoes pounded on cement. Eighth Army was coming to life.

Ernie found a cup and I shared half of my coffee with him. We sat like dazed prizefighters between rounds, sipping gratefully on life-giving fluid.

I tried to think of the case but nothing fit. Not yet.

When Riley stormed through the door of the Admin Office, he stopped and looked back and forth between us, pink tongue flicking between crooked teeth.

"Damn. The Honor Guard is already here."

There was so much starch in his fatigues that when he sat down at his desk the fabric crackled.

Ernie started fiddling with the coffee urn again. "Where can I get some coffee around here?"

Riley ignored us. He had already grabbed a stack of paperwork from his in-basket and, licking his thumb every third page, riffled through it.

"I need something from you, Riley," I said.

"Have to do with the Whitcomb case?"

"Maybe."

"Name it. At your service."

"We're looking for a former GI."

"Good. That narrows it down to about fifty million souls."

"He's here in Korea."

"Scratch forty-nine million."

"He might've been involved in black market operations. Phony Ration Control Plates. Stuff like that."

Without looking up, Riley reached for a pad of paper and a pencil and started making notes.

"I figure we should check the KNP Liaison blotter reports. Find out if any Americans have been arrested by the Korean authorities lately for customs violations, assaults, anything at all. If so, I want all the information we can find on them. Date they entered the country. If they've left yet. Anything."

"Won't be much," Riley said. "The ROK's don't arrest many tourists. Bad for the travel industry. If they get out of line, they just hustle them onto the next flight out of country."

"Yeah. But find out what you can."

"A former GI, huh? I'll check the AWOL register too."

"Great." I don't know why I hadn't thought about that. The brain wasn't functioning well this morning.

"And ROK immigration," Riley added. "See if we've got any *Miguks* who've overstayed their welcome."

"And other foreigners, too," I said. "There's always the possibility that he's not really an American. After all, it was an Englishman who was killed."

"Right you are. Anything else?"

"Don't say anything to the First Sergeant about this."

He looked at me.

"Not until I'm sure."

He nodded. "I'll make some calls."

I stood and grabbed Ernie by the elbow.

"Come on, pal. Let's go. I'll buy you some coffee at the snack bar."

That mollified him somewhat but he was still grumbling as we walked down the long empty corridor and hopped down the stone steps outside to the jeep.

I told Ernie about what Lieutenant Pak had told me and about the guy who'd been following us. He didn't like it any better than I did.

At the snack bar we bought two cups of coffee and sat down against the wall.

I thought about the Tiger Lady's *kisaeng* house and the deep caverns beneath the streets of Itaewon and the phoney ration control plate we had found at the Hyundai Print Shop. None of it did any good. I didn't know what we had. I didn't know how big it was. Or if any of what we'd learned had any importance at all. The case was wrapping itself around me like the tentacles of a giant squid, and I knew that if I didn't swim up for air soon it would drag me down into the slime and devour me bit by slowly chewed bit.

As if he were reading my thoughts, Ernie began to speak.

"Miss Ku didn't say much," he said. "Just that the guy was American and that he gave her real detailed instructions on what he wanted her to do. Go to Itaewon, find us, pretend she was a jilted girlfriend, and give us the note. She only saw him twice. The first night he came in with Print Shop Chong. Three or four nights later, he came back and made the deal with her. She doesn't even know his name."

Ernie glanced at me nervously. I knew what was happening. He was feeling guilty for having cheated on the Nurse. But that was his business. I had no opinion about it one way or the other, but he kept on chattering—unusual for him—as if he wanted to justify himself.

"I tried to pry more information out of her. But I believe that's all she knows. After all, it was a straight money proposition. She does a job for him, he pays her."

"But she saw him one more time," I said.

Ernie ladled more sugar into his coffee. "What do you mean?"

"In Itaewon. After she talked to us. To receive the second half of the money."

"Yeah. Then, too."

It bothered me. It was bothering both of us.

"Eun-hi saw him in the U.N. Club. Miss Ku saw him outside the Kayagum Teahouse. The guy was watching us."

Ernie nodded. "He sure was."

We sat in silence. I looked at him. No wiseass remark. No cynical sneer.

He felt worse about cheating on the Nurse than I had thought.

"We have to find out his name," Ernie said. "But how?"

I stirred my coffee and gazed into the black swirl. "There must be a way."

"How?"

"I'm not sure yet," I said. "I have to think about it."

Ernie respected that. He was never one to push. Still, he was worried.

"I think we might be getting close. And if we get close enough, this guy's liable to know it."

"And come after us, you mean?"

"It could happen."

Ernie shuffled in his seat and glanced around the crowded cafeteria. "Sure would be nice to know what he looks like."

"Sure would."

When we returned to the office, there seemed to be a lot of barking into phones and pacing back and forth.

Riley pulled us aside. "A call just came in from the KNP Liaison. You ever heard of a place called the Tiger Lady's?"

"Yeah," I said. "We've heard of it."

"Lieutenant Pak of the Namdaemun Precinct wants you two guys down there ASAP."

"What happened?"

"There's been a killing. Some gal. Something he called a *kisaeng*."

As we reached the doorway, the First Sergeant's voice bellowed down the hallway.

"Bascom! Sueño!"

I looked at Ernie.

"I didn't hear anything," I said. "Did you?"

"No. Not me."

We ran to the jeep.

24

THE KILLER SQUATTED NEXT TO THE BODY, KEEPING HIS FEET OUT of the blood, trying to fight back the rage that pumped into his brain—blinding him.

It was still dark out and bitterly cold. Snowflakes swirled in the gusting wind, like spirits endlessly tormented by the night.

With the back of his hand the killer cleared his vision, forcing himself to concentrate.

She'd been dumped here, an arm and a leg cruelly twisted beneath her limp body. She wore a nightgown and a robe. No slippers. Red welts stood out angrily on the soft flesh of her neck. Her fingernails had been shredded and, before her death, oozed crimson, which was now clotted and dark.

Tortured.

How much information had she given them? Probably everything. But it wouldn't do them any good. They still wouldn't find him. No one would.

Not, at least, until he took his revenge.

Cuts had been sliced along her arms. Not fatal. At the top of her flat belly gaped a long gash. Probably the final death-dealing wound.

The killer almost laughed.

So that was their game. Put the blame on someone else. An old trick.

She'd written a note and left it, as he'd instructed, at the message drop: *Contact. Two Americans.*

He was miles away when he received the transmission. Still, he'd dropped everything and returned immediately. As fast as he could, but not fast enough. He gazed down at the corpse.

She'd done her best. In her note she said that she would try to delay one of them. Apparently, she succeeded. Her only reward had been death.

He touched the dead woman's cold flesh. Just meat. Like so many he'd seen before.

When he first brought her into the operation, he'd used terror to train her. He showed her the photographs he'd taken of her younger brother and sister on their way to school, of her mother beating laundry with a stick at a stream near the family home. He'd demonstrated to her how he would kill them—running the edge of his blade lightly across her neck—if she didn't do exactly as he instructed. Or if she tried to run away.

At first she'd trembled with fright, but she was stronger than most. She accepted the situation. She even seemed to enjoy the work, especially after he paid her for the first completed missions.

He remembered the long nights they'd spent together. And her lust for pain. Ever more pain.

And now she was gone. Stolen from him.

A pot clanged against stone.

He swiveled in a crouch, ready to fight, and surveyed the darkness.

No movement.

Inside the big building, people were starting to stir. The sun would rise soon. He glanced back down at the body.

His fists clenched. They'd pay for taking this from him. This that was his.

Like a shadow blown by the wind, he floated into the gloom.

25

ERNIE AND I PUSHED THROUGH A CROWD OF GAWKERS OUTSIDE OF the House of the Tiger Lady. We entered the cool confines of the main ballroom. A uniformed policeman escorted us down the hallway.

The huddled *kisaeng*, their faces naked and raw in the morning light, almost leapt back in fright when they saw Ernie.

Outside in the alley, Lieutenant Pak was hunched over in a conference with some older men. Our blue-clad escort went out, conferred with him, came back, and asked us politely to wait here in the hallway.

Ernie was nervous, chomping on about three wads of gum, glancing back and forth, fidgeting with the knot in his tie. I told him to wait, took a few steps toward the back alley, turned a corner, and saw the body slumped in a puddle of blood.

Miss Ku. Her eyes still open, mouth slack. Her neck twisted and her stomach gouged with something sharp and long. Blood had dried like a frozen waterfall of cinnabar slime.

She was in her nightclothes: Silk gown with only a bathrobe wrapped around her slender body to protect her from the cold. The job looked familiar. The same long, deft jab below the sternum, slicing into the heart. Probably while holding her from behind with a powerful arm crooked around her frail neck. Then letting her go. Letting her slump to the ground in death.

There were cuts on her arms. Whoever had killed her had toyed with her, as Whitcomb had been toyed with. If it was the same killer, it made sense.

What didn't make sense were her fingers. The tips were raw and red. The nails had been ripped back one by one.

Another thing that didn't make sense was that the body was too close to the back of the Tiger Lady's *kisaeng* house. On the other side of the wall resided a couple of dozen women, and at least some of them must be light sleepers. Yet the killer had finished his bloody night's work while disturbing no one.

There was blood on the cobbled road but not much. Not as much as we found beneath Cecil Whitcomb.

I turned, took a few deep breaths, and returned to Ernie.

Something pushed through the crowded hallway. People were jostled, slammed against walls. The Tiger Lady, gray-black hair splayed like the mane of a lion, eyes as intent as the eyes of a viper, plowing through the bending reeds, heading right for us.

Ernie straightened himself and stood away from the wall.

She screeched. "*Shangnom-a!*" You bastard! And launched her crimson claws at his eyes.

Ernie twisted his head away just in time, but she sank her nails into his shoulder. He rotated his body and pushed her, slamming her into the wall. Like some enraged simian, she rebounded and renewed her attack.

Women screamed. Policemen cursed.

Ernie bounced back and grabbed her wrists as she came toward him again. Somehow he managed to retain his balance with her weight pushing against him.

I moved forward to help but three girls emerged from the crowd, swinging tiny fists, and simultaneously punched me in the stomach. I held my belly and looked at them.

"You stay back, Goddamn-uh!" one of them said.

Ernie and the Tiger Lady rocked back and forth like two bulls in a pen until finally the Tiger Lady collapsed and fell to her knees and covered her eyes with her withered palms. She started to cry.

"*Nuga, nuga, nuga kurei?*" Who, who, who would do this?

Two of the policemen pushed through the crowd of wailing *kisaeng* and helped the Tiger Lady to her feet. Another emerged from the hallway and called for Ernie and me to accompany him. The girls ignored us as we left, all their attention turned toward the moaning Tiger Lady.

When Ernie saw Miss Ku's body I thought he was going to collapse. I grabbed him around the waist and helped him down the alley past it, out into the coldness of the morning air. Lieutenant Pak and the other policeman were waiting for us. Ernie pulled himself together although his face was as pale as I'd ever seen it.

Lieutenant Pak strode forward and poked his nose in Ernie's face.

"You sleep with her," he said, pointing at the corpse.

I stepped between them. "Wait a minute. He's in no condition to answer questions. Not yet. He needs a chance to recover."

There is no right to immediate counsel in Korea. You either answer the policeman's questions or face the consequences—from a jail cell.

Ernie laid his hand on my shoulder. "That's okay, George. I'll talk to him. I need to." He unwrapped another stick of gum, put it in his mouth, and turned slowly to Lieutenant Pak.

"Yeah. I spent the night with her. I came late. She wasn't busy, we went to her room and talked."

Lieutenant Pak tried to keep his face from moving but the eyes crinkled involuntarily around the edges. Korean men weren't happy about Americans spending time with their women. But since fraternization was inevitable, they preferred that GI's stick to the business girls in Itaewon. The ones who'd been designated for the job.

"In the morning she let me out the back door." Ernie turned, pointing. "This door here. She was wearing the same clothes she has on now. The silk nightgown. The robe."

"After you left, did she lock the door?"

"No. She wore slippers and she followed me out into the alleyway." He pointed again, to a spot about ten yards in front of the back door. "When I reached the main road, down there, I turned one last time and waved. She waved back."

"So she was standing there, away from the door, alone, when you left her?"

"Yes," Ernie answered. "And it was still dark."

"We found sandals," Lieutenant Pak said. "They must've fallen off her feet in a struggle, and the tops of her feet are scraped raw, as if she'd been dragged."

Ernie shook his head. "I don't know anything about that."

Lieutenant Pak stared at him. Waiting to see if he'd fidget.

"Check her pockets," Ernie said.

"Why?"

"You'll find a stick of ginseng gum. I gave it to her just before I left. It probably has my fingerprints on it."

Lieutenant Pak studied Ernie some more. Without looking over his shoulder he shouted an order to one of the uniformed policemen. The policeman answered, trotted off to the body, and after bending over it and checking, returned to Lieutenant Pak.

"*Nei. Issoyo.*" Yes. It's there.

I spoke up. "He wouldn't have left such clear evidence if he was planning on killing her."

Ernie winced.

Lieutenant Pak half smiled. "I said nothing about killing."

He hadn't and suddenly I felt embarrassed. But it was what everyone was thinking.

"You know I didn't kill her," Ernie said.

Lieutenant Pak's eyes probed Ernie's face. "We'll see."

He turned to me. "This woman who calls herself Miss Ku, she is same woman you saw at Kayagum Teahouse. The one who wanted you to black-market?"

I didn't answer.

"And maybe she knew something that you didn't want anyone else to know."

A chill of fear went through me. Pak was close to finding out that we had been paid to deliver the note to Cecil Whitcomb, thereby demonstrating a motive for Ernie to murder Miss Ku. What with the way military justice works, just the suspicion was enough to get us both locked up. I had to give him something else to think about.

"Miss Ku was able to identify the American who followed us in the U.N. Club."

Lieutenant Pak thought about that.

"So the American's been following you," he said. "And he killed Miss Ku."

"Maybe."

"Who is this man?"

"That's what we all want to know."

He raised his finger and pointed it at me.

"I received your reports. They told me nothing. You are Americans, so I am patient with you, but if you keep me from this killer, your life in Seoul will be most miserable." He pointed his forefinger at Ernie. "*You* will not leave Korea."

Ernie nodded. "Can do."

Lieutenant Pak pivoted and walked back to the technicians in the alleyway, barking orders.

When they forgot about us, we slipped down to the end of the alleyway and disappeared.

On the ride back, Ernie couldn't stop jabbering.

"The son of a bitch!" He pounded his fist against the steering wheel. "He's been following us since this investigation began. First in the U.N. Club, then the Kayagum Teahouse, and even down here to Mukyo-dong. When we got close to Miss Ku, he took her out."

I leaned back in the seat, trying not to show my terror as Ernie whizzed within millimeters of careening kimchi cabs that charged like cavalry through the narrow streets. "He's been following us, all right. Whoever he is."

"Who does he kill next?" Ernie asked. "The guy who owns the print shop?"

"Maybe. Miss Ku saw his face. Now she's dead. So did Mr. Chong, the print shop owner."

"So we ought to tell Lieutenant Pak about it so he can get there first."

"The print shop guy can take care of himself. Besides, if we tell Lieutenant Pak, he'll have to go through regular procedures for search permission at the Namdaemun Police Station and this print shop Chong is liable to hear about it. He's making good money. Maybe somebody in the police precinct is on his payroll. If he gets wind of it, he hides any important information. I want to take another approach."

Ernie glanced at me. "You're not crazy enough to go back there and break in yourself?"

"No. Those boys in the shops are liable to lynch us. I'll send somebody else."

"Like who?"

"You'll see."

No sense letting Ernie know everything. This whole case was about to explode in our faces. And if we went down, the less he knew about my plans the better.

Ernie wasn't the type to press if I told him I didn't want to talk about something. We rode listening to the screech of brakes and the honking of horns and the pitiful pleadings of the dying Miss Ku.

When troubles start they don't stop. Back at the CID building Ernie let me off while he parked the jeep.

Inside, the Nurse sat in the First Sergeant's office, her dimpled knees peeking out from beneath the hemline of a neatly pressed brown skirt. Her long black hair was tied back in a bun and she clutched a cheap plastic handbag primly on her lap, nodding patiently as the First Sergeant spoke in loud English.

I hurried down the hallway and grabbed Riley.

"What's going on?"

"She came in a few minutes ago," he said, "demanding to talk to the Provost Marshal."

"About what?"

"About Ernie. And his 'crimes,' as she put it. The First Sergeant knew it was trouble. She looks so cute and innocent that if she latches onto the right colonel or one of the dorks over at the Inspector General's office, she'll make the whole CID look bad."

"What sort of 'crimes'?"

"Going out with girls. Not staying home. Drinking too much." Riley shrugged.

"But they're not even married."

"I don't think she sees it that way."

Korean women often went to their husbands' superiors to complain about off-duty behavior. In Korea, the role of the boss is so revered that he is considered to have the right—even the responsibility—to provide personal guidance to his subordinates. The Nurse was doing what came naturally. Trying to convince the men who controlled Ernie's professional life to control his personal life.

Miss Kim, the Admin secretary, kept her head down and pounded furiously on the keys of her electric typewriter. Having her rival here in the office, being treated like a queen by the First Sergeant, wasn't doing much for her mood.

"I have to warn Ernie," I said.

"Do that," Riley said.

I ran out to the narrow parking area between the buildings. Ernie had just parked the jeep and was walking toward the building. I grabbed him.

"The Nurse is here. Talking to the First Sergeant."

"Oh, shit. About what?"

"About you going out nights. Not coming home."

"Nothing in the Code of Military Justice says I can't."

"No. But the honchos don't like innocent-looking girls on their doorstep complaining about debauched GI's. Bad for the CID's image."

"Fuck the CID's image."

I squeezed his arm. Somebody had to lecture him. Somebody had to keep him from screwing up his life at every turn. If not me, who?

"Ernie. You have to make the First Sergeant happy. Let him

know you'll do whatever it takes to avoid embarrassment for him and the Provost Marshal. Otherwise, he might restrict us to compound or worse, who knows. Conduct Unbecoming is a court-martial offense. They could lock you up. What with this new murder, we have to keep our freedom of movement. You have to take care of it, Ernie."

"Shit, George. You worry too much about the small stuff."

"It isn't small, Ernie. You and I sent Cecil Whitcomb to his death."

He sighed.

"Besides, you ought to treat the Nurse better. She's a good chick. She deserves it. Get in there and make nice with her."

"I was going to anyway. Tonight."

"Do it *now.*"

"Relax, Reverend. I get the point."

He shrugged off my grip and stormed up the steps. Before I went back into the Admin Office, I watched him knock on the open door of the First Sergeant's office and enter.

I leaned over Riley's desk. "What'd you get on those former GI's?"

He handed me a stack of messages. "A couple hundred names. Seems that foreigners aren't as bashful as I thought about ending up on KNP blotter reports. Of course, a lot of them are just traffic accidents, things like that. But there's a few fights. Even a few alleged robberies. When you pick out some names, let me know and I'll ask for details."

"Thanks, Riley."

"What was all that shit about at the *kisaeng* house?"

"Woman got killed."

"Anybody we know?"

"A friend of Ernie's."

"He's not having a very good day, is he?"

"No. He's not."

Neither was I, but I didn't tell Riley that.

I thumbed through the blotter reports the Korean National Police Liaison had provided. As Riley had said, most were just traffic accidents or disputes over hotel bills. Of the serious incidents, four were alleged robberies by Americans, three of which turned out to be underpayment to prostitutes. Only one was an out-and-out theft, from a fellow traveler on a package tour. A Japanese camera. Virtually all the people listed, and all of those involved in the serious incidents, had already left the country.

The next stack of paperwork was a little more interesting. Each page was a short biographical sketch with a small black-and-white photo: GI's who'd gone AWOL in Korea and had not yet been apprehended. The fact that they hadn't been apprehended wasn't surprising, since we don't bother to look for them. The reason is that the ports of embarkation, either by ship or at the Kimpo International Airport, are so tightly controlled by the Korean authorities that we aren't worried about AWOL GI's slipping out of the country. And if they stay here, eventually they'll tire of scrounging for a living on the fringes of Korean life. Sooner or later, almost all of them turn themselves in, willing to accept court-martial as long as they can get a ticket back to the States.

Of course, I suppose a few of them went to all the trouble of getting phony passports and slipping out of the country, but the army wasn't worried about it. Now that the draft was gone and the American economy was in a shambles, men were fighting to stay in the army. Not to get out.

Still, the most likely way to make a living after going AWOL was by way of the black market. A phony military identification card, a phony ration control plate, and you were in business. The danger was that you had to go onto the compounds regularly to do the purchasing. That's why the guy who was shadowing us had short hair. So he'd look like an active duty GI.

I studied the pictures carefully. None of the faces seemed familiar. I tried to imagine each one in a smoke-filled barroom or on a street, lounging behind us, trying to look inconspicuous. Nothing clicked. Every face was a complete stranger.

I read the names and the biographical notes. Still nothing.

Heels clicked down the hallway. The Nurse marched past the door of the Admin Office, looking straight ahead. The big double doors of the exitway creaked open and slammed shut.

I thought of running after her, trying to console her, but she looked too upset. Anything I said would probably just come out stupid. Like most wives or girlfriends, the Nurse considered the running-the-ville buddy—me—the real cause for all her grief. Ernie was pure of heart. It was just evil guys like me who were leading him astray.

I damn sure wasn't going to betray Ernie and tell the Nurse the truth about his love life. And I didn't feel like telling any more lies today. So I stayed where I was.

The First Sergeant called Riley down the hallway, and after a brief chat the skinny Admin Sergeant returned. He was shaking his head.

"What is it?"

"I have to counsel Ernie on the dangers of promiscuity. And too much booze."

"You?"

"Hey, I'm a Staff Sergeant." Riley pointed to the yellow rocker beneath his stripes. "This gives me superior knowledge and virtue."

I thought of the bottle of Old Overwart he kept in his locker and the old hag business girls he sometimes picked up in the ville and dragged back to the barracks.

"Yeah. Virtue," I said. "You got that."

Miss Kim had had enough. Holding a handkerchief to her nose, she jumped up from her typewriter, ran out of the office, and clicked her high heels down the hallway toward the ladies' room.

"What's wrong with her?" Riley asked.

I shook my head. "I don't know."

Riley shuffled through a stack of paperwork. "Must be a virus."

26

Before the First Sergeant had finished with Ernie, I placed a call to the British Honor Guard.

The Sergeant Major confirmed for me that Cecil Whitcomb had indeed been the proud owner of a Gurkha knife. He'd bought it off a soldier in a British Gurkha unit in Hong Kong. For "five quid," whatever the hell that was. The knife was not listed in the inventory of his belongings conducted after his death.

The Sergeant Major told me that Whitcomb's body had been released by the Seoul coroner's office and had been flown out that morning via a specially arranged flight from Kimpo Air Force Base. I asked him for the name and address of Whitcomb's next of kin. He gave me an address somewhere in London, but of a woman with a last name other than Whitcomb. His mother, he said. Her husband, Whitcomb's father, had died a few years ago and she'd remarried.

I folded the address and stuck it in my wallet.

I went back to the barracks and waited until the firing of the cannon at 1700 hours that signified the close of 8th Army's official business day. When all was clear, I changed my clothes and went over to the snack bar and ate some chow. I just wanted to be alone. Have time to think about the case. Have time to think about what happened to Miss Ku. About what happened to Cecil Whitcomb.

Whoever we were dealing with had wanted Cecil Whitcomb badly. He'd used Miss Ku and Eun-hi and me and Ernie, and using us, he'd accomplished his objective. It made sense that he had to entice Whitcomb off the compound. In the nature of army life, whether in the barracks or on the parade field or out running the ville with his buddies, Whitcomb would never be alone. That night out in Namdaemun, he had been alone.

But why go to so much trouble in the first place? What was so important about Cecil Whitcomb, a part-time petty thief?

Why the killer wanted Miss Ku silenced was pretty clear. She knew who he was. She could identify him. She could testify against him in court. But not anymore.

The print shop owner knew who he was, too, but he was in less danger. From what we knew so far, there was no way Mr. Chong could link him to the murder of Cecil Whitcomb. So Chong was probably safe.

What about me? Was I safe? Was Ernie safe?

This guy knew who Ernie and I were, but we didn't know who he was. He was following us. If we closed in on him, he'd probably attempt to take us out, too.

Who was he working for? For himself or for someone else? Was he working for the slicky boys?

We hadn't heard from the slicky boys since the night they kidnapped us. I'd relayed a message that the secret of the location of their headquarters would remain safe with us. Had it worked?

Maybe.

I had no answers. Only questions that kept piling up, one after the other.

I felt for the .38 beneath my jacket. Still there.

I studied the faces in the snack bar around me. A lot of them were familiar because I'd seen them around compound dozens of times. Nobody out of the ordinary. Nobody who looked as if he'd ruthlessly tortured and murdered a beautiful woman.

That's another thing that bothered me. He'd tortured her. What information did she have that he didn't already know? I thought about it for a long time, but came up with nothing.

When I finished the chow, I wandered around the compound. Walking. Thinking.

If God gave me a chance to redo some things in my life, I'd have a long list. Number one would be canceling out the conversation Ernie and I had with Cecil Whitcomb.

With the approach of night the temperature dropped, but still no threat of snow. Somehow, I found myself in front of the PX. Standing at the taxi stand was Strange. He spotted me and stepped out of line.

When he came near he pulled his cigarette holder out of his mouth.

"Had any *strange* lately?"

I ignored the question. "Have you got anything for me, Harvey?"

He glanced to either side. "Not here."

"Okay. Where?"

He nodded toward the latrine. "Follow me."

He waddled through the crowd and back into the PX, toward the hallway that led to the men's room. I followed and pushed through the big wooden door. One guy stood in front of a urinal. Not Strange.

On the other side of the tiled wall was a row of commodes. Something hissed. I walked down to the last stall near the window and opened the door. Strange sat on the pot, pants up, staring down at a crumpled sheet of notebook paper.

"Four security violations in the last month," he said.

His cigarette holder waggled from side to side in his mouth.

"You inspected J-two?" I asked. J-2 was the place where Whitcomb had stolen the typewriter.

"Yeah."

The window above us was open and cold air billowed in like a small gray cloud. I was grateful for the fresh air.

"The violations wouldn't have been caught at all without surprise inspections," Strange continued. "They were small things. A safe left open during the workday while everyone was out of the room for a couple of minutes. A Top Secret cover sheet on a Secret document. Things like that. The only other thing I noticed was a couple of documents out of numerical order. Just slightly out of place. As if someone had been in a hurry and shoved it back into the file without checking the numbers. Not something many security clerks do. Finding an out-of-sequence document can be a bear. Take you all day. So you learn to be careful." He shook his head. "That wouldn't have bothered me at all if it wasn't for the rumors I've been hearing."

"What rumors?"

"Not violations, exactly. Just shit being tampered with. A guy down at Camp Market. He swears nobody but him touches his files, but when he comes in one morning, a couple of documents have been moved. He'd placed them in the file a certain way, flush up to the left side of the safe. In the morning, they were in the center."

"You security guys are a meticulous lot."

Strange ignored me. His cigarette holder quivered a little faster.

"Another guy at Army Support Command swears somebody came into his office. Dust that he leaves atop the filing cabinets on purpose was moved. Not much. Just like somebody had breathed on it."

"So why didn't he report it?"

Strange looked up at me wide-eyed, as if I were mad.

"And have a bunch of outsiders tampering with our files? We in security handle our own properties. Don't need a bunch of ham-handed MP's stomping around." He thought about that for a minute. "No offense."

"None taken."

Somebody new entered the latrine. We were quiet until he urinated and left.

"That pig didn't even wash his hands." Strange scowled.

"Some people," I said. "So tell me what happens. You security NCO's get together sometimes and compare notes. And if you find something suspicious going on you investigate it yourself?"

"Dick Tracy."

"So what've you found out so far?"

"*Nada.* Zilch. Not a goddamn thing. But we're keeping our eyes open."

"If somebody did break into those files, how would they do it?"

"Not from one of us, that's for sure."

I waited.

"All of our combinations have to be backed up. In case we're killed in the line of duty or smothered from muff diving or something. There's always a security officer."

The words "security officer" came out as if they were something unclean.

"Usually a young lieutenant assigned to keep an eye on an experienced security noncom. A young dick who doesn't know shit about security."

"So the security officer might've compromised the combinations?"

"Who else?"

"I don't know. There's no other way?"

"Had to be those young shitheads."

"But compromising each one of them, at all those different compounds . . ." I shook my head. "Sort of difficult, isn't it?"

"Only way. It couldn't have been experienced NCO's."

"I see you've given this a lot of thought."

"Sure have."

"Keep your ears open. Watch the security reports. If you hear anything else, especially about Captain Burlingame at J-two, let us know right away."

Strange nodded.

"Also, can you find out what the subject was of the documents that were tampered with at J-two?"

Strange looked at me from beneath raised eyebrows. "Do you have a need-to-know?"

"I might. In an investigation you're never quite sure what you need to know."

He lowered his eyes. "I'll see what I can do."

"Good. Can I buy you a beer?"

"No. No beer." His cigarette lighter waggled. "Had any *strange* lately?"

He was persistent, that's for sure.

"Not much. Only a couple of sisters out in Itaewon."

"Yeah?"

"Both of them skinny. Listen, I'd tell you all about it but I have to get out there."

"Pity."

"I'll fill you in completely next time we talk."

"That'll be soon?"

"Yeah."

"Good."

I left Strange in the latrine. As I walked out, the door to the commode creaked shut.

What with all the running around on the Whitcomb case, Ernie and I had fallen seriously behind on our black market detail paperwork. I wandered back to the CID office. It was dark now and cold, but when I strode down the familiar creaking hallways, there was still warmth left in the old brick building.

I turned on the lamp over Riley's desk, rummaged around for some typing paper and some carbon, and went to work.

It was quiet here. Relaxing. Sometimes I enjoyed working late. It gave me time to think. Time to review details that I might've missed early on.

But no matter how much I tried to concentrate on the black market paperwork, I couldn't keep my mind off the Whitcomb murder. And the murder of Miss Ku.

I wondered about what Strange had told me. About a bunch of paranoid security clerks losing sleep because a folder had been misfiled or a rat had knocked some dust off a safe. Security guys were a bunch of kooks. Every one of them weird in some way, and Strange was the weirdest of them all.

Still, there could be something to it. They were sensitive to these things. But what did it have to do with the Whitcomb case? Probably nothing. Cecil had gone to J-2 to swipe a typewriter. That's all.

I shoved it out of my mind and continued typing the reports on the black-marketeers we'd arrested.

After a while, I fixed myself a cup of coffee and sat down in a vinyl chair in the break area. Maybe I nodded off for a few minutes, I'm not sure, but what brought me fully awake was the sound of footsteps.

They seemed to be coming from down the hallway. I pulled the .38 out of the shoulder holster.

Holding the short barrel in front of my nose, I crouched forward through the doorway and out into the hall. Nobody. I squatted, listening.

More sounds. Something creaked. Not in the hallway, but down the stairway that led into the cellar.

I didn't remember the last time I'd been down there. Maybe the time we shuffled some furniture around the offices. There was nothing down there now but a big old cast-iron coal furnace and some supplies that the cleaning crew used.

Staying close to the wall so the old floorboards wouldn't squeak as much, I walked to the front of the stairway and listened again.

No sound now.

Whoever was down there must've heard me.

If it was one of the janitors working late, the light would be on. But it was dark down there. As dark as the night that embraced the ghosts of Cecil Whitcomb and Miss Ku.

I reminded myself that I had the revolver. It was loaded. Five shots. I stepped down the stairway.

At the first landing, I groped for a light switch. My fingers stumbled on it. I flipped the switch.

Nothing.

Somebody'd cut off the lights.

Not good.

Maybe if Ernie were here we would've charged down headfirst, kicked some ass, and taken names. But I was alone. And the only light in the building was a faint glimmer from the fluorescent bulb back in the Admin Office. If something went wrong, I had no backup.

I took a step backward, scanning with my eyes into the darkness.

"Dreamer."

It was just a whisper but it rushed through my body like a jolt of lightning.

I stood perfectly still, barely breathing. Wondering if I'd imagined it. The voice had been deep. And raspy. As if the inner lining of the throat was made of sandpaper.

It must've been my imagination. Nerves getting to me. Causing me to hear things. Psychosomatic.

I took another step backward.

"Dreamer."

My name, Sueño, means dream in Spanish.

It wasn't my imagination. It was real. Someone—or something—lurked down there in the darkness.

"Don't go," the voice said. "I came here to talk to you."

It was a flat drawl. American, no doubt. Southern, probably.

I tried to make my voice sound as steady and as firm as I could. "Who are you?"

"Who am I? That's a cop question. I thought you could do better than that, Dreamer."

The words slithered out of the void. The ramblings of an ancient serpent.

"What do you want?" I asked.

There was a long pause. "You."

My eyes darted through the darkness, hoping to discern one shadow from another. I didn't move. I was fairly safe here. If he tried to come at me, he'd have to climb the wooden steps and I'd hear him before I saw him. If he had a gun, he probably had a bead on me right now. Moving wouldn't do any good.

"You were at the Tiger Lady's this morning," he said. "I saw you. Strutting around like the buffoon you are. And that partner of yours. Bascom. Never has there been a bigger fool. I'll gut him some day, with my little blade."

I had to pry more information out of him. Keep him talking. If I fell for his insults, I'd lose my concentration and I'd learn nothing.

"You killed Cecil Whitcomb," I said.

Rocks clattered. He was near the coal bin. I turned slowly, raised my gun in that direction.

"It was necessary," the whisper said.

"Why?" I asked. "Why was it necessary."

He barked a short, brutal laugh. "You don't fool me, Dreamer. I know what you two did to Miss Ku. Tortured her. Let her bleed. Let her scream. And then killed her slowly."

"It wasn't us who killed her," I said.

"Didn't want to get your hands dirty? So maybe you turned her over to the KNP's. Same difference. Still, you're responsible. You're the ones who found her. You're the ones who betrayed her."

"We didn't betray anyone," I said. "You paid Miss Ku to give us that note. Then you killed Cecil Whitcomb when he went to Namdaemun. We went after Miss Ku because we're after you."

"So now you found me."

I heard shuffling over coal, moving to my left. I followed the sound with the barrel of my gun.

"There's plenty of room down here," the whisper said. "Come on down. I don't have a pistol, I don't even have a knife. Leave your .38 on the landing. It'll be a fair fight."

"Like the one you gave Cecil Whitcomb?"

"Sure. Just like that. But you're bigger than him and you think you're tough."

Down the hallway, a door slammed. I jerked back, my finger twitching on the trigger.

I wasn't sure but I thought I heard a hissing sound down below.

Footsteps clomped down the corridor. They were coming at me from two directions. Out of the darkness of the cellar something flew at me. I leapt back, twisting the gun barrel skyward, and fired.

The explosion of the shot reverberated in the stone-lined cellar.

Too late, I realized what had been thrown at me. A piece of coal. It rolled back down the steps.

The footsteps in the corridor started running, heading this way now. I crawled out into the hallway and aimed my revolver at the oncoming shadow. Moonlight drifting in through the doorway glinted off the barrel of his gun. My finger found the trigger.

The dark figure stopped suddenly.

"Sueño!"

"Top!"

"What the hell you doing shooting off your damn weapon in the goddamn building?"

"There's somebody in the cellar."

"Who?"

"The guy who killed Whitcomb."

The First Sergeant froze for a second, then turned his pistol toward the stairway and stepped past me.

"Wait!" I said. "There's no light."

He started down the stairs, but stopped and turned back. "You still have bullets in that thing?"

"Plenty."

The First Sergeant trotted off to his office and returned with a heavy-duty flashlight. Covering each other, we crouched our way down the darkened steps.

27

THE BEAM OF THE FIRST SERGEANT'S FLASHLIGHT BOBBED THROUGH dust and intricate cobwebs: disused office furniture, the coal furnace, ancient cardboard boxes filled with yellowing files, mops and buckets. Nothing else.

"Who'd you say was down here?" the First Sergeant asked suspiciously.

The odor of gunpowder drifted above the must and cobwebs.

"Somebody was here," I said. "I'm sure of it. I was talking to him."

The metal door of the fuse box stood open, a couple of plugs missing.

Behind the furnace, falling snow drifted into the cellar. The wooden hatchway where the workmen brought in the coal was wide open. A padlock hung loosely on the hasp. Busted.

The First Sergeant's face grew more grim but he didn't apologize for doubting me.

Outside, what looked like footsteps led off through the slush.

They were big, about size twelves, but whether or not they were sneakers or oxfords or combat boots we couldn't tell.

"You say this guy talked to you?" the First Sergeant asked.

I nodded.

"What'd he say?"

"He said we killed the gal down at the Tiger Lady's. And he virtually admitted to killing Whitcomb."

"Virtually?"

"Well, he didn't deny it."

"What else did he say?"

"He said he was going to kill me. And Ernie, too."

We followed the footsteps until they climbed back onto the sidewalk heading deep into the redbrick buildings of 8th Army Headquarters.

"You want back on the case?" the First Sergeant asked me.

"I never left it."

"Yeah. I didn't think you did."

From the CID office I dialed my way through the ancient phone exchange and finally was connected to a number off post. *Ajjima*, the Nurse's landlady, answered. Ernie and the Nurse were out she said—back together again, good news in itself—and she'd let them know about the threat to our lives as soon as they returned.

The landlady was a responsible woman. I knew she'd relay the message and make sure Ernie understood how serious it was.

Afterward, I walked back to the barracks through the softly falling snow. I drank a beer from the big vending machine. Even though I showered and changed into clean underwear I couldn't sleep. It was two hours past midnight. Still, I sat on the edge of my bunk in the dark. Thinking.

Footsteps down the hallway. I straightened. Pounding on my door. "Sueño!"

The voice of the CQ.

"Yeah?" I said.

"Phone call."

I slipped on my rubber thongs and slapped down the hallway, still in my skivvies. I grabbed the receiver.

"What?"

"Agent Sueño?"

"Yes."

"This is the Desk Sergeant at the MP Station. Your presence is requested in Itaewon."

"What is it?"

"Emergency. Someone hurt."

"Who?"

"I don't have a name."

"Where?"

"A hooch in Itaewon. The KNP Liaison Officer didn't give me an address. Said you'd know. Belongs to a woman called 'the Nurse.' "

I'm not sure what I did after that. I do remember the CQ talking to me. "Sueño. Sueño? You OK?"

I stumbled back to my room and threw on my clothes.

I ran to Itaewon.

The last glimmers of silvery moonlight disappeared behind floating clouds. The snow and slush had stopped, but the wind picked up and spirits whistled through dark alleys. I wound through a narrow pathway between brick and stone walls, listening for footsteps behind me.

Nothing.

At the Nurse's hooch, the front gate was open. Neighbors loitered in front, arms crossed, faces greedy with curiosity. Light from a street lamp streamed down onto the muddy walkway. A shrill wail ricocheted off the stone walls. The voice was tired, weathered. Not the Nurse. But it came from her hooch.

Then I knew who it was. Warmth drained from my face. I started to run again.

In front of the house I pushed through a small crowd. Without taking off my shoes, I leapt up onto the narrow porch.

Blue-suited policemen had already arrived. I saw something below me and stopped and almost stumbled. Blood streamed in a long trail across the vinyl floor.

She was on her back, and for the first time since I'd known her the Nurse's face was twisted in agony.

Ajjima, the landlady, knelt beside her, screaming through the dry reeds of what was left of her tattered vocal cords.

A young Korean policeman, pale, looked at me and then looked at the wall, as if bringing my attention to something.

Scribbled in blood, like the scrawl of an evil child's fingerpainting, were four dripping words. In English.

"Dreamer, dream of me!"

The landlady screamed again. I stepped back, smacking my shoulder against a cabinet. Jars shattered. Tins crashed to the floor and rolled crazily through the blood.

I knelt beside the landlady and reached for her. When my fingertips touched the cheap material of her sweater, a spark crackled between us.

She shrieked—again and again—as if someone had shoved a hot blade into her heart.

28

Captain Kim, the Commander of the Itaewon Police Station, strode into the chaos of the crime scene and started barking orders. Policemen jumped.

We'd worked together on many cases. Not always happily.

When Kim saw me he raised one shuttered eye, like a small brown bear coming out of hibernation, and spoke one word: "Why?"

I knew what he meant. Why was I here? Why was I involved with these people? Why did I let this happen?

I pointed to the pitiful remains of the Nurse.

"I knew her," I told him.

He scanned the room, taking in the landlady and the PX goods and the blood. He nodded his head and turned his back on me, writing me off as just another GI partaking of the charms of a Korean business girl.

He tried to interrogate the landlady, but all she did was swallow terrified gulps of air and let them out in something resembling a croak.

Captain Kim finally gave up in disgust and ordered she be taken to the hospital.

He asked me only a few questions. My story boiled down to two facts: that I'd known the Nurse for over a year now, and that she had been the steady girlfriend of my partner, Ernie Bascom.

That's when one of the uniforms interrupted and told Captain Kim that Ernie had been here, too, fought with an intruder, and been transported over to the military hospital on Yongsan Compound.

I didn't wait for a translation but asked my question in Korean. "Is he alive?"

"Yes," the policeman answered, nodding. "And conscious. But distraught about the death of this woman."

"Do you have a description of the intruder?"

The uniform frowned, not happy to be embarrassed in front of his boss. "We are working on that."

A pair of white-coated medical types came in with a long plastic bag. They laid it down next to the Nurse and rolled her into it. As they zipped it up and carted her outside, I looked away.

When the technicians arrived and Captain Kim started to direct their activities, I took advantage of his preoccupation, stepped out into the courtyard, and found a dark corner.

In the cold air I leaned over, hands on my knees. For a minute I thought I was going to be sick.

Who was this guy? This guy who was after me? With his "Dreamer, dream of me" and his two dead women and one dead man in his wake. Why had he targeted Ernie and me? He knew my name, that was clear. Sueño means to sleep or to dream. George the Dreamer. That's what the other Mexican kids in school used to call me. And now this guy was calling me the same thing. And taunting me, just like those kids. But the blood on the floor was no dream.

I had to do something.

Who was next? Maybe the print shop guy? Forget him. It was more likely that either Ernie or I was next, and since the killer had taken the trouble to visit me at work, it was probably me. I had to find this guy and find him quick. But how?

I turned. A few of the people in the crowd outside the gate were gawking at me, as if I were an attraction in a sideshow.

I waited until another small van of police officers arrived and all attention was directed to them. I scurried down the alley toward the Main Supply Route.

No taxis after curfew. I ran all the way back to the compound. Panting heavily, I was able to explain to the gate guard what had happened to Ernie. He called for an MP jeep and they drove me over to the 121 Evacuation Hospital.

The buffed corridors of the 121 Evac were dimly lit and silent this time of night. I tried to inhale as little as possible but the frightening smell of rubbing alcohol and disinfectant still needled its way up my nose. As I strode forward, I heard shouting in the distance.

The shouting grew louder as I approached the Emergency Room.

"Bullshit!" Ernie's voice.

"You have to stay for testing. Doctor's orders." A woman's voice. Patient.

When I pushed into the Emergency Room, a half-dozen blue-clad medics and nurses turned their eyes toward me. All of them looked tired and harassed. Ernie, still in street clothes, glanced over and continued talking as if I'd been a part of the conversation all along.

"They want me to stay overnight when I have work to do," he said. "Can you believe it? Just a few stitches, a little iodine, a bump on the head. In 'Nam we just patched them up and sent them back to the field, most rickety tick."

The nurse folded her arms, not liking the fact that Ernie now had reinforcements. He was hard enough to handle on his own.

"You might have internal damage," she insisted. "We won't know until tomorrow, when we run the tests."

Ernie held a bottle of pills up to the blue fluorescent light. "You gave me this shit. This'll take care of it."

"Antibiotics don't heal ruptured internal organs," the nurse said.

I put my hand on Ernie's shoulder.

"She's right," I told him. "Stay overnight. Let them run some tests."

He turned his bloodshot green eyes on me, lowering his voice for the first time.

"Where is she?"

"They're taking her to the morgue."

"Then I have to go see her."

"You have to stay here."

Ernie stood up. "No way."

I gazed helplessly at the nurse. "I'll bring him back tomorrow."

She nodded, finally worn down by his pestering. "You do that," she said. "If there's anything left of him."

At the front exit, Ernie tossed the antibiotics into a trashcan.

"Hey!" I said. "You're gonna need that shit."

"Why? Doesn't get me high."

Sometimes there's no reasoning with him. Especially after his steady girlfriend is murdered.

It was past four A.M. now, so getting through the gate was no sweat. I woke up a cab driver and he was happy for the early morning fare.

I helped Ernie into the cab. He wasn't nearly as strong as he was trying to pretend to be.

"*Odi?*" the driver asked. Where?

I wasn't sure how to say the word in Korean, so I just told him to take us to downtown Seoul. He rubbed his eyes. "Where in downtown Seoul?"

I said it as plainly as I knew how.

"The place where they keep the dead people."

. . .

As we rode through the sleeping city, Ernie started to talk.

"The son of a bitch knocked me out."

His voice sounded hoarse, as if he'd just come off a three-quart drunk.

"Who did?"

"A big guy. Almost as tall as you, but broader. Built like a fucking wildcat on protein supplements."

"American or Korean?"

"Made in the USA all the way. I was in the *byonso*," Ernie said, "squatting over the hole. It was those damn eels the Nurse and I ate downtown."

I remembered her telling him to send them back because they weren't fully cooked. As usual, he'd been hardheaded about it and refused.

"Must've been tainted or something," he said. "Anyway, it kept pouring out of me and you know how your knees can cramp up on you when you're squatting over a Korean toilet."

"Yeah."

"I heard a sound. Someone coming in the front gate. Quiet like. I figured it was *ajjima*'s husband, sneaking in from a *soju* house, liquored up again. Next thing I know there's a scream. The Nurse. A stick smashes against wood and glass and *ajjima*'s up screaming. I'm struggling to stand, pulling my pants up, and by the time I bust out of the *byonso*, people next door have opened their windows, yelling *Dodukiya! Dodukiya!*" Thief! Thief!

Ernie turned his head to look blearily at me. "You know how they do when there's a slicky boy in the neighborhood. So I'm still thinking it's a thief when something huge lurches out of the Nurse's hooch, and before I know what's happening a stick hits me in the stomach, but maybe it's not a stick but a boot and I take a couple of punches on the way down. The next thing I know some neighbors are carting me downhill to a GI ambulance."

I patted him on the shoulder. "Take it easy, Ernie. Calm down."

"I'll get the son of a bitch." His fists clenched. "I'll get him, George."

The Seoul City Morgue was big and made of cement, and we had to walk down a broad staircase that seemed as if it were leading into hell.

Nobody'd seen a foreigner down here in a long time—not a breathing one, anyway—and we received some surprised looks. The white-smocked attendant at the front desk was engaged in animated discussion with a well-dressed middle-aged man who seemed to be talking about the best place to spend his money to obtain the right kind of funeral for a revered grandfather. The man talking didn't notice us behind him and the attendant apparently thought it would be unseemly to interrupt the older man just to help a couple of foreigners.

Normally, Ernie would've raised some hell, but he just stood there leaning on me. Green around the gills and getting greener.

The morgue workers gawked at the awkward *yangnom*, foreign louts, waiting at the desk, made comments to one another, and giggled occasionally.

Finally the talker finished and when he turned around his eyes grew big, taking us in. But he recovered pretty fast and strode off in a huff of posed dignity.

I told the man at the counter that I was looking for a woman. Suddenly I realized how stupid that sounded, but as I looked around no one had laughed so I plowed ahead.

I didn't know the Nurse's real name. I'd heard it once or twice, but Ernie and I had become so used to just calling her the Nurse that at the moment it slipped my mind. Instead I described the circumstances: A beautiful young woman, knifed to death in Itaewon.

Only one corpse fit that description.

The man escorted us down another cement corridor. Ernie limped, holding his side. With each step the air became colder. On either side were more rooms. The attendant walked into one of them, strode down a row of metal cabinets, stopped, and pulled one open.

The Nurse was completely pale, as pale as I've ever seen anyone, and the smooth skin of her cheeks hung unnaturally limp. Her long black hair was matted behind her head and the smooth voluptuous contours of her body lay flaccid beneath the sheet.

Breath exhaled slowly from Ernie's body. He grabbed the edge of the cabinet and lowered his head.

I lifted the damp linen. Beyond the bare breasts, the flesh just below the center of her rib cage was hideously slashed. A knife had entered, twisting and tearing on its way in. There weren't many slashes on the arms. Apparently, the attacker didn't have time to complete his usual ritual.

I replaced the sheet and asked the mortician, "The knife went into the heart?"

"Yes."

"Then she couldn't have lived very long."

"After that? No."

He didn't ask me who had done it or who I was, and I was glad for that.

I gazed down at her, thinking that she and Ernie for months had been my only family. The only family I'd known for many years. My parents were lost to me at an early age, but I still had that reverence for family that is part of every Mexican's soul. I raised two fingers to my mouth, kissed them, and pressed the moist flesh against the Nurse's cold, soft lips.

Then I grabbed Ernie, turned, and helped him down the echoing hallway. We climbed the endless steps together.

The army didn't matter much to me anymore. Not the CID. Not my future. Not promotions. Not courts-martial. None of the things that most lifers put first. Only one thing mattered now. The only thing worth thinking about: Getting the guy who did this to the Nurse.

Outside, I hailed a taxi. I tucked Ernie inside. He didn't protest. Just went along with it. His body so limp, I wondered if the life was draining out of him too.

The driver shifted the cab into gear and we lurched forward into the sparse morning traffic.

Ernie leaned back in the seat and rolled his eyes. "She was a good chick, wasn't she?"

"The best."

"And nobody's ever seen anything like her. Not in Itaewon, not in Korea, not in the whole world."

"Damn right," I said.

"And we're gonna find the bastard who offed her."

"You better believe we are."

"And I'm going to personally rack his ass up and hang it out to dry."

"No doubt."

Ernie nodded his head vigorously, turned, and gazed out at a passing bus. Then he stared at his hands hanging limply in his lap.

Before we made it back to the compound, he was crying.

29

A TALL, BUSTY GIRL, HER BLACK HAIR TIED BACK IN A WHITE BANdana, brought me another frosty mug of beer.

"*Dasi hanbon?*" she asked. One more time?

"Yes," I said. "*Dasi hanbon.*"

She laughed, still amused by the fact that a foreigner could actually speak an intelligible sentence. As she turned away the skirt of her long blue dress swirled around her thick calves.

I was in the OB Bear House, on the outskirts of Itaewon, a spot where GI's don't often go. Plenty of Korean working men stood around at the small shelves against the walls or perched on tall stools surrounding high tables that were just large enough for three or four mugs of beer and a small plate of snacks.

This morning, Ernie had refused to return to the hospital. When I nagged him about it, he took a swing at me. I dodged it and later he apologized, but I knew the murder of the Nurse was about to drive him nuts. He just sat in his room, drinking beer, telling even the houseboy to get the fuck away from him.

There was only one way to pull him out of it: action.

I had to get a line on this killer and I had to get it fast. Eighth Army CID was too inefficient and relied too much on what they were told by the Korean National Police. There were just too many leaks in Lieutenant Pak's organization. Herbalist So was my last chance.

I needed direct action. I needed expertise in operating clandestinely in the city of Seoul. And I needed it now. Only So and his slicky boys could provide it.

The biggest stumbling block was, of course, that Slicky King So and the slicky boys had tried to murder us a couple of days ago.

But I'm a forgiving type of guy. I had to keep in mind that Ernie had pissed him off by slapping herbal tea into his face. And Herbalist So probably figured that if we escaped, we would betray his operation.

Since then, he'd had time to cool off. He must've come to realize that we weren't after the slicky boys, we were after the murderer of Cecil Whitcomb—and the murderer of Miss Ku and now the Nurse.

At least I *hoped* he'd come to realize that.

After all, he hadn't made any further attempts on our lives. This I took as a sign of goodwill.

The way I figured it there were two possibilities. If the slicky boys had nothing to do with the murder of Cecil Whitcomb, then Slicky Boy So would be happy to cooperate in tracking down the real killer. More murders could further excite the honchos of 8th Army, disrupting the slicky boy king's operation and costing him money.

That was the way I figured it. He'd want my help. Sure. No problem.

It was the second possibility that had me worried: Maybe the slicky boys *had* knifed Cecil Whitcomb.

Then, if we had drunk the potion that Herbalist So offered us in the dungeon, it probably would've proved fatal. And if I walked back into his clutches again, I'd probably never walk out.

Still, what choice did I have? I had to take the chance. I wasn't going to catch this killer, whoever he was, without help.

This afternoon, I'd gone to visit the retired slicky boy, Mr. Ma. I told him I wanted to meet with Herbalist So because I was sure that we could work out our differences and that we needed one another's help. He was noncommittal, but listened to me.

Finally, he sent his son Kuang-sok scampering away with a whispered message. When he came back, Mr. Ma told me to be here, at the OB Bear House, at eight P.M. Alone.

When I tried to drink the first beer at the OB Bear House, my hand shook so badly that I was forced to prop my elbow against the wall to raise the mug.

That had been two hours ago. I was still cooling my heels. No word yet. My stomach twisted like an undisciplined beast. This was my fourth liter of beer but I felt more sober than a chaplain at Sunday services.

A neat young man wearing thick, round-lensed glasses sat next to me, sipping on his beer and studying a textbook with a number of mathematical notations on its pages. He shifted his umbrella in his lap, recrossed his legs, and spoke to me in English.

"You shouldn't drink so much."

I looked at him. Amused. Good thing Ernie wasn't here. He was liable to pop him one for a remark like that. Me, I was just curious. Koreans don't usually interfere with other people's business, especially foreigners.

"Why not?" I asked.

"Herbalist So doesn't like it."

I set my beer down. "Why didn't you talk to me earlier?"

"We had to check you out."

I glanced out in the street. No sign of So's sentries, but they were out there somewhere.

"I'm alone," I told the neat young man.

"I know."

He picked up his umbrella, rose, and said, "Follow me. About ten paces behind."

Sadistic little bastard, I thought. He had waited until I ordered a fresh beer. I glugged down as much of it as I could and hurried after him.

• • •

Pellets of frozen rain spat against my face. Still, I managed to keep the swiftly moving young man in sight. He crossed the MSR, away from the main nightclub district, heading up a winding road that led into a somewhat higher class residential district. We turned down a number of narrow lanes. They were clean, well kept. Upturned shingle roofs rose behind high brick walls. Ernie and I never came up here because the debauchery of Itaewon didn't reach this high.

After we walked for about ten minutes, the young man snapped his umbrella shut and stepped into a small tearoom. I followed him in. The joint wasn't much bigger than a four-man room in the barracks.

We walked past a half dozen empty tables, pushed through a beaded curtain, and through another door into an outdoor garden with metal tables sheltered beneath a large canvas awning.

Herbalist So sat at one of the tables, an elegantly designed glass lamp in front of him. He wore a three-piece business suit and a huge wristwatch. A brand the PX never carried.

The neat young man with the umbrella disappeared. Shadows hovered beneath grinning demons carved into the stone-walled enclosure. Bodyguards.

I sat down in front of Herbalist So.

"You look good in that outfit," I told him. "On Wall Street you'd fit right in."

He stared at me for a moment, his lips tightening. "You're drunk."

"I had a couple of beers. Who wouldn't after what I saw last night?"

"I'll tell you who wouldn't. A smart man wouldn't."

I let the insult sit for a while. The rain pattered against the canvas above us. I needed him. I wasn't going to start an argument.

"You're wasting your talents, Agent Sueño," So said. "Stop drinking and you'll become somebody. We Koreans always knew you were smarter than the other CID agents we've seen. You've learned our language, you keep your word, you do not bully Koreans or think you're better than us. You don't look down at the things we've had to do since the war to make a living. All the other agents showed us nothing but false bravado and an inflated opinion of themselves. You have more than that."

I didn't particularly like being lectured by a thief. Sure, I drank more than I should, but that was my business.

"I may be a drunk," I said, "but I'm not a thief." I knew I'd lose his goodwill, but I was angry enough that I didn't care.

He studied me. A chill ran through my body and it wasn't from the cold wind. His eyes seemed to pinch into my soul.

I had been foolish. Maybe the men in the shadows didn't understand English, but they certainly understood that their leader had been insulted. The loss of face would make Herbalist So harder to deal with. Maybe impossible to deal with.

"No," the king of the slicky boys said softly. "You are not a thief, Agent Sueño. When you take money to do a job, you do it. Even if it results in death."

I lowered my head. So was right. We all have our shortcomings. Mine were legion.

I knew I had to be contrite to get what I wanted. Especially now that I'd mouthed off.

"This man I hunt has killed three people already: The British soldier, a young *kisaeng* called Miss Ku, and a former student of nursing. I need your help to find him."

"Yes. You do need my help. What do you want me to do?"

I told him about the print shop in Mukyo-dong and about the phony ration control plate we'd found there and how the owner had done business with the killer and claimed the man owed him money.

"I believe there's more information inside the shop," I told Herbalist So. "On the killer of these three people and his black market activities. Also I believe the owner knows more than he told me."

"And you wish us to talk to him?"

"Yes. Meanwhile, I will be doing everything I can to identify some sort of renegade American from our files. But so far we have nothing to go on. No fingerprints, no name, no identification numbers. Only a vague description."

"So this Miss Ku, the player of the *kayagum*, we led you to," So asked, "she has been killed? And this nursing student?"

"Yes."

"It seems that death follows in your wake, Agent Sueño."

I didn't answer.

"For our services there will be a price."

"It's in your interest to stop this man, too."

"It was," he said, staring at me, "when it was thought that we might have been responsible for the death of Lance Corporal Whitcomb. But with these new deaths, the trail of evidence will lead away from us. We are satisfied now. Our operation is secure."

I thought of telling him that if he didn't help me I'd bust his entire syndicate wide open. That I'd put everything I'd learned about the slicky boys into a report for the eyes of the 8th Army Commander, he'd assign a task force to the problem, and we'd put the slicky boys out of commission for good. But I knew it was futile. So's contacts ranged too widely. Even if the 8th Army honchos listened to me, Herbalist So would just keep his head down and when the staff changed at 8th Army and another crisis arose that seemed more important, he'd swing right back into normal operation. And, of course, there was always the possibility that in order to avoid the inconvenience, he and his boys would decide to drop me below the ice floes bobbing in the Han River.

Despite what he said, however, I knew he wanted to help. A murderer on the loose would cause everyone to be nervous. Him, 8th Army, the Korean National Police. It couldn't be good for his business. But I had insulted him. That had to be overcome.

"Yes," I said softly. "Your operation is secure. But, still, I need your help. What can I do to get it?"

He studied me without replying. I kept my eyes down, my hands folded in my lap.

Maybe it was my imagination but I thought I heard a sigh of approval coming from the shadowy men surrounding us.

Herbalist So's voice spread out clear and smooth amidst the clattering rain.

"Our assistance will require two things."

"Name them," I said.

"A favor, at an unspecified future date."

"What sort of favor?"

Herbalist So spread his fingers. "Only time will tell. When we need one, Agent Sueño, we will call on you."

I thought about it: the trouble helping the slicky boys could land me in. I also thought of the Nurse. Her slashed body, the life drained out of her beautiful face.

I nodded my head. "You've got it. What's the second condition?"

Herbalist So leaned back slightly in his chair. Overhead, the rain grew louder. "That will require a *seibei*."

I looked up at him. I knew what a *seibei* was. I'd seen it done in documentaries about ancient Korean life but I'd never heard of a foreigner being required to do it. But then I realized that although we Americans saw it as a form of degradation, Herbalist So thought of his offer as a compliment. Maybe some sort of an initiation. After all, if I was going to be doing favors for him in the future, I was, in effect, becoming a member of his organization. A slicky boy myself. But more important, if I turned him down, I would be insulting him again. I not only wouldn't receive his help, I would be lucky to get out of here in one piece.

"You honor me," I said, almost choking on the words.

Herbalist So barked some quick commands. I was still too stunned to understand exactly what he said, but the shadows came out of the rain and became men. One of the men rushed into the teahouse and came back with a straw mat. He placed it on the dirty cement of the patio. I stood up and someone told me where to stand, just off the edge of the mat. A cushion was placed on the other end of the mat and Herbalist So rose from his chair, slipped off his shoes, and sat down cross-legged on the cushion. The men backed away. All was quiet. They were waiting for me to begin.

I wasn't sure exactly how it went but I supposed they'd forgive me as long as I got the substantial portion of the ceremony correct.

A *seibei* is a method of showing respect from inferior to superior. At New Year's it was performed by the oldest son to his parents. Even a man who was seventy years old would bow before his mother or father if they were still alive.

I thought of the other instances in the history of the East and the West, when this sort of formality had caused so much trouble. Like when the British envoys of Queen Victoria had refused to prostrate themselves before the Chinese Emperor.

It's a fine way to act if you have gunboats to back you up. I didn't.

I slipped off my shoes and knelt on the edge of the pad. Still holding my upper body straight I shuffled forward until I was only a few feet from Herbalist So. Slowly, I bent forward at the waist and placed both my hands, palms flat, on the mat in front of me. I lowered my forehead until it touched the ground between my fingers and thumbs, then raised myself again. I repeated the movement three times. When I was finished, I squatted back, hands resting on my thighs.

"Well done," he said. "But you forgot the chant."

He spoke some Korean words of supplication for me. I didn't understand them, they were archaic language, but I repeated them as best as I could.

Finally, So nodded. Satisfied.

So I'd lowered myself to a common thief. A Korean one, at that. Most GI's would swear that they'd never do such a thing. But most GI's bubbled over with racial hatred and an inflated sense of pride that came from being part of a country that had been on the top of the heap for over a century. Such things didn't bother me. I was from East L.A. I'd been fighting my way up from the bottom all my life. Herbalist So had power. A lot more than I did. In certain areas, more than the Commander of 8th Army. He deserved respect. This little ceremony didn't bother me any more than standing at attention in a military formation and saluting some potbellied general with stars on his shoulder.

Herbalist So began to speak.

"Already, our minions are watching the village for the man you seek, Agent Sueño. But he seems to be intelligent and resourceful. We don't expect to capture him with such crude methods. As far as your print shop is concerned, that will be checked tonight. Tomorrow you will be contacted with the results."

"Where?"

"Wherever you are."

"Who will contact me?"

"Whoever we designate. Keep an open mind, Agent Sueño."

"I will."

Herbalist So nodded. The meeting was over. I stood up, put my shoes back on, bowed once more, and made my way out through the tiny tea shop. There were still no customers. And no one serving tea.

At the bottom of the hill I saw a familiar figure, wrapped tightly in a flowered raincoat. The Chinese girl. The same one I had seen inside the slicky boys' dungeon.

She held out her umbrella for me.

"*Irri-oseiyo,*" she said. Come this way.

I wasn't about to argue with her.

She led me by the hand to a tiny, immaculately clean *yoguan*, tucked back in an alley I'd never seen before. She paid for the room and, to my surprise, accompanied me down the creaking hallway. Once we were alone she told me to take off my clothes. It was an order she didn't have to repeat. She took me into the bathroom and scrubbed me down and rinsed me and dried me and soon had me lying naked on the warm sleeping pad under a silk comforter.

After washing herself, she turned off all the lights except for a soft red bulb in the entranceway and slipped into the bed with me.

She was slim and soft and completely naked. And as sweet as any woman has a right to be.

This woman, with her perfect features and her hairless, unblemished skin, and her supple body like a willow bending in the wind, seemed to be another species altogether from us regular human beings. She seemed too perfect. Too smart. Too gentle. Too dreamlike.

I still think of the night I spent with the Chinese woman as something that happened to me while floating in a world untouched by hatred or fear or cruelty or death.

Of course, she was being paid for her work. That took some of the edge off. Not much.

Before drifting off to sleep, I realized that working with Slicky King So wasn't half bad.

In the morning, the Chinese woman woke me. She held a breakfast tray: hot turnip soup, steamed rice, roasted mackerel. I washed my face and sat down on the floor to eat. As I wielded my wooden chopsticks, I noticed an envelope on the edge of the tray. When I reached for it she grabbed my hand with her soft fingers.

"Monjo pap mokku, kudaum ei ilkoyo." Eat first, after that, read.

I did as I was told. She had risen from bed early, and her hair was up and braided and she wore her bright red silk *chipao* with its high collar and the short skirt riding up above her round knees.

The turnip soup and the rice and the mackerel were delicious. I was hungry and finished it quickly. She cleared the bowls, asking me if I wanted more. I told her not to bother. She handed me the envelope.

Inside was a piece of blank paper with a neatly printed series of numerals.

"RCP's," she said.

Ration control plates. The numbers that had been on the phony ration control plates the print shop had embossed for the killer.

Also inside the envelope was a small black-and-white photograph, and a list of four names and serial numbers that had appeared on bogus military identification cards. Each name was associated with one of the ration control plates. When a customer approaches the door of the PX or commissary, an attendant checks his ID card and RCP to make sure everything matches.

I studied the photograph. Short, light brown hair. A square face with a crooked jaw. A nose that had been broken somewhere along the line, tight lips, lifeless eyes. The Chinese girl looked down at the photo and shuddered.

He seemed like any normal GI—but mean.

I twisted the photo so the light from the naked bulb above us would hit it more clearly. Tiny scars, barely visible, ran along his cheeks and the ridge of his nose. There were others on his chin and at the side of his jaw, extending back toward his ears.

I handed the photo to the Chinese woman, tracing the scars with my finger. She nodded, very solemn.

"*Orin i ddei, nugu deiryosso,*" she said. When he was a child, someone beat him.

She had to be right. It was obvious that no one would've been capable of whipping him that badly and leaving so many scars once he reached adulthood.

That's all I needed. A vicious, abused mongrel. The eyes in the photograph didn't look particularly intelligent, but that could be deceiving. His actions so far had been swift, brutal, and cunning.

I didn't want to leave, but the sun would be coming up soon and I had a lot of work to do. I kissed the hands and lips of the Chinese woman, trying to convince myself that she was real. She bowed as I left.

I strode out of the *yoguan,* her gentle fragrance still lingering about me, the killer's face clutched in my fist.

30

I ARRIVED AT THE CID OFFICE EARLY. WHEN RILEY SHOWED UP, HE pitched in and helped me. We compared the photograph the slicky boys had given me to MP mug shots and the long lists of AWOL GI's and the photos the Korean National Police had sent along.

It took us over an hour. When we finished we still had nothing. No match.

"He's not an AWOL GI," Riley said. "And if he mustered out of the army and came back to Korea, he hasn't raised enough hell, as far as the KNP's are concerned, for them to bother taking his mug shot."

"He's the cautious type," I said. "He wouldn't have let himself be picked up for anything trivial."

"No."

Miss Kim came in, silently handed us two steaming cups of coffee, and removed the old ones. We were too preoccupied to thank her.

"But the print shop guy told you he used to be a GI?" Riley asked.

"Yeah. What he said exactly was *Migun.*" I snapped my fingers. Most of the U.S. forces in Korea are army units. But there is a sizable air force presence and even a small contingent of navy. "What that means literally is 'American military person.' "

Riley was puzzled by my excitement.

"It doesn't necessarily mean army," I explained. "This guy could've been air force or navy."

"You're right," Riley said. "A sailor who jumped ship or a zoomie who got tired of rocketing around the universe."

Ernie walked in, a copy of the *Stars & Stripes* folded under his arm. Blue bags sagged beneath his eyes. Miss Kim swiveled on her typing chair and started pounding away on the keys, producing nothing coherent.

Riley studied Ernie. "Late night?"

"Couldn't sleep," Ernie said. He glanced at the paperwork in front of us. "What you got?"

I filled Ernie in on what we'd found, happy to have him back.

"How'd you get the RCP numbers?" he asked.

"I'll tell you later."

We decided that we had to check with both the navy and the air force liaison officers here on post. Ernie took the fly-boys. I took the squids.

"When the First Sergeant comes back from the command briefing," I told Riley, "tell him we're close. And we don't have time for any damn black market detail."

"Not to worry. I'll keep him happy."

As we were leaving, Miss Kim pulled a nail file out of her purse and slashed at red claws.

Ernie didn't seem to notice. On the other hand, he didn't offer her a stick of gum, either.

Sometimes you wear out shoe leather for days and come up with nothing, and other days you ask a simple question and people look at you like, "You didn't know *that*?"

I passed by the big black anchors on the front lawn of the Commandant Headquarters, Naval Forces Korea, and pushed through a heavy teak door into carpeted offices. I pulled out the black-and-white photo that Herbalist So had given me and showed it to the petty officer sitting behind a varnished desk. The brass in the office gleamed; the odor of disinfectant and boiled coffee hung in the air.

"This guy?" the petty officer said, fingering the photo. "Sure I know him. Lieutenant Commander Bo Shipton. Navy Seal." He shook his head. "Bad mother. Jumped ship about three, four months ago."

Bingo!

"When did you last see him?"

"Nobody's seen him since then."

"Do you have his personnel folder?"

"You'll have to talk to the commandant first."

"Can do easy."

The picture worked wonders. The commandant decided to see me right away. After a short chat, I obtained the information I wanted, assuring him that the integrity of the navy would be preserved. He was worried because anything that reflected badly on the navy could reflect badly on him.

The commandant offered me a cup of coffee but I didn't have time. I was out the teak door, past an old Korean man in a ragged khaki shirt. He silently scrubbed a huge brass ball with a sticky yellow fluid.

Children skated on frozen rice paddies and smoke curled from tubelike chimneys above the straw-thatched roofs of farmhouses. The roads were slippery and spotted with broad fields of black ice. Snorting oxen pulled wooden carts laden with giant turnips. Ernie sped around the obstacles as if he had every curve and hazard preprogrammed into his brain.

"Navy Seal, huh?" he said.

"Yeah. As bad as the Green Berets. On his way up, too. An officer, twelve years in."

"So why in the hell did he go AWOL?"

"That's what the commandant wouldn't talk about. His personnel folder was excellent. Beauregard Shipton, from south Texas, father a small-time rancher near the Mexican border who lost his land wildcatting for oil. Shipton had some problems with his father and wanted to be on his own. After Seal training he went to Vietnam. Served two tours there. A bunch of awards. Looks like he loved it."

"Those fucking Seals used to go up into North Vietnam. Right into Haiphong Harbor."

"According to Shipton's personnel record," I said, "he caught shrapnel in the jaw, couldn't breathe, and performed a field tracheotomy on himself. Sliced into his own throat, stuck a bamboo tube into his windpipe, and survived like that for three days until they managed to med-evac him out."

Ernie shifted into low gear and slowed for two farmers perched atop a rickety tractor. The tractor's ancient engine chugged doggedly forward, billowing black smoke into the gray sky. Ernie spotted an opening in the oncoming traffic, stepped on the gas, and swerved around the rattling machine. The two farmers stared.

When he built his speed back up Ernie asked, "So you gonna tell me now? About how you got those ration control plate numbers?"

I told him about the message written in blood above the Nurse's body and the tattered vocal cords of the landlady. I told him, too, about my meeting with Herbalist So, although I didn't mention the ceremony.

"So in the morning," Ernie said, "the Chinese girl gave you this information?"

"Right."

"This guy, Shipton, must be living off the black market, pulling down a grand or two every month."

"Probably."

"So why's he killing people?"

"I don't know."

"Who do you think is next on his list?"

"Us."

Ernie nodded. "Makes more sense than the people he's killed so far. At least with us he has a reason. We're trying to put him behind bars."

I moved my arm and felt the .38 rub against my chest. "Behind bars," I said. "That's one place to send him."

"Or to hell, huh?"

"Maybe better."

The road curved into a farm village. Ernie didn't slow much but blinked his lights on and off, and the white-gloved policeman on a platform in the center of town whistled us through. Schoolgirls with waist-long pigtails scurried out of our way, pointing and giggling at the long-nose GI's.

The road sign pointed toward Heing-ju Sansong, the fortified cliffs of Heingju, two kilometers away.

In the sixteenth century the Japanese Shogun, Hideyoshi, invaded Korea. The bulk of Hideyoshi's naval armada streamed up the Han River, past the cliffs of Heing-ju, heading for Seoul, the ancient capital of the Yi Dynasty. It was there at Heing-ju that the Korean defenders made their stand. They blockaded the river with pontoons filled with fighting men and huge sharpened stakes near the shore and from the cliffs of Heing-ju they launched fire arrows and blazing oil-soaked clumps of hemp and rock from wooden catapults.

Hideyoshi and his fleet took heavy losses, but in the end the Japanese landed successfully farther upriver. The Shogun's forces swallowed Korea whole, causing untold destruction and death. It might've happened a long time ago but the Koreans still remembered it, as they remembered every crime perpetrated on them by the Japanese.

In memory of the great battle, the ROK Navy's Central Headquarters was stationed here at Heing-ju, on the cliffs overlooking the blue expanse of the Han River Estuary. Lieutenant Commander Bo Shipton had been given a plum assignment—liaison officer to the ROK Navy, the only American serving with them at this headquarters. It was from here that he had gone AWOL three months ago. So far, no one had been able to tell me why.

Technically, Shipton was no longer AWOL. Thirty days after jumping ship his status had been changed. The U.S. Navy now officially classified him as a deserter.

• • •

The ROK Navy headquarters building was a rambling, single-story brick building with an elegant facade of inlaid brass and teak. A single pole stood out front. From it, the Korean flag fluttered in the breeze off the Han River. An expanse of lawn, brown and stunted now in the icy winter wind, spread toward the cliffs and dropped off into gray mist.

Ernie pulled in near the end of the parking lot and turned off the engine. I looked at him.

"You going in?"

"Too much brass. You take it."

"Okay."

He settled back in the canvas seat and pulled out a flat, brown paper sack stuffed with magazines from Scandinavia. Long legs, blond hair, pale skin.

"What's the matter, pal?" I asked. "Getting kinky on me?"

"No. Just need some shit to tell Strange."

That's Ernie. Always prepared.

I climbed out of the jeep and headed across the gravel parking lot toward a huge double door with brass handles in the shape of anchors. Two sailors dressed in black with white caps and white leggings raised their rifles and came to attention as I approached. One checked my identification and I told him I was here to talk to someone about the former U.S. Liaison Officer, Lieutenant Commander Beauregard Shipton.

Some quick words were whispered into an intercom, the door was opened, and I was waved in.

The carpeted hallways were paneled with varnished oak and hung with painted scenes of historic Korean sea battles. In a glass case a metal astrolabe, one of the earliest in human history, invented by some ancient Korean scholar, glistened. I was trying to decipher the brass plaque below it when a Korean lieutenant in a dress naval uniform hurried down the hall, all smiles, holding out his hand.

"Good afternoon. You're here about Shipton?"

"Yes."

It turned out he was Lieutenant Lee, the Public Affairs Officer, and spoke excellent English. He took me back into his office and after checking my identification he told me the usual: that they had already given a full statement to the U.S. authorities concerning the disappearance of Lieutenant Commander Shipton, and they didn't see anything more they could add.

"I want to speak to the people Shipton worked with," I said.

"That would be Commander Goh, his former supervisor. Unfortunately he is very busy."

I explained why we were after Shipton; about the three murders. And I told Lieutenant Lee that if I didn't receive cooperation immediately more innocent people could be killed.

His eyes narrowed at that and there was some more hushed conversation on an intercom. Lieutenant Lee was clicking back on his intercom when a stout man in a naval officer's uniform stormed into the room.

He had a craggy, square face and broad shoulders, and his chest was loaded with ribbons. The Public Affairs Officer stood up immediately and bowed.

"This," Lieutenant Lee said, "is Commander Goh."

Goh's hard eyes studied me, the creases around his nose and mouth tight, as if he were having a terrific bout of indigestion. His Korean was gruff. Guttural.

"*Shipton rul allago shipyo?*" he said. You want to know about Shipton?

I nodded. "*Nei. Allago shipoyo.*" Yes. I want to know.

"*Kurum. Kapshida.*" Well, then. Let's go.

The Public Affairs Officer seemed perplexed—maybe by my speaking Korean—but he made no effort to stop us. I followed Commander Goh down the carpeted hallway.

He made a couple of turns past busy offices with typewriters clattering away and gorgeous young Korean secretaries serving tea to bored-looking Korean officers. He pushed through a door with a large window in it that looked out toward another vast expanse of lawn behind the building, striding straight for the cliffs.

For a moment I thought he was going to keep going and see if I'd follow him over the edge. Instead, Goh veered toward a massive bronze statue of an ancient Korean warrior in metal helmet and brass-plated vest. Just beneath the huge sword leaning against the warrior's leg, the commander stopped abruptly.

"Yi Sun Shin," he said, gesturing toward the statue.

I knew who he was. The Korean admiral who'd invented the ironclad, sulphur-spewing *kobuk-son*—turtle boats. With his daring tactics and guerillalike forces, he had almost single-handedly stopped the invasion of Hideyoshi's naval forces through the straits and isthmuses of the islands off the southern coast of Korea. Even in Japan, his military genius is revered.

"Yes," I said, speaking in Korean. "He's very famous."

Commander Goh nodded. Satisfied.

He turned and clasped his hands behind his back and stared across the Han River below us.

"So you've come about Shipton," he said in Korean.

"Yes. We have reason to believe that he's killed three people."

Commander Goh nodded. "He's a very disturbed man."

"You knew him well, then?"

"Very well. We worked together every day. We traveled together around the country to inspect naval fortifications. After work I showed him what life was like in our teahouses and in the floating world of the night."

The military elite ran this country. They had money and they had prestige. And when they decided to visit a *kisaeng* house or some other place of pleasure, you can bet they received the very best. For a moment, I envied Lieutenant Commander Shipton. To run with them. Why would anyone go AWOL from a setup like that?

"What went wrong?" I asked.

Commander Goh breathed deeply of the salt air and took a few steps closer to the cliff. Twenty or thirty yards below, the churning waters of the Han River Estuary lapped against jagged rocks. He studied the low-lying fog.

"Shipton became very friendly with us. We all liked him. He even started to speak some Korean. Not as well as you, Agent Sueño, but he was progressing."

He paused and gazed at distant clouds hovering over the Yellow Sea. The old habits of a sailor.

"One of our admirals had a daughter. She was a very well brought up young woman with a good education, but maybe she wasn't the most attractive girl in the world. So the family was having trouble finding a suitable husband for her. It was decided that since she wasn't going to find the very best of Korean husbands, she could settle for an American. She was introduced to Shipton.

"Besides," Goh said, turning away from the water, "the admiral and his family had dreams of emigrating to America."

He raised and lowered his broad shoulders.

"None of this, of course, we told to your previous investigators, Agent Sueño. We thought it would do no good. Now that he's killed—killed again—we must tell you the full truth."

"Killed again?"

"Yes." He swiveled his craggy face toward me. "Can you keep what I'm about to tell you out of your report?"

"I don't know. It depends on what it is."

His expression didn't change but he nodded. "We cannot afford for any of this to ever come out."

"It will be kept strictly confidential," I said. "Classified. No one outside of our investigative services will ever see it, unless it needs to be used in a trial."

"But you will try him for these three murders he's recently committed?"

"Yes."

He seemed to reach a decision. "You won't need what I'm about to tell you for that." He glanced at my hands. "I notice you don't take notes."

"I have a good memory."

"If I'm to tell you what I know about Shipton, it must never come up in his trial and it must never come up in your official reports."

"You're protecting this Korean admiral, the father of Shipton's fiancée."

He looked at me steadily. "Yes."

It was a tough bargain, but I needed all the information I could gather if I was to have a chance of finding Shipton. We already had him pegged for three homicides. Maybe the evidence would be questionable in a high-class stateside trial, but for a military court-martial, here in 8th Imperial Army, it was plenty. I could get by without what Commander Goh was about to give me.

"All right, then," I said. "No notes. No recordings. And what you tell me will never appear in an official report."

"Or a trial?"

"Or a trial."

He let his breath out slowly and turned away again, as if searching for strength in the distant sea.

"The girl's name was Myong-a. Her family name isn't important. She spoke English well, and she and Shipton liked each other immediately. It seemed as if she did something for him. Shipton had been a lonely man. He left his family years ago and had never returned home. He spoke of his mother only when asked and of his father not at all. But Myong-a was a bright girl. She knew how to make him smile and make him laugh, and it seemed that he was forgetting the horrors of the war he had left behind."

A fisherman and his son rowed slowly on a splintered prow down the river, heading for the verdant waters of the estuary. As they slipped out of the fog Commander Goh watched them, and when they were once again covered in mist he resumed his speech.

"What Shipton didn't know, and what most Americans don't know, is that we Koreans are a very practical people. Marriage, to us, is primarily an economic union, a union designed to continue the growth and prosperity of the family. Love, if it comes at all, comes later and grows slowly. Marriage proposals don't usually start with love for us. But they did for Shipton.

"Myong-a, however, was a spirited young woman, and as such she had been in love with a Korean man, one of her former classmates at middle school. A man who wasn't suited for her. A common laborer. Even though she was planning on marrying Shipton and leaving the country, she—foolishly and to the shame of her father—continued to see this man.

"Shipton, although somewhat befuddled by your American notions of love, was also observant and shrewd. It didn't take him long to realize that not all of Myong-a's devotion was directed toward him."

Commander Goh opened his palms toward the heavens. "Shipton followed her, waited to see what she was planning to do, and broke in on them while she was in a room in a cheap *yoguan* with her young man."

He shook his head, his eyes crinkling, as if he were fighting back tears.

"He killed them both! Why? So foolish. So rash. And then he was gone. We never saw him again. The National Police found the bodies, but when they discovered the identity of the girl we were notified and we immediately assumed jurisdiction of the investigation."

Korea had been under virtual martial law since the Korean War. A few strings, pulled in the right places, and the navy could have what it wanted. Even a murder investigation.

"Why didn't you notify us?" I asked.

"Ah, don't you see? This became a personal matter. Between the officers here at Navy Headquarters and Shipton. We wanted to catch him before he somehow slipped out of our country. We wanted our own revenge."

"But you failed?"

"Yes. Lieutenant Commander Shipton is a very resourceful man."

"And as a consequence, three more people are dead."

Commander Goh's eyes burned into mine. "Would you have been able to stop him, Agent Sueño?"

I thought of our own contacts on the Korean economy. Slim to none. If the ROK Navy investigators hadn't been able to find Shipton, we were unlikely to.

"No," I said. "We probably wouldn't have."

The commander nodded. "So don't put the blood of these new victims on our hands."

Bureaucratic shuffling. Even when the entrails of sweet young ladies are being sliced out of their soft bodies. I thought of the Nurse and I got mad. Mad at their arrogance, their willingness to keep things covered up, their overbearing desire to have their integrity protected, no matter what the cost. Even at the cost of blood.

"If the blood is not on your hands, whose hands is it on?" I asked bluntly.

"Shipton's."

He was right, but he was also wrong. With more manpower, maybe we would've stumbled onto Shipton by now. Maybe Ernie and I would've been less gullible. Maybe we would've been more likely to protect Miss Ku and the Nurse. But I was too angry to argue. It was useless now. I only wanted one thing. To bring Shipton down.

"I want everything your investigators have uncovered."

"They will brief you."

"Now," I said.

"Yes," he said. "Now."

We marched silently back into the headquarters building.

They showed me photographs of the two bodies. The young woman laying naked in an alley, her neck snapped. The young man with sliced arms, razorlike cuts to the legs and torso, a deep killing gash in the center of his chest below the sternum.

A couple of Korean sailors in dungarees were standing next to the jeep, goofing off from a work detail. Ernie was leaning out of the jeep, showing them the pictures in the magazines, pointing and making comments that had them laughing uproariously.

It was good to see his spirits lifting.

When he saw me coming, he folded up the magazine and handed it to one of the sailors. The sailor tried to refuse but Ernie insisted and also presented both of them with a couple of sticks of gum. They chomped happily with their big square bronze jaws.

"Took you long enough," Ernie said.

"You should've gone in there with me. Some of the secretaries are finer than moon goddesses."

"Yeah?"

Commander Goh strode quickly across the lawn. Both sailors snapped to attention, saluted, bowed, and got back to work. Commander Goh ignored them and stopped at our jeep.

"You also are an investigator?" he asked, staring at Ernie. His English was accented but understandable.

"Yes," Ernie said.

Commander Goh shook his forefinger at me and resumed speaking in Korean.

"He, too, must abide by our bargain. Silence on the murder of the daughter of one of our brother officers."

"*Kokchong halgossi oopsoyo,*" I said. You have nothing to worry about.

He nodded, took another hard look at Ernie, turned, and strode away.

"Who was that asshole?" Ernie asked.

"His name's Commander Goh. He wanted to make sure you and me are operating on the same sheet of music."

"Why?"

"Let's get out of here. Then I'll tell you."

The two sailors in faded dungarees waved as we drove off.

I filled Ernie in on what I'd learned. About how the ROK investigators had followed Shipton around the country, how he'd eluded them by only minutes in a couple of spots, but eventually he'd disappeared entirely from their radar screens. They figured he was receiving help. Possibly from one of the organized crime syndicates in the country.

Ernie frowned. "The slicky boys?" he asked.

"I don't think so. They're not the only hoodlums in the country."

If Shipton was receiving help, he would've been a natural for mobsters to use to obtain phony identification and buy black market items out of the commissaries and the PX's. And that's what we could've been checking out all this time, but the ROK Navy hadn't notified us. I complained about that, but it didn't seem to bother any of the stoic Korean investigators. The fact that a *kisaeng* and a business girl had been slaughtered cut no ice with them. And they were only vaguely disturbed by the murder of a British soldier.

As usual, Ernie summed up the situation.

"So we still don't know where in the hell he is?"

"You got that right."

"So what's our next move?"

I pulled out the slip of paper the Chinese girl had given me this morning.

"Eighth Army Data Processing," I told Ernie. "We live in an age of computer punch cards."

Ernie shifted into low gear, gunned the engine, shifted back into high, and swerved around a farmer riding a rickety wooden buggy pulled by a flea-bitten pony.

"Fuck a bunch of computers," he said.

31

THE NCO IN CHARGE OF THE DATA PROCESSING UNIT WAS A nervous type with thick glasses and a habit of biting on his lower lip and brushing back his brown-and-gray mustache.

"This'll be hard," he said. "Four numbers. All bogus. And they could've been used anywhere in country."

"Start your search in Seoul first," I said, "and spread out from there."

"Not normal procedure," he insisted. "And we have other batches to run. I'm already working everybody overtime."

"I'll call the Provost Marshal, if you want, and have him call your boss."

"No." He waggled his nervous fingers. "That won't be necessary. Three murders, you say? Yes. That'll get priority."

"We thought so, too."

He scurried off toward the clattering machines busily processing punch data cards. Ernie and I walked back into the waiting room and poured ourselves overly cooked coffee into white foam cups.

As we waited, I watched the stream of young GI's, all with sheaves of paperwork in their hands, parading in to get a new ration control plate issued or an old one renewed. The time and money and effort the 8th Army put into ensuring that nobody sold a jar of instant coffee down in the village was enormous. Still, millions of dollars of black market goods found their way onto the Korean markets. The whole reason behind the system—supposedly—was to protect fledgling Korean companies from the unfair competition of duty-free goods from the U.S. Army compounds. The only problem was that there weren't any Korean companies that grew bananas or bottled maraschino cherries or distilled Scotch whiskey, as far as I knew. So the demand was tremendous. And although the honchos of 8th Army went at their task with all the vigor of Hercules cleaning out his stables, they weren't able to do much more than cause a ripple in the flow of contraband.

I think, if the truth were known, they were more concerned with making sure a bunch of foreigners didn't get their grubby hands on the products that, by divine right, belonged to Americans. Brainwashed by Madison Avenue, the army hoards consumables like gold.

A courier came in carrying three oblong boxloads of data punch cards, stacked one atop another. He hoisted them onto the counter. Another bored clerk signed a receipt for them, then lifted them onto a long table with other stacks of boxed cards. I stood and wandered over to the end of the counter.

Each box was marked in black grease pencil: Wonju, Osan, Pyongtaek, Waegwan, Taegu, Pusan. The cities near all the major U.S. bases. Every few minutes, from the other end of the table, a listless clerk picked up a box and fed the cards into one of the whirring machines.

I sat back down and waited.

"This coffee's for shit," Ernie said.

"They use it on the printers when they run out of ink."

"I believe it."

He shuffled through a news magazine looking for pictures of naked women but didn't find any.

"Don't they have a *National Geographic* around here?" he said.

I helped him look. No dice.

It took about a half hour but finally the harried sergeant came back out, holding a sheet of paper with the four numbers Herbalist So had given us on it.

"Checked everywhere," he said. "No luck. None of these numbers turned up. Not even in the history files. Which doesn't surprise me because all of them are of a sequence that we haven't even issued yet."

"Then they made a good guess when they chose those numbers."

"All four?" He frowned. "More likely they knew something."

"How could anyone determine what number sequences you use?"

"Beats me. It's strictly classified." He handed the paper back to me. "Sorry we couldn't help."

I pointed to the boxes on the table behind the counter. "What about those?"

"Those? Cards from PX's and commissaries around the country. They're just in."

"How about running them for us? Checking for these numbers?"

"But they just came in."

"It's a bother, that's for sure. But, you know, murder and all that . . ."

He sighed, looking extremely tired and harassed. "Okay. But it'll take a while."

"We'll wait."

He went back into the noisy bowels of the data processing unit and I sat back down next to Ernie.

"Dick," Ernie said.

It was almost midafternoon by the time the sergeant reemerged, and both Ernie and I were grumpy because with all the activity today we hadn't been able to squeeze in lunch. The sergeant handed me a three-page computer printout. Rows of numbers were printed on it. The numbers were so light, I had to squint to read them.

"Don't you guys ever change your ribbon?"

"Every week."

"What's all this supposed to mean?"

"Your number."

"Where?"

"One of them anyway." He pointed an ink-smudged finger at the second page. "Card was used once in the PX on Hialeah Compound. And again, less than an hour later, at the commissary on the same base."

"How long ago?"

"This morning."

"Where's Hialeah Compound?"

"Pusan."

"How'd these cards arrive here so fast?"

"Flown up by helicopter."

"They bring them in every day?"

"Every day. Unless the weather grounds the aircraft."

So Shipton had murdered the Nurse and then hopped on a train or a bus and headed down to Pusan, the southernmost city on the Korean Peninsula, a trip of about five hours. He'd appeared bright and early this morning at the PX and commissary, making purchases, knowing that we wouldn't be looking for him that far away.

I grabbed the printout. "Can I keep this?"

"Sure."

"Thanks for your help, Sarge."

Before he could say anything, Ernie and I were out the door, running for the jeep.

It was finally time to level with the First Sergeant. Not about everything, but about most things.

Before I had given him the whole story he raised his hand and said, "Hold it."

He checked on his intercom, received clearance, and the three of us marched down the slickly waxed hallway to the Provost Marshal's office. The receptionist eyed us suspiciously but the Provost Marshal, Colonel Stoneheart, was waiting for us and waved us on into his office. We took seats in comfortable leather chairs. The flags of the United States, the United Nations, and the Republic of Korea stood behind his desk.

The Provost Marshal relit his pipe.

"Okay," the First Sergeant said. "Go ahead."

I cleared my throat, hoping I'd be able to play this right. Ernie was tense; I needed to make sure they didn't ask him any questions. With two of us answering, they could trip us up.

"Cecil Whitcomb was a thief. You saw that, sir, in our preliminary reports. We have reason to believe that whoever killed Whitcomb down in Namdaemun knew him, or at least had seen him before."

"What reason?"

"We're not sure yet. We just don't think it was random."

Ernie shuffled in his chair. I continued.

"We got a lead that a woman in Mukyo-dong, a *kisaeng*—"

"A what?"

"A *kisaeng,* sir. A professional entertainer. Like a geisha girl."

"Oh." The Provost Marshal fiddled with his pipe. "And where in the hell is Mukyo-dong?"

"Downtown Seoul."

"Go ahead."

"So we got this tip—"

"Where'd you get this tip?" This was from the First Sergeant.

"Sources in Itaewon."

"Sources in Itaewon? You mean gossip from business girls."

I didn't answer.

The First Sergeant folded his arms. "Go ahead."

"So we went and talked to this girl. She knew a Korean man who owns a print shop, and he had an American friend. She thought this American guy was black-marketing, so we went to the print shop owner and got the guy's picture." Actually, the slicky boys stole the picture. But I didn't want to tell the colonel that I was working with *them.* "We also found some phony ration control plate numbers."

The First Sergeant and the Provost Marshal looked at each other.

"Good work," the First Sergeant said. "But you're not on the black market detail. You're investigating a murder."

"So this *kisaeng,* the next morning, ends up dead."

The Provost Marshal shuffled through some papers. "I saw something about that in the blotter reports. And another one in Itaewon."

"Yes. This American guy's next victim."

"What'd this Itaewon girl have to do with it?"

"She knew us."

The Provost Marshal puffed furiously on his pipe, but it had gone out. "Corporal Sueño, would you please explain yourself?"

"This guy somehow found out that Ernie and I were investigating the murder of Whitcomb. Although our lead in Mukyo-dong wasn't a very solid one, this guy, for reasons of his own, thought it might lead to something. He killed the *kisaeng* so she wouldn't be able to identify him, and then he killed the woman Ernie has been seeing in Itaewon, probably trying to scare us off the case."

The Provost Marshal looked at Ernie. Ernie remained completely stoic, as if he hadn't even heard what I said. The Provost Marshal turned back to me.

"It's sort of thin."

"You're right, sir, but if we can pick this guy up, interrogate him, we'll probably be able to pin the Whitcomb murder on him. If he hadn't been involved, why would he be murdering these women we talked to?"

I hadn't thought out very clearly what I was going to say to the First Sergeant and the Provost Marshal, but I was warming to the explanation now.

"He's getting desperate. He probably thinks we know more than we do, and even if he didn't kill Whitcomb, he certainly has information that will help. We can already bust him and turn him over to the KNP's for the murders of those two women."

"Okay," the Provost Marshal said. "We pick this guy up for questioning. But where can we find him?"

I pulled the folded computer printout from my pocket.

"We just got this from Data Processing. One of these phony RCP numbers, one of those associated with his photograph, was used down on Hialeah Compound in Pusan this morning. He probably thinks he's safe down there for a while. Ernie and I can go there now. Pick him up when he makes his next purchase."

The First Sergeant didn't like it. "Why not just notify the Pusan MP's?"

"How are we going to get the photograph down there to them that quickly? We'd have to send a courier down with it, anyway. Might as well be me and Ernie. Besides, the Pusan MP's have other things to worry about. Ernie and I wouldn't have anything else to concentrate on, other than busting this killer."

"What's his name?" the Provost Marshal asked.

"Beauregard Shipton. Lieutenant Commander, U.S. Navy. Former Liaison to the ROK Navy headquarters. Been AWOL for about three months."

The Provost Marshal set down his pipe. "An officer?"

I nodded.

He shuffled some papers, probably hoping it would give him time to think. Apparently it did.

"Okay. Very good report, Corporal Sueño. You and Bascom can go now. First Sergeant, you stay here."

The First Sergeant followed us into the hallway. "Wait in my office," he told us. He went back into the Provost Marshal's office. The door closed.

"Dick," Ernie said.

"Yeah. The world's full of them."

Instead of the First Sergeant's office, Ernie and I waited in the Admin section, shooting the breeze with Riley. Miss Kim still hadn't thawed out, so Ernie didn't know what to do with himself. And he was out of gum.

Riley pulled something out of his desk. "The KNP Liaison gave me this."

It was a color photo of the blood scrawled on the wall at the Nurse's hooch. He handed it to Ernie. Ernie didn't flinch.

He was acting tough. But that's all it was: an act. Deep down inside he was burning about the Nurse's death.

Ernie studied the photograph. "Goddamn," he said. " 'Dreamer.' That's your name, isn't it, pal?"

"One way to translate it."

"This guy's really got a hard-on for you."

I shrugged. Hearing it said that baldly didn't make me feel exactly warm and secure.

Lights blinked on Riley's phone. Carefully, he lifted the receiver, keeping the mouthpiece covered. After a few seconds he put the receiver back down.

"The honchos're burning up the wires."

"What for?"

"Getting clearance from the head shed. Making sure this doesn't embarrass the navy too much."

"Jesus," Ernie said. "What the hell's to clear? The guy's a stone killer."

"But he hasn't killed anybody important yet," Riley pointed out. He saw our grim faces.

"Sorry," he said.

A few minutes later the First Sergeant's heavy oxfords thundered down the hallway.

"Sueño! Bascom! I thought I told you to wait in my office!"

We rose but didn't answer.

"Never mind that now." The First Sergeant checked his wristwatch. "Go pack your bags. The last Blue Line leaves Seoul Station at seventeen hundred hours. I want you two on it."

Riley unlocked the bottom drawer of his desk. "I'll issue them some petty cash, Top."

"Fifty bucks should do it."

We all stared at the First Sergeant.

"Okay. A hundred each—but that's it."

As Riley counted out the greenbacks and filled out receipts for us to sign, Ernie made eye contact with Miss Kim. She looked worried and didn't seem to know what to do with her hands. Finally, she pulled out a handkerchief and scampered down the hallway to the ladies' room.

Ernie shrugged. As if to say, "Who can understand them anyway?"

32

THE SEOUL TRAIN STATION IS A BRICK MONOLITH COVERING A full city block with a huge dome towering above its center. The station looks like something out of Czarist Russia. Which in a way it is, since the "bears to the north," as the Koreans call them, built the station as a gift to the Korean king in the 1890's. The Russians' motives weren't completely pure, since at the time they were locked in a power struggle with Japan over influence in the Far East.

We pushed through the surging crowds of men in business suits and kids in school uniforms and old ladies with huge bundles balanced atop their heads. In all this madness there was a small sea of tranquility with the red-and-white cloverleaf of the 8th United States Army above its door. The RTO. The Rail Transportation Office. It had a lounge and a PX, and a ticket counter so GI's wouldn't have to stand in the long lines with the masses.

While Ernie went over to the counter to get our tickets, I grabbed the military phone on the green shelf and looked up a number in the narrow U.S. Forces Korea phone book.

After I dialed the number it rang twice, then a voice squeaked, "Distribution Center."

"Harvey?"

"Who's this?"

"George."

"Hmmm," he said. "Had any *strange* lately?"

"Last night, as a matter of fact."

"Anyone I know?"

"How could it be someone you know if it was strange?"

He didn't have an answer for that.

"Listen," I said, "do you have anything new? On that J-two business?"

"Some."

"What?"

Strange hesitated. "This line isn't secure."

"I'm on my way to Pusan. I don't have time to come in and talk. You questioned the security NCO at J-two. Nothing was missing, but he was going to double-check the items that had been disturbed."

"Hmmm."

"What were they?"

"Hard to say."

"I mean what was the subject of the documents? All I need is a general idea."

I heard a tapping on the phone.

"What was that?"

"Checking for bugs," Strange said.

"We're not being bugged, for Christ's sake. I just need the general subject."

Another long silence.

"Okay," I said. "She was Chinese. From Fujien Province. Came here with her family after Mao took over the mainland. Speaks Korean because she grew up here and went to school here, but right in the middle of things I had her lay a little Chinese on me. Just to see what it was like."

"And?"

"She reminded me of a beautiful bird in a tree singing a song of happiness."

"Perched on your branch?"

"Yeah. Perched on my branch. Now gimme the subject!"

"Tunnels."

"What? Did you say 'tunnels'?"

The line clicked and buzzed and went dead.

I thought of calling him back but decided against it. We didn't have much time until the Blue Line left and besides, Strange probably wasn't going to tell me anything more over the phone anyway.

Security guys. They're all a bunch of whackos.

We hustled out of the back door of the RTO down the long, covered corridors of the Seoul Train Station. The layout is massive, with signs everywhere written in Korean and English and crowds rushing through the overpasses and the underpasses heading like lemmings for the various trains that find their hub there.

The Blue Line is the only deluxe accommodation that runs nonstop all the way down the Korean Peninsula, from Seoul to Pusan. Well, not exactly nonstop. It stops for exactly four minutes each at the two major cities along the route: Taejon and Taegu. The entire trip of about 340 kilometers takes about five hours. Leaving at five P.M. would get us into Pusan a little after ten, enough time to scrounge accommodations before the midnight curfew. The government won't allow trains to travel any later.

We stood on the platform waiting with the other passengers, mostly well-dressed Koreans; ladies in fine western outfits or the colorful flowing skirts and blouses of the traditional Korean *hanbok*, men in suits. Vendors shouted the benefits of their wares: candy and snacks for the kids, or dried cuttlefish and a tin of orange juice to wash it down, or baskets of fat winter pears ready to be peeled.

Ernie stopped one of the saleswomen and bought two large packs of ginseng gum. He was ready now for any adventure.

The train pulled up in a shriek of billowing steam. We climbed aboard on the wrong car but managed to push our way through the crowded aisle until we found our seats. We stowed our bags in the overhead rack and leaned back in the comfortable seats. Plenty of legroom.

After ten minutes, the whistle sounded, the conductor bellowed, and slowly we started to chug forward.

The blue-suited stewardess came by, checking to make sure everyone was seated and comfortable. Ernie stared at her and twisted his head 180 degrees as she passed, zeroing in on her butt.

When she was gone, he leaned back in his seat and closed his eyes.

"Wake me if she comes back."

"Will do."

Out the clean plate glass window, I watched the city of Seoul roll by. Warehouses, residential apartments, the blue expanse of the Han River, and the trees and red tile roofs of Yongdungpo. We were heading south and gaining speed. Soon the buildings of the city's suburbs gave way to vast tracks of frozen brown rice paddies and blue hills in the distance and little straw-thatched huts huddling amidst patches of frozen snow.

I thought of this guy named Shipton and I thought of Cecil Whitcomb. What was it that had brought these two together? What was the deadly connection? Whatever it was it seemed just out of reach, on the other side of a wall of mist, waiting for me to reach out and grab it. I thought of a *kisaeng* named Miss Ku and a beautiful young woman who only wanted to be Ernie's wife.

And I thought of tunnels.

Strange had said "tunnels." Something classified in J-2 had been about tunnels.

Of course there were all sorts of tunnels. A new one for commuter traffic had been built beneath Namsan Mountain just south of downtown Seoul. There was one being carved beneath the city, the beginning of a subway system that should be finished in about twenty years. But most of all, I thought about the ones dug by the North Koreans and just discovered by our side about a year ago. Three of them. Right under the DMZ. With a track down the center and wide enough for three armed soldiers to march abreast. The newspaper stories had estimated that the North Korean People's Army could move a fully equipped infantry battalion through each of these three tunnels in about two hours.

But what in the world did that have to do with this case?

Probably the whole thing—dust disturbed on the top of a filing cabinet, folders moved from the edge of the drawer to the center, the feeling that someone had tampered with their documents—was strictly the overheated paranoia of a bunch of half-nuts Security NCO's.

If they were all like Strange, who could trust any of them?

I watched a white crane wing slowly across a frozen field. What was he doing here this late in the winter?

A strange bird.

Everything I looked at—the distant hills, the huddled farm communities, the gently rolling rivers—faded into the bloodied body of the Nurse.

The trip took longer than we thought because the ROK Army was conducting war games in the hills just south of Taejon. The train screeched to a halt amongst the frost-covered peaks and soldiers hopped aboard, holding their M16 rifles pointed toward the sky, spot-checking identification and searching the baggage for evidence of enemy commandos.

It was all pretty silly, but in this country citizens put up with any indignity from the military. For one thing, they remember the horrors of the Korean War. For another, they don't have any choice.

When an armed party approached us, Ernie opened one eye and growled at them. The soldiers must've thought that messing with an irate American would make their officer-in-charge unhappy, so they ignored us. After about forty minutes we started moving again.

When the train finally pulled into the big cement bulwark of the Pusan Train Station, it was already after eleven. Less than an hour until curfew.

We were both worn out, and at the moment I didn't give a damn about Shipton or Whitcomb or the murder case—all I wanted to do was get my butt off that damn rattling platform. We slung our AWOL bags over our shoulders and plowed through the milling crowds to a long row of kimchi cabs outside. The drivers loitered in front of their cars, smoking, exchanging banter, hoping for one more good fare before the world closed up at curfew.

"Where to?" Ernie said.

It wasn't as cold down here but still our breath billowed before us.

"Probably too late to get billeting at Hialeah Compound. Best we find a *yoguan*."

Across the broad road that ran in front of the train station were rows of two- and three-story cement and brick buildings, some with blinking lights advertising warm floors and baths.

"Over there," Ernie said. "Maybe they offer girls, too."

"Maybe."

Always thinking, that Ernie.

We trotted across the big road against the light and entered the maze of alleys between the buildings. *Soju* houses and soup joints were still doing a good business at this hour. Sandwiched between a teahouse and a dumpling shop was a doorway that led upstairs to the Hei-un Yoguan. Upstairs, an old woman sat on the floor in a little room watching a Korean comedy show on a TV that was turned up way too loud. She lowered it when she saw us.

I greeted her and asked about rooms, and she said she had two. After setting the price, we gave the money in advance and she gave us keys and pointed down the hallway.

Our rooms were small but comfortable enough. Each had a flat hard bed and a cylindrical bead-filled pillow and a bathtub with a nozzle on a long rubber hose for a shower.

Luxurious accommodations for a former field soldier.

Neither of us felt like going outside and elbowing amongst the natives for some chop, so we ordered Chinese food from the old woman. In about twenty minutes a boy brought a tin box filled with fried rice and sweet-and-sour pork and a plastic pot of barley tea.

After we ate, we shoved the plates and utensils out in the hallway. Despite Ernie's protestations of wanting to find a girl, he didn't do anything about it.

Shortly after midnight the city quieted down and I lay beneath my half-open window, moonlight streaming in, and pulled the covers over my head. A few minutes later, I passed out.

Something pounded on my door.

"George! Reveille! It's oh-dark-thirty."

Ernie's voice. I looked around. He was right. It was still dark.

I climbed out of bed, unlatched the door, and let him in.

"I don't know about you," he said, "but I want to get out of this roach coach, make it over to the compound, and find some real chow. You know—coffee, toast, all that shit. And read the *Stripes*."

"Yeah. Let's do that."

We had a lot of work ahead of us. No sense putting it off.

Ten minutes later we were outside. When we found a cab, I told him to take us to Hialeah Compound. The driver roared through broad, wide-open streets, not nearly as crowded as those in Seoul. The compound was farther inland than I thought. About five miles from the Port of Pusan.

The Japanese Imperial Army, for some reason, had been big on cavalry. The compound that is now Hialeah had been used by them to race horses. When the U.S. Army took it over, some wiseacre decided to call it Hialeah Compound, after the famous racetrack in the States. The name stuck.

A narrow road lined with shops and bars led straight into a dead end that was the front gate of Hialeah Compound. A big cement MP guard shack sat on the side, and barbed wire ran along the top of the closed chain-link fence. We got out, paid the driver, and marched into an open door marked "Pedestrian Entrance."

A bored MP wearing a gleaming black helmet liner sat behind the counter. A stenciled sign behind him instructed us to show our identification and pass upon entering or leaving Hialeah Compound, by Order of the Commander.

Friendly place.

We showed him our ID's and he gave us directions to the billeting office. Just outside the MP shack sat the NCO Club. Not open yet, but reassuring to know that it was there.

"Ice cubes and cold beer," Ernie said. "Who could ask for more?"

The Korean clerk at the billeting office had us fill out a couple of forms, took copies of our temporary duty orders, and finally gave us the key to a section of a Quonset hut. He told us there were two bunks in there and we'd have to share. It didn't bother us. We didn't plan to spend much time there anyway.

After dropping off our bags in the room, we forgot about breakfast and went straight to the PX.

It was a good-sized building, which made sense because although the population of the compound was small—only about two thousand—there was still a big demand for the PX products off base, so everybody bought their full ration every month.

The front door was locked. We walked around back and found a door open at the loading dock. After wandering around for a while we found an administrative office and a Korean secretary sitting at a desk in front of a door marked "Manager."

The manager was a small American man, a slight paunch under his business suit, and prematurely balding on top. He nodded enthusiastically when we told him why we were there. No, he said, the courier hadn't picked up the ration control data cards from last night.

He took us into a storage room marked "Layaway," cleared a table for us, and plopped down three oblong boxes of computer punch cards.

"You'll keep them in order, won't you?" he asked. "If they are out of order it causes them a terrible time up at Data Processing in Seoul, and I always receive a nasty phone call from their officer in charge."

"We'll do our best," I said.

"Got any coffee?" Ernie asked.

"Of course. Just ask Miss Lee. She'll be happy to get some for you."

I wondered how happy Miss Lee would be about serving two strangers, but I didn't say anything. The manager left, and Ernie followed him out and came back a few minutes later with two steaming cups of coffee in mugs marked "Army & Air Force Exchange Service."

"That Miss Lee is one fine-looking mama," Ernie said.

I was worried that he'd disappear on me but instead he took off his jacket, draped it over the back of one of the folding chairs, and rolled up his sleeves.

The coffee wasn't bad. Strong and hot, which is what I needed.

We went to work. We compared the printed numbers across the top of each card in the boxes with the four numbers we had that we expected Shipton to be using. It was tedious work. Every few minutes I had to take a break, sip on some coffee, and let my eyes uncross. Ernie took off his round-lensed glasses and set them on the table next to him.

A couple of PX employees—Koreans—wandered in, staring at us curiously. They took off their coats, hung them on the rack, and went back out onto the floor.

While we worked, the store opened, soft music was turned on out in the main room, and we heard the buzz of consumers doing their part to keep the international economy humming.

When I finished my coffee I decided to go after some more, but Ernie said he'd do the honors. Trying to keep Miss Lee all to himself.

It took us another hour and a half to go through the cards but in the end we had nothing. Not one card matched any of the numbers that had been provided to me by Herbalist So. I had the nagging feeling we'd screwed up somewhere. Maybe missed one of the cards. But we'd been careful as we went through them, pulling each one out, holding it up to the light, passing it across the table for a double check. There was no sense going through them again.

The manager came in.

"Ration Control's here to pick up the cards." He smiled. "I hope you're about finished."

"Yeah, we're finished."

Finished for good, I thought.

Ernie walked out into the main part of the PX, put his hands on his hips, gazed around, and walked back in.

"Goddamn shoppers," he said. "Don't they ever get tired of it?"

The PX manager looked at him as if he were a bona fide madman.

"Maybe we ought to go through the new cards," Ernie said.

"What?"

"You know, the cards that have been anviled this morning. The ration control plate guy's packing them up now."

"But he's in a big hurry," the PX manager said. "He has to make rounds of all the outlets."

"Come on," I told Ernie.

At the row of cash registers we found a guy in fatigues. His armband said "Ration Control" below the 8th Army red-and-white cloverleaf patch.

He was a Spec 4, and after I showed him my CID identification and loomed over him for a few seconds he docilely brought the new cards back into the room.

We leaned over the table, working, and suddenly Ernie stiffened his back.

"Goddamn," he said. "I got one! The son of a bitch was just in here!"

I snatched the card from his fingertips and compared the number to my list.

"You're right. It was him." I turned to the PX manager and pointed to a code number in the upper left of the card. "Which cashier was this?"

"Fourteen. I don't know. I'll have to look it up."

Number Fourteen turned out to be a middle-aged Korean woman who'd been a PX employee for years, and when we pulled her off the cash register and escorted her back into the office, she was not only worried but her hands were shaking.

I handed her the card. Two cartons of cigarettes and a hundred dollars of miscellaneous items had been marked off.

"Do you remember this sale?"

She gazed at it a few seconds, then shook her head. I pulled out the photograph.

"How about this man?"

"Yes," she said. "I think so. Very big man. He wear hat." She reached up to her ears and jerked down, as if pulling on a cap.

"Did he say anything to you?"

"No. Just buy and go."

"Have you ever seen him before?"

She shook her head again. "I don't think so."

We checked with the ID card checker at the front door, but he didn't remember the man at all.

"Looks like we screwed up royally," Ernie said.

"But he's still nearby," I said. "If you wanted to make as much money as you could—fast—on the black market, where would you go next?"

"The package store."

"And then?"

"The commissary."

Without any good-byes we were out the door, jogging across the brown grass of the parade field, heading toward the little building that sold GI's in Pusan all the duty-free booze they could drink.

There was only one cashier at the package store and not much traffic. He recognized the photograph immediately.

"He go. Maybe thirty minutes."

"Where?"

"I don't know. PX taxi wait for him."

"What did he buy?"

"Here." He pulled out the ration control card and showed it to us. Four quarts of Johnnie Walker Black Label. The most expensive brand the store carried, and a full ration for the month. Also two cases of beer and two cases of soft drinks.

"Where's the commissary?"

The man pointed and we were out the door.

A row of black Ford Granada PX taxis stood in front of the Hialeah Compound Commissary. We checked to see if any of them were already loaded with goods and waiting for a customer to return, but none were.

I showed the drivers the photograph of Shipton. But nobody

recognized him or remembered a cab waiting for a fare. Either Shipton hadn't arrived yet or we'd missed him completely.

Ernie kept watch outside while I went in. Without bothering to check with management, I interrupted each one of the Korean cashiers right in the middle of her work, flashed my badge, and showed her the photograph. Each woman shook her head until I reached aisle number seven.

"Yes," she told me. "He go. Maybe fifteen, twenty minutes ago."

"Did he say where?"

Her forehead crinkled. "No."

"Let me see his card."

"No can do."

The ration control punch cards here were dropped into locked metal boxes with two padlocks on the top. If they operated like they did in Seoul, the Ration Control representative would have the key to one lock and the store manager would have the other.

"What did he buy?"

"Everything."

"Everything?"

"Every ration item. Also a lot of oxtail and bananas."

Prime black market stuff.

"Did he say anything? Anything at all?"

"No. He very quiet. Pay cash."

"Any hundreds?"

Bills of fifty dollars or higher have to be recorded on a sheet of paper with the serial number listed and the name and social security number of the presenter. Another of the unbelievable steps 8th Army takes in their attempt to stop black-marketing. Not that it works.

"No," the cashier said. "Just twenties."

"Did you see a cab outside waiting for him?"

She shook her head emphatically. "No way. I'm too busy for that."

She glanced down the line of waiting shoppers and my eyes followed her. The women behind loaded carts stared at me with dull, resentful eyes.

I smiled, waved at them, and ran out the door.

Ernie stepped out of the shadows.

"Shipton's already been and gone," I said, "with a big load. Only thing to do now is try to find the taxi."

I jumped into the cab on the end of the line and told the driver to get his dispatcher on the radio. The little box clicked and buzzed and when a Korean voice came on the line, the driver handed the mike to me, pointing at which button I should push.

"This is Agent Sueño," I said. "Criminal Investigation Division. Do you speak English?"

"Yes," a crackling voice said tentatively.

"We're after a man who picked up a PX cab, probably at the main PX. Then he went to the package store and then the commissary. He is a big man, light brown hair, and wearing a wool cap."

Suddenly I caught myself. If Shipton was in a PX cab right now, he might've had the driver turn his radio up. He could be listening to this conversation.

I switched to Korean, hoping Shipton didn't speak it well enough to follow me, and told the dispatcher that I'd made a mistake. I told him I wanted him to inquire on a general broadcast if anybody had a passenger who fit that description but I wanted him to use only Korean (which he normally would have anyway) because I didn't want the man to know we were after him.

He told me he understood. I heard conversation in the background, chatter amongst the other dispatchers, then he came back on the line.

"We can speak English," he said. "Man no can hear."

My heart sank. "He's already out of the cab?" Once Shipton hit the streets, we could lose him again.

"No. He's in the cab, but cab too far away to pick up signal."

"Where in the hell is he going?"

"To Texas Street."

Texas Street. The nightclub and red light district that ran along the strip right in front of the Port of Pusan, catering to sailors of every nationality. Less than a half mile from the train station district, near the little *yoguan* we'd stayed in.

"Do you have an address?"

"No. Driver just say he go Texas Street."

"I want to talk to that driver. Now!"

"No can do. Too far away."

"If we take another cab down there, when we get in range, we'll be able to talk to this driver, won't we?"

"Yes," the dispatcher answered. "That's fastest way. It's cab number one-four-five. Pak-si is the driver."

"Good. We're leaving now."

I glanced at our driver. He was about forty, heavy lines in his face, and he looked worried. I spoke back into the mike. "Explain the situation to our driver. Tell him we want to find Pak-si and find him *fast.*"

I handed the mike to the driver. He and the dispatcher chatted away for a few seconds. Ernie sat in the front seat. I climbed in back.

After his conversation with the dispatcher, the driver didn't seem any less worried than he had been but he backed the cab up and put it in gear. We slid past the line of shoppers loading bagfuls of groceries into the trunks of the waiting cabs.

Once we passed through the main gate of the compound and were out on the broad roadways heading into downtown Pusan, Ernie patted the driver on the shoulder.

"Don't worry, *ajjosi.* My partner and me, we're *taaksan* number-one policemen. We catch bad guy, no sweat."

The worried man nodded, flashed a wan smile, and turned back to the road.

I patted the .38 under my coat and wished I felt as confident as Ernie.

Chasing a murderous Navy Seal. On Texas Street in the red light district. Not the best way to round out your morning.

33

IT DOESN'T SNOW AS OFTEN DOWN SOUTH IN PUSAN, BUT THERE'S more rain and it can still get awfully cold. The roads were slick, and fat clouds swept into the city off the choppy gray waters of the Straits of Korea.

When we were halfway to Texas Street the driver clicked on his radio and tried to contact Pak-si. No dice. About a mile farther on he tried again: This time the little speaker in the metal box crackled to life. The two drivers spoke so rapidly I didn't catch most of it but I did learn that Pak-si had already dropped off his fare and was returning to Hialeah Compound. I told our driver to set up a rendezvous point. I had to talk to Pak-si.

Five minutes later, we sat at the curb of a huge circular intersection with a statue in the middle. It was a granite replica of men and women striving forward together in an heroic effort to fight back the Communist hordes who had surrounded this city in the winter of 1950.

These big round traffic circles dotted the flat topography of the city and were responsible for a lot of accidents. Whoever the genius was who had designed them should've been run over by a speeding kimchi cab.

"Are you sure he's coming?" I was becoming impatient.

The driver clicked on his radio, spoke briefly to Pak-si, and turned back to me.

"Maybe five minutes."

Ernie climbed out of the cab and trotted through the rain to a little open-front store displaying the usual soft drinks and dried cuttlefish and discs of puffed rice. He bought three bottles of Bacchus D, a concoction of fruit drink and painkiller designed to ward off headaches, and came back and offered some to me and the driver. As soon as we twisted the caps off the little brown bottles and drank them down, another bulky Ford Granada with a plastic light atop pulled up behind us.

Our driver hadn't turned on his meter—police business—but I handed him three dollars anyway. He nodded, started his engine, and sped out of there as fast as he could.

We climbed into the cab with Pak-si. He was a younger driver with straight black hair and a brown, leathery face and one eye that seemed to have been damaged in some way.

"*Kapshida!*" I said. "*Bali!*" Let's go! Quickly!

"Where?"

"To wherever you dropped off the man with the hat."

He revved up the engine and started to click on the meter, but Ernie showed him his badge and held up the palm of his hand.

"*Kongja,*" he said. One of the few Korean words he knew, but one of his favorites: Free.

Pak-si's face soured but he drove resolutely forward, fighting his way into the flow of circling traffic.

On the way I interrogated him.

He told me that a man had come out of the PX with two large bags and he had helped him load them in the trunk of the cab. I flashed the photo. He glanced at it, then turned his concentration back to the road. Yes, that was the man.

After leaving the PX, they'd gone to the package store and after that to the commissary.

A routine black market run. Nothing the drivers weren't used to.

I asked him if the man had acted strange in any way. If he'd seemed nervous.

No, Pak-si said. He was very relaxed.

After loading up at the commissary the man had told him to take him to Texas Street. This was a little unusual because most of the Hialeah Compound GI's did their black-marketing close in, at some of the joints near the compound. Still, going to Texas Street wasn't unheard of. If a guy has a girlfriend who works one of the clubs on Texas Street, he might deliver the goods to her hooch. That's what Pak-si expected, but that's not what happened.

I asked him what did happen.

Pak-si's passenger seemed to know the back alleys of the Texas Street district well. He guided Pak-si to a residential area on the hills behind the nightclubs and had him stop in a narrow alley.

"Did you help him unload?"

Yes. And he carted all the stuff into the home of an old woman who obviously wasn't his girlfriend but must be a black market mama-san.

I asked Pak-si how long he'd been driving a PX cab. He told me eight years. If he'd never been to that joint before, it couldn't be a usual selling spot for Hialeah GI's. He agreed with that. It was the first time he'd ever been to the place and seen the old woman.

Pak-si pulled off the main road, zigzagged through alleys, and suddenly we were cruising down the main drag of the district known as Texas Street.

How it got its name I wasn't sure. The street's real name wasn't Texas. In fact, most streets in Korea don't have names. Only districts are named, and they are divided into smaller compartments called *dong* and *bonji*. Then *ho*, the actual address numbers. I had to believe that the nickname Texas Street came into existence because at night, when the place was crawling with business girls and drunken sailors, it reminded Koreans of what they thought the Wild West must've been like.

Now the district was quiet, and the unlit neon signs dripped with rain. Almost all the doors of the dozens of nightclubs were bolted. Only a few were open, beaded curtains rustling in the wet breeze from the sea.

Pak-si turned up another alley and then down another and another. I put my hand on his shoulder and told him to pull over before he reached our final destination, so we could walk up. He turned down one more street and found a spot to park against a high stone wall.

"Go up there," he said. "And turn right. Second door on the left."

We thanked him.

Did he have to wait, he asked.

No. All I had left were twenties and a ten and two bucks. I handed him the two bucks. He shrugged. Easy money.

As soon as we climbed out of the cab, he released the brake, shifted into neutral, and rolled back down the hill.

We walked up the road and peered around the corner. Nothing moved.

"You think he's still here?" Ernie asked.

"Probably not. He seems to have a habit of moving fast. But let's not take any chances."

I pulled the .38 out of the holster. "You go in first. I'll come in behind you."

"Right."

The walls were too high to see anything. When we reached the doorway in the metal gate, Ernie kicked it in, which was sort of unnecessary since it was unlocked anyway. It crashed back on itself with a great bang. Ernie ducked through the door. I was right behind him.

A tiny old woman in a sweater and a long gray dress emerged from the hooch and stood on the narrow wooden porch.

"Migun isso?" I asked. Is there a GI here?

"Oopso," she said. *"Imi kasso."* Not here. He already left.

We searched the little room anyway and checked out back. No sign of a six-foot-two Navy Seal. Plenty of PX goodies, though.

"How much did you pay him?" I asked the old woman.

"Not your business."

I showed her my badge. "We could have you arrested."

"Go ahead."

She was a pugnacious little crone.

"Where'd the American go?"

"I don't know."

"What's his name?"

"I don't know."

"How did he find you?"

She raised and lowered her narrow shoulders. "Girls on Texas Street. They know me."

"Which club?"

"Any club."

"When's the American coming back?"

"I don't know."

"Has he been here before?"

"First time."

"What'd he look like?"

"Big. Like you. But light skin. Like him." She pointed at Ernie.

I pulled out the photo. "Is this him?"

She looked at Shipton's picture and then up at me.

"Yes." For the first time concern edged her wrinkled face. "What did he do?"

"He killed three people."

Her eyes widened. She sat down on the porch without bothering to wipe off the droplets of rain.

"Three people?" she said.

"Yes."

"Koreans or Americans?"

"One Englishman. Two Koreans."

"English?"

I nodded. The old woman shook her head. Her voice became less strident. Soft. Almost as if she were in awe.

"I never see this man before. He come this morning. First time. I paid him two hundred and thirty thousand won." She waved at the black market goods piled in the back of her hooch. "Not bad price. I wanted to pay less, but he said he would put them back in the cab and go somewhere else. So I give him a little more. Anyway, I make money. He was very quiet. Very serious. Didn't seem like GI. Most GI just give black market stuff to girls. Girls bring to me, sell. I always get good price from the girls because they not smart. Think only of today. Of new hairdo. Of new makeup they want to buy. This man, he very patient. Wait until finally we settle on price. He count money, put in his pocket, and go."

She looked up at me and then at Ernie, as if she were puzzled. The mistlike rain splattered on her face and dress. "I never see before. It's true."

She crossed her arms over her withered chest and shivered.

"I never want to see again."

The thought of murder had somewhat chastened the old woman, and before we left she told us the names of the clubs from which she received referrals. They were clubs nearby on the strip.

As we walked down the hill toward the sea I breathed deeply of the salt air, fighting off the disappointment at having been so close to Shipton and yet missing him again. But we weren't back to square one. Shipton was in the neighborhood somewhere. Maybe just a few hundred yards from where we stood right now. We had his photograph and we had plenty of shoe leather.

"Is it possible that he'll make another black market run today?" Ernie said.

"I don't think so. He maxed out his monthly ration on that card, so now he'd have to use a different card and a different ID. Too risky. Somebody on the compound might remember him, call the MP's."

We stepped gingerly on the wet cobbled streets, which sloped down to the sea. Gulls soared in graceful circles above us.

"So what would you do," I asked, "if you'd just cleared over a hundred thousand won on the black market and you didn't have to go to work and you were right smack dab in the middle of Texas Street?"

"I'd get laid," Ernie said promptly.

"So would I. Which sets out an interesting course for this investigation."

Ernie rubbed his hands together. "Time to get cracking, pal. What we gotta do, we gotta do."

"That's what I like about you, Ernie. Dedicated to your tasks."

"You got that right."

We checked the open bars on Texas Street first, hoping Shipton would be spending some of his hard-earned money. No luck.

We wandered around, trying to look like horny sailors—which wasn't hard except for the sailor part—and, as we expected, we received a few propositions. All of which we accepted. Every hooch we went into, though, was full of willing girls but no Shipton. We showed his photograph around, but all we received in return were blank stares. And disappointed scowls when the business women realized they weren't going to make any money.

It was noontime now and the district was starting to come alive. A few merchant marines prowled the streets: Filipinos, Greeks, Dutchmen. They were off watch now—or whatever their work shifts were called—and it was time for a little fun. Neon crackled and sparked to life under the drizzling rain. Jukeboxes started up. Girls in miniskirts appeared in dark doorways.

Ernie and I never had gotten that breakfast we wanted on the compound so we decided to break for some chow at a noodle shop with big steamed windows. We sat up front where, after rubbing a couple of portholes on the plate glass, we had a pretty good view of the street.

A girl of about thirteen took our order. She looked like she should've been in school. Two bowls of *meiun-tang*. Colas. No beer.

"He could be anywhere," Ernie said.

"Yeah. He might've gone to the train station and caught the Blue Line heading north or he might've hopped on a bus or he could be next door taking a nap. The only thing we got going for us is that he doesn't know how close we are."

"At least we don't *think* he knows."

"Sure. But it doesn't seem likely. And if he doesn't know, he'll do what he wants to do."

"Which is stay here on Texas Street for a few days?"

"Wouldn't you? He doesn't know we have the stolen ration control numbers. If I were him, I'd use the four plates to the max, then head north."

"So maybe we can stake out the PX tomorrow and catch him when he comes through the door."

"Yeah. Maybe. But since we can't count on it we have to stake out Texas Street for now."

"Tough duty."

The girl brought our steaming bowls of red broth. A glassy-eyed mackerel stared up at me, surrounded by three clam shells atop a pile of onion shoots. The girl set down the bowls of rice and the plates of fermented cabbage and diced turnip while Ernie and I unwrapped our wooden chopsticks and pried them apart. After pouring our colas, she left us and we dug in; all the while keeping an eye on the people parading through the lively drizzle of Texas Street.

After we finished eating, we paid the girl, left her a little tip which sort of surprised her, and went back to work.

The Texas Street district was composed of one main drag stretching about three blocks, with side streets shooting off from it. We decided to start on the northernmost end, near the black market mama-san's hooch, and work our way south.

As more and more joints opened, we had more and more opportunities to ask questions and flash Shipton's photograph. Apparently he hadn't made a big splash in town because every bartender and business girl and boy mopping floors swore they'd never seen him before.

We also checked *yoguan*s. Climbing up creaking staircases that smelled of urine and charcoal smoke, flashing the black-and-white photograph to old men and women who looked as weathered as the wooden buildings they lived in, always receiving the same unknowing stare.

I was beginning to understand why even the ROK Navy investigative services hadn't been able to collar Shipton.

At midafternoon, a truck with workmen came by and made a big to-do about climbing up power poles and unraveling a cloth banner across the roadway. The wind and rain fought them but they finally unfurled the long canvas, and it rippled out its message: *Welcome,* U.S.S. *Kitty Hawk!*

We asked some of the girls in the bars about it and they bubbled with excitement. The *Kitty Hawk* had already entered the harbor. Tonight the liberty launches would be pulling into the port loaded with American sailors, all wearing tight pants bursting at the seams with three months' pay.

Girls were pouring in from all over the country, they told us, from as far north as Seoul and Inchon, to get in on the easy money.

"Just what we need," Ernie said. "Three thousand horny sailors getting in our way. And half of them who look just like Shipton. Or close enough so a bunch of busy Koreans won't be able to tell the difference."

I thought about it for a minute. "He planned it this way," I said.

"What do you mean?"

"I mean what better time to make a bunch of runs on the PX than when there's an aircraft carrier in town? The squids'll go right over to the compound, load up on cigarettes and scotch, and sell it here on Texas Street to pay for their three days of liberty. The clerks on the compound won't have time to notice a guy going in and out three or four times a day, each time using a different name."

"Yeah," Ernie said. "He'll just be another sailor."

"And maybe he plans to run Texas Street, too. The MP's and Shore Patrol will be too preoccupied with breaking up fights and keeping sailors from tearing down the town to notice what one quiet guy might be up to."

"So he heard that the *Kitty Hawk* was on the way in and decided to take a working vacation?"

"That's what it looks like."

"But he's not expecting us to be searching for him."

"I hope not."

"So we'll find him in the crowd." Ernie thought about it for a minute. "Have to wade through a lot of squids, though. Up to our assholes in squids."

By the time the sun went down we'd checked out every bar or flophouse or brothel that ever existed on Texas Street. I'd come to the conclusion that Shipton wasn't here; he was hiding out somewhere else. Still, I believed there was a good chance he'd show that night.

We found a cozy bar where the girls wore their hair up, held in place by jade pins, and floated around the room in the rustling silk of their full-skirted *Hanbok* gowns. Texas Street catered to just about every taste. Even if you were strange enough to prefer your women elegant and well-dressed.

The girls spoiled the effect of their appearance, however, when I listened to their conversations in Korean. They talked about how to get the most money out of a sailor and how to avoid VD and what to do if you got pregnant.

They were just as foulmouthed as any of the other girls on the street. But I liked the joint. The music was soft and the bar stools comfortable and fish floated in blue aquariums. The gentle notes of a Korean love song warbled out of the sound system. The women here probably serviced over-the-hill bosun's mates who could hardly get it up anymore.

Another reason I liked this place was that they had draft OB Beer served in frosted mugs. It had been a hard day. Ernie and I were putting them down pretty good. We were both hungry but didn't feel like leaving the tap, so we gave one of the girls some money and sent her out for "cut bait."

That's what we called it because it attracted business girls like schools of fish.

What she brought back was actually small bundles of grease-stained newspaper. She set the bundles down on the bar, unwrapped them, and the aroma of hot onion rings and batter-fried tempura billowed upward. The girls swarmed around us, picking away greedily at the hot slices. Somebody poured soy sauce onto a plate and we all dipped and munched and talked.

We ate as much as we could and enjoyed the girls rubbing their silk-covered bodies against us. After the chow was gone, however, Ernie seemed a little morose. I wondered if it was the fatigue of traveling. After the fourth beer, he started talking.

"She was pregnant," he said.

"The girl who bought the onion rings?"

"No. The Nurse."

I set my beer down. Looked at him. Waited.

"She said she wanted to 'present' the baby to me, but I didn't answer her right away." He sipped on his beer and looked over at me. "That's why the Nurse said she'd kill herself if my extension didn't go through."

"Because the marriage paperwork takes six months?"

"Yeah." Ernie looked at me, studying my face. "You think we'll catch this guy?"

I nodded. "We'll get him."

He studied my face for a while longer. "Okay," he said, "I believe you."

A pack of American sailors burst into the room like Irish banshees on New Year's Eve. Their black uniforms were neatly pressed and their spotless white hats sat at jaunty angles on their heads. I saw the patch on their left shoulders: U.S.S. *Kitty Hawk.*

The girls beamed as if a host from heaven had just floated down from the sky. Soon the place was crammed with sailors and every girl was on somebody's lap, being pulled and tugged and handed around.

The bartender was too busy to even refill our beer mugs. We tossed down the last of the suds and left.

Texas Street was like what I imagined Rio de Janeiro must be like during the Carnival season. Except nobody was half naked because it was too cold, and almost all the men wore the uniforms of the U.S. Navy. They traveled in packs. The doors to the clubs were wide open and music and screaming roiled out onto the street and every seat inside was taken and so was every girl.

There weren't any Hialeah Compound GI's around. They had a tendency to stay away when a big ship was in port, resenting the squids for running up the prices.

Since we weren't in uniform and wore only our blue jeans and nylon jackets, we were a little conspicuous ourselves. We stayed in the shadows. Scanning the road for anyone who looked like Shipton.

A couple of times we thought we spotted him, but when we got close we realized it was someone else. We bought bottles of beer from street vendors and drank under awnings, protected from the sporadic rain, keeping an eye on the street scene.

As curfew approached, things didn't seem to be slowing down, but a phalanx of a dozen burly guys with batons and Shore Patrol arm bands plowed through Texas Street, warning everybody to get off the streets or back to the ship by midnight.

We were going to have to find shelter, too. There weren't any girls available so we faded back a few blocks from Texas Street until we stumbled into a little place that advertised sleeping accommodations. The Koreans call it a *yoin-suk*, not as high-class as a *yoguan* and not nearly as luxurious as a hotel.

The woman who owned it said she had one private room left and Ernie and I could have it for only seven thousand won. About ten bucks. I thought it was a little steep for this kind of joint, but the *Kitty Hawk* was in, so what the hell. We paid her and told her we had to go back out for a few minutes, and she promised to keep the front gate open for us as long as we weren't out too late after curfew. I told her we wouldn't be.

Back on Texas Street the crowds were beginning to thin. Sailors wandered down to the pier and caught launches that were lined up to take them back to the ship.

Back in the bar district there was nothing new. No sign of anybody who looked like Shipton.

Korean National Police had now joined the Shore Patrol and were helping to shoo everyone off the street in the last ten minutes before the world shut down. Bars closed their doors and shuttered their windows.

When the Shore Patrol reached us, I showed my badge to the guy in charge and asked if he'd seen anyone who looked like the mug in the photograph. He shook his head, but showed it to the other Shore Patrol guys. Nobody remembered Shipton.

The Korean policemen I asked hardly glanced at the photograph. With a city teeming with foreigners they weren't likely to be able to tell one from the other—unless he had three arms and horns.

But they were curious as to why we were looking for him. I told them that he was a deserter, which seemed to satisfy them. Koreans take desertion a lot more seriously than we do. In fact, you can be executed for it.

When the streets were almost empty, we wound our way through the dark alleys back to our little *yoin-suk*. Anywhere from six to ten workingmen and poor women lay on the floor of each room sleeping, their possessions jumbled nearby.

Being rich foreigners, we were ushered into our private accommodations in the back. The old woman even handed us our own porcelain pee pot.

We rolled out the sleeping mats. After folding my clothes and setting my wallet and badge and pistol under the bead-filled pillow, I turned off the bulb. The room was stuffy but warm, and we were both too exhausted to do anything but go straight to sleep.

I awoke with a start.

"Ernie." I nudged his shoulder. "Wake up."

"Huh?"

He tried to pull the cotton comforter over his head.

"Wake up. We have to go."

He propped himself up on his elbow. "Go? What're you talking about? It's still dark."

I looked at the fluorescent dots on my wristwatch. "It's almost four-thirty. A lot of sailors will be up and on their way back to the *Kitty Hawk*."

"So what?"

"So I finally realized what Shipton's doing here in Pusan."

"I'm glad you figured it out, because apparently he wasn't getting laid."

"No. He has bigger plans in mind."

"George, I wish I knew what in the hell you were talking about."

"No time now." I turned on the bulb. "Come on. Get dressed. We have to get down to the waterfront."

"Oh, Jesus. You really are nuts."

"No arguments."

In less than five minutes we were up and out into the hallway. The mama-san heard us and emerged from her room and unbolted the front door for us.

She bowed as we left but I didn't have time for formalities. I just plowed into the shadows, Ernie close on my heels.

34

MIST LACED WITH SALT RUSHED IN FROM THE SEA, SLAPPING THE warm flesh of my face and waking me up with each step we took down the dark streets.

I wasn't sure if it was a dream I had or just some sort of sudden brainstorm. Whatever it was, it pushed its way up from my unconscious and screamed at me to get up and *do* something! Ernie was still grumbling, so as we emerged from the alley and turned down Texas Street, I started to explain.

"It's always bothered me," I said, "Strange's accusation that somebody'd been tampering with classified documents. And right there in J-two, at the same time that Whitcomb was stealing office equipment. But it didn't seem logical. Whitcomb was a petty crook, not some sort of foreign agent. And even if he had been an agent, why steal a typewriter?

"Maybe Strange and his buddies are just hysterical, I thought. They get together, exchange suspicions, and work each other up into a frenzy. But still the coincidence bugged me."

Ernie snorted through his nose, head down, not saying anything. We walked quickly past the shuttered shops and nightclubs.

"Remember the note Miss Ku gave us?" I said. "There was something in there about 'I haven't told anybody yet' or something like that. As if whoever wrote the note knew something incriminating about Whitcomb. What would anyone know that was incriminating?

"At first I thought it was that Whitcomb was messing with an innocent girl. Well, that's out now. But there's something else the person who wrote the note might've known. He might've known about the only real crime Whitcomb committed. Namely, that he stole typewriters. How would he know that? If he was a fence, he might know, but a fence would be making money from Whitcomb—he wouldn't be threatening him. So maybe it was somebody who was there when he stole the typewriters. Somebody who caught him red-handed."

"Why wouldn't he have turned Whitcomb in?"

Ernie was starting to wake up now. We reached the end of the row of dark nightclubs and started down the long slope that led to the pier. A few shadows were clustered on the quay. Sailors waiting for the next launch to take them out to the *Kitty Hawk*. In the distance the harbor was pitch-black. Shrouded by mist. I could see nothing.

"He wouldn't turn Whitcomb in," I said, "because he was there in the J-two office in the middle of the night for no good reason himself."

"*He* was the one after the classified documents," Ernie said. "Whitcomb's killer."

"Exactly. And he stumbled into Whitcomb."

"And Whitcomb wouldn't realize right away that he was talking to another thief, because the man was American, maybe even dressed in a military uniform. He would've bluffed Whitcomb into thinking that he was straight."

"So when Whitcomb received the note, he thought the guy wanted to deal somehow. Maybe get in on his action. Maybe even open the door to richer hunting grounds."

"And instead he wanted to gut him and leave him for the rats."

"Right," I said.

"And this man was Shipton?"

"Right again."

"And Shipton wanted to kill him because Whitcomb was the only person living who could link him to the theft of those classified documents. Why didn't Shipton just kill him in the J-two office?"

"Might not've had a chance. Whitcomb would've been nervous, on guard, backing away. Killing him then might've attracted too much attention, proved there was another man there that night."

"So he used Miss Ku to get in touch with us and hand the note to Whitcomb." Ernie nodded his head in thought. "But why us?"

"Shipton wanted somebody official to contact Whitcomb, to add to the threat, make it more likely that he'd show up. And do you know of any other CID agents who hold court daily in Itaewon?"

"Just us."

"Besides, if he had us involved in some way, he figured we couldn't pursue the case wholeheartedly."

"He had that wrong."

"Yes, he did."

Three sailors emerged from an alley, laughing and exchanging lewd stories. Ernie and I slowed to let them get a few yards ahead of us.

Ernie furrowed his brow. "But Shipton has already shown us that he has no trouble slipping on and off military compounds. Why wouldn't he just kill Whitcomb himself? Why involve us and Miss Ku?"

"You saw how Whitcomb lived. In a barracks with a dozen other men. They sleep together, shower together, eat chow together. Even run the ville and pick up girls together. Getting Whitcomb alone would be Shipton's main problem."

"But the meeting in Namdaemun involved his thievery operation, so Whitcomb wasn't sharing that with any of his pals."

"Right. So he'd come alone."

"But why kill him at all? Whitcomb was just a long-nose slicky boy. He wasn't likely to blow the whistle on Shipton. He probably didn't even know his name."

"But he saw his face."

"So?"

"You'd be right if this was just one thief spotting another. But Shipton was after military secrets. And for those to have any value, you have to sell them to somebody who can use them."

"Like the North Koreans?"

"Yes. And they wouldn't want to jeopardize a guy with as much potential to steal prime information for them as Shipton."

"So maybe the North Koreans ordered Shipton to kill Whitcomb."

"Maybe. And they probably have big plans for Shipton. Very big plans."

"If they have such big plans for him, why are they allowing him to black-market?"

"After he committed the first murders, of his Korean fiancée and her boyfriend, he was living on the lam. Black market was a natural way for him to support himself. It's easy money. He probably grew to like it."

"So maybe the North Koreans don't even know he's black-marketing."

"Maybe not. Or if they do, they don't want to force him to stop and piss him off.

"He's arrogant."

"Wouldn't you be? After evading everybody these last few months?"

"But it can't last forever."

"That's why I think he's building up to a big score."

"Hit the big one and then slip out of the country with the loot?"

"That could be it."

"I'm glad you figured all this out, George," Ernie said, "but I still don't know what we're doing up this early."

"Going to the *Kitty Hawk*."

"To the *Kitty Hawk*? What in the hell for?"

"Classified documents," I said. "You forget, Ernie. That's what Shipton was after at J-two. That's what he'll be after here."

"Why go after such a difficult target when he's been doing so well on the army compounds?"

"That part I haven't figured out yet. Unless it has something to do with the tunnels Strange told me about."

"Tunnels and an aircraft carrier? That doesn't make any sense."

"No, it doesn't. But the *Kitty Hawk* is a mother lode of classified information. Shipton and his North Korean handlers will see it as a gold mine too good to pass up."

"And he was a squid himself. He'll know his way around."

"Right."

"So maybe you're right and he'll go after Top Secret info while they're in port. But how the hell are we going to get on the ship?"

"Bogart. Like we usually do."

"Yeah," Ernie said. "But usually we don't do it before breakfast."

A crowd of sailors had gathered at the pier, laughing and playing grab-ass and talking about the Korean girls in the bars last night. Ernie and I stayed close to them, trying to blend in, which wasn't too hard because the guys with overnight liberty could wear civilian clothes and were dressed pretty much like us.

Deep in the mist a steady churning grew. The sailors moved toward a metal gangway. We moved with them.

With a final roar of its engine, a large flat launch with the U.S. flag waving at its tail edged expertly up to the bottom of the slippery steps. Sailors filed down. There was a little shoving, but we shoved back, and found ourselves sitting on one of the hard benches of the launch.

Luckily nobody tried to talk to us and Ernie and I stared grimly forward; two sailors too hung over to bother messing with this early in the morning.

As the engines fired up and we moved away from the quay, I felt the rolling swell of the sea beneath the metal hull. It was invigorating. I liked it right away and decided I felt at home on the sea, although I'd never been in a boat before. Except for one time. During a summer program sponsored by the County of Los Angeles, when they'd taken me and a lot of other orphans to Pacific Ocean Park. We rode around the pier and back. I got seasick. Where I grew up, in East L.A., there wasn't much opportunity to earn your sea legs.

The little launch plowed through the waves but we could only see about twenty yards to our front. The impenetrable curtain of mist seemed to recede before us, and the faster we moved the faster it ran away.

Twenty minutes later a huge metal wall appeared without warning in the center of the sea. Sailors started to shuffle in their seats and I realized that the wall must be the aircraft carrier, the U.S.S. *Kitty Hawk.* The launch moved down the wall until it found another metal staircase, this one leading up to a hatch in the hull. Light poured out of the opening and was diffused into a golden haze by the millions of airborne droplets of seawater.

Beneath the ladder, the sailors secured the launch with hooks on the ends of chains, and one by one we clambered off the rocking platform and climbed the stairwell. I went first. Ernie right behind me.

At the top of the stairs we finally met the inevitable: officialdom.

I had been watching the sailors above me. Each flashed his identification card and gave a halfhearted salute to the navy chief in his crisp white uniform. When it was my turn I mimicked the sailors as well as I could, trying to act as bored and as hung over as everybody else. The chief hardly looked at me. I stepped past him.

Out of the corner of my eye, I saw Ernie going through the same motions. He took a step away from the chief, and then a gravelly voice erupted through the morning stillness.

"Where the hell did you get that army jacket?"

Ernie stopped. I turned.

The chief was talking about the dark blue nylon jacket Ernie wore. Mine just had a map of Korea with a dragon coiled around it. Ernie's had a map of the Korean Peninsula, too, but instead of a dragon he had a dagger stabbing through the heart of Seoul, dripping blood. Beneath was the embroidered statement, "I've already done my time in hell," and the dates of Ernie's first tour in country.

Sailors only spend a few days here, not twelve months.

Ernie grinned at the chief. "Stole it off a drunken dogface."

A howl of laughter went up from the squids behind us. The chief laughed too.

"*All right!*" the chief said, waving us on through.

Ernie caught up with me as we walked down a long metal corridor.

"Quick thinking, Ernie."

"No, it wasn't," he said. "It's true. I did steal it off a drunken dogface."

I didn't bother to ask for details.

Actually, I had no idea where we were going. The *Kitty Hawk* seemed immense; loaded with armaments and aircraft and big enough to house three thousand sailors. We passed a barber shop and a room with a fat color TV in it, and in the distance I smelled the usual aromas of a military chow hall in the morning. Coffee, bacon, sizzling sausage.

"I haven't had a decent breakfast since we left Seoul," Ernie said.

"No time."

"So where are we going?"

"We have to find the bridge."

"What bridge?"

"That's where the captain is and probably where they keep all the classified documents."

"Watch your head!"

A thick metal pipe ran across the roof of the passageway as if someone had set it there as a booby trap. I ducked beneath it.

We found a ladder and climbed. And kept climbing until I started to smell salt air again. Suddenly there was dark sky above me and we stepped out on the metal deck.

At the railing, the mist had started to lift. Out to sea a band of deep blue lit the horizon. A crescent moon sat slightly above, as if overseeing the impending sunrise. Toward land, the lights of Pusan twinkled on, one by one.

I took a deep breath of the fresh air and held it.

"Maybe I joined the wrong service," I told Ernie.

"You?" Ernie said. "A squid? Floating for months at a time? You couldn't stand it."

"Maybe you're right."

Light filtered through huge plate glass windows in the metal superstructure looming above us. Behind them, shadows scurried.

We wandered below deck, peeking in offices, until I saw a tired-looking sailor slumped behind a desk.

"Who handles classified documents?" I asked.

"Who wants to know?"

I slipped out my badge and flopped it open.

"Investigative Services," I said.

I was stretching the truth a bit. Naval Investigative Services was the navy's equivalent of the army's Criminal Investigation Division. No sense advertising that soldiers were aboard the *Kitty Hawk.* You might as well tell them they'd been infected with the bubonic plague.

He barely glanced at the badge.

"This must be about Harrelson," he said.

"Yeah, that's right." I tried to hide my surprise. "What's the status?"

"Still in sick bay. Whoever did it cracked his skull wide open."

"Will he live?"

He lifted his hand and rocked it from side to side. "They're not sure yet."

"What did the guy get?"

"How in the fuck should I know? They don't tell me shit."

"But Harrelson worked with classified documents, didn't he?"

"Damn right. That's why Chief Longo is so pissed."

"Longo's in charge of classified documents?"

"In charge of security for the whole ship."

"Where can I find him?"

"Down to the next ladder, one deck above. The office is marked."

"Thanks."

We left the clerk, found the ladder, climbed upstairs, and wandered the hall until we found an office with the stenciled letters: Security.

It was a roomy office, with six desks and a dozen filing cabinets. A heavyset man was on the phone. He wore the uniform of a chief. A group of sailors milled about, trying to look busy. Everyone seemed upset.

"Yes, sir. Yes."

The chief slammed down the phone. I walked toward him.

"Chief Longo?"

He checked us out, letting his eyes linger on our wrinkled blue jeans.

"Yeah?"

I pulled out my badge and the identification behind its plastic holder and barely opened it, asking the question as I did. "How's Harrelson?"

"Stable. That's about the best they can say." He scowled.

"I'm Investigator Sueño. This is my partner, Investigator Bascom."

Ernie nodded slightly.

"So fast?" The scowl hadn't left his face.

"We happened to be in the area. I need a rundown of the type of documents that were compromised."

The chief rubbed his forehead and eyes with a big hairy paw. The man was obviously exhausted. Good.

"You know you need clearance, even an investigator needs clearance, before I can discuss weaponry."

Weaponry! What the hell was Shipton after? I took a chance. "Only if it's nuclear," I said firmly.

The chief snapped, "What the fuck do you think I'm talking about?"

He looked around, as if suddenly realizing that he'd shouted.

"Oh, sorry. It's just that Harrelson was a good kid." He shook his head glumly. "Right here on the *Hawk*."

"Did anybody get a look at the perpetrator?"

"Nobody. I doubt even that Harrelson did. The blow came from behind. It was twenty-three hundred hours, maybe he wasn't as alert as he should've been. The guy broke into the classified locker."

"But only went after the documents concerning weaponry?"

"That's what it looks like so far. Jesus, I don't know. I think we'd better go talk to the captain." The chief rubbed his eyes again. "So you guys just happened to be in the area." He was looking at Ernie. "What detachment are you with?"

"Seoul."

His big hand stopped rubbing. "Seoul? There isn't a Naval Investigative Detachment in Seoul."

"Temporary duty," I said. "From the Philippines."

"They sent a whole detachment on temporary duty from the Philippines?"

"Listen," Ernie said. "You got a head around here? We been wandering around the ship and all I've had so far this morning is coffee. My eyes are about to turn yellow."

"Sure. Down the hallway."

Ernie took a step toward the door.

"I got to piss like a racehorse myself," I said. "Be right back, Chief."

He grunted and picked up the phone again.

When we reached the hallway, voices drifted after us.

"Those guys can't be navy," somebody said. "Did you see those jackets?"

"Naval Investigation didn't say nothing about agents arriving this soon."

We strode quickly toward the ladder and slid down it without touching any rungs.

"When those squids realize we're army," Ernie said, "we'll be in a world of shit."

"And we have too much to do to sit in a brig until it gets sorted out."

"Shipton could be on his way to the PX right now."

Somehow I doubted that, not here in Pusan. It would be too risky so soon after hitting the *Kitty Hawk*. But we didn't have time to argue the fine points.

We kept dropping down ladders and sprinting down hallways, not caring anymore who saw us or what they thought. When we finally reached the hatch in the side of the hull, a launch was shoving off.

"Hey!" I shouted. "Hold that boat!"

"Aren't you supposed to say 'belay' or something like that?" Ernie said.

That Ernie, always a stickler for the right word. The chief at the gangplank made a hand signal that held the boat.

"All right, you two," he said, frowning. "You're lucky I held it. Let's see your liberty chits."

I pulled out my CID identification.

"We don't need liberty chits," I said. "We're Criminal Investigation agents and we're on a case, Chief. A man's life could be at stake."

The chief stared at all the stamps and squiggles and officialese in my leather wallet. Ernie opened his badge, too, and slammed it shut impatiently. The chief was surprised, but too much of a lifer to want to fight all that documentation.

"Army?" he said. "What are you doing on the *Kitty Hawk*?"

"You don't have a need-to-know!" Ernie snapped.

We scurried down the ladder and climbed aboard the launch. It pulled away and the startled face of the chief receded and grew blurry in the mist. About thirty yards out, a siren sounded aboard the ship.

"Step on it, Smitty," one of the sailors said to the helmsman. "Get us ashore before they cancel liberty or some such shit."

Smitty nodded and the engine roared.

35

FIRST WE CAUGHT A CAB BACK TO HIALEAH COMPOUND. I wanted to get as far away from the U.S. Navy as possible.

After showing our ID at the pedestrian gate, we went over to the MP Station. No unusual blotter reports. Everything had been quiet on Hialeah Compound last night.

"That's because Shipton was busy elsewhere," Ernie said.

Busy is right. Possibly offing his sixth victim, Seaman Harrelson, of the U.S.S. *Kitty Hawk*, and stealing who-knows-what kind of top secret information.

I wasn't sure what to do next. The PX office wasn't open yet, so we finally did the sensible thing and grabbed a couple of trays at the post snack bar. We went through the line and ordered ourselves some breakfast.

As I sipped on hot coffee and listened to the tinkling of glassware and the rustling of newspapers, I tried to put things in perspective.

Shipton's primary goal was the theft of classified documents.

Who knew how much he'd gotten away with in the last three months? Maybe the suspicions of Strange and his ilk were blown way out of proportion. Or maybe they were just the tip of the iceberg. Hard to tell. But what I did know for certain was that Shipton now had access to information on "tunnels" from the army and "weaponry," probably nuclear, from the navy. Valuable stuff.

Why was he doing this? Because he was AWOL and broke and somebody was paying him to turn over the documents. Who? Not much doubt. The North Koreans.

So why did he black-market, too? Because there was good money in it. And maybe the North Koreans paid only upon delivery. And since Shipton was probably in no position to run an auction, the North Koreans probably paid him only what they wanted to pay him. And that might not be all that much. After all, they wanted to keep him hungry. Keep him feeding them stolen information.

Maybe they helped him get the phony ration control plates. Maybe that was his payment.

But that was speculation. We had a highly trained navy commando on the loose in Korea. He was a killer, he was after top secret documents, and he would stop at nothing to get what he wanted.

Shipton knew the military community intimately and he could blend right in. Buy uniforms, obtain phony ID's, waltz in and out of classified areas with just bluff and bravado.

What would he do next?

Probably continue to make all the easy money he could off of those ration control plates until they became hot. Did he have any idea yet we were onto him? If not, in a couple of hours, when the front doors of the PX opened to shoppers, he might stroll right on through as if he owned the place. And we could be right there to finally bust him.

Maybe. But nothing else in this case had been easy. Something told me picking him up wouldn't be easy either.

He hadn't been subtle with the navy. Hit somebody over the head and steal what you need. But maybe he had no choice. The *Kitty Hawk* was only in port for a few days. Hard to establish an inside contact in that time. Besides, Shipton was probably counting on interservice rivalry to keep our exchange of information down and make it less likely that we would link his naval activities with the security compromises in 8th Army. And he was probably right.

I didn't think he would just randomly keep stealing classified documents and black-marketing until one day we got lucky and he got caught. Something told me there was a master plan to all this. Bo Shipton was too intelligent, too well trained, to drift along in crime without some sort of overall goal. Maybe it was just to make enough money so he could slip out of the country and retire on the Riviera. Or did the classified information he was gathering, looked at as a whole, represent some sort of clandestine mosaic?

Whatever his motive, I knew in my heart that he had a mission. I just had to figure out what it was.

On the way to the snack bar, we had stopped at billeting and shaved and now, with bellies full of scrambled eggs and hash browns, we both felt a lot more human.

"This Shipton is one bold dude," Ernie said, his mouth full of toast.

"Killing Miss Ku. Killing the Nurse. Not very bold. They were both helpless."

"Yeah," Ernie said. "And he tortured Miss Ku. At least Whitcomb was more like a fair fight, wasn't he?"

"Even that wasn't fair when you consider all the combat Shipton has been through."

"It won't do him any good when *we* catch him," Ernie said. He glugged down the last of his coffee. "Don't sweat it, George."

I checked the clock on the wall. Almost eight hundred hours. Riley would probably be in. So would Strange. We left our dirty plates on the table and walked back to the snack bar manager's office.

He was a Korean man in a neat white shirt and tie, hunched over a stack of invoices. I showed him my badge and he pointed to a phone at a table loaded with purchasing regulations. I lifted the phone and got through to the base operator and told her what I wanted. Ernie stood in the doorway and watched the short-order cooks in the kitchen.

Strange answered on the first ring.

"Distribution."

I asked him a few questions that he couldn't answer, but he said he'd try to get the information and I should call back in a couple of hours. He made me promise to tell him all about the girls on Texas Street once he had what I wanted.

I hung up and thought of calling Riley. But what would I tell him? That Shipton was more dangerous than I'd figured? Besides, we weren't supposed to be on the *Kitty Hawk* at all—supposed to go through channels for that sort of thing—and I didn't want to mention our little naval adventure if I didn't have to.

We walked around the compound for the next couple of hours, keeping our eyes open, until the PX manager unlocked the front door of the store. Korean dependent wives streamed in, along with a few GI's, but nobody who looked like Shipton. Ernie found a secluded spot across from the parking lot, and I went in the back door to use the nervous manager's phone.

He wasn't happy to see me again but was relieved that this time I didn't want to go through the cards. I borrowed his copy of the AAFES phone directory and started calling PX managers in the compounds leading north from Pusan.

At each place I got a raft of shit, but gradually I convinced each manager that he'd be in serious trouble if he didn't cooperate. If someone else was murdered, I promised to put the blame directly on him. In the end, each consented. Most even gave me a Korean secretary who took down the four stolen RCP numbers Shipton was using and promised to check all the ration cards before they left the store. If they found anything, they would call me here at the PX manager's office.

The calls took over an hour. When I finished, I told the manager that if I received any calls he should keep the person on the line and bring me to the phone right away. I'd be in the parking lot or in the store somewhere.

He frowned but agreed.

I grabbed a couple of paper cups, filled them with coffee from the manager's large urn, and carried them out into the parking lot.

Ernie was still slouched against the cement wall.

"If we were on the black market detail," he said when he saw me, "we could make a year's worth of quota today."

I handed him the coffee and turned to look at the GI's and Korean women pushing carts of merchandise out of the store toward the line of PX cabs. "They're at it hot and heavy."

"This is a big city," Ernie said. "Only one military base. A big demand." He sipped on his coffee. "I think we're wasting our time here."

"I do, too."

"After a big score like the *Kitty Hawk*," Ernie said, "Shipton wouldn't take any chances. He'd leave Pusan."

"You're probably right. But where would he go?"

"Depends on what he's after."

"Yeah."

We finished our coffee. As goods were loaded into the backs of taxis and customers climbed aboard and sped off, more people filed into the end of the cab line. It was endless.

"Maybe I ought to call Riley," I said.

"Maybe you should."

"You want to go in? It's cold out here."

"No. I'll wait. You're better with the bureaucratic bullshit."

"Thanks for the compliment."

"You deserve it."

I went back inside, and after my talking to the Korean female operator and listening to a lot of clicking and buzzing, the phone rang and someone picked it up.

"Criminal Investigation," the voice said, but it wasn't Riley. It was the First Sergeant.

"This is Sueño."

"Where in the fuck *are* you?"

"You know where we are," I said. "In Pusan. Doing our job."

"Is that what you call it? Now listen to me carefully, Corporal Sueño . . ." The First Sergeant always used our ranks when he was busy trying to cover his own ass. "I want you and Sergeant Bascom to hop on the first train heading north and get back to Seoul ASAP! You understand that?"

"Understood. But why?"

"Because I *say* so! That's why. The head shed is just about to shit a brick. Two army investigators aboard a goddamn naval vessel!"

"What are you talking about, Top?"

"Don't *give* me that innocent shit! I know it was you two shitheads. Nobody else would be stupid enough to pull such a stunt."

"But we're onto something here."

"Who cares? Get your tails back here!" He paused. "What are you onto?"

At least the First Sergeant was enough of a cop to suppress his bureaucratic instincts for a moment and show some interest.

"We know Shipton is here. He could turn up any minute."

"The MP's down there have his photo and they've put out an alert for him. You're not needed there, Corporal. If he turns up, they'll find him."

Not likely, I thought. Not unless he jumped up and down and shouted his name and the date he went AWOL at them. They mostly had their thumbs up their asses.

"We're more effective down here," I insisted.

"You're more effective where and when I *tell* you to be goddamn effective."

Another phone rang. The Korean secretary picked up, listened for a moment, and glanced at me. She pointed at the receiver and mouthed the word "Taegu."

"Just a minute, Top. I have another call coming in."

"No 'just a minute' about it! You and Bascom get your asses back here and you get them back here *now*! You read me, Corporal?"

"Yeah. I got it, First Sergeant."

Something slammed and the line went dead. I sighed, set the phone down in its cradle, and grabbed the other one from the secretary's hand.

"Agent Sueño," I said.

"This is Miss Chong from the Camp Henry PX. We found one of those numbers you gave me."

"When was it used?"

"This morning. He must've been buying something at just about the time you called."

"Have you told anyone else about this?"

"No. Just our manager."

"Please don't mention it to anyone, Miss Chong. How late do you stay open?"

"Until six this evening."

"We'll be there as soon as we can."

To my surprise, Ernie didn't seem excited by the news. Instead, he leaned against the brick building, a few droplets of perspiration dotting his upper lip. He acted as if he hadn't even heard me.

"The Nurse's funeral," he said. "They're holding it tomorrow, at a Buddhist temple. I'd like to be there."

"You'd be about as welcome as a rat in a kimchi pot," I said.

"Yeah," he answered. "Still, I'd like to go."

For the first time that morning I looked at him carefully. He seemed more pale than usual.

"You never went back to the One-twenty-one Evac for those tests, did you?"

"Who needs 'em?"

"You do," I answered. "You don't look well."

Ernie rubbed his stomach. "Probably just that cut bait we ate last night."

Suddenly, his cheeks bulged and he swiveled and lurched away from me, clutching his stomach. He barfed his guts up, retching painfully. Finally, he wiped his mouth and turned back to me.

"So much for those scrambled eggs and hash browns."

I examined the color of the goo. "You're barfing blood, Ernie."

He nodded. Then he lurched sideways. When I grabbed him, he seemed as weak as a rag doll. I helped him over to the Hialeah Aide Station.

The Physician's Assistant there looked at me as if I were nuts. "They wanted to run tests on him at the One-twenty-one Evac but instead he came down here?"

"It's a long story," I said.

"And I don't want to hear it," he snapped at me.

Within twenty minutes they had strapped Ernie to a stretcher and wheeled him out to a medical evacuation helicopter for the flight back to Seoul.

If I went to Taegu on my own, the First Sergeant would almost certainly court-martial me. But with only a routine MP dragnet, Shipton would find some way to slip out of the country before we caught him. He'd proved awfully resourceful so far. If he escaped, we'd never see him again and I'd have to live with what he'd done to Whitcomb and Miss Ku and the Nurse—and my part in their deaths—for the rest of my life.

I checked out of billeting, still undecided. I used their phone and called Strange. After running down some bullshit story about the girls on Texas Street for him, his voice shuddered and he told me two words: "Mining equipment." I didn't know what the hell that was supposed to mean and he hung up before I had a chance to ask.

Outside of Hialeah Compound I caught a cab and rode it to the bus station. I pushed through the bustling crowd and waited in line to buy a ticket.

If I showed some results, if I caught Shipton, the First Sergeant wouldn't be able to burn me for not returning to Seoul. Maybe.

When I reached the window the ticket girl asked me, "*Odi?*" Where to? I slapped down a five-thousand-won note and bought one ticket for the express bus to Taegu.

The trip from Pusan to Taegu is through beautiful countryside covered with groves of pomegranate trees and gracefully terraced rice paddies clinging to the sides of sloping hills. The trees were naked and the hills were draped with a thin layer of ice.

At about the halfway point, my bus passed the city of Kyong-ju, the capital of the ancient Kingdom of Silla. Silla was one of the powers on the peninsula, along with Peikchae and Koguryo, when Korea was divided during the Three Kingdoms period more than thirteen centuries ago.

I gazed at the blue-tiled pagodas and the upturned roof of the museum, wishing I could stop and spend a few hours immersed in the artwork and craftsmanship of the ancients.

Instead, I stayed on the bus. When it stopped in downtown Taegu, I caught another cab that sped me across the flat terrain of the city to the U.S. Army's Camp Henry, home of the 19th Support Group.

On the way, I thought of Shipton and Slicky King So and what Strange had told me. No sudden insight flashed into my brain but slowly a pattern started to emerge. As I looked at its hazy outlines, I couldn't believe it at first.

Maybe I'd been listening to army propaganda films too long or reading only the honeyed versions of world events in the *Stars & Stripes* to be able to believe what I was guessing. But I thought of the secrecy of the military brass—even routine crime statistics were classified—and their absolute belief in their own infallibility. Gradually, I began to think that what I was thinking might be true.

If I was right, Shipton did have a goal. And maybe, if you set aside his killings, I would've been rooting for him to attain it.

Maybe.

Probably not.

Tunnels. Nuclear weapons. Mining equipment.

The North Koreans had dug tunnels beneath the Demilitarized Zone. No question about that. And tunnels could only be used for offensive military operations. So what were we going to do about it? Passively sit by and try to find the tunnels one at a time? Harder than it seemed. Sensing equipment was only so good. It couldn't penetrate hundreds of feet of granite, and there were thousands of square miles of mountainous terrain to cover and no theoretical limit to how deep the North Koreans could dig. And we are Americans, after all. Everybody knows that the best defense is a good offense.

This is not to say that we were going to start a war, conduct a preemptive strike, or anything like that. Our political leaders wouldn't stand for it. But 8th Army did have to take protective measures, didn't they? They were responsible for the lives of fifty thousand soldiers and sailors and airmen and their dependents. Not to mention the defense of South Korea. What could they do?

Tunnels. Mining equipment. Nuclear weapons.

The North Korean mechanized armor units were overwhelming. A much greater force than the South's. Some magazines said double or triple that of our side. Our current strategy, if the North Koreans decided to come south, was saturation bombing by B-52's from Okinawa. But it would take time for those planes to arrive on the scene. And bombing, by its very nature, is a hit-or-miss affair. And bombing certainly couldn't affect anything that was underground.

So maybe we were digging our own tunnels.

And what would we put in them? Maybe a little surprise for the North Koreans' armor battalions. Maybe nuclear weapons.

Had the *Kitty Hawk* been transporting A-bombs? Maybe. But it was navy policy never to confirm or deny such a thing. I couldn't possibly know for sure.

Or was I all wrong about this? Even if I was right, maybe our tunnels were just in the contingency planning stages, only on paper. But contingency or not, the North Koreans would certainly want to know. And when someone with Shipton's training deserted his post and was wanted for murder, how difficult would it be to recruit him as an informant?

Maybe that's why the South Koreans hadn't told us anything. They wanted to capture Shipton themselves, interrogate him using their persuasive methods, then work backward to his controller and maybe to other North Korean agents. If they let the U.S. in on it, we'd demand he be turned over to us right away. And because we paid most of their defense bills, they'd be under tremendous pressure to comply. But if they kept the whole thing secret, we'd think that Shipton was nothing more than another guy gone native. We wouldn't worry about him. Even if we never heard from him again.

Maybe I was wrong. Maybe there was a simpler explanation for all this. But in my gut I didn't think so.

When Cecil Whitcomb had stumbled into Bo Shipton that night, both of them stealing at the 8th Army J-2 building, he'd stumbled into a secret war that would mean life or death for millions of people. And, by doing so, he'd signed his own death warrant.

At Camp Henry I went straight to the PX. The manager and the secretary, Miss Chong, showed me the data card. It was the right number. Maxed out on the ration.

"But we got a call from the MP's," Miss Chong said. "After I talked to you on the phone. Apparently this person went over to the commissary using the same ration control plate and the same identification card."

"What happened?"

"The ID card checker noticed that the photo looked as if it had been tampered with. He called the MP's."

"And?"

"They arrested him."

"Arrested him? They've got him in custody? And no one was hurt?"

"Hurt? Of course not." Miss Chong looked indignant.

I would've bet that taking Shipton down would've caused a slaughter.

"Where is he now?"

"At the MP Station." She pointed. "One block down. On your left."

I ran out the door.

The MP Desk Sergeant was surprised to see a guy toting a canvas bag and all out of breath burst into his office. I showed him my badge. "Where's the guy you arrested at the commissary?"

"With the phony ration control stuff?"

"Right."

"Back here."

He led me down the hallway to a holding cell and I peered through the one-way glass.

A chubby buck sergeant in wrinkled fatigues slumped on a wooden bench, his elbows on his knees. His brown hair was cut short and a narrow mustache drooped from his round nose.

"This is the guy?" I asked.

"That's him," the Desk Sergeant said proudly. "Caught him red-handed."

A wave of nausea rumbled through my gut. For a minute I thought I was going to throw up but I fought back the feeling. The head of the buck sergeant lolled listlessly from his shoulders.

He wasn't Bo Shipton. He wasn't even close.

36

THE GUY REMINDED ME OF AN OVERWEIGHT CHIPMUNK. HE KEPT rubbing his hands and wouldn't make eye contact with anybody; really ashamed of what he had done.

"I thought it would be easy money," he whined. "I'd seen the guy around compound once or twice, couple of months ago. He asked me where I worked and we shot the breeze, but this morning he sits down with me at the snack bar and shows me this ration control card and asks me if it looks like the real thing. It did. So he tells me I can have it. Cheap. I tell him it won't do me any good without a phony ID card. So he pulls one out and shows me how the plastic is already slit and I can slip my photo right in there. So I ask him how much and he says a hundred bucks, but I can tell he's in a real hurry so I get him down to forty and I figure I have a pretty good buy."

"You did," I said. "But you should've had the ID card re-laminated."

"Yeah. Now you tell me."

"Did this guy give you his name?"

"No. Just a passing acquaintance, you know? Said, 'hey,' ya know?"

"You saw him in the snack bar a few times? Anywhere else?"

"On the shuttle bus going to Camp Walker. In the PX." He shrugged.

"What'd he tell you? Was he retired? Active duty? Civilian? What?"

"He didn't say. I just figured he was on leave."

I pulled out the photograph. "Is this him?"

The buck sergeant took it with the tips of his fingers. "That's him," he said sadly.

I snatched the photo back. "Did he say where he was going?"

"No."

"Did he hang out with anybody around here?"

"Not that I know of."

I slipped the photo in my wallet and stood up to leave. The guy looked at me, his big brown eyes starting to water. "Say, how much trouble am I in?"

I said, "Enough to fuck up your whole career."

His mustache drooped all the way to his knees.

"I was afraid you were going to say that."

For some reason Shipton had tried to draw me to Taegu. Was it to pull me away from Pusan, or to keep me away from Seoul? Or was it for some other reason altogether?

Or was it so he could lure me into a secluded spot and slice me up like he'd done Whitcomb and Miss Ku and the Nurse? And the two lovers before them.

One thing was for sure: there was no sense chasing ration control numbers all over the country anymore. Shipton had probably sold them all off, scattering them to the wind like a flock of pheasants exploding from a bush.

He knew I was following. Maybe he'd had a scare on Texas

Street. After all, we'd been right on his heels, hadn't missed him by much on the *Kitty Hawk.* But he'd be more cautious now. He'd be a lot harder to catch.

The First Sergeant was probably right. I needed the resources we could pull together in Seoul. Now that Shipton was onto us, I could no longer do this alone.

Bo Shipton was trying to manipulate me. The best way to avoid that was to go back to what he was after. Secrets. Classified information. All the black-marketing stuff was just to make money to support his operations.

Had the *Kitty Hawk* been his last big score? Would he disappear for good now, his mission accomplished?

I didn't think so. If it was, I didn't think he would've murdered Miss Ku. Instead, he would've run to Pusan, stolen what he wanted, and vanished. If Miss Ku had given us information, he would've been gone before it did us any good.

Of course, I was assuming he was still rational. Which maybe he wasn't. After all, he'd had no good reason to kill the Nurse. He killed her just to warn me off. Or was there maybe another reason she had to die? One I hadn't thought of yet?

It took two hours for me to interrogate the buck sergeant the Camp Henry MP's had arrested and write up my report. The sun was just going down and I was half starved when I stopped in the NCO Club and had half a chicken and a mess of greasy french fries. Afterward, I wandered toward the front gate.

It was nice here. The rain and snow had stopped. The wind had died down. The sky was clearer than in Seoul. The moon and stars blinked at me between banks of drifting clouds.

At the pedestrian exit an MP stopped me and checked my ID card. After he glanced at it, I showed him Shipton's photo.

"Do you recognize this guy?"

He shook his head and stepped past me to check the trunk of a PX taxi that was leaving compound.

Black market. Eighth Army was so preoccupied with it that we let all the big stuff slide.

Outside the compound, four cabs sat in front of the cement

block walls. I told the driver of the first one to take me to *Mikun piheing chang.* The American army airfield.

Thirty minutes later I had bummed a ride in a helicopter heading north. We floated through billowing gray clouds and gathering dusk. After forty-five minutes, I lifted the visor on my helmet. Lights sparkled in the distance.

The Emerald City of Seoul.

We landed on the helipad on the south post of Yongsan Compound. I thanked the pilots, hiked the long mile back to the main compound, and wound through the brick buildings of the headquarters complex. The lights of the CID building were off, but the front door was open. So much for security. The Admin Office was locked, however, so I pulled out my key and opened it.

I switched on the light, tossed my bag into a chair, and started puttering around with the coffee maker. I wasn't really sure why I was here. Maybe just to check the blotter reports, see if anything unusual had happened, anything that might lead me to Shipton.

The coffee started to perk and I sat down in one of the vinyl-cushioned lounge chairs.

I'd lost my best chance on Texas Street. Shipton would be hard to find now. Maybe impossible.

The only thing I could do was to anticipate his next move. But how the hell would I do that?

I was mulling this over when all the faces I'd been dealing with in this case started to swim before my eyes: Cecil Whitcomb, Eun-hi, Miss Ku, the Nurse, Herbalist So, Shipton. When I got to the Chinese woman, I imagined her offering me a steaming bowl of tea. I sipped on it and suddenly felt totally relaxed. She studied me with her almond eyes. Then I was gone.

I jerked awake, twisting around, struggling to remember where I was.

Moonlight filtered down, illuminating the coffinlike shape of

Riley's desk. The pot of coffee was full now. Untouched. I could smell its gentle aroma.

What had awakened me had been a loud noise. A door slamming, as if someone were leaving the building. Or entering?

All was silent now. No noise, not even the clanging of the rusty pipes of the radiator. The heat was turned off. I was cold.

I strained to pick up any sound. Nothing. Still, I felt as if there was a presence out there. I reached inside my jacket, pulled out the .38, and clicked off the safety.

The gun felt heavy and reassuring in my palm. Cold. Loaded with death.

Footsteps. Slow at first but then faster, with more authority. Heading this way.

I slid out of the chair and stepped behind a filing cabinet next to the door. If someone entered the room I'd have a straight line of fire. Into the back of his head.

The footsteps stopped in front of the Admin Office. Hesitated. As if the intruder were peering into the room. Then the footsteps came closer and I pointed the business end of the pistol at the back of a skull. It was fuzzed with close-cropped gray. As I was about to squeeze the trigger, he turned and I saw the wrinkled face. The bleak eyes.

"Sueño!"

"Top! What are you doing here in the middle of the night?"

"Put that goddamn pistol away, will ya?"

Slowly, I lowered it and stuck it in the shoulder holster. "Sure."

He switched on the light. Our eyes blinked.

"That's the second time you almost goddamn shot me," he said.

I grinned.

"I thought someone had broken in here." The First Sergeant looked at me more carefully. "About time you showed up, Corporal."

"Look, I can explain that. One of the ration control numbers turned up in Taegu. I had to check it out."

"Did it come to anything?"

"No. Turned out Shipton sold the card and phony ID to some gullible buck sergeant down there."

The First Sergeant's eyes drilled into me. For a minute I thought he was going to start cursing. "I told you to get your ass back here."

"Yeah, well, I was on a case."

"I don't give a shit about your damn case. When I tell you to get back here, you get back here! You understand?"

I could've argued with him. I could've told him that he'd just put his finger on the trouble with the entire army. The army didn't care about the cases. Bureaucratic shuffling, the next promotion, how it looks in the newspapers. All those things are more important than the case. More important than catching a murderer. I could've told Top all that; I wanted to. Instead, I shut up.

In the army, taking an ass-chewing is a lot easier than accepting a court-martial.

"Yes, I understand," I said.

Top glared at me, trying to gauge my sincerity. In the end he decided to accept what he got.

"Don't let it happen again," he said.

I nodded.

He noticed the perked coffee and walked over and poured himself a cup. As he stirred in the creamer he kept staring at me.

"You guys must've spent a lot of time carousing in Pusan."

I walked back over to the chair and flopped down. "Yeah. Carousers. That's Ernie and me."

He kept studying me, not coming to any conclusions but getting more and more suspicious.

"What the hell did you do down there?"

"Came close to catching Shipton," I said. "But he got away."

The First Sergeant perched on the edge of Riley's desk, spreading his fingers, studying his stubby knuckles.

"I got some bad news for you," I said. "Ernie's in the hospital."

Top scowled. "I know. The One-two-one notified me. I just came from there."

"How's he doing?"

"In intensive care." The First Sergeant shook his head. "The asshole should've listened to the doctors in the first place."

"You're not taking me off the case again, are you?"

"No. Stick with it. But the next time I tell you to get back to Seoul right away, you get back to Seoul, you understand me, Sueño?"

"I understand, Top."

"Good."

I shrugged on my jacket and left the First Sergeant. I trudged through the thick snow toward the 121 Evac.

The big double doors of the Intensive Care Unit blared in stenciled red: Authorized Personnel Only.

When you want to do something in the army, don't ask for permission. I didn't.

The room was dark, with only little red lamps on the nightstands next to the beds. I scanned the charts rather than trying to make out the bandaged faces. Ernie was third bed on the left.

When I leaned over him, he seemed to be asleep.

I stood there for a moment, silently. He was hooked up to tubes. One eye cranked open.

He croaked. I didn't understand but I knew he was trying to say something. He shook his head from side to side, then lifted his arm, grabbing the tube in his mouth.

As he pulled, an endless plastic serpent emerged from his throat. Finally, it popped free and he rotated his jaw as if to get the muscles working again.

"Son . . . of a bitch . . . busted . . . my spleen."

His voice sounded as if he'd been wandering through the desert for three days.

"You mean to tell me," I said, "that you've been running all over Texas Street, chasing after a half-crazed killer, with your insides rattling around?"

Ernie grinned. "I guess I have. Give me some . . . water."

It didn't sound like a good idea. If they were feeding him intravenously it was because they didn't want anything in his stomach. He saw my hesitation.

"Just enough to . . . rinse . . . my throat."

There wasn't any water on his bedstand. I tiptoed across the aisle, found some next to another guy's bed, poured a little into a small paper cup, then sipped it to make sure it was water. I held the cup to Ernie's lips. He sucked greedily until it was all gone. Then he leaned back and convulsed his throat as if enjoying the full magnificence of the life-giving fluid.

"Did you catch him in Taegu?"

"False lead," I said. "He was there but sold the ration control plate to some dumb buck sergeant."

"Clever."

"Yeah," I agreed. "Now he knows we're onto him."

Ernie groaned. I don't know if it was from pain or from thinking about Shipton.

The skin around his nose and mouth twisted, his stomach moved like a rising bowling ball beneath the sheets, and suddenly blood and water squirted from his mouth. I ran around the bed and grabbed a towel, and now he was retching yellow bile and I handed him the towel and ran out of the ward.

Down the hall a sleeping medic sat behind a counter. I yelled, "The guy in the third bed, Intensive Care, he's vomiting up blood!"

The medic pressed a button, jumped up, and a few seconds later three people in green smocks and I stood around Ernie's bunk. He'd stopped throwing up but his breath still sounded bad.

One of the medics turned to me.

"You didn't give him any water, did you?"

"A little."

The medic's chest puffed out and he was about to read me my rights as a prisoner or the riot act or something when we heard a knock against the bedside table.

"Get the . . . *fuck* away from me."

It was Ernie, growling. Somehow, he'd yanked out his tubes, tumbled off the bed, and pushed away the medic who was trying to restrain him. From the locker behind his bunk, he grabbed his socks.

The medics kept jabbering away but Ernie put on his shirt and his blue jeans, then reached for his shoes and his jacket. He turned to me.

"You ready, pal?"

"You should stay here, Ernie. You're not well."

"We have to catch that asshole Shipton."

He slid on his shoes, raised his arms and put on his jacket, and started down the hallway. The medics ran after him. One grabbed his arm; Ernie swiveled and punched him in the nose.

The medic howled and grabbed his face, and I ran in front of him and his buddies and held my hands up.

"Sorry. Sorry. He's not himself."

"He can't *do* this," one said. "He'll be busted down a stripe for sure."

"I know. I know."

Ernie bounced around on the balls of his feet for a few seconds, eager to throw another punch. Suddenly his fist fell, his head rolled, and he collapsed in a heap.

I helped the medics take off his clothes and we hoisted him back onto the bunk. One shot him up with some sedative and another stuck the rubber tube back down his throat.

When I left, he was snoring soundly.

37

THE KILLER LURKED IN THE ALLEYS OF NAMDAEMUN-SI, THE GREAT South Gate Market, checking the eyes of strangers.

Farmers shoved wooden carts loaded with fat cabbages and winter turnips into a bewildering maze of canvas-covered corridors. Squatting over an open coal stove, an old crone fried *pindae-dok*, fragrant pancakes made of flour and garlic and green onion. Workmen waited for the sizzling delicacy, stomping their boots in the crusted snow.

When he was satisfied that he hadn't been followed, the killer strode deeper into the catacombs of the market. Merchants in bloody aprons pounded hatchets on wet boards, wailing out the prices of their fresh catch from the sea. In the distance, dogs yipped. Their barking grew louder.

Behind a plywood partition, a small kennel was hidden from the regular flow of pedestrian traffic. A Korean man crouched in front of one of the bamboo cages, scratching behind the ear of a frisky mutt. The man's face was like brown leather stretched across a craggy ridge of granite; his body hard, from years of training as an agent of espionage in the secret enclaves of Communist North Korea. He stood and turned slowly—warily—as the killer approached.

"*Kei sago shipo,*" the killer said. I want to buy a dog.

The Korean nodded. "We have the best stock."

"It must be a pup but old enough to mate."

"We have just the thing. And since it hasn't yet mated, the meat will be most beneficial to the health."

The obligatory code words over, the Korean squatted back down and pulled the large pup out of its cage.

"You have been busy," he said.

It was not an accusation, merely a statement. The killer didn't answer.

The Korean said, "Your mission is too important to be endangered by some personal vendetta."

The killer's face hardened. "The mission is important to you. To me, only the money is important."

"If you want your money, you will not jeopardize this mission."

The killer took a step forward. "The Americans killed a woman who was mine."

The Korean cocked an eyebrow. "Are you sure it was they who killed her?"

"The ROK Navy long ago gave up on me. It could only have been them."

The Korean turned back to the dog and shrugged. "Perhaps." He found a loose leather thong and deftly tied it around the back legs of the pup. "But now," he said, "since you returned the favor and killed *their* woman, this 'nurse' in Itaewon, they are after you with more fervor than ever."

The killer shrugged again. "It will do them no good."

The Communist North Korean yanked the knot tight and lifted the dog by its hind legs, tying it to a wooden crossbar. The puppy whined, its front paws barely touching the ground. The Korean rose and turned back to the killer.

"Do you eat dog meat?"

The killer shrugged. "Meat is meat."

The Korean tied another leather thong around the dog's snout and ratcheted the crossbar higher, until the pup's front paws scratched wildly in the air. Canine eyes whirled with panic, the muffled screams of the dog slicing through the cold morning air. The Korean jerked down on the front paws and the joints of the back legs cracked. Ignoring the animal's frantic yipping, he glanced back at the killer.

"You Americans love dogs, they say. Certainly you will enjoy this meat."

They stared into one another's eyes. Suddenly, the killer stepped forward, a knife appearing from the folds of his coat. He squatted and, with one swift movement, sliced the sharp blade across the pup's throat. Blood exploded onto dirty ice.

Ignoring the Korean, the killer slashed vertically up the dog's quivering torso, reached in, and peeled back the hide. The knife continued to probe. Guts snaked onto the pavement like steaming serpents.

The killer carved and peeled until what had once been a pup was nothing but a hanging lump of raw meat. He carved off a chunk of flank, rose, and offered it to the Korean.

The Korean smiled but shook his head. "I prefer mine cooked."

The killer gazed into the Korean's eyes and popped the still bloody dog flesh into his mouth. Chewing with the big, knotted muscles of his jaw, his eyes never wavered from the eyes of his Communist handler.

The Korean didn't flinch. He reached into his pocket, pulled out a slip of paper, and handed it to the killer. On it were etched four numbers.

"Memorize this and destroy it."

The killer glanced at the paper, soaking up the information. When he had it locked in his memory, he popped the paper into his gory mouth and swallowed it whole.

"Only a few days," the North Korean said, "and the operation will be ready."

The killer nodded.

"There have been inquiries," the North Korean said. "Discreet but unmistakable. Someone is planning to set a trap for you."

The killer stared at him, chewing slowly, waiting.

"When you go in, this man, this Sueño, he will come after you."

The killer snorted with contempt. "Let him."

"Do not be overconfident. We cannot eliminate him now. That would only alert the Americans, make our job more difficult. You must ensnare him in his own trap. Once you have the documents we need, killing him will be of no consequence. But make sure that no one realizes that it was our work."

The killer growled. "I am not an amateur."

He swallowed the last of the dog meat, turned, and vanished back into the endless maze of the Namdaemun Market.

38

STRANGE HAD A HABIT OF ARRIVING AT THE OFFICE EARLY. SO DO a lot of NCO's who have no life outside their work. He stumbled into me at the back entrance of 8th Army headquarters, snapped his head around, and almost poked me in the eye with his cigarette holder.

"What happened to you?" he asked.

"Long night." I took him by the elbow and guided him toward the Distribution Room. "Let's talk."

He held a cup of snack bar coffee in one hand and fumbled for his keys with the other. Once inside, I shut the door behind us.

"I need everything you've got on the recent security violations."

He placed his coffee on a desk and sat down. "You guys finally starting to take this stuff seriously, eh?"

"Let's just say *I'm* taking it seriously."

He fiddled with the empty plastic in his mouth. "Had any strange lately?"

I took a quick step forward, leaned across the desk, and lifted him by his khaki lapels halfway out of his chair.

"I have a serial killer on my hands," I said, "and people I know and love have been killed, and I'm not going to put up with any more of your shit. You start giving me the information I want and you start giving it to me right now!"

I didn't think Strange's gray pallor could grow any grayer but somehow it did. The stained cigarette holder tumbled from his lips.

"Okay," he croaked. "Okay."

After that, things went a lot smoother. I asked the questions, and he answered. When he didn't know something he picked up the phone and called one of his buddies in the far-flung network of army security wienies.

The picture I put together was composed of suspicions and anomalies that would never stand up in a court of law. But these guys knew their business and they took it seriously. What they had wasn't enough for them to pass along an official report to the head shed, but it was enough for me.

I ran my theory about the tunnels and the nuclear devices being placed beneath the DMZ past Strange. He had no direct knowledge of it, but it didn't seem too farfetched to him. Even if it wasn't true, it was the type of scheme the North Koreans would believe in—and would want to check out.

On the wall of Strange's office hung a large map of Korea. We charted the places that had been hit by Shipton. His method of operation seemed pretty straightforward. Somehow, he obtained inside help—maybe a combination to a filing cabinet or a copy of a key to a door—and then, either by putting on a uniform and impersonating an American officer or by using his commando skills, he gained access to the information he wanted. Each place he had hit was a potential gold mine for certain types of information: orders for heavy equipment, disposition of explosives, personnel records for mining engineers, acquisition of contract excavators.

Shipton knew exactly what he was after and he'd gone about it systematically. We were looking for any missing pieces of his puzzle, the parts Shipton still needed to fill in. If we could figure them out, we might be able to anticipate his next move.

Strange shook his head. "Looks like we're too late. He's already put it all together."

"Except for one thing," I said.

"What's that?"

"The actual location of the tunnels."

Strange ran his finger across the map until it pointed to an area here, at 8th Army Headquarters, in the south of Seoul.

"What's that?" I said.

"Geological Survey."

"Have they reported any security problems?"

"Not a one."

I lifted his clipboard off his desk and thrust it at him. "They're about due for their annual security inspection, aren't they?"

He gulped. "As a matter of fact, I was planning on doing that today."

"Good."

He reached for his cap.

I read the *Stars & Stripes* and drank about four quarts of coffee in the snack bar. I didn't even bother to call the office. They knew Ernie was in intensive care and the Nurse was dead and I was after her killer. If they couldn't figure out why I didn't report in, screw them. At noon I called Strange.

"They're clean," he reported. "But mighty nervous."

"About what?"

"They're handling documents with a higher classification than they've ever received before."

"How high?"

"Top Secret Crypto."

Crypto. Secrets transmitted in a cryptographic code so highly classified that even talking about it was a crime.

"When did they get them?" I asked.

"Yesterday. And they have a suspense date of five days."

Which meant their survey work had to be completed and turned in to the head shed in five days. "What happens then?"

"What do you think happens?"

"That's what I'm asking you."

"They select the final list of sites."

I thought it over. "And after the site list is out of their hands?"

"First it goes to the Eighth Army commander for his approval. After he chops off on it, it's locked up down in the War Room, four stories below ground, armed guards twenty-four hours a day, tighter than a chaplain's ass."

"Good work, Harvey."

He paused a minute, then said, "Had any strange lately?"

I told him something. About women and debauchery and long nights. I don't even remember what it was now.

That night Mr. Ma didn't seem surprised when I asked for another meeting with Herbalist So. Two hours later, I was in the patio behind the teahouse, sipping on herbal tea, when I was graced with the presence of the King of the Slicky Boys.

His bodyguards stayed just out of earshot as I told him what I knew and what I suspected, leaving out the details of my conjectures on the classified information. So nodded thoughtfully as I talked, but when I mentioned Ernie he raised his hand.

"We already know about that. And the unfortunate death of the young woman. The question is, Agent Sueño, what do you plan to do about it?"

I let my fists unknot, took a deep breath, and outlined my plan.

While the Top Secret information was at the Geographic Survey office it was vulnerable. Shipton and his North Korean handlers would certainly know this. Once the decision on where along the DMZ to implant the nuclear devices was finalized, and it went back to the War Room, it would be much harder—probably impossible—to obtain. Now was the time to strike.

What I proposed to Herbalist So was that he find a way to feed this information to the North Koreans. I doubted that the slicky boys had direct contact with the North Korean Communists, but when you're buying secrets—and the penalty for dealing in secrets in Korea is death—there's going to be a tight network that handles the sale of such dangerous information. Over the years, the slicky boys, although they might not deal in such information themselves, would've developed conduits into that network.

When I proposed it, So didn't bat an eye. I'd been right. He knew how to contact them.

If a way could be arranged to feed the information indirectly to Shipton, then I could be waiting for him at the Geographic Survey office with a nice MP escort when he arrived.

Herbalist So seemed to like my plan, as far as it went, but wanted to make modifications. He assured me that once Shipton and his handlers were put onto the Geographic Survey building, they would check the scene out carefully before acting. Any sign of increased security, any sign of extra checks at the front gate, any sign of stakeouts or extra security personnel planted in the area, and they wouldn't take the risk.

For a North Korean agent—especially one as valuable as Shipton—to be caught right in the middle of the 8th Army Headquarters complex was something the North Korean Communists would avoid at all costs. The international repercussions would be too great.

If I couldn't wait for him, I asked, how could we catch him?

Herbalist So had an answer.

I would enter the compound, he said, clandestinely. Like a thief in the night. No one, including the authorities, would be aware of my presence. Not until it was too late.

I had no idea how I could do this but he told me not to worry, I would be contacted. An escort would be provided.

Finally, I agreed. I wasn't happy with it but he was right. It was probably the only way.

We settled on details and, in Western fashion, shook hands.

"We will contact you," he said. "When the moment arrives."

I bowed deeply to him and he bowed back, then left with his boys. I finished my tea and wandered out into the empty street. At each intersection I searched for the Chinese woman. She wasn't there.

• • •

The waiting was the hard part.

To make it easier, I went down to the arms room and took a little target practice on the firing range. Palinki stood behind me, red plastic muffs over his ears.

"You're getting better, Sueño," he said, "but bend more at the knees. And try to relax your shoulders."

I managed to hit the target a few times. Once, when I imagined it was Shipton, right through the heart.

After about thirty rounds, Palinki clapped me on the back.

"Keep at it and one day you'll be the best in the detachment," he said.

Not likely. Where I grew up nobody knew anything about handling guns, because nobody could afford them. The teenage gangs in the neighborhood went in for knives and baseball bats. Traditionalists all.

After I cleaned the .38, I asked Palinki if he had a few more bullets he could spare—off the inventory.

"No sweat, brotha. You just keep me straight if you catch me down in the ville."

"Will do."

Palinki didn't drink often, but when he did his big Samoan face flushed red and he went on a rampage, like a mindless caveman suddenly trapped in a world of maddening intricacies. Now he was in the program, attending meetings and trying not to drink. He was doing real good, but he had decided to get out of the army. The army, what with the NCO Clubs and the Happy Hours and the bars off post, was set up for drinking. Too much temptation, Palinki figured.

He was going back to Samoa and fish, he said. I hoped he made it.

I grabbed the extra rounds, popped them in my pocket, and climbed back up the cement stairwell toward the daylight.

The days slipped past slowly. Ernie was still in the 121 Evac, and at night I hung out in Itaewon expecting any minute to be contacted by Herbalist So or one of his boys. Or, better yet, the Chinese woman.

I heard nothing.

Meanwhile, the weather had cleared, the skies were porcelain blue, but the thermometer had dropped like a fighter going down from a kick to the head. Dirty snow clung to the edges of rooftops, hardening into bizarre shapes like soot-covered gargoyles.

I didn't give up on the ration control numbers Herbalist So had provided. I stayed on the phone during the day, checking with local MP's where the numbers had turned up, and they even made a couple of arrests. Each time, however, the story was the same. Some guy had sold the GI the ration control plate—cheap—guaranteeing that it was safe.

It looked as if Shipton was trying to keep our attention diverted. The phony ration control plate incidents worked up the spine of Korea. From Taegu to Taejon to Pyongtaek to Songt'an—up to Seoul.

He was getting closer.

I checked on Ernie every day. His condition had stabilized, and the doctors hoped he'd be up and about in a couple of weeks.

They talked about taking judicial action against him for leaving the hospital without authorization. But it was just talk. Designed more to keep him in bed and on his medications more than anything else.

Ernie passed the time by hobbling around the hospital and watching medics administer injections. And asking a lot of questions about prescriptions.

"A pharmacist," he told me. "That's what I should've been. A pharmacist."

I laughed. That would've been like a glutton guarding the cream puffs.

We talked about the Nurse. He asked me a lot of questions that I couldn't answer. No, there was no reason why she should've died. She was young and had much to live for. Shipton had been after us, not her, I told him. She'd just gotten in the way.

That didn't make it any easier for him. He conned one of the medics into slipping him a few extra capsules of tranquilizers, and when I left him that day his eyes were calm, staring off into space.

. . .

The intensity of Shipton's lust for revenge haunted me. He had killed Ernie's girlfriend and tried to kill Ernie. All because we were chasing him or because, as the voice in the cellar had said, we had killed Miss Ku. But why did he accuse us of having killed her when it was obvious that he was the culprit? I couldn't explain it. However, it was a topic I was looking forward to discussing with him.

Four days dragged by. Tomorrow the list of sites for the buried nuclear devices would be shipped out of Geographic Survey and their Security NCO could breathe a sigh of relief.

I was tense. I couldn't understand why Herbalist So hadn't contacted me. Alternate plans started in my mind. Maybe I should spill the whole story to the First Sergeant, get a few reliable MP's assigned to accompany me, and stake out the place myself. If we played it right, maybe Shipton or his comrades wouldn't spot us and we'd be able to trap him. I didn't like the idea but it looked as if my request for help from the slicky boys was a bust.

I was on my way down to the snack bar for lunch, staying away from the go-go girls at the Lower Four Club. They reminded me too much of Miss Ku and the Nurse. My hands were thrust deep into my pockets, my head down.

A coal cart whizzed past me, pushed by a sturdy Korean in a cast-off wool uniform. These were the men who delivered coal to the big furnaces that kept the barracks and the public buildings on 8th Army Headquarters warm. It was a dirty job and done mostly in the wee hours of the morning when everyone else was fast asleep. It was unusual to see a coal cart during the day.

By the side of the road a group of Koreans, men and women, chopped ice to clear the sidewalk. They heaved the big chunks into a growing pile.

As I passed, one of the women jumped in front of me, brandishing a wickedly curved metal scythe. I stopped instinctively, ready to pull my hands out of my pockets and protect myself. Within the folds of the white bandana wrapped tightly beneath her chin, her wrinkled face smiled broadly.

"Greetings from Herbalist So," she said.

For a moment I thought she was going to swing the scythe and stab the sharpened point into my heart. She read my concern and laughed.

"Tonight," she said, "you are to visit the home of Kuang-sok's father. Just before curfew. Be prepared."

Kuang-sok's father, Mr. Ma, the retired slicky boy.

The other workers were still bent over, hacking at the ice, seemingly oblivious to our little confrontation. The woman smiled again, gaps flashing in white teeth, lowered her scythe, and rejoined the line of workers.

I wanted to ask her questions but it was clear that no one had anything more to say to me. They chopped and hacked, ignoring me as if I'd never existed. I watched her broad back for a second, then continued on.

In the distance, steam rose from the snack bar's long tin roof. Clouds rolled in. The afternoon sky started to darken.

Tonight I would invade the U.S. Army's compound with the retired slicky boy Mr. Ma.

It had to happen tonight. This would be Shipton's last chance to steal the information on the tunnels. And my last chance to catch him before his mission was complete and he disappeared into the mist.

I patted the .38 under my jacket. Suddenly I wished I'd spent more time on the firing range.

39

SNOW BEGAN TO FALL EARLY IN THE EVENING. JUST A FEW SCATtered flakes at first, but it picked up as the night went on. By the time I left the barracks, the crystals were coming down in fat, wet chunks that lingered on my shoulders like sloppy drunks who don't know when to go home.

Flurries charged through the crooked alleys of Itaewon, chased by shifting gusts of wind. The pathways looked different in their white shroud of lace, but I managed to find the old wooden building after recovering from a couple of wrong turns.

The stone walkway was slick with ice but after descending one flight, I pounded on the door of the basement. Thirty seconds later, the door creaked open. No light flooded out. The inside was black. I slipped into the warmth.

The shadowy figure of Mr. Ma guided me through the cellar and slid back the door to the hooch he shared with his son. A stained yellow light filtered out. The boy lay facedown on a sleeping mat, a silk comforter pulled up to his shoulders, sound asleep.

Mr. Ma whispered to me. "Take off your jacket."

I did as I was told. He inspected me.

I wore blue jeans, black combat boots, and a black turtleneck pullover. The .38 formed a lump below my left armpit. Beneath the outer layer of clothing I had on underwear and thermal long johns. Mr. Ma tugged on the tight material of the pullover, letting it spring back into place, and motioned for me to tuck it into my pants.

When I finished he nodded approvingly.

"Good," he said. "But no jacket."

It would be cold as a son of a bitch out there.

There was still some time before curfew so we sat on the narrow wooden porch. I asked him how Herbalist So had maneuvered Shipton and his North Korean handlers into making their move tonight.

He didn't have all the details but claimed that one of the workmen on compound, the man who changed the glass bottles of drinking water, had managed to obtain copies of the keys to the inner security rooms of the Geographical Survey building. At Herbalist So's instructions, this man had approached certain brokers in clandestine information and put the keys on the underground auction block. Someone had snatched up the offer right away. Discreet inquiry indicated the buyers were the same agents who were handling Shipton.

"Why wouldn't Shipton have gone in earlier?"

"The keys were just sold today."

Talk about cutting it close.

"How can we be sure he knows the information he seeks will be gone tomorrow?"

"We can't. We're hoping he obtained that information from other sources. If we offer him too much knowledge, he will become suspicious. Besides," Mr. Ma said, "the Communist habit is to act immediately. Before they are betrayed."

Ma slapped me on the knee.

"*Kapshida*," he said. Let's go.

. . .

The snow hadn't let up. It was past curfew now so everyone was off the street. Occasionally, in the dark alleys, we saw another set of footprints, silently erased by the falling flakes.

We wound through pathways that were new to me, and after a few minutes I was completely lost. Without my jacket the cold bit into the bones beneath my flesh and held on, gnawing at the marrow with a fierce pleasure.

Finally, we emerged on the MSR. Mr. Ma peeked out onto the main road, looking for the white jeeps of the curfew police. When he saw that all was clear, he waved me forward. Ahead loomed the stone wall, topped with a chain-link fence and barbed wire, that surrounded the south post of Yongsan Compound.

Without hesitation, Ma picked up speed, running as if he were going to smash face-first into the wall ahead. Instead, he bounded forward, caught a toehold, and kept his momentum, moving his body up the wall like a crab scuttling over a sand bank.

Why hadn't he told me about this? Probably because he didn't want me to think about it. I didn't. I hit the wall running, moved easily up the craggy rocks about halfway, until my trailing foot slipped and I plummeted down to the ground, tumbling backward on my ass into the snow.

My head snapped against the soft pack.

I lay dazed for a time, I'm not really sure how long. Finally, I heard Mr. Ma hissing at me. I raised myself on my elbow and fingered the back of my skull. No blood. I'd live. I looked up.

Ma sat atop the wall like a cat, motioning for me to move forward. Shaking my head to clear it, I rose unsteadily to my feet.

I took it more slowly this time, checking my handholds and testing my foot placements before entrusting my entire weight. After what must've been five minutes of struggle I finally made it. Ma grabbed my arm and, with surprising strength for a man of his size, yanked me up to the top of the wall.

No congratulations, no words of encouragement. We just moved forward.

We still had the chain-link fence to get over—the metal posts of which were imbedded in the stone—and the barbed wire coiled atop it.

Prongs at the summit stuck out at wicked angles. The thought of trying to climb over that, with almost a twenty-foot fall below, caused a spasm of fear in my stomach.

But Ma didn't make any moves to climb up. Instead, he slid along the top of the wall toward a juncture where the cliff rose even higher. When he reached it he paused and grabbed two loose stones, about the size of bricks. I wondered if he'd planted them there. Working quickly, he shoved the flat side of one of the stones beneath the taut chain-link fence. The muscles on his neck strained as he twisted it up. Miraculously, despite all the tension in the fence, he pried the linked wire up about three inches from the stone wall.

I glanced down at the road. No pedestrians. No traffic. But it wouldn't last long. The curfew police would be along soon.

He grabbed the other stone and, about a yard away from where he had set the first one, he twisted it skyward. Now, there was about four inches of space between the chain-link fence and the stone wall. Twisting his neck at a painful angle he forced his head beneath the fence. I thought for sure he'd be trapped that way: his head on one side of the fence, his rib cage on the other. But he kept wriggling forward, pushing up as much as he could with his hands, and slowly the razor-sharp bottom of the chain link dragged itself over his chest. Once he had wriggled in up to his waist, the rest was easy. He kicked forward, twisted his ankles until his feet popped through, and he was in.

I almost applauded. I'd never seen anything like it, even in a circus.

Mr. Ma squatted in front of the fence, checking over his shoulder for guards. He jabbed his finger forward, pointing for me to crawl through the same opening he'd just squeezed through.

He had to be insane. No way I'd ever fit. I was twice his size. But he kept pointing and he grabbed the fence with his fingers, showing me that he'd be lifting up on it.

In the distance I heard the purring motor of a jeep, heading our way. I lay down on my back along the cold stone fence, twisted my head, and started pushing with my feet. It scratched and it hurt and every inch forward was accompanied by pain. Ma squatted above, jerking with all his strength on the thick wire. I must've sliced half my nose off pushing my head through but finally it was in and when the fence scraped along my chest I thought for sure my shirt would be shredded. Ma kept lifting and tugging until I wriggled through to my waist and kicked forward and scraped my pelvis bones and finally my thighs and my knees and my feet.

I was in! I gazed down at the fence, now pressed firmly against the stone, and couldn't believe I'd squeezed through the tiny opening.

Ma slapped me on the shoulder but suddenly twisted his head. Footsteps. We ran toward the tree line.

Squatting behind a row of snow-covered birch trees, we watched as a guard in heavy gloves and fur-lined parka sauntered by, an M1 rifle slung carelessly over his shoulder. He was Korean. One of the contract hires who guard the compound at night.

When the guard's footsteps faded, Mr. Ma turned and stalked off through the trees. I followed.

Many of the redbrick buildings on military compounds in Korea—and all throughout Asia—had been built by the Japanese Imperial Army prior to World War II. After Emperor Hirohito's surrender ending the war, the U.S. Army had moved right in.

Mr. Ma and I stood amongst a grove of trees on a small hill overlooking a cluster of brick buildings surrounded by a high wall. The old Japanese stockade.

We moved down the hill.

Nowadays, the U.S. Army used the buildings for storage only, but I'd heard stories about this place. About how the Korean partisans had been imprisoned here by the Japanese, and how they'd been tortured and killed.

We entered the brick archway into the square courtyard. I glanced at the walls. The bullet holes had never been covered over. Koreans had been executed right here, right where I stood, for wanting nothing more than the freedom of their country. Possibly, Herbalist So's father had been one of them.

A small building sat off by itself. Ma tried the door. It wasn't locked. Inside it was dark but instead of sitting down and resting as I hoped, Ma motioned for me to help him move a large crate. We both leaned up against the splintery wooden box. It didn't budge. I noticed the stenciling. A diesel engine. Made in Detroit.

I braced my legs against the wall and we tried again. This time the crate budged slightly. We leaned into it, straining with everything we had, and slowly it started to move. It let out a groan as it slid across the floor, and after a few feet Ma straightened.

"Deitda," he said. Enough.

He knelt and brushed off dust. In the dim moonlight I made out a thin line on the floor. A rectangle. Almost identical to the trapdoor Ernie and I had discovered when escaping from Herbalist So's dungeon. Using a loose board, Ma slowly pried it up. In the depths were the ruins of a ladder and cobwebs and more darkness. A tunnel. They kept popping up in this case.

Whispering, he took mercy on my dumbfounded expression and started to explain.

Before the Second World War, many Koreans had been held in this stockade, sometimes hundreds at a time, awaiting interrogation or even execution. The Japanese guards were ruthless but still there was occasionally trouble. Once, the prisoners rioted, and overcame their guards. The warden, who lived in this small building, had been slaughtered by the inmates.

The Korean insurrection was put down by Japanese force of arms but, in view of his predecessor's bloody demise, the new warden decided to add a little life insurance. He dug an escape tunnel, the one we were looking at now.

When the American army took over in 1945, Herbalist So gave orders for the tunnel to be kept secret and had it extended until it reached beneath the new road connecting south post to north post. In all the years since, the tunnel had been used only by those slicky boys approved in advance by Herbalist So.

Apparently, Mr. Ma and I were two of those so approved.

The tunnel reeked of decayed rodents. I thought about snakes. There must be plenty down there. I asked Ma about it. He laughed.

There are no poisonous snakes in Korea, he said. I wasn't so sure that was true.

Ma told me to wait. He dropped down the ladder and fumbled in the dark amongst stones. Suddenly, a light flared upward. He smiled up at me, the flickering flame of a lighted candle making his bronzed face look like a death mask. He motioned for me to follow.

I swallowed and lowered myself onto the ladder, and pulled the trapdoor shut above me. Mr. Ma told me that first thing in the morning, laborers in So's employ would enter the building and replace the crate we had moved back over the tunnel's mouth.

How were we going to get back out?

He grinned again in the eerie light. That was the easy part.

We crouched through the tunnel. It was circular and lined with brick. After about twenty yards the brick gave way to unfinished cement.

The air became thicker. There wasn't much oxygen down here and we'd use it up soon. In a barely controlled panic I started to wonder if there was another crate sitting atop the trapdoor on the other side. I whispered my question forward to Ma. It's already been arranged, he replied.

I hoped so. If anybody fumbled an assignment we'd be in a world of shit.

The cement ended, the tunnel narrowed, the air grew stale, and something crashed into my toe. Pain shot up my leg. I stumbled forward, cursing, and fell flat on my face on the rock. I'd tripped over an outcropping of stone.

Mr. Ma called back. "*Bali bali,*" he said. Hurry.

I crawled forward. The tunnel was too small to stand up in now. All I could see was the flicker of Mr. Ma's candle ahead of me. Water began to seep out of the walls of the tunnel. I cursed some more. My hands and feet and knees became slathered in mud. Sweat began to sting my eyes and seep from my armpits.

Unbelievably, the tunnel became even narrower. Soon, I had to lie flat on my belly and slither forward like an eel. I could no longer see Mr. Ma's light and I kept wriggling forward quickly, frightened that he might leave me behind.

The mud and the water soaked the front of my sweater and my blue jeans and began to seep into my long underwear. The tunnel was so narrow now that I felt as if I were crawling into the belly of an enormous python made of granite. I was having trouble breathing.

Something squeaked and scurried through the darkness. Without thinking, I slapped at the rolling fur and felt its plump body twist and writhe beneath my hand. A sharp pain jabbed my finger. I jerked backward. A rat. It scampered farther into the darkness.

I couldn't see the puncture wound but I knew I'd been bitten. I sucked blood off my fingertip. I wasn't sure which was worse: dying of suffocation or from the bubonic plague.

Finally, the tunnel started to widen. With great relief I found myself crawling on hands and knees. The air grew lighter, almost breathable.

At last we reached the end of the tunnel. Ma handed me the candle and climbed up another ladder. At the top he creaked open another trapdoor, peeked out, pushed his way through, and told me to bring the candle up with me.

I climbed out into the open space, taking greedy breaths of dusty air. The space we stood in was dark and dank but, compared to the tunnel, I felt as if I'd stepped into a springtime meadow.

We were in another warehouse. But this one was different. It was made of finely finished cement, no windows, and the crates around us were of cardboard rather than wood.

Ma closed the trapdoor and we piled a few of the boxes atop it. Each was stenciled with English lettering: Water, canned, ½ gallon, 12 each.

The other boxes were filled with nonperishable foodstuffs and medical supplies. It finally dawned on me where we were. An air raid shelter. Somewhere deep beneath 8th Army headquarters.

A thick coat of dust covered everything.

Ma opened one of the crates. He told me to douse the candle and hide it in there. I hesitated. Without light, we would be blind. He took my hand and had me grasp the back of his belt. I blew the candle out and placed it where he told me to. The world was pitch black. He pulled me forward.

I stumbled after him through the darkness, clinging to his belt like a lifeline, touching objects with my hand, occasionally bumping like a blind man into a box or a chair. After we crossed what seemed to be a short hallway, we entered another room. Here, moonlight filtered through a narrow window covered with metal bars. Light had never looked so beautiful.

Mr. Ma shoved the heavy door forward and it scraped on the cement floor. Outside, he lifted the padlock that hung open over the doorknob and locked it into the eye of the metal hasp.

Red lettering on the door in Korean and English said *Authorized Personnel Only! Do Not Enter.*

We walked quickly through a large room that I recognized as the regular air raid shelter used during the monthly drills, and we climbed a flight of stairs and finally out into the open sky and stars.

Ma crouched low and checked around us. We were about ten yards behind the headquarters building, less than a block from Geographic Survey.

Scurrying like an Arctic wolf across the snow-covered lawns, Ma made his way through the moonlit complex. I followed. After a few yards, under the caged red bulb of a firelight, I spotted the sign: *8th U.S. Army Geographic Survey, Colonel J. Ramrock, Commander.*

A short flight of steps on the side of the building led down to a cellar door. Ma scurried toward it. We crouched in the darkness. He tried the door. It was padlocked from the outside. We'd have to find another way in. But he grabbed my arm and pointed to the rusty metal hasp.

He pulled on it. The door swung open. The hasp had been sawed neatly in half, but the padlock had been left in place. From a distance, the door looked secure. At least enough to fool a half-asleep security guard.

Ma pointed into the darkness and his somber face took on a seriousness that was unusual even for him. I immediately understood what he meant.

Shipton was already inside.

I reached beneath my pullover, unsnapped the leather holster, and pulled out the .38. Ma nodded in approval.

He opened the door. We entered.

The long hallway was like a tomb. Still, at each doorway we stopped and listened. Ma gently twisted each doorknob. Locked from the inside. Shipton had to be downstairs. Underground, where Strange had told me they kept the classified documents. I pointed toward another stairway leading down. Ma nodded and took the lead.

Although I took each step as silently as I could, my hard-soled combat boots seemed to be making way too much noise. Ma turned, frowning.

I knelt down and unlaced the boots, took them off, and set them against the wall. Ma shook his head. I picked them up, knotted the laces together, and drapped them around my neck. He nodded.

As we inched our way downstairs I thought about running back up, sprinting through the headquarters complex to the MP's at Gate 7, and ordering them to call for about five jeeps full of backup. It would be a lot safer, but I knew it wouldn't work. By the time I arrived back with help, Shipton would've sensed something was wrong. He'd be long gone. Besides, he probably had escape routes planned, escape routes I knew nothing about. We had to catch him now. While he was busy photographing the documents or trying to break into a safe. Now, while he was close.

When we reached the bottom of the landing, my knees were shaking. Down the hall, at the last doorway, light filtered out. A flashlight. Someone was inside.

Ma's face was grim. He motioned me forward. I had to admire him: the guy was fearless.

At each door we passed, we stopped and listened but now Ma didn't try the doorknobs. Any whisper of sound would betray us. The glow of the light in the last room grew brighter as we inched forward.

At the edge of the door we both froze. Ma pointed to his chest and motioned that he would go in first, veering to his left. He signaled that I should follow, moving to the right and taking aim with the pistol. My hands shook and I hoped that my lips weren't quivering but I knew they were. Ma placed one hand on the doorknob, held out three fingers with the other, and started to count them down.

One. Two. Three!

We slammed through the doorway.

Ma moved left, I moved right, both of us scanning a room lined with file cabinets, searching for anything that moved. I held the .38 in front of me but I saw only a safe, untouched, and a lighted flashlight resting atop it, its beam reflecting off a coffee cup of burnished bronze. I realized what had happened but before I could turn, Ma was moving back toward me, his hands waving frantically, and something dark burst through the door and lunged at Ma. I saw only a gleam of silver and heard Ma grunt and then he was flying, lifted through the air, his squirming body heading straight toward me.

I swiveled and pointed the gun. But there was nothing to shoot at except Ma's stomach. I stepped backward, but the soaring body arched toward me and slammed into my hands and my chest and I saw the gleaming blade and a hand around its hilt and the knife slashed toward my chest. I rolled but it was no good, the blade slammed into me with a thud, and I expected a searing pain but I felt nothing. I knew that was probably because I was in shock and that the pain would come later.

Then the laces of the boots jerked at the back of my neck.

I realized the blade hadn't reached me, it had slashed into the boot hung around my neck.

Still, I was on my back and Ma was on top of me and someone was on top of him. Something heavy stomped my wrist. The pain flamed up my arm like molten lead.

The gun. The gun!

It was gone. My hand was useless, probably busted. I rolled, trying to get away from the monster above me and the pain, until I slammed into the wall. When I looked back I could see in the steady light of the flashlight that Ma lay sprawled beside me, blood seeping out a huge gash in his back. Above loomed a man. A man holding a bloody Gurkha knife.

Shipton.

I scrambled for the gun, found it in the dark. But before I could turn and fire I heard his heavy footsteps pounding out the door.

No time to think now. I tried to rise, pushing with my free

hand, but pain exploded up my arm. Something was broken. I rolled. Using my knees, I managed to struggle to my feet and stumbled forward.

At the door I paused. Listened. Nothing.

Shipton could be just around the corner, holding his breath, knife raised to strike again. Unsteadily, I raised the pistol and charged into the hallway, slamming backward into the far wall. Turning. Aiming. Nothing. I scanned the corridor. He was gone.

I moved forward. Could he have escaped that quickly? I remembered the corridor of doorways. We'd checked inside none of the rooms. Shipton must've emerged from one and now had ducked back in. I crept forward, keeping my back pressed against the wall, darting my eyes constantly to the right and left.

At the first door I held my breath and listened. Silence. Reaching out with my injured hand, I turned the knob. Fire shot up my arm. Grimacing, I twisted. Finally, slowly, the door opened.

I gazed into a pitch-black vacuum. Shipton could be just inside. Waiting. Quickly, I reached in, felt for the switch, snapped it skyward, and stepped back out. Nothing happened. The lights were out.

I remembered the glowing bulb of the red fire light out front. Shipton hadn't cut the electricity, that might've set off an alarm. But unscrewing the fluorescent lamps inside the building would've been easy enough.

Mr. Ma might still be alive, bleeding to death back in the other room. He needed help and he needed help *now.* It might take me hours to flush out Shipton. I decided I couldn't let Mr. Ma die.

I backed down the hallway, twisting and turning with each step, keeping the pistol pointed in front of me.

I slipped back into the file room and knelt beside Ma's body. Hot blood seeped into the denim of my blue jeans. Keeping my eyes on the doorway, I shoved the pistol in my belt, and reached for his neck. His eyes were wide open, staring at the ceiling. I gave it two minutes, pinching deeply into the loose flesh of his throat, searching for an artery. No pulse. He was dead.

When I stood, the blood on my knees dripped down my pant-legs to my socks. I remembered my boots. I unraveled them from around my shoulders, fingering the ugly gash made by Shipton's knife. Then I heard the shouts of panicked men.

I forgot about trying to slip on the boots and just strapped them over my shoulder. I pulled the revolver out of my belt, staggered back to my feet, and hobbled forward, out of the room and down the hallway. It seemed like a long trip. As I climbed the stairs, pain rocketed up my arm, slamming into my skull like exploding artillery shells.

Outside, flames licked the winter sky. A fire in the Aviation Battalion offices, about thirty yards away, on the far side of the headquarters building. I pushed through the door and emerged into the cold night air. I wasn't worried about Shipton popping out at me. He couldn't be here. He'd started that fire. It couldn't be a coincidence.

The flames swelled, enveloping the building. Men shouted and ran toward the conflagration. I scanned the scurrying faces in the dark. No Shipton.

A couple of men were decked out in dress uniforms. One in red with a white sash across his chest, a British Honor Guard soldier. The other in green, ROK Army. The night guard at the 8th Army Headquarters building. They joined the frantic crowd, searching for hoses, yelling for buckets.

Then it dawned on me what must've happened.

Once Shipton had tricked Mr. Ma and me into entering the Geographic Survey file room, why hadn't he just disappeared down the hallway, left us searching for him in the dark like a couple of dimwits? Why had he come back and attacked? He must've known that I'd be armed—and attacking us for no reason was too big a risk. He'd attacked because he wanted to delay us. Or kill us. When that hadn't worked, he'd set the fire. It was clear to me now. It was a diversion.

Strange had told me that after the Geographic Survey people completed their final list of possible tunnel sites, they would pass the documents on to the 8th Army Commander. That's what had happened. When Shipton couldn't find what he wanted in the Geographic Survey files, he realized the papers must've been moved earlier than scheduled.

Shipton had killed Ma—and would've killed me too—so he

wouldn't be interrupted while continuing his search. And now he'd set a fire to pull the Honor Guard soldiers away from their posts. The Headquarters building was unguarded.

I started to run.

The men responding to the alarm were too busy, too fascinated with the flames for me to bother asking for their help. It would've taken too long to explain what was wrong, what I needed. Shipton would work fast. I couldn't risk delay.

The corridors of the 8th Army headquarters building were dark. A red lamp glowed in the carpeted foyer.

A few yards in, I stopped and peered down the hallway. Nothing. I stood for a moment, listening. No sound. I crept forward.

The commander's office was back in the corner of the building, in a position of honor. I'd never been inside, but I'd heard about it. Plush furniture, valuable paintings, an outer office with a gorgeous Korean receptionist, a small conference room next door.

I stopped in front of the big double-door entrance to the commander's office. A replica of the 8th Army cloverleaf patch, bigger than a basketball, had been carved with loving care into varnished teak.

Everything was quiet. No sign of Shipton. He must be inside.

He had to be.

I stepped forward, grabbed the brass handle of the door, and pulled it open.

In the receptionist's office, moonlight filtered in through open curtains, glistening off leather chairs and gleaming coffee tables.

I slipped my finger into the trigger housing of the .38 and took another step forward.

The noise was like a great ripping of wood. I swiveled instinctively but saw nothing. I tried to locate the sound. It seemed to be everywhere and nowhere. I had only a split second to look up but as I did, I realized that the sound I had heard was plywood sliding above me, and the heavy darkness that crashed into me was Shipton.

He had dropped on me from the ceiling.

40

THE KILLER REPLACED THE PANEL IN THE PLYWOOD CEILING AND dragged the tall Mexican into the 8th Army Commander's office. After leaning the CID agent's limp body against a file cabinet, he knelt and felt for a pulse. Still strong. This man who'd been hounding him—this Sueño—would regain consciousness soon.

Prying one of the bayonets off the rifles the Honor Guard soldiers had left, the killer ran the sharp tip along the agent's neck. Flesh rippled beneath the gleaming blade. Waste him now, he decided. Take no chances.

Something made him hesitate.

Angel and Chuy. Two ranch hands from Matamoros—perched on the edge of the corral. He could still see them. Watching.

This Sueño had proved to be the same type of Mex. Watching. Always watching.

And the killer remembered the woodshed. The door slamming behind him. The foul reek of cheap rye whiskey. His father turning, slowly, hatred filling his eyes. Unraveling a black leather belt from his emaciated waist. Swinging the huge silver buckle, slapping the weight of it into his palm.

And he remembered the crying, the pleading—the way his little boy whimpers seemed to enrage his father. And most of all he remembered the relentless battering.

After his father had left the shed, the boy who was not yet a killer staggered out, covering his eyes, trying to hide his injuries, into the bright noonday sun. Into the pitiless stares of Angel and Chuy.

It was their eyes he couldn't stand. Always watching. Always knowing. Their faces showing nothing. Like two vultures feeding off his soul.

When his father died, the killer inherited a pile of debt and a worthless ranch. But he was big now. And strong. After he'd disposed of everything that had ever belonged to his father, he disposed of two more things: Angel and Chuy.

He'd gutted them. Using a hacking blade he found in the toolshed. And left their bodies in a thicket of mesquite.

The killer shook his head, bringing himself back to the business at hand.

He poked gently into the soft flesh below the chin of the CID agent. A bubble of blood rose to the surface, burst, and started to trickle toward the collar of the black shirt.

This agent—this Sueño, this dreamer—had been like Angel and Chuy. Always watching. Always knowing. Waiting patiently to witness the beating that would surely come.

Suddenly, the killer slapped his knees and rose to his feet, his decision made. He'd kill this agent slowly, like he'd killed Angel and Chuy, like he'd killed Whitcomb. He'd watch the silent knowledge in Sueño's eyes change to surprise at his great prowess. And then to terror.

Always terror.

When I came to, I was no longer in the receptionist's office but in the 8th Army Commander's office itself. I finally made it, I thought. The corridors of power.

A green lamp glowed above a work counter. Bo Shipton hunched over it, shuffling through papers, his narrow eyes glancing up occasionally at me. His big paw clasped my .38.

Muscles rippled through his arms and shoulders as he worked. He wore a plain dark brown poplin shirt and dark khaki work pants. Good camouflage for a thief. With his short haircut and his neatly shaved mug, he could've easily passed for a military officer in civvies putting in some late hours.

He must've dragged me in here and propped me against this cabinet. I wasn't tied up, which was a nice touch—but he didn't have any rope, so maybe he was less generous than I thought.

Neither of us spoke for a while. He was too busy, I was too stunned. Finally, the ringing in my head subsided and I started to lift myself up.

"Don't move!"

The voice was a low growl. Raspy. As if his throat was lined with gravel. I remembered the field tracheotomy I had read about in his records. The tube of bamboo he'd stuck in his own windpipe. His jawline was jagged and rippled with scars; reconstructed after the wounds he received in Vietnam.

"If you move," Shipton said. "I'll shoot you right now."

Keeping the gun on me, Shipton edged toward the safe. He swirled the combination dial back and forth until the ball bearings clicked. He grabbed the handle, twisted, and swung open the heavy door. He riffled through the papers inside, found a blue folder marked TOP SECRET, and carried it back to the lamp. He pulled a tiny camera from his pocket. When he was finished photographing its contents, he stuffed the folder back into the safe, closed it, and locked it shut.

He stepped toward me.

"Sueño," he said, lingering on the word. "You're a Mex. And like all Mexes you hang out in *las cantinas* and you take money to do low jobs. You and your partner, Bascom, were the only CID agents greedy enough to bring Whitcomb to me. *¿Entiendes, cabrón?*"

His Spanish came out in a flat drawl. An Anglo trying to impress somebody.

"Stick to redneck American," I said, rubbing the cut above my collar. "Your Spanish is for shit."

Shipton's big body tensed. "You're a lowlife," he said. "On the take."

"It was a few bucks for a favor. At least I never killed one of my own girlfriends."

He raised the gun. "I could pull this trigger right now. End it all."

My bowels just about unraveled. When the gun didn't go off, I thought I might have a chance.

"Too many guards around here, Shipton. A gunshot would make it real hard for you to get away."

He smiled. "You're right. Besides, it would be less enjoyable. And I owe you one."

"Owe me for what?"

"For killing Miss Ku."

"Are you mad? I never touched the girl."

He shrugged. "Maybe it was your partner then. Doesn't matter. That's why I killed that Itaewon bitch he was shacked up with. I would've offed him too if she didn't have so many noisy neighbors."

"They know how to treat a thief."

The scars on the side of Shipton's head swarmed toward his eyes like a school of hungry fish. "You got a sharp mouth for a lowlife, on-the-take CID asshole."

He lowered the gun and slid it behind his waist.

"Get up!" he said.

I rose unsteadily. I ached all over but especially in my right hand, which was shooting thunderbolts up my arm.

Shipton grabbed two rifles, M14's, the type the Honor Guard uses, both with shiny, stainless steel bayonets glimmering in the green light. He loosened the carrying strap on one and slung it over his powerful shoulders. The other he pointed at me.

"Out the back, Dreamer," he said.

We stepped into the commander's conference room. In the far wall was a door locked by a long brass bolt. Shipton jerked it back, pushed the door open, and shoved me through. I missed the first stair and fell facedown into the snow.

Shipton poked me with the bayonet.

"Move," he hissed.

I lifted myself up and staggered along the big brick wall of 8th Army Headquarters.

Behind us, the flames at the Aviation building crackled. Men shouted. All activity was centered down there. We were moving away from all that, into the shadows.

No chance to run away. He'd pop me in the back before I made three steps. Best to keep him talking.

"Why'd you kill Whitcomb?"

"Keep moving."

"Is it because he saw you that night in J-two?"

"You're a real sleuth, aren't you?"

"How long you been working for the North Koreans?"

He jabbed me again with the bayonet. "Shut the fuck up."

We turned a corner, and in the distance I spotted a shadowy figure pushing a cart. Coal delivery. The workman wouldn't be much help. Anyway, he moved away, not even glancing in our direction.

"You better hope nobody shows up," Shipton said. "If they do, I'll shoot you and end it quick."

But for some reason he had decided not to shoot me right away. I considered asking why but thought better of it. Instead, I concentrated on finding a means of escape. Anything. A loose brick, an old piece of pipe, anything I could use as a weapon. The M14 in Shipton's hands was loaded. I'd heard the rifle's bolt clack forward before we left the Headquarters building. The odds against me were long, but I wasn't dead yet.

He poked the tip of the bayonet into my back.

"Over there," he said.

With the blade, he motioned toward a gap between two buildings. When the narrow pathway opened up, we were standing in the center of a small, courtyardlike space with the backs of four brick buildings facing us. Four more narrow pathways ran off like spokes from a wheel, all of them uphill, giving the impression that we were in an enclosed bowl. Once, the Japanese Imperial Army had used this space as a garden. But with typical American efficiency we'd blacktopped it over.

It was like the spot in Namdaemun where Cecil Whitcomb had died. In the center of things but isolated: Shipton's method of operation. Ice crunched beneath my stockinged feet. My toes were frozen—I'd left the boots back in the Headquarters building—but I hadn't even noticed the discomfort until just now. Too many other things to worry about. The snow had stopped falling and a few stray trails of footsteps crossed this small field of frost.

"Hold it right there," Shipton said. I had reached the center of the courtyard. "Turn around."

I turned.

Before I could react, he popped the magazine out of the M14, ejected the live round from the chamber, and tossed the weapon to me. It slipped out of my grasp, clattering to the snow, and as I bent to pick it up he whipped the other rifle off his shoulders and pointed it at me. He clanged a round into the chamber.

I hefted the M14 in my hands. He had bullets, I didn't. But at least I had the bayonet.

"Go ahead," Shipton taunted. "I'll even give you a chance. The same one I gave Whitcomb."

Some chance. To die with a knife in the gut or a bullet through the head. I braced the rifle butt against my hip. Pain roared from my wrist.

"Too bad you're hurt," he said. "Makes it less challenging."

"I'll kick your ass anyway."

His eyes widened. "Is that what you said to Miss Ku?"

What the hell was he talking about? Why did he think I killed Miss Ku? But if he didn't kill her, who did? No time to think about that now. Only time to find a way to stay alive. I had to get under his skin somehow. Force him to make a mistake.

"You really cared for her, eh?" I said. "The way you cared for the admiral's daughter?"

His face didn't flinch.

"Not an admiral," Shipton said. "Not yet, but she was an officer's daughter, all right. I thought maybe she wouldn't be like those bitches in Vietnam, just using GI's while they're still fucking their old boyfriends. But I was wrong."

"They're not all like that, Shipton. Only the ones who hook up with you."

Keeping his eyes on me, he stepped in a slow semicircle, checking all the pathways leading into our private coliseum of death. Not a sound. No one. Only the distant hollers of men battling the fire. Shipton looked back at me.

"What's the spirit of the bayonet fighter?" he asked.

It wasn't a question I was expecting. I knew the answer. Everyone who'd been through basic training knew the answer.

When I was silent, however, he raised his rifle. "What's the spirit of the bayonet fighter?"

I stared into the black hole of the bore. "To kill," I answered.

That seemed to satisfy him. "And what are the two types of bayonet fighters?"

The rifle was still pointed at my head. I had no choice but to go along with his sick fantasy. "The quick and the dead," I answered.

"That's right." He lowered the rifle. "The quick and the dead, Dreamer. Now, let's see what type you are."

Hope rushed through my body like an electric shock. Maybe he was crazy enough not to shoot me. At least, I'd have a chance. I gripped the rifle butt tighter, ignoring the pain in my right arm.

Keeping his eyes on me, he popped the magazine out of his M14 and ejected the round from the chamber. Run, I thought. Before I could make a move, he shuffled forward in the snow, holding the bayonet pointed straight at my eyes. He jabbed.

I backed up, but the tip of the blade caught my forearm. Blood started to trickle.

"You're an oaf, Sueño," he said. "I thought all you Mexes could knife-fight."

That's why he was after me. Why he followed me into the CID building at night and why he wrote "Dreamer" in blood on the wall of the Nurse's hooch. Not just because I had been assigned to his case, but because I'm Mexican. He was from the south of Texas. His prejudices were probably inbred.

"Go fuck yourself, Shipton," I said.

I backed up faster now. He followed. We circled each other, bayonets pointed.

He moved like a cat, smooth, agile—as if he'd been born to bayonet fighting. Throw him off stride, I thought. Make him angry. Do something.

"Mexicans are too tough for you, Shipton. Did they know how weak you really are? Is that what you've been trying to hide from all your life?"

He didn't respond, but the features of his scarred face hardened into stone. With a yell that curdled my chilled blood, he hopped forward, jabbing the bayonet at my solar plexus. I moved to my side, not backward as he expected me to, and thrust out with a jab of my own.

I missed him completely. He parried easily, then swung the butt of his rifle around in an arc toward my head. I saw it coming and dodged. The wooden stock slammed into my shoulder, knocking me backward.

Even though my socks were soaking wet, somehow I kept my footing, but he was on me now—jabbing, thrusting, parrying. It seemed as if he had three blades on the tip of his rifle. It was all I could do to stay on my feet and keep moving away. The bayonet slashed into my wrist, into my forearm, and every time I tried to make a counterthrust, my damaged right arm failed me. Even if I'd found an opening in his awesome assault, I wouldn't have been able to take advantage of it.

He came at me remorselessly, slashing with the bayonet, not plunging it forward for the kill, but slicing along my wrists and my arms as I tried to fend off the blows. Blood splattered in the snow. He bounced back, smiling.

"Trickier than Whitcomb," he said softly. "But still not worth a damn."

He closed in and slashed again. I grabbed at his bayonet with my fingers but the sharp blade bit into bone and slid free. He swiped at my arms and, with the blood flowing and my flesh shredding, he cut into my shoulder, then backed off. I leaned against a wall, gore gushing down my side and leg.

"You better think of something quick," he suggested. "Pretty soon you won't be able to lift your arms."

As he came at me again, I stepped away from the wall and backed off, protecting myself as best I could. He jabbed and sliced at will. Sweat blinded me. Loss of blood was making me dizzy.

He was playing with me now, taking his time to kill, enjoying himself. Cutting me on the hands and arms as he'd cut the Nurse, and Whitcomb before her.

His piercing green eyes watched me, knowing every move I made before I made it. As if he were searching into my soul. Searching for terror.

Something rattled and crashed.

Shipton hesitated. It was a mistake.

Sometimes when you're terrified, there's also a sense of rage. A rage you're hardly aware of at the time. How could he do this to me? How could he do it to the Nurse?

I leapt forward, ramming my bayonet toward his throat with every ounce of strength I had. His eyes widened as he saw the cruel blade closing in but somehow—miraculously—he swiveled his head. By a quarter of an inch, the bayonet slashed past his skull.

I charged forward blindly, completely off balance, consumed by rage. Shipton sidestepped and poleaxed me with the butt of his rifle as I passed. I crashed to the snow. Shipton pointed his bayonet down at me for the kill but something rumbled, growing louder, and he looked up.

Coal struck his cheek, opening a small blossom of blood. An old wooden cart was building up speed, rolling down the narrow pathway toward us. Atop a black pile of soot perched the cross-legged Ernie. Screaming. Chucking chunks of black rock.

The cart careened across the frozen snow of the courtyard and slammed into Shipton. He went down. Ernie leapt out of the cart, screaming and pummeling him with his bare fists.

I kicked in the powdery snow, searching for the bayonet.

Knuckles cracked on bone. Ernie was down. Shipton was up. Where the hell was the bayonet?

Shipton had his back to me, scrabbling for his weapon. He was standing now, trying with frigid fingers to jam the magazine of live ammunition into its slot.

My rifle! Where was my goddamned rifle?

Ernie scrambled to his feet, yelling. With a metallic snap, Shipton's magazine clicked into place. He pointed the M14 at us.

Thunder rained down. I looked up.

Down each pathway more coal carts rolled. Hooded men behind them, crouched and shoving. The carts burst out of the mouths of the narrow lanes and clattered across the courtyard, all heading straight for Shipton.

He swiveled the M14 wildly. A round exploded—but the carts didn't stop.

Like a herd of enraged musk ox, the carts slammed into Shipton. He crumpled. The rifle flew into the air.

With his head down like a bull, Ernie charged. Screaming, he grabbed Shipton's rifle, slipped in the slush, and crashed to the deck.

I was up, plowing toward Shipton. He regained his feet amazingly fast, but as he rose I kicked for his face. He dodged, caught my unbooted foot in his chest, and threw me back. I flailed wildly with my arms, lost my balance on the slick ice, and went down again.

The men who had pushed the coal carts backed up toward the safety of the brick buildings, as if to observe the outcome of the battle between these crazy foreigners.

Breathing heavily, Shipton braced himself on the edge of an overturned cart. He pulled the .38 from his belt, cocked the hammer, and aimed the barrel at me.

All over now, I thought.

His eyes focused, his big paw seemed to tighten around the .38, then something dark leapt out from behind the pile of coal.

Shipton's eyes widened. Behind him, I saw Ernie, holding something between them like an offering. The M14.

Ernie thrust upward. Shipton let go his grip on the .38 and it tumbled to the ground.

Ernie shoved up—and kept shoving—ramming the bayonet deeper into Shipton's neck. Shipton's mouth opened in a scream that had no sound. Slowly, like a metal tongue emerging from hell, the spike of the bayonet appeared between his teeth.

Pushing with all his might, Ernie lifted him higher into the air until Shipton let out a sort of groan and then a growl of agony rattled over the frozen snow.

Gore bubbled from his throat and flooded out of his nose. Finally, Ernie jerked back on the bayonet and Shipton flopped face-down into the snow, shuddered, and lay still.

I staggered to my feet, stumbled over Shipton's body, and picked up the .38. I pointed it at Shipton. His head lay twisted on the ice. Blood poured from his neck and mouth. I felt for a pulse. Then, I dropped the .38 and sat down next to him.

Ernie was on all fours, breathing heavily, drooping his head, saliva streaming from his lips.

One of the men who had pushed the coal carts now approached. A few feet away from us he stopped and shoved back his hood. Herbalist So. The King of the Slicky Boys.

"Are you hurt, Agent Sueño?"

I surveyed my body. The cuts I'd received all seemed to be superficial. Plenty of blood but no gushing from an arterial wound. My wrist, even if it was broken, could wait until we reached the 121.

"I'll live," I said. "But you'll find Mr. Ma's corpse in the Geographic Survey building."

No emotion showed on Mr. So's face. He barked swift orders to the hooded men behind him. Two grabbed a cart and shoved off, heading for Geographic Survey.

I studied So's face, thinking of how he'd manipulated me. How he'd manipulated all of us.

"The slicky boys have their compound back," I told him, gesturing toward Shipton's body. "No more North Korean agents to worry about. No more Whitcomb. The Eighth Army honchos will be satisfied. Everything can go back to normal."

The leathery features of the Emperor of the Slicky Boys didn't move but somewhere, maybe it was at the corners of his mouth, I thought I saw a trace of a smile.

He turned back to his men. "*Kaja!*" Let's go.

They grabbed their carts and rumbled into the night.

Ernie and I lay in the snow like two victims of a plane crash. A few minutes later, a pair of heavy boots pounded toward us. An MP skidded to a halt.

"Jesus Christ!" he said. "What in the hell happened to you guys?"

Ernie rolled over—groaning—and flipped him the bird. "Dick," he said and passed out.

41

THE JEEP ENGINE PURRED ALONG THE COUNTRY HIGHWAY. ERNIE had the heater turned up full blast and insisted on driving, telling me that he was feeling a lot better. We wound through rising foothills terraced with frozen rice paddies. Farmhouses huddled in companionable clusters, their thatched straw roofs frosted with ice.

Last night, the MP's had taken us over to the emergency room at the 121 Evac. After he stopped the bleeding, the medic on duty put a brace on my forearm saying that nothing was broken, just a few nasty ligament tears. He patched up all the cuts and bruises Shipton had perpetrated on me, and stitched up a few more.

"Just meat," the medic told me. "It'll heal."

He gave me a shot of antibiotics to ward off infection and a tetanus shot for the rat bite. Finished, he stood back and gazed proudly upon his handiwork. From the shoulder down I looked like something constructed by Dr. Frankenstein. Nothing I couldn't hide inside a coat, though. Except for the brace.

Ernie was supposed to stay in the hospital to allow his spleen rupture to finish healing, but after all he'd been through, no one had the nerve to tell him again he couldn't leave.

While Mr. Ma and I were struggling with Shipton, a Korean janitor at the 121 Evac had woken Ernie and told him that I was in trouble. After he'd sneaked out of the hospital, the slicky boys hid him under a canvas tarp and wheeled him in a coal cart over to the Headquarters complex.

On 8th Army compound, Slicky King So had his thumb on the pulse of everything.

After the medics patched Ernie and me up, they released us from the emergency room and I made a few early morning phone calls. Things were beginning to become clear to me. I explained to Ernie, but despite my protestations that I could take care of the problem myself, he had insisted on coming along.

Maybe I was all wet. Maybe there was something else behind this. But since last night, when Shipton told me that he hadn't killed Miss Ku, I hadn't been able to think of anything else.

I'd always been troubled by the circumstances of her murder.

Miss Ku had been tortured, as if someone had been trying to pry information out of her. And she must've been abducted, because you can't torture someone in the little alley behind the Tiger Lady's *kisaeng* house and not have anybody notice.

So if Shipton hadn't been the one who killed her, who had?

Using old-fashioned deductive logic, I'd been eliminating each possible suspect.

Except one.

One of the things that still bugged me in this case was that the ROK Navy had never notified us about Shipton being wanted for the murder of the daughter of an admiral. If they had, maybe we would've picked him up earlier and none of this shit would've happened.

Also, when Ernie and I went to the ROK Navy Headquarters in Heing-ju, this admiral—the father of a murdered daughter—hadn't even bothered to come out of his office and talk to me. I know if my daughter had been killed, and some investigator was offering to help, I wouldn't have missed the chance to talk to him.

The other thing that nagged at me was Commander Goh's language ability. When he'd first seen me, he'd spoken in Korean. I'd responded and we had a long conversation. But when he walked out to the jeep before we left, he immediately spoke to Ernie in English. How had he known that I speak Korean and Ernie only speaks English?

At the time, it seemed like mere coincidence. Now, I wasn't so sure.

The highway rose higher into the mountains. Ernie passed an overloaded country bus, flashed his headlights, and sped into a tunnel carved into the side of a granite cliff.

Despite all that had happened to him recently, he honked the horn and hooted at the echo, laughing in the darkness like a demented child.

The calls I had made this morning were to set up an appointment with Commander Goh at ROK Navy headquarters. As it turned out, that would be impossible. Today, all the brass would be attending a reenactment of one of Admiral Yi Sun Shin's victories over the forces of the Japanese Shogun Hideyoshi in 1592. The entire celebration, complete with replicas of the old sailing vessels, was being held on the coast of Kanghua-do, an island across a narrow inlet west of Seoul.

When we emerged from the tunnel, a natural harbor curved like a half-moon around the choppy gray waters of the Yellow Sea. A long wooden pier extended from the shoreline. Nearby, a parking lot was chock-full of military vehicles.

An elegant Japanese junk with folded sails lay low in the menacing waves. Closer into shore bobbed the iron-plated shell of the Korean *kobuk-son*, the turtle boat, the world's first armored ship.

Ernie guided our jeep through the village. Near the pier, the streets were lined with men in white pantaloons and brightly colored vests, sporting stovepipe horsehair hats tied atop their heads. The women drifted like flowers in their *chima-chogori*, flowing silk gowns.

"Looks like they're about to have a party," Ernie said.

"And we're going to ruin it."

The citizens of Kanghua waved as we cruised by. They don't see many foreigners out here.

We'd made sure to wear our civilian coats and ties. We were on official business and besides, I had a hunch a lot of people would be looking us over before the morning was through.

Ernie pulled up in the parking lot and backed the jeep into an open slot. We strode out toward a group of ROK Navy brass gathered at the base of the pier. All wore their black dress uniforms and gold-rimmed caps. Below them on the beach, sailors in dungarees hustled about near the turtle boat, preparing for their mission.

As we approached, the faces of the Korean officers turned toward us. Near the center stood a tall, gray-haired man with more gold on his brim than anyone else in the crowd. Two stars on his shoulders. An admiral.

In front of him, talking earnestly, stood Commander Goh.

I stopped three feet in front of them, flashed my identification, and spoke in Korean. "I'm Inspector Sueño," I said. "Eighth Army CID. Here to ask a few questions of Commander Goh."

The admiral's mouth almost fell open—the American military was not often seen in these remote areas. Ernie positioned himself a few feet away from me, hands on his hips, making sure that everyone understood that he wasn't intimidated by all this rank.

"*Wein irri issoyo?*" the admiral said. What is it you want?

"There was a murder," I said in Korean. "The daughter of an admiral, Commander Goh told me. But I've checked into this murder more thoroughly. It wasn't the daughter of an admiral who was killed."

Commander Goh took a step away from the admiral. I continued talking.

"Lieutenant Commander Shipton is dead. He was killed by Agent Bascom here"—I nodded toward Ernie—"last night, during the commission of a crime."

Air seemed to escape from Commander Goh. He edged farther away from the admiral. I stepped closer.

"The woman who was murdered," I said. "She wasn't the daughter of an admiral. She was the daughter of a naval commander. She was your daughter, Commander Goh. It was your daughter who was killed by Shipton."

He lowered his head, for what seemed a long time. Finally, he looked back up and spoke in English. Maybe hoping some of his fellow officers wouldn't understand. He spoke loudly. Forcefully. Unashamed.

"Yes. Myong-a was my daughter. Our little baby. Our only child." He shook his head, fighting back demons. "She was given over to a foreigner. He was a strong man, and I hoped that he would make her a good husband. But she had already changed her mind about him when she went back to her old boyfriend. Myong-a had seen the evil in him. She had walked away from his evil."

The admiral patted him on the shoulder, told him he didn't have to go on. Goh shrugged him off, ignoring him. A tremendous insult in a society that reveres hierarchy.

"Myong-a was afraid to tell Shipton that she would not marry him. Why didn't she come to me? I would have protected her. But she didn't want to cause trouble. Myong-a didn't want to hurt my chances of being promoted to admiral."

The strong lines of Goh's face started to melt before my eyes.

"And after she died, her mother became sick. She died only a month ago, willing death to come to her, refusing medication."

The officers stood frozen, hushed and embarrassed. Ernie shifted his hips, fondling the handcuffs at the small of his back, snapping his gum. The only person in the crowd who wasn't impressed with Commander Goh's story.

"So I am like you now, Inspector Sueño," Commander Goh said, looking straight at me. "I too am an orphan."

"And the rest, Commander Goh," I said. "Tell us the rest. Tell us about the *kisaeng* in Seoul. Tell us about Miss Ku."

He continued to stare at me, his face unchanging. He said nothing.

"The ROK Navy investigation had failed," I said. "Shipton had completely disappeared. But then, you heard about the murder of a British soldier in Namdaemun. You recognized it right away as the handiwork of Shipton. Who else would've wanted to kill—or been capable of killing—a foreigner in such a brutal manner? When you found out that Agent Bascom and I were assigned to the case, you had us followed. We led you to the Tiger Lady's *kisaeng* house."

He took a step backward.

"You killed her," I said. "You killed Miss Ku. Didn't you?" When he didn't answer, I continued. "She had known Shipton. She had slept with him. When she told you that she didn't know how to find him, you didn't believe her."

I longed to smash the side of his big square head with my metal brace. I was enraged by it all. By all the killing.

"You sliced sharp knives into her fingernails. And then you ripped them off. When she still didn't talk, you kept torturing her. And when you finally realized she knew nothing, you murdered her. Dumped her in the alley. Murdered her in a way that would make us believe that Shipton had done it."

The admiral had had enough. He barked an order. Two of the younger officers stepped between me and Commander Goh. Another laid his hand on Ernie's elbow. Ernie flinched as if he'd been buzzed by high voltage wire, hopped back, and punched the Korean officer with a right cross to the nose.

All hell broke loose. Goh backed away, out of my line of sight. Officers shouted, grabbing me and Ernie, and we shoved back, trying to break free.

Down below, someone fired a gun.

The oars of the turtle boat churned into the choppy waters, and the long-necked prow of the antique ship headed past the breakers toward the Japanese junk, the grimacing head of the turtle glaring at its doomed prey.

A deep voice boomed through the melee.

"*Shikkuro!*" Shut up! It was the admiral.

Everyone stopped and looked at him and then followed his eyes.

Commander Goh had slipped away from the crowd and was backing down the pier toward the sea. He stopped, reached inside his coat, and pulled out a German Luger.

Ernie shook himself free and ran to the far side of the wooden pier, taking cover behind a post. He pulled out a .45.

I pulled my .38. Holding it in my good hand, I ran to the other side of the pier.

Commander Goh backed away from us, waving the Luger from side to side.

Ernie's gum clicked rapidly. "There's nowhere for you to go," he said. "You're trapped."

"I will go to the sea," Commander Goh said in English. "Where a sailor always goes in time of trouble."

The three of us strode down the pier. Commander Goh walking backward, Ernie and me following. All with pistols drawn.

A horn, like the bellow of a dragon, sounded below. The turtle boat was picking up speed, moving alongside the pier, heading toward its victim, the Japanese junk.

There were no sailors visible; they were all inside, hidden beneath the iron shell. Protected.

Commander Goh glanced down at the metal plating floating low in the water. Oars peeked out of portholes just above the waterline. Huge metal spikes stuck straight up into the air. Sharpened, to discourage boarders.

Commander Goh kept backing up. Only a few yards of wooden pier were left.

I started to sweat, trying to control the shaking of my hand. It wasn't working.

On the other side of the pier, Ernie seemed relaxed. He'd killed a man last night. He was ready to kill another today.

Behind us, the admiral's voice barked. I glanced back. Where the pier met the shore, a row of Korean MP's had taken firing positions.

"Put the gun down," I told Commander Goh. "You've hurt enough people."

He shook his head.

"My daughter is dead, my wife is dead. What else do I have to live for?"

I had no answer for him.

He reached the end of the pier.

Wisps of sulphur drifted out of the mouth of the turtle's head on the bow of the spike-backed boat. Medieval chemical warfare. The turtle boat glided quickly through the water, along the length of the pier, the pointed end of its prow aimed straight at the Japanese junk beyond the breakers.

When the turtle boat pulled even with us, Commander Goh stopped at the wooden railing and glanced back along the pier. He pointed the Luger at me. Ernie knelt, bracing his pistol with both hands.

"Drop it!" he shouted.

Commander Goh kept his eyes on me. "Admiral Yi Sun Shin died at sea," he said. "Aboard his command ship. Shot through the heart by a Japanese arrow. I too am a sailor. I will not rot in prison. I will die at sea."

Sulphur gas billowed into the air. The turtle boat crashed through the waves below us.

I'm not sure, but it seemed as if Commander Goh flashed me a half-smile. He turned, tossed his gun into the sea, and, spreading his arms, leapt gracefully off the edge of the pier.

Ernie and I sprinted forward. Footsteps pounded behind us.

I reached the edge first. Down below, spread-eagled on the iron shell of the turtle boat, sprawled Commander Goh. A metal spike stuck wickedly out of his back. Blood streamed down his black coat and pants.

His arms and legs still kicked. A beetle pinned by a tack. He coughed, blood flooded out of his mouth, he stiffened his body one last time, and lay still.

The turtle boat continued its headlong charge through history and the waves. Sulphur still exploded out of its mouth in a great yellow cloud.

When it rammed the Japanese junk, the sound of ripping lumber tore through the sea air. On the shore, civilians and sailors cheered.

The turtle boat plunged ever deeper into the junk, seawater rushing into the open gash. As one, the line of oars started churning backward and the boat strained to withdraw. As it did so it rocked from side to side. Commander Goh's bloodied body slid off the metal spike.

The corpse tore free and slithered down the hull into the choppy gray waters of the Yellow Sea.

42

A COLD WIND SWEPT ACROSS THE BROAD EXPANSE OF THE HAN River.

We stood in the National Graveyard of the Republic of Korea; the sky above was placid and clear, as if even the spirits of the ancients were hovering in solemn observance. A military honor guard in crisply pressed white slacks and green tunics fired a volley into the air.

Slowly, the corpse of Ma Jin-ryul, the career slicky boy, was lowered into the frozen earth.

I had pitched a bitch back at CID Headquarters and forced the ROK Liaison to listen to me. Finally, because he had helped stanch a potentially disastrous rupture in military security, and because he was a veteran of the Korean War, the Korean government had consented to give Slicky Boy Ma a burial with full honors.

Kuang-sok stood at my side, his ten-year-old face as unmoved as one of the stone statues that guarded the great archway that led into the cemetery. He didn't appreciate this honor now, but I hoped that when he was older he'd treasure the memory. His foster father, who had been denied respect while he was alive, had finally received the respect he'd been due.

After the casket was lowered, workmen stepped forward and hurled shovelfuls of earth onto the flag-draped coffin.

Kuang-sok and I walked down the hill. Halfway to the bottom, his fingers curled around mine.

I searched my notes of the case and found the name and address of Cecil Whitcomb's mother. It took me most of the day to write a letter to her. In the first few drafts I told the truth about how Ernie and I had taken money to lure her son to his death. But each time I hesitated before putting it into an envelope, drank some coffee, and looked at what I'd written again. It didn't make sense to burden this woman I didn't know with all these painful things. It didn't make sense to burden myself. It wouldn't do any good. I scratched out sentences and paragraphs and the letter kept getting smaller. At the end of the day it was so short it might've been one of those prefabricated cards people buy in the PX.

Before Happy Hour I looked at the draft one more time, tore it up, and threw it in the trash.

Ernie's spleen healed up okay and he pressured the doc into giving him a complete rundown on how the damage would effect his drinking.

"You have to stop," the doctor told him.

"Stop drinking?"

"Yes."

"Come on, Doc. Give me the real story. Not the propaganda."

"Your spleen will never again function at peak efficiency, Bascom. Alcohol could do tremendous damage."

"But it's the liver and the pancreas that process the poison."

That's Ernie. Leave it to him to argue with a guy who spent six years in medical school.

The doctor ran some impressive-sounding words past him and did his best, but in the end Ernie remained unconvinced. The next time he went to Itaewon—with me and Riley along to watch out for him—he slammed home as many shots of *soju* as he ever had before.

Same old Ernie.

Unless somebody mentioned the Nurse.

Ajjima, the Nurse's landlady, couldn't rent the Nurse's old hooch. People were afraid of her ghost. I don't believe in that stuff. I carry plenty of ghosts around inside me but I don't believe in the ones on the outside. I rented the room and told Kuang-sok he could stay there.

He moved his father's old furniture over and I visited three or four times a week and brought him food from the commissary on post. But it wasn't working.

Ajjima pulled me aside one day and told me that the boy wanted to go to an orphanage.

"Why didn't he tell me that himself?" I asked.

"He embarrassed," she said. "Maybe you feel bad."

She was right. It did make me feel bad. But I made the arrangements, and the next weekend we loaded up all his stuff in a truck Ernie borrowed from 21 T-Car and carted Kuang-sok out to a Catholic orphanage past Kimpo.

After Ernie and I unloaded everything, I went into the office and made a substantial contribution to the orphanage. About half my monthly paycheck. The Korean priest was grateful and told me that he didn't expect Kuang-sok to be here long. A healthy young boy like him should get adopted and go overseas within a matter of months.

Outside, Kuang-sok bowed to Ernie and me, but he turned and walked away with the priest without bothering to thank us.

Ernie started up the truck. "You figure he blames us for the death of his father?"

"Sure he does," I said. "Don't you?"

"Naw. Not me. I blame Shipton."

He swung the truck down the dirt road until we hooked up with the main highway and sped back to Seoul.

I wished, sometimes, that I could accept things as easily as Ernie. But I still saw Mr. Ma's face when he realized that Shipton's knife had sliced into his back. And I saw the Nurse. And I saw Miss Ku. And sometimes I even saw Cecil Whitcomb.